Spindle's End

Spindle's End

Robin McKinley

DAVID FICKLING BOOKS

OXFORD   NEW YORK

SPINDLE'S END
A DAVID FICKLING BOOK 0385 60419X

Originally published in the US by G.P. Putnam's Sons, a division of
Penguin Putnam Books for Young Readers

First published in Great Britain by David Fickling Books,
a division of Random House Children's Books

This edition published 2002

1 3 5 7 9 10 8 6 4 2

Papers used by Random House Children's Books are natural, recyclable products made from
wood grown in sustainable forests. The manufacturing processes conform to the
environmental regulations of the country of origin.

Set in 11.5/14 pt Granjon

DAVID FICKLING BOOKS
31 Beaumont Street, Oxford, OX1 2NP
a division of RANDOM HOUSE CHILDREN'S BOOKS
61-63 Uxbridge Rd, London W5 5SA
A division of The Random House Group Ltd.

RANDOM HOUSE AUSTRALIA(PTY) LTD
20 Alfred Street, Milsons Point, Sydney,
New South Wales 2061, Australia

RANDOM HOUSE NEW ZEALAND LTD
18 Poland Road, Glenfield, Auckland 10, New Zealand

RANDOM HOUSE (PTY) LTD
Endulini, 5AJubilee Road, Parktown 2193, South Africa

THE RANDOM HOUSE GROUP Limited Reg. No. 954009
www.randomhouse.co.uk

A CIP catalogue record for this book is available from the British Library.

Printed and bound in Great Britain by
Clays Ltd, St Ives plc.

To the Lodge, my Woodwold
and to the other Dickinsons who love it too

PART ONE

Chapter I

The magic in that country was so thick and tenacious that it settled over the land like chalk-dust and over floors and shelves like slightly sticky plaster-dust. (Housecleaners in that country earned unusually good wages.) If you lived in that country, you had to de-scale your kettle of its encrustation of magic at least once a week, because if you didn't, you might find yourself pouring hissing snakes or pond slime into your teapot instead of water. (It didn't have to be anything scary or unpleasant, like snakes or slime, especially in a cheerful household – magic tended to reflect the atmosphere of the place in which it found itself – but if you want a cup of tea, a cup of lavender-and-gold pansies or ivory thimbles is unsatisfactory. And while the pansies – put dry in a vase – would probably last a day, looking like ordinary pansies, before they went greyish-dun and collapsed into magic dust, something like an ivory thimble would begin to smudge and crumble as soon as you picked it up.)

The best way to do it was to have a fairy as a member of your household, because she (it was usually a she) could lay a finger on the kettle just as it came to a boil (absentminded fairies could often be recognized by a pad of scar-tissue on the finger they favoured for kettle-cleaning) and murmur a few counter-magical words. There would be a tiny inaudible t h o c k, like a seed-pod bursting, and the water would stay water for another week or (maybe) ten days.

De-magicking a kettle was much too little and fussy and frequent a job for any professional fairy to be willing to be hired to do it, so if you weren't related to one you had to dig up a root of the dja vine, and dry it, and grate it, producing a white powder rather like plaster dust or magic, and add a pinch of that to your kettle once a week. More often than not that would give everyone in the household cramp. You could tell the households that didn't have a fairy by the dja vines growing over them. Possibly because they were always having their roots disturbed, djas developed a reputation for being tricky to grow, and prone to sudden collapse; fortunately they rerooted easily from cuttings. "She'd give me her last dja root" was a common saying about a good friend.

People either loved that country and couldn't imagine living anywhere else, or hated it, left it as soon as they could, and never came back. If you loved it, you loved coming over the last hill before your village one day in early autumn and hearing the corn-field singing madrigals, and that day became a story you told your grandchildren, the way in other countries other grandparents told the story of the day they won the betting pool at the pub, or their applecake won first place at the local fête. If you lived there, you learned what you had to do, like putting a pinch of dried dja vine in your kettle once a week, like asking your loaf of bread to remain a loaf of bread before you struck it with a knife. (The people of this country had developed a reputation among outsiders for being unusually pious, because of the number of things they appeared to mutter a blessing over before they did them; but in most cases this was merely the asking of things it was safer to ask to remain nonmagical first, while work or play or food preparation or whatever was being got on with. Nobody had ever heard of a loaf of bread turning into a flock of starlings for anyone they knew, but the nursery tale was well known, and in that country it didn't pay to take chances. The muttered words were usually only some phrase such as "Bread, stay bread" or, in upper-class households, "Bread, please oblige me," which was a less wise form, since an especially impish gust of magic could choose to translate "oblige" just as it chose.)

Births were very closely attended, because the request that things stay what they were had to be got in quickly, birth being a very great magic, and, in that country, likely to be teased into mischief. It was so common an occurrence as to occasion no remark when a new-sown field began coming up quite obviously as something other than what was planted, and by a week later to have reverted to what the farmer had put in. But while, like the pansies and the thimbles, this kind of magic was only a temporary aberration, it could be very embarrassing and onerous while it l asted. Farmers in that country worried more about falling asleep during the birthing times of their stock than they worried about the weather; the destruction a litter of baby taralians caused remained, even after it had reverted to piglets. No-one knew how the wild birds and beasts negotiated this, but human parents-to-be would go to extreme lengths to ensure a fairy was on hand to say the birth-words over their new little one.

Generally speaking the more mobile and water-dependent something was, the more likely magic was to get at it. This meant animals – and, of course, humans – were the most vulnerable. Rocks were pretty reliably rocks, except of course when they were something else that had been turned into rocks. But rocks themselves sort of slept through magic attacks, and even if some especially wild and erratic bit of magic decided to deck out a drystone wall as a marble fountain, you could still feel the drystone wall if you closed your eyes and touched the fountain, and the water would not make you wet. The lichen that grew on the rock, however, could be turned into daisies quite convincing enough to make you sneeze if real daisies did so; and the insects and small creatures that crept over the lichen were more susceptible yet.

(There was an idea much beloved and written about by this country's philosophers that magic had to do with negotiating the balance between earth and air and water; which is to say that things with legs or wings were out of balance with their earth element by walking around on feet or, worse, flying above the earth in the thin substance of air, obviously entirely unsuitable for the support of solid flesh. The momentum all this inappropriate motion set up in their liquid element unbalanced them further. Spirit, in this system, was equated with the fourth element, fire. All this was generally felt to be a load of rubbish among the people who had to work in the ordinary world for a living, unlike philosophers living in academies. But it was true that a favourite magical trick at fêtes was for theatrically-minded fairies to throw bits of chaff or seed-pods or conkers in the air and turn them into things before they struck the ground, and that the trick worked better if the bits of chaff or seed-pods or conkers were wet.)

Slower creatures were less susceptible to the whims of wild magic than faster creatures, and creatures that flew were the most susceptible of all. Every sparrow had a delicious memory of having once been a hawk, and while magic didn't take much interest in caterpillars, butterflies spent so much time being magicked that it was a rare event to see ordinary butterflies without at least an extra set of wings or a few extra frills and iridescences, or bodies like tiny human beings dressed in flower petals. (Fish, which flew through that most dangerous element, water, were believed not to exist. Fishy-looking beings in pools and streams were either hallucinations or other things under some kind of spell, and interfering with, catching, or – most especially – eating fish was strictly forbidden. All swimming was considered magical. Animals seen doing it were assumed to be favourites of a local water-sprite or dangerously insane; humans never tried.)

There did seem to be one positive effect to living involuntarily steeped in magic; everyone lived longer. More humans made their century than didn't; birds and animals often lived to thirty, and fifty was not unheard of. The breeders of domestic animals in that country were unusually sober and responsible individuals, since any mistakes they made might be around to haunt them for a long time.

Although magic was ubiquitous and magic-workers crucially necessary, the attitude of the ordinary people towards magic and its manipulators was that it and they were more than a bit chancy and not to be relied on, however fond you were of your aunt or your next-door neighbour. No-one had ever seen a fairy turn into an eagle and fly up above the trees, but there were nursery tales about that, too, and it was difficult not to believe that it or something even more unnerving was somehow likely. Didn't farmers grow more stolid and earthy over a lifetime of farming? Wasn't it likely that a lifetime of handling magic made you wilder and more capricious?

It was a fact much noticed but rarely discussed (and never in any fairy's hearing) that while fairies rarely married or (married or not) had children, there never seemed to be any fewer fairies around, generation after generation. So presumably magic ran in the blood of the people the way it ran in all other watery liquids, and sometimes there was enough of it to make someone a fairy, and sometimes there was not. (One of the things ordinary people did not like to contemplate was how many people there might be who were, or could have been, fairies, and were masquerading as ordinary people by the simple process of never doing any magic when anyone was around to notice.) But there was a very strong tradition that the rulers of this country must be utterly without magic, for rulers must be reliable, they must be the earth and the rock underfoot for their people. And if any children of that country's rulers had ever been born fairies, there was not only no official history of it; there were not even any stories about it.

This did mean that when the eldest child of each generation of the ruling family came to the age to be married (and, just to be safe, his or her next-younger and perhaps next-younger-after-that siblings) there was a great search and examination of possible candidates in terms of their magiclessness first, and their honesty, integrity, intelligence, and so on, second. (The likelihood of their getting along comfortably with their potential future spouses barely rated a mention on the councillors' list.) So far – so far as the country's histories extended, which was a little over a thousand years at the time of this story – the system had worked; and while there were stories of the thick net of anti-magic that the court magicians set up for even the cleanest, most magic-antipathetic betrothed to go through, well, it worked, didn't it, and that was all that mattered.

The present king was not only an only child, but had had a very difficult time indeed – or his councillors had – finding a suitable wife. She was not even a princess, finally, but a mere countess, of some obscure little backwater country which, so far as it was known for anything, was known for the fleethounds its king and queen bred; but she was quiet, dutiful, and, so far as any of the cleverest magicians in the land could tell, entirely without magic. Everyone breathed a deep sigh of relief when the wedding was over; it had been a wait of nearly a decade since the king came of marriageable age.

But the years passed and she bore no children.

Certain of the king's cousins began to hang around court more than they used to – his generation was particularly rich in cousins – and one or two of these quietly divorced spouses who were insufficiently nonmagical. There had not been a break in the line from parent to child in the ruling of this country for over five hundred years, and the rules about how the crown was passed sideways or diagonally were not clear. Neither the king nor the queen noticed any of this, for they so badly wanted a child, they could not bear to think about the results if they did not; but the councillors noticed, and the king's cousins who divorced their spouses did themselves no good thereby.

Nearly fifteen years after the king's marriage the queen was seen to become suddenly rather pale and sickly. Her husband's people, who had become very fond of her, because she was always willing to appear at fairs and festivals and smile during boring speeches and to kiss the babies, even grubby and unattractive ones, which were thrust at her, were torn between hoping that whatever she had would kill her off while the king was young enough to remarry (and there was a whole new crop of princesses grown up to marriageable age outside the borders as well as a few within), and hoping that she would get well and come to more fairs and festivals and kiss more babies. The givers of boring speeches especially wished this; she was the best audience they had ever had.

The truth never occurred to anyone – not even when she began to wear loose gowns and to walk more heavily than she used to – because there had been no announcement.

The king knew, and her chief waiting-woman knew, and the fairy who disguised the queen's belly knew. But the fairy had warned the king and queen that the disguise would go so far and no further: the baby must be allowed to grow unmolested by tight laces and the queen's balance not be deranged by high-heeled shoes. "A magician might make you a proper disguise," said the fairy, whose name was Sigil, "and let you dance all night in a sheath of silk no bigger around than your waist used to be; but I wouldn't advise it. Magicians know everything about magic and nothing about babies. I don't know nearly as much about magic as they do – but I know a lot about babies."

Sigil had been with the king's family since the king's mother had been queen, and the king loved her dearly, and his queen had found in her her first friend when she came to her husband's court, when she badly needed a friend. And so it was to Sigil the queen went, as soon as she knew for sure that she was pregnant, and begged for the disguise, saying that she had longed for a child for so many years she thought she could not bear the weight of the watchfulness of her husband's people, who had longed for this child all these years, too, if her pregnancy were announced. The king, who had wanted to declare a public holiday, was disappointed; but Sigil sided with the queen.

The poor queen could not quite bring herself, after all the long childless years, to believe it when her friend told her that the baby was fine and healthy and would be born without trouble – "Well , my dear, without any more trouble than the birth of babies does cause, and which you, poor thing, will find quite troublesome enough." And so the birth of an heir was not announced until the queen went into labour. The queen would have waited even then till the baby was born, but Sigil said no, that the baby must be born freely into the world, and freely, in an heir to a realm, meant with its people waiting to welcome it.

The country, that day, went into convulsions not unlike those the poor queen was suffering. An heir! An heir at last! And no-one knew! The courtiers and councillors were offended, and the highest-ranking magicians furious, but their voices were drowned out in the tumult of jubilation from the people. The news travelled more quickly than any mere human messenger could take it, for the horses neighed it and the trees sang it and the kettles boiled it and the dust whispered it – an heir! The king's child is born! We have an heir at last!

It was a girl, and the names chosen to be given her on her name-day were: Casta Albinia Allegra Dove Minerva Fidelia Aletta Blythe Domina Delicia Aurelia Grace Isabel Griselda Gwyneth Pearl Ruby Coral Lily Iris Briar-Rose. She was healthy – just as Sigil had said she would be – and she was born without any more trouble than the birth of babies does cause, which is to say the queen was aching and exhausted, but not too exhausted to weep for joy when the baby was laid in her arms.

The eldest child of the reigning monarch was always next in line for the throne, be it boy or girl; but it was usually a boy. There was a deeply entrenched folk myth that a queen held this country together better than a king because there is a clear-eyed pragmatic common sense about an unmagical woman that even the most powerful – or rather, especially the most powerful – magic found difficult to disturb; it was thought that a man was more easily dazzled by pyrotechnics. Whether this was true or not, everyone believed it, including the bad fairies, who therefore spent a lot of their time making up charms to ensure the birth of male first children to the royal family. The royal magicians dismantled these charms as quickly as they could, but never quite as quickly as the bad fairies made them up. (As it was difficult to get any kind of charm through the heavy guard laid round the royal family, these charms had to be highly specific, with the knock-on effect that third children to a reigning monarch were almost always girls.) But the folk myth (plus the tangential effect that first-born princesses were rare enough to be interesting for no reason other than their rarity) guaranteed that the birth of a future queen was greeted with even greater enthusiasm than the birth of a mere future king; and so it was in this case. No-one seemed to remember, perhaps because their last queen had been nearly four hundred years ago, that that queen had left some unfinished business with a wicked fairy named Pernicia, who had sworn revenge.

The princess' name-day was going to be the grandest occasion that the country had ever seen, or at least that the oldest citizen could remember – grander than the king and queen's wedding sixteen years ago – grander than the king's parents' wedding, almost fifty years ago, and certainly grander than the king's own name-day because he'd been born eighteen months after his parents' wedding and no-one had realized he was going to be the only one.

The king and queen wanted to invite everyone to the name-day. Every one of their people, they felt, should have the pportunity to join them on their day of joy and celebration. They were talked out of this ridiculous idea by their councillors – uncharacteristically in agreement on this particular topic – with some difficulty.

It had been the queen's idea to begin with. Her native country was just about small enough that everyone could be invited to a major royal occasion (although the royal list-makers and caterers and spare-chair-providers would hope that not everyone came), and the king and queen recognized by sight a substantial minority of their subjects. While she found her husband's country rather intimidatingly larger (and it seemed all wrong to her that many of his subjects would never meet their king), in times of great importance she reverted to her upbringing. The king was lucky enough to love his wife, and had been rather struck by her tales of a king and queen who had open court days, when anyone who wished to speak to them could turn up and do so. He thought an open name-day a splendid notion.

It will not do, said the councillors and courtiers. (The magicians were still nursing their snit about not having been told of the queen's pregnancy, and refused to attend the discussions about the name-day. What they were really outraged about, of course, was that a mere fairy had successfully thrown fairy dust in all their eyes.) You must, said the councillors, have the sort of name-day that other countries will send emissaries to – we will need their good wishes, their favourable memories, in nineteen or twenty years' time. And you cannot make the sort of fuss that an emissary is going to remember pleasantly if a hundred thousand or so of your people are milling around the city walls, trampling the fields into mud, and demanding to be fed and housed.

This made the king and queen thoughtful, for the king remembered the long difficult search for his wife, and the queen remembered what a shock it had been when the envoy had presented himself at her father's rather small and shabby castle, and she had had to be rushed out of the kitchens where she was boiling sweetmeats and up the back stairs to wash her face and comb her hair and put on her best dress to meet him. (He had been eating her sweetmeats with a look of great concentration and contentment, when she had made a stately entrance into the front room, slightly out of breath from having hopped down the corridor on one foot and then the other, pulling on her shoes. She hadn't realized that her sweetmeats, excellent though she knew them to be, would render even a king's envoy happy to wait.)

A compromise was reached. It was the sort of compromise that made the councillors gnash their teeth, but it was the best they had been able to wrest from their suddenly obstinate rulers, who would keep insisting that their daughter belonged to her people. Heralds would be sent out to every village – each and every village – to proclaim at the town centre, which might be anything from the steps of the mayor's house in the larger to the town well or watering-trough in the smaller, that one person, to be chosen by lot (if the magicians had recovered from their snit, they would provide cheat-proof lots; otherwise Sigil would find fairies to do it), was invited to the princess' name-day. And that one person, whoever he or she was, need only present the lot, as good earnest of the invitation, to be allowed entry into the royal grounds on the name-day.

The councillors and courtiers could only see the fabulous amount of organizational work, and, magicians or no magicians, the infinite amount of cheating that would go on – or at least would try to go on – as a result of this plan. And while the court folk were applying court mores to many ordinary people who wouldn't know a political intrigue if it grew butterfly wings and bit them, it was true that the heralds, who were themselves ordinary people under their livery, tended to let it be known, especially at the smaller villages, at the local pub after the official announcement was made, that the king and queen had wanted to invite everyone, really everyone. And that if the person with the royal lot showed up with a friend or two, chances were they'd all get in.

That took care of the common citizens, and, barring the number and manner of them, that was the easy part. Much harder were the high tables: who would sit near the king or the queen, who would have to make do at a slightly less high table headed by a mere prince or duke or baron, which countries were to be invited to send emissaries, and whether the fuss made over the emissaries should have more to do with the size and status of the country, or the number of unmarried sons in the royal family.

But hardest of all was what to do about the fairies.

Court magicians were members of the court, and there would be special high tables just for them, where they could compare notes on astrological marvels, cast aspersions on the work of other magicians not present to defend themselves, and be slightly world-weary about the necessity of coming to so superstitious and ridiculous an event as a royal name-day.

But fairies were a different kettle of imaginary watery beings. Some fairies were nearly as powerful as the magicians, and what they thought and did was much more varied and unpredictable. Magicians had to attend the Academy for a number of years, and anyone calling himself a magician – since it was usually a he – had a degree in hippogriff leather to show for it, although no-one but another magician would be able to read the invisible writing on it. Magicians could make earthquakes happen if they wanted to, or a castle go up (or down) in a night, and a properly drawn-up magician's spell could last a lifetime. Mostly they were hired by powerful people to spy on their powerful neighbours, and to demonstrate their existence, so that the powerful neighbours didn't try anything with their own magicians. (Fêtes where the magicians of rival families would be present were always well attended, because the spectacles were sure to be exceptionally fine.) Magicians without a taste for this sort of flash stayed at the Academy, or at other academies, pursuing the ultimate secrets of the universe (and philosophies concerning the balance of magic), which were, presumably, dangerous, which was why

Academicians tended to have long sombre faces, and to move as if they were waiting for something to leap out at them. But the point was that magicians had rules. Fairies were the wild cards in a country where the magic itself was wild.

Even the queen was a little hesitant about issuing a blanket invitation to fairies. Several hundred fairies together – let alone several thousand – in one place were certain to kick up a tremendous dust of magic, and fate only knew what might be the outcome.

"But most fairies live in towns and villages, do they not?" said the queen. "So they are, in a way, included in the invitation our heralds are carrying." The fact was that no-one really knew how many fairies – even how many practising fairies – there were in the country; the ones people knew about were the ones who lived in the towns and villages with other people and visibly did magic. There were known to be fairies who lived in the woods and the desert places (and possibly even in the waters), but they were rarely seen, and it was only assumed that they were fewer than the known ones.

There were also, of course, wicked fairies, but there weren't many of them, and they tended to keep a low profile, because they knew they were outnumbered – unless someone angered them, and people tried very, very hard not to anger them. It was the malice of the wicked fairies that gave the good ones a lot of their most remunerative work putting things back to rights, but generally speaking, things could be put back to rights. People were diligently cautious about bad fairies, but they didn't worry about them too much; less than they worried about the weather, for example, a drought that would make crops fail, or a hard winter that would bring wolves into the towns. (It was actually easier if droughts or hard winters were caused by a bad fairy, because then what you did was very straightforward: you hired a good fairy to fix it. The capriciousness of real weather was beyond everybody, even the united efforts of the Academy, who periodically tried.)

"I think," said the king slowly, "I think that's not quite enough."

The queen sighed. "I was afraid you'd say that." There had

been relatively little magic in her father's country and she had never quite adjusted to the omnipresence of magic, and of magical practitioners. Magic had its uses, but it made her nervous. Sigil she loved dearly, and she was at least half-friends with several of the other fairies strategically employed in the royal household; the magicians she mostly found tiresome, and was rather relieved than otherwise that none of them were at present speaking to her because they blamed her for the secrecy of her pregnancy.

There was a pause. "What if," said the queen at last, "what if we invited a few fairies to be godmothers to our daughter? We could ask twenty-one of them – one each for her twenty-one names, and one each for the twenty-one years of her minority. Twenty-one isn't very many. There will be eighty-two magicians. And it will make the fairies seem, you know, wanted and welcome. We can ask Sigil whom to invite."

"Fairy godmothers?" said the king dubiously. "We'll have a time getting that past the court council – and the bishop."

Sigil had been worrying about the fairies, too, and thought that inviting one-and-twenty fairies to be godmothers would be an excellent idea, if they could hedge it round first with enough precautions.

"No gifts," said the king. "Too controversial."

"Oh, godmothers must give gifts!" said the queen. "It would be terribly rude to tell them they mustn't give their godchild anything!"

"The queen's right," said Sigil, "but we can tell them they must be token gifts only, little things to amuse a baby or flatter a baby's parents, nothing – nothing – difficult." What she meant, the king and queen both knew, was nothing that would make the princess unduly visible on the ethereal planes. That sort of thing was the province of heroes, who were old enough to choose it and strong – or stupid – enough to bear it. "And I think we should invite at least one man. Male fairies are underappreciated, because almost no-one remembers they exist."

" You must be the first of the godmothers, dear," said the queen, but Sigil shook her head.

"No . . . no," she said, although the regret was clear in her voice. "I thank you most sincerely. But . . . I'm already too bound up in the fortunes of this family to be the best godmother for the new little one. Give her one-and-twenty fresh fairies, who will love the tie to the royal family. And it can be quite a useful thing to have a few fairies on your side." The king remembered a time when he was still the prince, when one of the assistant chefs in the royal kitchens, who was also a fairy, was addressed by a mushroom, fried in butter and on its way to being part of a solitary late supper for the king, saying, "Don't let the king eat me or I'll poison him." There was always a fairy or two in the royal kitchens (the rulers of this country did not use tasters) and while it took the magicians to find out who was responsible for the presence of the mushroom, it was the fairy who saved the king's life.

Sigil took the queen's hands in her own. "Let me look after the catering. What do you think the cradle should be hung with? Silk? And what colours? Pink? Blue? Lavender? Gold?"

"Gold, I think," the queen said, glad to have the question of the fairy godmothers agreed upon, but disappointed and a little hurt that Sigil refused to be one of them. "Gold and white. Maybe a little lavender. And the ribbons should have pink and white rosettes."

Chapter 2

The shape of the country was rectangular, but there was a long wiggling finger of land that struck down south-east and a sort of tapering lump that struck up north-west. The south-east bit was called the Finger; the north-west lump was called the Gig, because it might be guessed to have some resemblance to the shape of a two-wheeled vehicle with its shafts tipped forward to touch the ground. The royal city lay a little north of the Finger, in the south-east corner, nearly a month's journey, even with frequent changes of horses and a good sprinkling of fairy dust for speed, to the base of the Gig.

The highways that bound most of the rest of the country together gave out at the beginning of the Gig. The local peer, Lord Prendergast, said, reasonably, that he (or his forebears) would have built a highway if there had ever been any need, but there never had been. Nothing exciting ever happened in the Gig, or at least hadn't since the invasion of the fire-wyrms about eleven hundred years ago, before the days of highway-building. So if you wanted to go there you went on cart tracks. (The lord's own travelling carriages were very well sprung, and he would upon occasion send them to fetch his less well equipped, or more easily bruised, friends and associates outside the Gig.)

And what you needed, muttered the royal herald, bearer of a little pouch of cheat-proof lots (almost empty now) and important tidings about the princess' name-day, was not swift horses but six-legged flat-footed ponies that could see in thick mist and the green darkness of trees. He had given up riding, after his fancy thoroughbred had put its foot in a gap of root and stumbled, for the umpty-millionth time, and he was now leading it, half an eye anxiously upon it, for he thought it was going a bit lame. He sneezed. Also needed were human beings impervious to cold and damp. The Gig was a damp sort of place, and most of its village names reflected this: Foggy Bottom, Smoke River, Dewglass, Rainhill, Mistweir. Moonshadow didn't sound very promising either, although at least it didn't utterly guarantee wet; and the last village of the Gig, right out next to the wild lands where no-one went, was called Treelight. He had thought this was a very funny name when he was setting out from the royal city. It was less funny now, with the leaves overhead dripping down his neck, and he not yet arrived at the first village of this soggy province. He sneezed again.

To think that Lord Prendergast preferred to live out here and leave his seat at court empty from year's end to year's end! There must be some truth in the stories about that family, and the house they lived in, Woodwold, a vast mysterious place, a thousand years old or more, full of tales and echoes of tales, and with some uncanny connection with the people that lived in it. But it was still a grand and beautiful house – grand enough for a highway to have been built to get to it. Except it hadn't been.

The herald blinked, distracted. The sun had suddenly cut through the leaf cover and a gold-green shaft of light fell across his path. He looked at the sunbeam, scowling; there was no reason, this far off the highway and with soggy leaf-mould the chief road surface, for there to be so much dust to dance in a sunbeam. The thick dust and moist air would conspire to leave ineradicable chalky smudges on his livery. He sighed again. Maybe Foggy Bottom – which should be the first village he came to – would have a blacksmith who could look at his horse's foot.

Foggy Bottom had heard of the princess' birth as quickly as the rest of the country; one of the village fairies had a particular friend who was a robin whose wife's cousin's sister-in-law was closely related to a family of robins that lived in a bush below the queen's bedroom window, and had heard the princess' first startled cry. Foggy Bottom was expecting something like the herald (and was accustomed to travellers who had never been to the Gig before, by the time they reached Foggy Bottom, looking cross and rather the worse for wear), but was not at all expecting his announcement.

They had turned out eagerly to hear him – this was one of those villages where the herald stood at the public watering-trough to make his proclamation – but they were only expecting some cushiony, royal adjectives to ornament the known fact of the young princess' birth. They were so startled by the invitation to the name-day they forgot to relish her name.

"From every village?" said Cairngorm, who ran the pub. There was a square, although it was not square, at the centre of the village, and the watering-trough stood across from the blacksmith's, with the pub at ninety degrees, and the wrights' yard opposite. The herald stood next to the watering-trough, as he said the familiar words, his natural inclination towards the pub in this case counterbalanced by his anxiety to learn if his horse was sound enough to go on.

The herald stopped thinking about his horse and nodded. He still enjoyed this part, enjoyed creating astonishment, enjoyed watching the faces in front of him shift from pleased anticipation to surprise, even shock, enjoyed handing out the special cheat-proof long straw that would instantly look like all the other, ordinary straws as soon as it was laid among them. In the bigger villages the straw had to go to the mayor; the little villages were his call. He favoured pub proprietors; he thought Cairngorm would do nicely. "Every village. Heralds have been sent to every village – at least," he amended, "every village we know about from the last census."

"If that don't beat all," said Grey, who had a farm outside the village and was only in town today because he had a broken plough-handle that had to be mended before he could get on with business. "Well, I can't go."

"Make yourself popular by selling your lot!" shouted a friend across the heads of the crowd; several people laughed, and then the conversation became animated and general. Katriona, who had been standing with Cairngorm's elder daughter, Flora, the two girls holding each other's hands in excitement, said to her friend, "I must go!" ducked under a few arms and round a few bodies and fled back to her aunt's house. "I told her she should come for the herald's announcement!" she muttered between breaths. "I told her!"

But when she burst in through the door and babbled out her news, her aunt was unflustered, and her hand holding the spindle, and her foot on the pedal, never faltered, and the woollen thread went on spinning itself fine and true. "I'm not at all surprised," she said, although she let her wheel come to a stop so she could hug her frantic niece into some calm. "I've always liked the queen; robins don't nest outside just anyone's window." Katriona's aunt was the fairy whose robin friend had told her of the princess' birth. She was generally considered the best fairy in Foggy Bottom; some said in the entire Gig.

The herald was gone the next day after a merry evening telling stories about the royal family (some of them true) in Cairngorm's pub, and a beautiful sleep in her best feather mattress. He had been able to give himself over to jollity because the blacksmith had told him his horse would, after all, be able to go on the next day – although he had had a funny way of putting it, almost as if some magic would be worked overnight, which in a smith's forge was, of course, nonsense. Smiths were often rather enigmatic – it was one of the perquisites of the job – as was the face-obscuring thatch of beard which this smith did not have. Perhaps that was the reason the herald had found him odd; he had never seen a clean-shaven smith before.

The herald was a little sorry about the early start in the morning – wistfully recalling the beer of the night before, thinking that perhaps there was something to be said for some bits of the back of beyond – but his horse was waiting for him, snorting red-nostrilled at dust motes and dancing round on all four feet uniformly. The herald looked at him a bit waspishly; he wanted a riding-animal, not an adventure. The smith said neutrally: "He'll have got used to our roads by now. You just climb on and point him." And hang on, thought the herald, and was catapulted down the village street in the direction of Smoke River.

The lot-drawing was held that same evening in Foggy Bottom. There was some joshing with Katriona's aunt and Nurgle, the laundress, and especially Snick, who wasn't a real fairy but couldn't help winning at cards, and one or two other of the local fairies, about not using magic to mind how the lots went – and with Katriona herself, although she kept shaking her head and saying, "I don't do that, you know I don't do that," while her aunt, who could but wouldn't (and was privately rather disparaging about the magicians' supposedly tamper-proof lot), only smiled and said something bland, and Snick, who didn't think he could but wasn't sure and couldn't do anything about it if he did, looked worried. Foggy Bottom liked its fairies – Nurgle was even married – and didn't make them hold sprigs of hawthorn and rowan as charms against magical meddling, as some towns had done – although Snick had a bit of both in his pocket, just in case.

There was a hush as everyone drew – Grey held the straws, because he had declined either to have a lot or to bestow it on anyone else – and as more and more were drawn, and fewer and fewer were left in Grey's fist, the tension was pulled tighter and tighter. But Gash, who had drawn last, held up his straw, the same length as all the other losing straws, and said, "Then who has it?"

There was a silence, and Katriona burst into tears. Cairngorm made her way to the girl's side – her aunt already had an arm around her – and prised her fingers open. There lay the single long straw.

"You knew," Katriona said to her aunt later, when they were back home again. Katriona was sitting so close to the fire that her face was starting to scorch and in a minute her heavy petticoats would start to burn her legs. The heat and brightness were reassuring, as if she were about to be drawn away to some cold dark unguessable fate. The tap and whirr of her aunt's spinning wheel went on behind her. "You knew. I thought it was funny you came to the drawing. I knew you'd never go to the name-day even if you drew the long straw. You knew I was going to."

" Well, yes," admitted her aunt. "It was a surprise to me — knowing, I mean; I haven't had a pre-vision since you were a tiny child and I saw you would come to me. I hadn't known about the invitation till you told me, but it stood out so very clearly that you would draw the long lot I knew it must be true. I thought it might come as rather a shock to you, and I wanted to be there when it happened."

"Maybe I won't go."

Tap. *Whirr*. "Why not?"

" You admitted you wouldn't go."

Her aunt laughed. "I'm an old lady, and I like to sleep in the same bed every night, and . . . I hear more from my robin than I tell you, not because I don't want to, but because I can't." Katriona knew about this. Beast-speech often didn't translate even when you'd think it should. "I know as much about the royal family as I need to. I think you'll like the little princess. I think you should go."

"I won't get near enough to like or dislike her," said Katriona. "She'll just be a lot of gold and white and lavender silk with pink and white rosettes." One of the translatable things the robin had told her aunt was how the cradle would be decorated.

"I'll give you a safety charm," said her aunt. "So you won't be eaten by bears or attacked by robbers. I can even give you a charm so that there are never stones under your blanket when you lie down to sleep at night." Katriona laughed, but the laugh quickly faded and her face was moody as she stared into the fire.

"My dear," said her aunt. "It's a rather overwhelming enterprise, I know. "

Katriona moved abruptly away from the fire and began to flap the front of her skirt to cool it off. "I haven't been further than Treelight since . . . since. . . "

"Since your parents died and you came to live with me," her aunt said gently. "Yes, I know. "

"And I've never been off the Gig since then."

"What better reason to go farther than the invitation to the princess' name-day? You go, dear. Go and have a wonderful time.

I'll be very interested to hear what you have to say about everything. Robins tend to see the big and the little and leave out all the human-sized bits in the middle."

And so Katriona went.

Barder, who was the wheelwright's First Apprentice, offered to go with her – "Not the whole way," he said, peering at her anxiously. "I'm not trying to take what isn't offered," – although the herald had made the usual unofficial announcement that a friend or two of the person with the long lot would not be turned away. "But – it's a long road, all on your own. He'd let me off, if I asked," he added, meaning his master, Sarkon.

"Thanks," she said. "But I'll be all right. Aunt's giving me charms for everything, from robbers to midges."

Barder smiled. The entire village called Katriona's aunt Aunt; hardly anyone remembered her real name, which was Sophronia.

"Luck, then," he said, and held out his hand, the fingers curled round something. Katriona held out her own, and felt the something dropped gently in her palm, and then his fingers closed hers over whatever it was he had given her. She resisted the urge to look at it immediately, but felt herself blush, for they were not declared sweethearts. Barder said lightly, "Did Aunt give you a memory charm so you'll remember everything to tell us when you come back?"

"I'll ask her for one."

Barder's gift was a little flat medallion of ash, carved, like the plaque over the door of Cairngorm's pub, in the shape of an egret; but while the pub's egret stood, gazing over the green marsh at its feet, Barder's egret curled into the small oval space, its long neck folded gracefully back against its body, its long legs tucked out of sight. Even in so tiny an area Barder had cut the feathers to perfection; Katriona half-expected them to yield under her touch as she stroked them. "A memory charm, eh?" said Aunt, admiring the egret. "He's given you his own charm, I think, a charm for remembering where to come back to."

"Barder isn't—"

"Not that kind of magic," said Aunt. "But real for all that."

There was quite a little party gathered outside the pub to see Katriona off; she would rather not have been seen off by anyone but Aunt, but too many people asked when she was leaving, and Aunt said, "You're going for all of us, you know. You can bear a few extra hopes and wishes."

She was going on foot; she carried a blanket and a few extra clothes, and she would be swifter on her own feet than on any pony she and her aunt could afford to hire. Local beasts (barring Lord Prendergast's) tended to be the stolid sort. What money they could spare was done up in a small secret parcel hidden in her petticoat. Her major encumbrance, though they were no burden, were her aunt's charms; there were so many of them she had tied them to her belt with bits of string, and they fanned and dangled and shimmered out round her as if she wore an extra skirt curiously made of what looked like the contents of a magpie's nest. But these would feed and comfort and protect her on her journey; and of course she had her own odd talent, although she had rarely found it what anyone could call useful, herself especially. She waved self-consciously as she turned to go, and everyone waved back. Even the smith, whose name was Narl, came to the front of his yard and lifted the sledge he was carrying in acknowledgement of her adventure.

The long green tree-tunnel the herald hadn't liked was pleasant to her; when she came upon the first highway at the end of the Gig and the beginning of the great sprawl of her native land, she was amazed. The plains before her seemed to stretch out for ever, or almost for ever, for there were mountains at one end of them, and she had never seen mountains before. Nor had she ever seen anything like the meandering muddle of buildings and yards that made up the towns she passed through. She had been too young to remember the journey to her aunt in the Gig after her parents died, but she would have sworn she had never seen anything like what she saw now in her life.

She met other people on their way to the name-day, although she was the only one she saw who went alone, a fact that gave her a certain dubious satisfaction; some people seemed to have brought their entire villages with them, or at least their entire families. Many people were well hung round with charms from their own fairies; she began to suspect that first-time travellers were recognizable by the number and elaborateness of their charms.

Katriona made good time. She was a quick walker, and deft, and easily wove her way through slower, larger, and clumsier processions. When the high roads were too crowded she took to the fields and forests; animals never troubled her, and she was too well-bred a country girl to tread on anyone's crop. At first she foraged for her food, but the closer she came to the royal city the fewer wild lands there were; she was not sorry for the excuse to buy herself the occasional hot cooked meal at a pub or inn, but mostly she fed herself from market stalls. One of her aunt's charms let her know which stall-keepers were honest.

Another of her aunt's charms let her sleep in trees without rolling out, so when she could find no haystack nor barn nor hedgerow she liked the look of, she found a tree instead. Sleeping in trees always gave her a stiff neck, but she preferred this to sleeping unhidden on the ground, marauder-charms notwithstanding .

It took her fifty-one days to reach the royal city, where, possibly on account of the excellence of another of her aunt's charms, she found herself a tiny cubby of a private room at a pub on the outskirts of the royal city, and prepared to wait the nine remaining days till the name-day.

The cubby gave her claustrophobia, but the swarming streets were worse; she was by turns glad she was alone, and longed for a familiar face. She thought oftenest of Barder and Flora as companions, but she missed her aunt the worst. The noise of the crowd went on even at night. Every street performer in the entire country seemed to be here: tumblers, actors and singers; and the constant rising excitement of holiday with the known culmination of the royal name-day meant that more and more people got drunk and lively every night as well. Katriona took to sleeping with a pillow over her head, but it wasn't enough. The pub gave her a special rate on her cubby in exchange for dish-washing and assisting the cook, and this helped to preserve her tiny stock of cash and to pass the time.

But it was still a long, edgy nine days.

Chapter 3

Katriona was up at dawn on the name-day, feeling as anxious as if she were a crucial part of the day's events instead of a small undistinguished member of an audience of thousands. She was determined to be through the gates as soon as the gates opened, and to get as near to – to whatever – as she could. She kept remembering her aunt saying, "I think you'll like the little princess," and while she was sure that what she had replied to her aunt at the time was the truth, it also felt as if a geas had been laid upon her, and that she must try as she could.

The gates were still closed when she arrived, but there were many people waiting there already, the crush somewhat impeded by the late travellers who had decided they would save valuable time in the morning by sleeping there, and, such had been the gaiety of the night previous, could be neither awakened nor moved. But Katriona was among the first few hundred through and out upon a great dazzle of lawn. She had never seen grass so smooth and beautiful; it distracted her from the tall poles garlanded with ribbons and flowers, the vast white tents with the royal banner flying from their peaks, the beautiful liveries of those who were moving slowly over the platform where the rows of lavishly decorated tables for the court were placed. (This stage was high enough so that even sitting down no courtier or peer would be shorter than the tallest member of a crowd which might be standing on its feet and straining for a glimpse of its betters.) At the centre was a taller platform where the princess' cradle stood, almost invisible among the gold and the lavender and the rosettes.

But she came to herself as she was jostled by the rush of people behind her, and made a dart towards the barrier that stood a few feet out from the court tables. The barrier was made of mere rope and ribbons, draped from narrow white posts, but its purpose was made clear by the guards that stood behind it. Although the guards themselves looked perhaps more ornamental than practical, still, guards were guards, and there were swords hanging from the gorgeous belts that crossed the splendid livery. The crowd looked at them, and steadied a little.

People began to find where they would sit down, the first-comers pleased with themselves and resistant to inroads by late-comers. More royal guards appeared to sort out disagreements before they became heated.

Katriona found herself a corner of an aisle close enough to the barrier to count the gems in the hilt of the sword of the guardsman nearest her and the ruches in the tablecloth of the nearest court table. She heard commotion ebb and flow in the empty aisle beside her and then a large bare leg and foot planted itself next to her. She was eye level with the backward sweep of an unsheathed sword that swung by the leg. Lord Prendergast had a dress sword he sometimes wore – sheathed – at fêtes and things, but it was straight, like those of the guards behind the barrier; this one was curved, and, more important, only about half a hand's-breadth distant. She was rather preoccupied with its nearness, for the first time thinking that as a small young woman alone she was vulnerable to displacement by larger rowdier elements. She observed that the bare leg was bare only to just below the knee, and then, rather more reassuringly, that the curiously wrapped and looped trousers disappeared towards the waist under a livery coat similar to those the guards were wearing.

The man she looked up at was probably not so tall as he seemed, standing next to her as she sat on the ground. His arms were crossed, and he was scowling, and she glanced over her shoulder at a group of young men, their colour somewhat heightened, looking at the sabre-bearer and visibly changing their minds about coming any farther. The sabre-bearer was directly beside her, as if it were she he was specially guarding.

The sabre seemed to whistle past her ear as the man turned and bent over her. She flinched. He was bald as well as barefoot, and his skin was a deep, shining grey-brown, rather like wet shale. He gazed down at her, and while he was still scowling, he no longer looked angry but puzzled. Katriona wanted to say, I am no-one, I am no-one from that no-place, the Gig, because his gaze seemed to be trying to make her into someone; but her tongue was stuck to the roof of her mouth. He straightened up, his eyes moving away from her and towards the dais, and she watched as his line of sight rose, and she could guess he was now looking at the cradle. She expected him to leave her now, and she drew in the first half of a deep sigh of relief.

But her breath caught in her throat when with a sudden, impulsive movement, he pulled something off over his head and bent over her again. He was holding the something down towards h e r, and as she looked up, he dropped it round her neck. She felt the weight of it at once, although it had drifted through the air as if it were made of gossamer. She touched it gently, feeling the half-exciting, half-irritating buzz of magic against her skin, thinking, Oh dear. This is not just a little charm, for sleeping in trees, or keeping your place in a queue.

There was a buzz in her ears, too; the amulet hadn't been made for her, she was too small for it, and it was having trouble finding her within the larger space it was accustomed to. She fingered it, waiting, dazzled, helpless, glad she was sitting down. She hadn't noticed before the shimmer of magic behind the barrier; well, of course, it would be there, in a crowd like this you could never know . . . but this was a lot of magic, a very large lot of magic, what were they expecting?

The buzz began to subside, and she heard the man say to her, "You wear that, child, and you stay just where you are, it'll hold you safe."

Still a little dazed, she said, "But—"

The man was already turning away – the sabre twinkled past

her eye – she reached out and grabbed his ankle, banging her head on the flat of the blade. It was cold against her skin, and for a moment she saw . . . lace, tiny delicate holes and large drooping arches, squares and triangles and shapes she had no names for, webwork from thread fine as spider silk to stout rope like a carter's, layers and layers of it, hung like an infinity of veils; soon she would be lost among them. . . She felt the man's hand on her head, tipping her upright again, brushing the tangle away. "Little maid, I am sorry. Eskwa is dangerous unsheathed, but I want him dangerous today; and I would rather he bound than he cut. Putting things to rights tomorrow if I have guessed wrong will be easier. But Eskwa does not like binding; he says it is not his work, and it makes him short-tempered."

She shook her head to clear it, pulling the string of the amulet against her neck till it bit into her skin as if saying to it, *Here. This is where I am. This is all of me there is*. She said unsteadily, "I know – how magic works. My aunt is a fairy." For some reason he laughed when she said this. "There must be an – exchange."

She could not refuse so great a gift, but what did one do in a case like this? There were rules for the basic things, salt for saving a life and wine for bringing one safe into the world; if you had no salt you licked the back of your hand; if you had no wine you offered an empty cup; if you had no cup, you offered your cupped hands. She didn't know the ritual response for having a queen's ransom dropped round your neck by a stranger when you hadn't a king's ransom to give. She was groping in the secret pocket inside her skirt for something to offer him; she did not want to give him one of her paltry charms, she thought it might be rude; and Eskwa made her nervous.

Her hand closed on Barder's wooden egret. She hated to lose it, but somehow that made it less meagre a token. She held it up, and the man took it solemnly, and looked at it, and as he looked at it he smiled, and with his smile Eskwa made her less nervous. "I think you are right, child," he said, "that there must be some exchange between us; Nagilbran always told me I was too light-minded. He would call me very light-minded indeed for this whim of mine," and he touched his collar-bone with the hand that did not hold Barder's egret, where his amulet had hung. "This is a very beautiful thing, and the man who made it for you loves you with a love that even magic cannot improve upon. I will not take it away from you. Listen, child. The necklace is a loan. I'll come back for it when you don't need it any more. Tomorrow, perhaps, when I have my wrong guesses to mend. And I thank you now for the loan of your medallion."

He laid it gently into her hand again, and left her, walking quickly away down the aisle. She turned her head just in time to see one last fierce glitter from Eskwa as she gratefully tucked the egret away; but then the crowd set up a shout and she turned back.

The king, queen and princess had finally arrived, last of all. The princess was being carried by a small, surprisingly drab person. The queen hovered over her, not so much, Katriona thought, that she had any fear for her, but because she found it difficult to tear herself away from the contemplation of her daughter, even at the expense of her own grand entrance. Katriona had her fingers curled round the centre stone of the sabre-bearer's amulet, and it throbbed gently, like a small beating heart. She could see the king's face, and the queen's, and the small drab person's, although they were some distance from her, but not the princess's; the princess was just a froth of ribbons and drapery.

The crowd leaped to its feet and shouted and waved their hands, Katriona borne with them, although no-one touched her. The little party mounted the half-dozen low steps to the cradle-dais, and then the small drab person handed the princess to the queen, who herself laid her tenderly in the cradle. And so Katriona saw nothing of the princess at all, just as she had predicted to her aunt two months ago: nothing but a bundle of gold and white and lavender. She thought she had a glimpse of one small waving fist just before the princess disappeared below the sides of the cradle.

Then there were the speeches, and Katriona felt she probably wasn't missing much by not being able to hear them on account of the noise of her neighbours, the wind, and the tendency of the speech-makers to mumble. The bishop, who was the first, and most resplendently dressed, and had the most sonorous mumble, had gone on the longest; maybe there was more to say over a princess than over an ordinary baby. Name-days in Foggy Bottom lasted as long as the lighting of two candles and one stick of incense, and the laying on of one pair of hands. Of course the Foggy Bottom priestling was muttering away like anything as he did these things, and the bishop was in no hurry. His satellite priests pulled out a series of little wallets and satchels of dried herbs and other unguessable crumbs and particles, adding a pinch here and a pinch there as if the princess were an outlandish sort of broth. They would have smothered her in the smoke from their censers as well, except the wind kept snatching it away.

It was funny about the wind; there had only been enough to make the banners show their colours a little while ago. But there had been an odd, almost brutal gust as the queen had laid the princess in her cradle; not only had the princess' own long trailing robes and wrappings suddenly wafted out, the queen's headdress had as well. Katriona glanced over at the fairy godmothers' table, where the wind was having a very good time among the headgear. And now the pennoncels flying high above the dais were struggling against their ropes as if they wished to fly away from here, from the name-day, from the royal city; and dark clouds were beginning to roll up. It had been a beautiful day, a day suitable for a princess' name-day; but now there were thunderclouds gathering in the north-west. The heartbeat against her palm quickened.

Katriona looked with some puzzlement towards the First Magicians' table. She found it hard to believe that the king and queen hadn't asked particularly that the weather today be fine; even her aunt had been known to make a tiny break in the clouds for a wedding-party to make a dash from the church to the pub where the food was without ruining the bride's finery (village bridal dresses could afford to be as grand as they often were because fairies saw that the weather didn't ruin them from one generation to the next), and her aunt in general didn't believe in messing with the weather. While it seemed to Katriona that conversation at the First Magicians' table had lapsed, she could not be sure that the number of magicians looking thoughtfully at the sky was not merely on account of the slow plod of the speeches.

Well, at last. The final orator shuffled away, and the king – trying not to give the impression of a person waking from a nap standing up – turned to the fairy godmothers' table and smiled. The first fairy was halfway up the dais before he'd finished turning his head.

Katriona leaned forward now, straining her ears, because she wanted to hear the sort of thing fairy godmothers gave to royal goddaughters; but the fairy, perhaps having taken instructions from the failure of the speech-givers to be heard, was careful, after she had bent over the cradle, to turn back towards the audience and shout: "To our very own princess, Casta Albinia Allegra Dove Minerva Fidelia Aletta Blythe Domina Delicia Aurelia Grace Isabel Griselda Gwyneth Pearl Ruby Coral Lily Iris Briar-Rose, I give the gift of golden hair, as gold as corn-tassels in August."

Katriona nearly fell over. Golden hair! Golden *hair*? What an utterly idiotic gift! Aunt had always taught her that you were *respectful* of your magic! And here, the very first – golden hair! from a fairy godmother, who could give you anything – well, almost anything. They would only have invited the best to be the princess' godmothers. But here was the second godmother. Surely she would do better.

Wrong. "To our princess, I give the gift of eyes as blue as love-in-a-mist, or summer sky after rain." Katriona put her head in her hand. "Skin as white as milk." She'll have to live under a royal parasol all her life, then; skin like that burns indoors, with the shutters closed. "And as flawless as the silk woven by the royal silkworms." She'll look like a *doll*. No *person* has flawless skin. "Lips as red as cherries." "Teeth like pearls." Katriona missed a few, by dropping the amulet and pressing her hands over her ears in despair. "Feet that never stumble at dancing." "Fingers that never falter upon the flute." "A singing voice sweeter than the first birds of spring" and "A laugh like a silver bell." "Her golden hair will fall in long ringlets wide and round as goblets."

Katriona wished her aunt were there. She found herself

thinking over all the charms her aunt had given her, wondering if there were anything she could give to the princess. Would she like, when she was a little older, to be able to sleep in a tree? While they're at it, she thought sourly, hearing the bestowal of eyelashes as long and fine and silky as the hairs at the tip of a fleethound's tail, they could at least give her fingernails that never break off below the quick, eyes that never get dust in them, a digestion that is never upset. They hadn't guaranteed her not to have flat feet yet either; weren't they worried they'd end up with a princess with feet like a duck's? . . . "Her embroidery shall be peerless"; "her sweetmeats sublime."

Poor princess. Was Katriona imagining it, or did the queen look the tiniest bit dismayed? Did she shiver? Or was that only the wind? Katriona remembered the popular story that the queen had been in her father's kitchens overseeing dinner when the emissary had come to offer her the king's hand in marriage; perhaps she had been looking forward to teaching her daughter her own recipe for sweetmeats.

As the twentieth gift was uttered – something to do with spinning woollen thread as fine and strong as the slender reedy leaves of the maundry, much loved by basket-weavers – there was a burst of thunder so near overhead that everyone, except possibly the king, ducked; a number of people stretched themselves flat on the ground, with the concomitant effect of a lot of boots going into a lot of faces; cries of pain and protest combined with the next blast of thunder. Katriona was suddenly the only one near the barrier still sitting up; and she clutched the sabre-bearer's amulet with both hands.

In the aisle in front of Katriona, just before the boundary, a black cloud was creating itself. Its centre twisted and writhed and began to take on a shape somewhat human, and as it did so, the outside of the cloud began to organize itself into a long grey cloak, and the cloak began to send up streaks of purple and magenta and cerise from its hem, as if the air were a vat of dye it trailed in. And then the human form within it gave a final jerk and shudder, and a woman stood there, a woman as tall as the king, and with a face more dangerous than an army waiting for the command to attack, and she wore black and grey streaked with purple and magenta and cerise, and a necklace of black stones.

She turned slowly in a circle, holding the edges of her cloak against her bent arms so that the material hung down like wings; and as she finished her circuit and again faced the dais, she dropped her hands and arms, and laughed.

"So: a fine day for a princess' name-day, and a fine crowd to see. Well! I wanted to see, too – but I was not invited. I live alone near a wood – perhaps not quite alone – but no herald came to me; and when one-and-twenty fairy godmothers were chosen I was not among them. But I wished to see the princess' name-day – and so I came."

She paused, but no-one said anything. Even the First Magicians sat as if stricken; perhaps they were. The queen had bent over the cradle as the black cloud formed itself out of nothing, but she seemed frozen, reaching for her child but not able to touch her. One of the courtiers, at the end of the table by the aisle Katriona sat beside, held a bit of bread to his mouth, but he neither ate it, nor laid it down, nor closed his mouth. Katriona was rigid in what she thought was nothing but sheer terror; if she moved, the tall woman might notice her.

As the black cloud had become a woman, Katriona had watched the magic barrier behind the ordinary barrier flame up till the faces of the people she saw through it were patched and mottled with its colours: reds and red-purples and mauves and greys. As the tall woman spoke, each word seemed to glance off that undulating barrier, but it left a little black streak behind it, so that the barrier began to look spotted, like fine sheer cloth with soot.

When she finished speaking, the tall woman reached out a hand towards the barrier, and the sooty black streaks extended into smudges and dapples, till the barrier became piebald, and the clear colours were all shadowed. But she dropped her hand at last, and the shadows began to fade; but Katriona fancied, as they faded, that they shimmered grey-brown, like wet shale, and that instead of spots and mottles, they were woven, like cord or rope. The woman laughed again, but it was a laugh like the sudden knowledge of your own death, and many of the people who lay on the ground whimpered or cried out.

"I, too, have a gift for the princess," said the tall woman, "and while it pleases you not to seek it, I will give it to her nonetheless; but perhaps . . ." and here the woman's voice grew silky with malevolence, "perhaps I will alter it just a little. I was not in a good mood when I arrived, you know, for I had expected an invitation to the name-day; I was still hoping right up until this morning that this would be put right. I might still have forgiven you, this morning.

"But I am quite a . . . quite an important fairy, and you cannot have overlooked me, except by deliberation. I do not like to be overlooked. And now, when I have humbled myself to you by coming anyway, not only do you not ask me to sit at the high table, you hold me here with your rabble of subjects. . . No, I am not in a good mood.

"I wish the country to remember me, too, as one of the fairies who gave the princess a gift on her name-day." She had been facing the barrier, but now she turned round, towards the crowd – the rabble of subjects – and threw her arms out wide. "My original gift was this: that the princess will grow in all those beauties and virtues she has been so adorned with this day. But on the day she reaches her majority – on the day that her father should crown her his heir – on her one-and-twentieth birthday, she shall fall down in a poisoned sleep, and die, and nothing anyone can do will save her."

Katriona stopped breathing.

"But that now seems to me so – simple. And so I think I will alter it – a little. What was it I heard some magic-trifling buffoon giving her as I arrived? Some sublime ability to spin the dense stinking hair of a sheep into something resembling the thin drab tumescences of an unlovely marsh plant? How charming. I think I shall say – on her one-and-twentieth birthday she shall prick her finger on the spindle of a spinning wheel; and this prick shall cause her to fall into that poisoned sleep from which no-one shall rouse her."

Not breathing wasn't enough; Katriona wanted to be a grass blade, a lump of gravel, an earthworm, anything but a person listening to this curse, shaping itself implacably over the baby princess' tiny, oblivious head.

"Perhaps you will say that is mere ornamentation. And it does still give you one-and-twenty years to enjoy her. I think . . . I think it shall be that *my disposition of her future may happen at any time.*" Again the woman laughed, and the people lying on the ground outside the barrier writhed and flinched as if the laugh were a lash across their flesh. "Perhaps I shall even come to her, in secret, tonight, and pick her up out of her cradle, and press her tiny soft hand against the sharp spindle end. . ."

Thunder groaned in the distance in a terrible harmony to the moans of the crowd; the queen gave one shriek, and fell fainting across the cradle. The king, moving as if he were tearing himself free from iron chains, stooped beside her, and took her in his arms. The tall woman smiled. "Burn all the spinning wheels in the kingdom, should you choose; it will not save her. Lock her up in your deepest dungeon for the rest of her short life, and that will not save her either. Delight in your princess while you can, for you shall not have her long!"

The tall woman threw up her hands, and she was a black cloud again, tumultuous as a tornado, spinning, spinning, spinning like a kind of maniacal wheel, where she had been standing, and the banners above the dais were torn free, and the poles that had held the silken hangings crashed down upon the king and the queen and the cradle with the princess still in it – and Katriona, with no recollection of how she got there, found herself kneeling by the cradle and snatching up the now-crying princess in her own arms and patting the little back and stroking the little head and saying, over and over, "No, no, it shall not happen, it can't happen, they won't let it happen, you can have all my aunt's charms, I'm not much of a fairy yet although my aunt says I will be, but you can have my gift, it's only baby-magic so it won't last, and it isn't very useful anyway, I can talk to animals, sometimes it is a little useful, and it is the only useful gift anyone has given you all day, sometimes if someone has put a spell on you or on something round you, if you have an animal you can ask, animals aren't so mixed up by magic as we are, it's only baby-magic, it's only – but you're only a baby yourself, oh, oh, it *cannot* happen," and she realized the tears were streaming down her face and down the back of the princess' neck, which might be part of why the princess was crying so hard. The sabre-bearer's amulet thrummed against her breast like the beating of many small heavy hammers, and as she rocked the princess she saw that there were shreds of red and red-purple and mauve and grey draped over her arms and strung through her fingers like torn fabric she had clawed her way through, and streamers of it hung as well from her hair and tickled her face, but she had no hand free to brush them away.

There was an uproar round her, and to the extent that she was thinking clearly about anything, she was expecting the princess to be taken away from her at once; but what happened instead was someone's arm round her waist, helping her to her feet, hustling her, with the princess still in her arms, down the back of the dais, and under the wreck of the poles and the name-day hangings. Here there was a little corner of quiet, and the hustling stopped, and Katriona found herself looking down into the face of the small drab person who had carried the princess and stood behind the queen, and her face, too, was streaked with tears.

"My dear, do you have any idea what you have done? I would thank you for it, only I doubt that you do know. "

Katriona balanced the princess awkwardly so that she could sweep the worst of the flapping, confusing streamers out of her face with one hand; she might have thought to offer the princess to the small person, but she did not, and the small person did not offer to take her. The small person did, as the amulet was revealed from behind the now only whimpering baby, reach out and touch it delicately with one finger. "Well. That explains one thing."

Katriona found herself smiling, the desperate smile of someone who has no idea what is going on, is frightened, and wishes to please or at least to placate. The small person's eyes rose from the amulet to Katriona's face, and she smiled back, but it was a gentle and understanding smile. "You are still only a child yourself. My poor dear. . . Oh, I do not know what to do!" The small person's face lost its smile as if it would never find it again, and she pressed a hand briefly over her eyes, and a few tears crept out from under her palm. Speaking as if to herself, she said, "What I told the queen is only the truth – I'm too bound up in this family – over many years and three generations of kings and queens I have sunk my power deep here, too deep to be got back. . . There were to have been one-and-twenty gifts, and only twenty were given when Pernicia appeared – Oh yes," she said, speaking directly to Katriona again, "yes, I know who she is; but I did not know she was so powerful. I hoped, as one always does hope until catastrophe strikes, that it would not come. I hoped that the years had worn her out, the years since our last queen. . .

"Listen. There is no time. I will try to see to it that no-one remembers you. Take the princess and go – take her and go. That is her only chance – because by the time it is quiet enough that one might be able to think, it will be too late. I will give you a charm so that you can escape the royal city unseen; then you are on your own. I dare not let you carry any smell of me or my magic beyond the walls of the city – ah! I dare not so much as kiss her good-bye; I dare not touch her again, now that you have taken her— Do not tell me where you are going, do not say it aloud in this place, in this air, that Pernicia so recently disturbed for her own ends. The fewer traces you leave the more easily I can erase them."

"I – but—" began Katriona, appalled, but unconsciously easing the princess against her till she fitted comfortably against her own breast and shoulder. The princess had one small fist wrapped in the neckline of Katriona's dress, and was beginning to experiment with pulling her hair with the other one.

"Yes, I know," said the small drab fairy. "I'm sorry. But you will do it, will you not? I cannot force you any more than I can keep her safe myself. But it is truly the princess's only hope. Take her home with you. Raise her as if she were your own."

"*Raise* her? But what—"

"You will hear from me later. I will find you when I can – when

I dare. It may not be for some time. Pernicia is . . . we must find out everything about her, and this will not be easy. Listen to this — memorize it — anyone coming from me will tell it to you, and that is how you will know who they are. Words are the only token we can risk. And — and — a poem is the most I can give her, my dear, my only darling!" The fairy's voice faltered, but then went on firmly: " 'Small spider weave on a silver sleeve, Oh weave your grey web nearer, From a golden crown let your silk hang down, For lost, lost, lost is the wearer.' "

" '. . . is the wearer,' " repeated Katriona obediently. "But what will you tell the poor queen?"

But she never knew the answer, for as she raised her head from the effort of memorization — her mind felt like a field of rabbits bolting in panic from the sight of the hunter — to look again at the small person who had just destroyed her life and given her some other, far more dangerous life for which she was totally unprepared, she found herself on the outskirts of the royal city, in a small stand of oak trees. It was near sunset, and the princess was asleep on her shoulder.

Chapter 4

"Small spider weave. . ." Katriona murmured; by the sun, the small fairy had recited the poem for her to learn several hours ago. She gave a hitch upward with the arm that bore the weight of the sleeping princess; babies always weighed more than you thought they would. And . . . she would be carrying this one for a long time.

She sat down. She had to sit down. If Pernicia herself had appeared in that little grove and ordered her to hand the princess over, Katriona would still have sat down. She tried to arrange the princess on her knee, but sleeping babies are intransigently floppy, and Katriona, while she had had a good bit of experience with babies, was not at her best, and her hands were shaking. The princess lay like a little crushed parcel, snoring faintly.

Katriona tried to take stock. Most of her few possessions were back in the little cubby at the pub with no chance of reclaiming them. She would have to hope that no conclusions were drawn about their abandonment. She was wearing her charm-skirt (now tucked tactfully under her ordinary skirt, so that she didn't look such a bumpkin), and her few remaining ha'pennies, her small folding knife, and her flint and tinder were in her pocket with Barder's egret. She was wearing her best clothes, which she had been a little ashamed of as not at all best enough for a princess' name-day, but their lacklustre appearance now would be useful, when she had no others, and they were, furthermore, both comfortable and durable. Better yet was the fact that she was wearing her cloak, not because she had thought she would need it, but because it was the newest thing she owned; she would miss her blanket at night, but at least with the cloak they wouldn't freeze. Nearer home even in midsummer there was no guarantee of warm nights. She unwound the scarf that went round her neck, crossed her breast, and tied at her waist; it was not ideal for the purpose, but she could use it for a baby-sling.

Then she lifted her outer skirt and detached one of the charms, the one that made the wearer look too poor and ordinary to be worth a passing glance. She hoped that all her charms would include a baby that she carried – not a contingency she had thought to verify with her aunt beforehand – but this one she tucked down inside the princess' clothing. It had been made up with robbers and thugs in mind; she hoped it would include royal messengers desperately searching for some sign of the missing princess and her kidnapper. It was the best she could do.

She unwrapped, and snipped off, the long ribbons of gold and lavender, and the pink rosettes, that the princess was wearing; even her smallclothes were so white as to be dazzling, and far too finely made to be anything other than what they were, clothing for a princess on her name-day. Well, there was nothing to be done about that; she didn't have a charm for producing baby clothes out of oak leaves; and after a few days they would be as grimy as she could wish – rather more grimy than she could wish – and she wasn't planning on letting anyone near enough to examine the quality of the stitching. After a moment's hesitation she stuffed the bright ribbons into another pocket in her petticoat. She didn't want to leave them to be found, and she had no good way of disposing of them; furthermore she had some unhappy sense that they might be the only symbols of her heritage the poor little princess had remaining to her.

Lastly she tucked the sabre-bearer's amulet under her dress, wondering what the small person – she didn't even know her name – had meant by "That explains one thing." Did the small person know the sabre-bearer, and his tendency to befriend undistinguished strangers with gifts of great magic? Or was she only referring to the fact that the amulet had let Katriona cross the barrier Pernicia had not been able to break? At least the weight and throb of it were gone; it rested lightly against her, almost too lightly, as if the string that held it together were all it was made of, and the queerly translucent stones were mist or imagining.

Then she stood up and started walking. She did not know what else to do. The sun told her which way to walk; she was going home.

There were, that evening, surprisingly few people on the roads, and those there were seemed absorbed in their own concerns. There was an air of tension everywhere, but Katriona was not sure if this might merely be the tension she carried with her. Her legs were used to heavy loads, but she was accustomed to panniers or backpacks to carry them; after a few hours of carrying the princess her shoulders and arms were tired, and her back sore. She would get used to it; she had to.

When a flying wedge of horsemen wearing the royal livery shot past her – the bugler giving warning for everyone to fall out of the way – it was all Katriona could do not to shriek out loud; and she wasn't at all sure that what she wanted to shriek wasn't, "Here, I've got her! It's all a terrible mistake! Please, take her back to her poor parents!" But she didn't; and no-one looked twice at the young woman with the anguished face carrying the sleeping baby in a sling.

As twilight deepened into night and Katriona trudged on, she thought, I must have milk for her. I dare not ask to buy milk while we are still so close to the city because I do not want anyone to wonder why I am carrying an unweaned baby not my own; but. . .

Perhaps it was some lingering effect of the small fairy's charm; perhaps it was merely Katriona's own dogged determination. But she did not stop that night, and the princess never woke. Katriona knew she should wonder if the princess were sick; but she was too grateful for the respite. Once they were out into wilder country it would be easier.

*

It was easier, but it was not easy. At the end of that first centuries-long night, Katriona struggled into a bit of hedgerow with a shaggy bank that hid them from the road, and fell into an exhausted sleep. She was awoken too few hours later by a thin, miserable, hungry wail from the princess, who was sopping and dirty besides. Katriona dealt with the more immediately disagreeable problem with a few strips hacked from her petticoat, and then, since she couldn't spare anything potentially reusable, rolled up the smelly, disgusting mess of the princess's underclothes, wrapped it in another strip torn from her petticoat, and tucked it grimly into the sling under the baby. The princess, still fretful, found motion distracting, and only whinged and grizzled as Katriona staggered down to the road again and set off, looking sharply round her for any sign of water.

There was a stream, fortunately, not far away, and she fought her way upstream through low-hanging shrubs till they were a little out of sight of the high road, drank deeply herself, splashed her face savagely in an attempt to wake herself up, laid the princess's discarded nappy in the stream and put a stone on it to soak, and set about trying to persuade the princess to drink a little water. It wasn't food any more than it was for Katriona, but neither of them had had even water since midday the day before, and breakfast was still somewhere in the future.

She contrived a twist out of another bit of her petticoat – it was disappearing fast, and she needed its pockets – which the princess seized on with no hesitation and sucked eagerly till she discovered it wasn't what she wanted, whereupon she spat it out and began to scream with real rage, turning red with effort and throwing herself round.

"Oh, magic and glory, what do I do now?" said Katriona aloud, beginning to panic; but her ear registered certain little rustlings in the bushes and forced her mind to take note. *Good morning, sir,* she said, because the old dog-fox was watching her and the princess with interest.

Hungry baby, he said, surprising her; foxes generally wanted to talk about butterflies and grass and weather for a long time while they sized you up – if they would talk to you at all. Even in that country foxes didn't much like having human beings who could talk to them – and even in that country those who could were rare enough – and were not inclined to be helpful to any fairy. Katriona was already a little surprised that this one had brought himself to her attention in the first place; but she was always polite to animals, and a fox might know where the nearest field with calved cows in it was. *Yes*, she said sadly, *and I have no milk*.

Not your baby, said the fox.

No, she began, and then said firmly, *I am not her mother, but she is mine to care for*.

Foxes have a sense of humour, and she felt this one expressing his, since she manifestly was not taking good care of the princess at present. She looked at him, scowling, reminding herself that she still had a favour to ask him.

Wife had pups, fifteen days ago, said the dog-fox.

Katriona managed not to say, Well how nice for you both, but she thought the fox could guess what she hadn't said, and if foxes laughed, he would have laughed louder. She had picked the princess up, and was trying to cradle her, but the princess wasn't having any of it: she wanted breakfast – she wanted yesterday's tea and supper – and she wanted them now. Tiny fists can hurt quite a lot when they hit you in the face. Katriona lowered her to her lap, and hung on. Maybe she would wear out soon.

Wife has milk, said the fox.

Katriona's head shot up and she stared at him. He was crouched on the bank above her, his red coat perfectly camouflaged by the last winter's leaves still caught in the hedgerow, below this year's green. She was so startled she forgot to be polite. *Why do you want to help us?* she said.

Not foxy, to help human? said the fox, smiling a fox smile. *No. Like babies. Even human babies. Yours makes too much noise.*

Katriona knew what he was saying; noise in the wild was dangerous – and he didn't know the half of it. *I don't know how to make her quiet. She's angry because she's hungry.*

The fox jumped down from the bank and put his nose to the

princess' screwed-up, beetroot-coloured, shrieking face, and stoically withstood two bashes from those heavy little fists before she registered the arrival of another presence. Katriona held her breath. The princess opened her eyes, and her shrieks fell off into more hesitant wails. She grasped one of the fox's ears and pulled. He flinched, but put his tongue out and licked her, and she laughed. It was rather a hoarse laugh, but it was a laugh.

Quickly now, he said, withdrew his head (giving it a shake, as if to resettle his ears, and his nose, where the princess had struck him), and trotted off, upstream. The princess gave another cry at her new toy being so abruptly withdrawn, but her tantrum had worn her out, and on a too-long empty stomach she didn't have the strength to start in again. Almost as suddenly as blowing out a candle she fell asleep again, although she grizzled in her sleep, and her little face was frowning, her mouth set and the corners turned emphatically down, in the unequivocal way of unhappy babies.

Katriona snatched up the nappies from the water, and held them at arm's length while they streamed—at least the running water had cleaned them fairly well—supporting the baby sling with the other arm. She ached all over, and was herself dizzy with hunger, and her held-out arm kept dropping involuntarily to her side, wetting her skirt and that ankle and foot. The foot began to squelch in its shoe.

Katriona expected an argument from the fox's wife, but she followed him out of their den almost as soon as the fox had gone in, with motherliness radiating off her like heat from a fire. She licked the princess' face, and the princess woke, and obligingly pulled her ears, but she was weeping before she was properly awake, a thin, despairing wail, and it hurt Katriona's heart to hear her.

Put her down beside me, said the vixen. *Lay her as if she were — a puppy. She's too big for me to move. I'll do the rest.*

And she did. Katriona wondered if the fox cubs whimpered for their breakfast that day, for the princess emptied the contents of several nipples before she fell asleep again, this time smiling and rosy. *Thank you*, said Katriona. *Thank you, thank you. Can I . . .* she hesitated. *Is there anything at all I can do for you? I – I'm not a real fairy. I can't do much. I'm sorry.*

What's your name? said the dog-fox.

Katriona, Katriona said in surprise.

Well, Katriona, said the dog-fox, *if a fox ever calls you Katriona, you must come to its rescue. Will you do that?*

Yes, said Katriona, and felt the fox's sense of humour again, although it had a bitter edge. *Yes*, said the dog-fox. *I believe you. I had been watching you some time before I spoke, this morning, and I might not have let you know I was there.*

Sleep here now, said the vixen, as Katriona wearily began shrugging herself back into the sling. *We'll keep watch. I can give her one more meal before you set out again. But only one. Or my babies will howl.* Fox cubs didn't howl, but Katriona acknowledged the joke. She fell asleep so quickly she cracked her head against the ground lying down.

She opened her eyes to the sound of delighted infant laughter: the princess was playing catch with the dog-fox's tail. The rest of him was lying just out of her reach – she couldn't quite roll over yet, although she was trying – and he tickled her face with his brush, and then flicked it away as she grabbed for it. She thought this was a delicious game, and waved and kicked, and sneezed. Katriona couldn't see any obvious tufts of fur gone, and she rather thought the old fox was having a good time. Fleas, she thought. Never mind. I will find some wild garlic for the fleas.

The thought of wild garlic made her stomach give a sudden shriek of its own, almost as loud as the princess' as she once again missed her grab, and equally suddenly Katriona realized she was smelling food. Fox dens do tend to be a bit redolent of past fox dinners, but this was . . . she sat up and turned round and saw a meat pie lying on a bit of bare earth near her. It looked as if it had had a rather hard journey, but it was indubitably a meat pie.

The dog-fox said, *It's for you. Sorry about the teethmarks. I was in a bit of a hurry.*

Katriona had eaten it all almost before the fox finished speaking. She sighed. *I can only thank you again, she said. And again and again.*

I could grow accustomed to being thanked, said the fox, half joking and half serious; thanks as humans understood them were not usual in animal cultures. (Nor were apologies. The fox's pride had evidently been offended by an insufficiently clever snatch at the stolen meat pie. Pride was very important. It was one of the things that kept you alive.) *I feel you are hiding from your own kind for a good reason*, said the fox after a pause. *It was the princess's name-day yesterday, and at midday the sky darkened, and the wind smelled wrong, and later on the king's horsemen galloped down the roads with angry, frightened faces. And then you came.*

Yes, said Katriona, and the fox asked no more; secrets were another of the things that kept you alive. Katriona could hear muffled squeaks and rustles from inside the den; presumably the vixen was feeding her own children.

I thank you for your thanks, the dog-fox said at last, almost primly, and she had impulsively half reached out to touch him, a caress or a hug, before she remembered what brutal bad manners that would be, and flinched back. The fox was looking at her thoughtfully. *Like this*, he said, rolled to his feet, walked over to her, and laid his long narrow furry cheek briefly against her wide smooth round one.

Chapter 5

There were fleas, but the wild garlic helped, and the reek of it kept certain other inevitable odours a little at bay. And she began to think that one or two of the fairy godmothers' gifts that she had missed while her hands were over her ears must have been about good nature, because the princess was astonishingly good-natured during their long difficult journey; the tantrum she had their first morning was the only tantrum she ever had. Maybe it's something in the milk, Katriona thought a little wildly, for the princess drank not only fox's milk, and goat's, and cow's and ewe's and mare's and a variety of domestic cats' and dogs' (mostly sheepdogs' and collies'), but also doe's, badger's, otter's, polecat's, pine marten's, wolf's, lynx's, wildcat's, and bear's (some of these more tactically difficult to achieve than others). She knew, although she had not been told, that some kind of word had gone out among the animals that there was a baby walking west and north in the arms of a fairy woman not her mother, who couldn't do much fairy work but could talk to animals – she hoped they said she was polite – and she often found when she huddled down by a farmyard at evening or very early morning (one of the extraordinary adaptations the princess had made without fuss was to the necessary regime of only two meals a day) and asked, *Goat, goat, can you spare me any milk?* the goat – or whatever milking mother was on offer – was half expecting her, and could often tell her where to look for the princess' next meal as well.

Katriona preferred the bigger farms, when she was lucky

enough to find a farm she thought she could risk approaching (hedgerow or haystack near the field with the animals she wanted in it; farmhouse far from the farmyard) because the princess, especially since she only had the chance to slake it twice a day, had a mighty appetite, and a small householder would miss what she took. A few times Katriona left one of her last ha'pennies on a doorstep, or tied up in the farmer's kerchief hung over his pitchfork, or by the sink in the dairy for the farmwife to find. This was the sort of thing that happened in this country, but then the ha'pennies left were usually silver, or sometimes, if someone was very lucky, something called fairy metal, though no-one (including fairies) knew where it came from, iridescent in sunlight, and strangely warm in the hand even in winter. Katriona's ha'pennies were just the ordinary copper ones struck by the king's mint; but then you never got to spend the iridescent ones. They became family heirlooms. Which was all very well *after* the day you had to go hungry because someone had pinched your milk. (The story that went with the fairy-metal coins was that the animals milked better and the crops grew better and the human farmer and farm family were healthier for the whole season after. She couldn't do anything about that, either. All she could do was leave a plain dull ha'penny.)

But often enough there was no farm, or there was a too-populous village too near even a good large spread-out farm, or something else was wrong, often nothing Katriona could even describe, only a prickle between her shoulder-blades that made her clutch the princess more closely and keep on.

And then she had to listen for the sound of wild animals talking among themselves, which was as difficult as picking out a fox's red coat among last year's beech leaves, and for similar reasons. And then, having managed to orient herself to a sound not made by wind or water or will-o'-the-wisp (wills-o'-the-wisp in that country could be quite noisy, if dancing lights and minor visions weren't alluring enough and the wisps were beginning to feel frustrated), she had to try to move in that direction, till she could say, *Pardon me, gentle persons, I have a favour to ask*, before they disappeared because a human was approaching them. Not always, even then, would they wait for her, but usually they did: the word had gone out.

She wished she could ask why there had been that word: there weren't any stories that weren't obviously nursery tales about animals organizing to feed an orphaned baby. Did the animals know that this baby was the princess? Was that part of the word that was passed among them? No-one had ever asked who the baby was, but then animals wouldn't. The baby was the baby and the mother was the mother, even when she wasn't. (The dog-fox had been rude in suggesting the princess was not Katriona's baby, but foxes are brash creatures, and gratuitously inquisitive. Katriona couldn't imagine any animal but a fox – except, possibly, a few of the cheekier birds – remarking as he had remarked on the princess' name-day.) Animals always wanted to know – their lives too often depended on it – but they rarely asked questions. You weren't supposed to have to ask questions; language was a weak and unreliable means of taking in information, and many wild animals dispensed with it; your ears and nose and eyes were much preferable.

And because the animals did not question her, she could not ask them: Why are you doing this for us?

There were stories that didn't sound like nursery tales, about companies of leopards and lynxes and dragons and wolves that had fought at the sides of various kings and queens many years ago; but maybe those were merely nursery tales for grown-ups. History was as unreliable as almost everything else that was influenced by magic in this country – which was nearly everything – and those stories could have been true or they could have not been true. Did the animals know about Pernicia?

But Katriona did have to go in search of animals to help her; they might expect her, they might wait for her, but they rarely came to meet her. She had had no warning, one evening, and was beginning to feel some anxiety that she had gone so far into a plausible-looking wood without hearing any animal speech, when a hummock of darkness had risen in front of her in the twilight and shadows, and become a bear. She had gripped the princess so tightly she gave a little squeak and then began to cry, and even after the bear had addressed them in a voice as kind and loving as Katriona's aunt's, saying, *I have milk for your baby*, Katriona had not been able to make any reply for at least a minute. The steady yellow eyes of wolves appearing out of the darkness between blink and blink was nothing compared to the revelation of the bear.

The bear sat down, quietly, and crossed her immense, dagger-clawed paws over her broad breast, and waited for Katriona to recover herself. Not wishing to appear rude, but still struck dumb, Katriona took a wavering step forward; and then the princess, who had stopped crying, gave one of her delicious, crowing chirrups, and held out her arms – to the bear.

There was this also to say about the bear: She was big enough, presumably, to spare milk for a human baby without much shortage to her own. It had taken most of a riverbank of otters to feed the princess, another evening, though the otters had seemed to think it all a great joke. The nursing mothers had hung round talking among themselves about the adventure of feeding a human baby while one after another had her turn with the princess, and before each had slid silently back into the river to return to her own territory and her own children. That had been a long night, because many of the otters were coming from a considerable distance, and the princess's dinner had a number of hiatuses, or perhaps merely courses – with which she put up with her usual good humour.

The princess was undoubtedly thriving. She wasn't very clean, but she was bright-eyed – and alarmingly cheerful – and apparently robustly healthy. And energetically putting on weight. Katriona's mind and eye noted this with satisfaction; her back and shoulders were less pleased.

It took them three and a half months to return to Foggy Bottom. Katriona had decided that she had best travel mostly at night, and off the main road; and with the (increasing) burden of the princess as well, she did not move very quickly. She began to feel as if the journey were her entire life, and that she would never come to the end of it; she felt that way particularly at the end of every night's walk, because she was always tired and hungry, and worried whether this would be the night that their luck ran out, and she would find no milk for the princess. There was always a slightly dreamlike quality to talking to animals, both because it happened in your head, like you might make up imaginary conversations with people, and because the way animals' minds worked was so different from the way human minds worked. The disorienting quality of beast-talking was that much more bewildering when you were tired.

Katriona was also always short on sleep because she woke often every day, thinking she heard the sound of Pernicia's creatures creeping near them (and what would they be? Dark and scaly, with poisoned spines? Slithery and slimy, with too many legs? Or more beautiful than anything kind and good, with eyes that killed you quicker than basilisks? Would it be worse if Katriona could talk to them, too? Or maybe she didn't use creatures at all; maybe Katriona would wake up drowning in a swamp or having been turned into a giant hogweed or a troll. Or – worst thought of all – possibly Pernicia would come herself, in person; Katriona often saw her, tall, deadly, stooping down to seize them both. . .). Or at least the king's hunters.

Why hadn't the royal magicians found them? A really good magician could find anything that was lost by looking into the palm of the hand he usually carried his wand in; even a not very good magician ought to be able to find something large and important and specific, like a baby princess, with a few drops of farseeing and a bowl of water. If the small person, the fairy who had given Katriona both the princess and a poem, was powerful enough to keep them invisible to the best searchers in the realm, why wasn't she powerful enough to protect the princess at home where she belonged?

Or could the sabre-bearer's amulet be hiding them?

Katriona couldn't bear to think about any of it too closely.

She often thought of trying to find a robin who could get a message to her aunt – robins always seemed to have family in areas you wanted to get a message to or from – but she couldn't think of anything to say that wasn't more dangerous than remaining silent and continuing to trust to luck. It was bad enough she was leaving a trail of stolen milk between the royal city and the Gig. Perhaps their luck was merely that magicians scorned talking to animals; animal thoughts weren't nearly orderly enough to suit magicians, and were always full of large untidy preoccupations, like sex and death and the next meal.

She had seen no-one in the royal livery in weeks. She often had to follow the main road for a little while, because it was the only way through; and sometimes they had to sleep near it because she was too tired to look for better shelter, and then she would be awakened by the sounds that travellers made, and peer through leaves or shrubbery to see them, half hoping she would overhear some conversation about the missing princess, about the ten-foot giant who had snatched her out of her cradle at the name-day and been seen striding south with her, which was where the king's trackers were concentrating their efforts. She hoped it was a good thing, to see no-one in the king's livery.

She was always hungry. She was often too tired to forage for herself properly after she'd found milk for the princess, and she was desperately weary of the sort of things you could scrounge in wild land in summer, and eat raw; only a few times, when it had been raining and they were both wet and cold, did she risk a fire (one of her aunt's charms persuaded wet wood to burn, although the wetter the wood, the sooner the charm wore out. Her aunt sold many of these charms in the fenny Gig) and then only if she could find a place far enough from the road and with the wind in the right direction. Once or twice the ha'pennies she left in dairies were for cheeses she'd stolen; but the only milk she was willing to drink was goats' and cows' and ewes', although it was sometimes offered elsewhere (including by the bear). She was tired of sitting on the ground; and even with a no-rocks charm, there was an infinity of difference between sleeping on the ground and on the oldest, roughest, lumpiest, and most-in-need-of-restuffing mattress, made by human hands, and sheltered by four walls and a roof – and furnished with blankets and pillows. (They never slept in trees. Katriona didn't want to find out the hard way that that particular charm would not include a baby she carried.)

She was also, of course, very, very tired of the princess, but the first time she had leant over her to pick her up for their evening's walk, seen her eyes focus gravely on the face above her, and then, after a thoughtful moment, watched her face break out into a smile as bright as daylight – a smile just for *her*, Katriona, as clear as if the princess had called her by name – she had to admit she was also rather terrifyingly fond of her. Even if she did weigh too much. And always needed changing. I didn't have to rush up to the cradle and start babbling to her like a loony, Katriona thought testily; nobody forced me. I just did. But if I hadn't, who would have her now? The small fairy would have found someone else . . . wouldn't she? She would have found someone *better* . . . wouldn't she?

What had she told the poor king and queen?

The last thing before Katriona fell asleep every morning, she recited to herself the verse the small fairy had taught her. She often fell asleep murmuring, weave your grey web nearer. . . And woke up murmuring, lost, lost, lost is the wearer. . . "Your golden crown is certainly lost," she said under her breath one evening, dunking the grubby baby in a shallow pond, fairly warm after the sun had been on it all afternoon. The grubby baby laughed, and pulled up a handful of bottom-of-shallow-pond mud and decomposing slime, and rubbed it into her hair. This was excellent fun, so she pulled up another. "Oh, you're a lot of help, you are," said Katriona, making a dive at her with a reasonably clean piece of flannel, and rubbing her face. The princess put up with this indignity stoically. "Sometimes I think I miss soap even more than bread. But, you know, we'll be home soon." She paused, and the baby, catching her mood, also paused, and looked at her anxiously.

"Home for you, too," Katriona said, catching one of the muddy hands and applying her flannel to it. "Home for you, too."

It rained steadily the last day and a half to Foggy Bottom. Katriona used the weather as an excuse not to stop either. She had run out of ha'pennies a sennight ago – despite how frugally she had hoarded them – and was hungrier than ever; and she was too tired to do anything but stay on the main cart track into the Gig when the dawn came. It had been empty all night, and she managed to get off the road before any of the other occasional travellers saw her during the day.

Her aunt would know how to tell everyone that Katriona had come back from the princess' name-day with a baby of a suspicious age (she assumed that the news of the princess's disappearance would have flown round the country as quickly as the news of her birth had); although could anyone entertain so ludicrous a notion as that someone like Katriona had successfully kidnapped the princess? If the princess had disappeared on account of the threat from Pernicia, it was because she had been hurried off to some royal stronghold where the most powerful magicians, the wisest fairies, cleverest scouts, and sharpest troops could keep her safe.

When Katriona felt she couldn't walk any further, she stopped and sat down under a tree for a few minutes, and leant against it, and fell into a kind of semi-conscious drowse; and as soon as she could struggle to her feet again she did so. The princess, for the first time, was not feeling well, and wasn't hungry, but was restless and whimpery, and Katriona was therefore even more anxious to get her home to her aunt. Oh, Aunt, she thought. You won't believe how much I have to tell you. . .

The rain and wind among the leaves made enough of a din on the second evening that she couldn't hear her own footsteps, although she could feel the mud sucking at her feet, trying to pull her shoes off, trying to unbalance her till she fell down. She often stumbled. She kept the edge of her cloak pulled over the feverish baby, for it was wool, and warm even as wet as it was; but, being wool, it also became heavier and heavier as it grew wetter and wetter. Katriona sneezed. It's summer, she thought drearily; I shouldn't have a head-cold in high summer.

She knew all the back ways in and out of Foggy Bottom, but she was too tired to choose; she took the first turning off the main road that would lead her to her aunt's house – to her house. If she met anyone she knew, she didn't know what she would say, with the baby in her arms. She didn't know, and she was too tired to care. She was home at last. She was nearly home at last.

Her aunt had the door open, and was looking out. "Oh, Katriona," she breathed, and embraced her before she was over the threshold, and in spite of the rain – and the baby. She made room for the baby in her hug as she might have made room for any other impediment. Katriona sneezed again.

"I'll give you something for that," said her aunt, and pulled her filthy wet cloak off her, and drew her to the fire; and Katriona felt the fingers at the back of her neck, untying the ragged scarf that had valiantly withstood its unsuitable occupation as baby-sling for so long, and still her aunt asked no question and made no exclamation. As the sling came loose, and Katriona settled the princess in her lap in the way she had settled her in her lap any number of times over the last three and a half months (but in a chair! said a small internal voice refusing to be daunted by head-colds and exhaustion. In a *chair*! In a chair you will be able to sit in again tomorrow, and the day after that!), she reached up and grasped her aunt's hand – her aunt was occupied drawing the little table and another chair to the fire.

"Aunt," said Katriona, and her voice shook a little. "Aunt – this is the princess. They – they *gave* her to me." And then all the last three and a half months rose up together and fell on her, and she put her free arm on the table and leant her head against it and cried and cried and cried and cried, and she only stopped at last because the princess started crying, too. When Katriona had reassured her and the princess had fallen into a heavy doze (drooling fondly down Katriona's neck), Katriona told her aunt everything she could remember about the name-day, about Pernicia, about the small drably-dressed fairy and the verse she had taught her, about the king and queen, about the sabre-bearer and his amulet, about the gold and white and lavender streamers with the pink and white rosettes, which were still, ruinously wrinkled, in the bottom of one of her pockets, and how she hadn't been able to bear to throw them a way. About how she had been afraid to send any message to her aunt. And about how it was that while Katriona had often gone hungry, the princess had always had her milk.

Her aunt listened to everything, occasionally patting Katriona's hand, and apparently not noticing the increasing reek of wet unwashed person and wet unwashed baby that rose from Katriona and the princess as the fire warmed them and the rain came off them as steam. Katriona was still talking, hoarsely, when she fell asleep.

When she woke up, she was both clean and in bed. In her own bed. In any bed. For a moment she thought she had dreamed; and she struggled not to wake up . . . no. She felt her way down to the foot of her bed and looked over the rim of the loft and saw the cradle by the fire. There had never been a cradle by the fire since Katriona could remember; and she could see her aunt's foot rocking it gently. Most of her aunt was hidden behind the back of her chair; but she must have heard her niece stir, because she put her head round the chair and saw her sitting up and looking down.

"How are you feeling?" said her aunt.

"Good," said Katriona, after a moment, in surprise. "Better than I've felt since – since the name-day. Aunt, I've had a *bath*."

Her aunt smiled. "Only as much as I could arrange. You can have a proper bath later; there's only so much you can do with an unconscious, snoring body, even with cooperative water. And I had to save some of my energy for persuading the ladder to carry you up to the loft. But I thought you'd be more comfortable, clean and in your own bed. How's the cold?"

"Gone, I think." She stood up, waveringly. "I'm so hungry I can't think."

"Don't think, eat," said her aunt. "We'll think together later."

There was bread and chutney and a salad of greens and new potatoes on the table, and Katriona ate it all. Only then did she approach the cradle.

She knelt beside it. The princess, also looking very clean, was asleep. For the first time Katriona really noticed that her hair was blonde and curly, her skin pale but rosy; and she looked lovingly at the long silken eyelashes lying sweetly against the little satin cheek. "Aunt," she said softly, "I don't even know what to call her. Her name is Casta Albinia Allegra Dove Minerva Fidelia Aletta Blythe Domina Delicia Aurelia Grace Isabel Griselda Gwyneth Pearl Ruby Coral Lily Iris Briar-Rose. I've been calling her baby, or – when we were far enough away from everyone – princess, because I didn't want – I didn't want her to forget, I know that's silly when she's only a baby, but – and besides, you can't call a princess by name, can you?"

"Briar-Rose," said her aunt. "Rose. Rosie. Rosie is a good name for a little village maiden. We'll call her Rosie."

PART TWO

Chapter 6

The next time a royal herald appeared in Foggy Bottom, shortly after the arrival of Aunt's second niece, Rosie, it was a far more subdued and apprehensive occasion. The villages of the Gig had heard of the events of the princess's name-day from the returning attendees – fortunately no-one asked Katriona why it had taken her more than twice as long to make the journey home as it had the journey away – and had looked at their spinning wheels and hand spindles in alarm and dismay. Every home in the Gig had at least one tool for spinning; the weavers in Smoke River paid real coin for good thread, and Lord Prendergast, as well as most of the local smallholders, raised sheep.

The herald brought instructions that no spindle, iron or wood, should have a point on it thinner than the forefinger of a three-month-old baby – which had been the age of the princess on her name-day – and the herald here brandished a wooden peg that looked unsettlingly like a baby's forefinger. Katriona shivered, and needlessly rearranged the contentedly sleeping princess in her new baby-sling. The princess gave a little moan of objection and lapsed back into unconsciousness.

Aunt had said firmly that the entire village was ordered to attend the herald's announcement, and that the entire village had to be there – including Katriona and Rosie.

"I'll carry her, if you wish, but be there you both must be." She looked into Katriona's drawn, unhappy face and said, "My dear, think about it. No sane grown-up would leave a baby home alone, and the one thing we absolutely cannot do is call attention to ourselves by staying away. There is nothing about Rosie to suggest she is anything but our Rosie."

Katriona took comfort in the presence of several other women clutching babies of various ages and looking frightened – and in the reassuringly large and solid proximity of Barder, who had worked his way through the crowd to stand next to her for the herald's proclamation. This herald, too, was gone the next day, but there was no celebration in the pub the previous evening.

The herald had brought other news: that the king and queen were offering a fantastic reward for any news of Pernicia, of her whereabouts, her situation, her plans, her powers – anything – any news at all. Squadrons of the king's armies and parties of the king's magicians were still scouring the countryside for any trace of her; but so far as the herald, and Aunt's robins, knew, they had found nothing.

Nor had anyone else. No-one had come forward to claim a portion of the king's reward. No-one was able to say anything about where she had been before the name-day, nor where she was and what she was doing now. No-one. Not one of all the court fairies and magicians, who were among the most powerful in that country; not one of the magisterial seniors at the Academy, not one of the dangerously wayward fairies of the wild lands who could see through stone and talk to fire-wyrms and hear the stars singing.

Pernicia, people murmured. Wasn't that the name of – ? There were tales that people's grandparents and great-grandparents had told them, that they had had from their grandparents and great-grandparents. The story was of a wicked fairy with a name like Pernicia, who had sworn revenge on the queen of their country, many generations ago, a queen who had been unusually clear-sighted and unshakable by any magical means, even for a queen. Pernicia – if that had been her name – had said to her, "It is true, you have defeated me for now; but one day I will throw your heirs' heir down, and shatter your country with the shock, till no stone stands on any other stone that human hand set together, and the animals flee underground to the deepest roots of the mountains, and the birds will not sit in the trees, and the trees themselves bear no leaves and no fruit."

And the wicked fairy – whose name might have been something like Pernicia – went away into some wilderness where no-one could find her, for she set magical guardians around it, so that the wilderness appeared even wilder than it was, and people stayed away without knowing why they stayed away. And – the stories said – she set herself to learning how to live past the usual span of human years, so she might have her revenge in the time that suited her best, and that she should be there in the full strength of her pride and malice to enjoy it. Perhaps she was powerful enough, and wicked enough, to have learnt it; for it was said that if you were powerful enough, and wicked enough, there was a way.

But that country was full of magical wildernesses where no-one went; and even if you did go there – even if you were a very clever fairy or a very wise magician – you were very unlikely to see or to find everything that was there.

And that country was full of tales of fairies and magicians and magic. Many of them were just tales.

But Katriona remembered the small fairy saying to her: *Oh yes, I know who she is; but I did not know she was so powerful. I hoped, as one always does hope until catastrophe strikes, that it would not come. I hoped that the years had worn her out, the years since our last queen.*

If the tale about a wicked fairy with a name like Pernicia was more than just a tale, and if that Pernicia had returned from her long exile, then the country was in the gravest danger it had been in since the plague of fire-wyrms had set upon it from the north. Pernicia had nearly defeated the queen she had faced long ago, and if the queen had been merely an ordinary queen, she would have defeated her. And if Pernicia had learnt the secret of long life, she would have spent the years while she waited for her opportunity learning new wickedness, and nursing her hatred. King Harald had thrown the fire-wyrms back, but the Gig's terrain still showed the scars of the conflict in high tors and sudden valleys where the battles had been fought, and the fire-wyrms had melted the landscape in fury when the magician-wrought armour of Harald's regiments withstood them. What might Pernicia do that would batter and buckle the entire country?

The princess must be kept safe, not only for her own sake, but for the sake of the country. Even the king's conniving cousins, who had gone home in disgust upon the birth of the princess, showed no signs of wishing to return to the court now that she had disappeared. The princess yet lived; Pernicia's own disappearance proved that. But the princess must be kept safe – wherever the king and queen had her hidden. The heralds had no news about that; but then the people did not expect it. It was not a thing to speak aloud, with Pernicia listening.

Everyone all over the country went home after hearing the heralds' announcement, and at once knocked the pointed ends off their spindles and threw them on the fire, or bashed them with mallets and gave them to their local smiths who threw them on the hotter smithy fires; and then they looked sadly at the mutilated spindles. Weavers temporarily found their thread supplies short, while spinners adapted to shorter and thicker spindles. Later on spinners and toolmakers began to develop new spindles and new ways to cast their thread on and off them; over time, in a mixture of anger and fear and resentment, and a fuzzy but sincere desire to show support for their royal family, a new art form was born: spindle ends.

At first these were only rough shapings of the beheaded ends, merely to make them look less wrong. Spindles became readily detachable from wheels and handles, so that one shape or another could be tried and fiddled with and remade and tried again. Iron spindles were discarded altogether. Spindles and spindle ends became objects interesting in their own right; people argued as passionately over which woods made the best spindle ends as they did over which made the best bows and hafts.

Over more time – and obstinacy – the new spindle ends became not merely necessary adaptations of an old system, but the way things were: and the offhand whittling of them became both elaborate and beautiful. A spindle was now a rounded, palm-sized end tapering to a slim graceful rod no thinner than a three-month-old baby's forefinger. Little loops began to appear on spindle posts, where out-of-use spindles were dropped, point down; doorways and chimneypieces sprouted similar loops for hand spindles. Spinners grew much more organized about finishing off, so that their spindle ends were free for display when not in active use; the broad blunt ends of wheel spindles, in particular, were intricately carved.

Eventually, in later generations, a hand-carved spindle end was a favourite wedding gift, believed to confer good luck and healthy children on the bride and groom; and especially fine examples of the spindle-carving art were highly prized heirlooms. In neighbouring countries, people who saw the spindle ends that people of this country began carrying with them for luck adapted their own spinning wheels so that they too could use their neighbours' beautiful spindle ends, and spindle ends became one of this country's most sought-after exports. No-one outside seemed able to learn the knack, although many tried; but in areas that had never seen a carved spindle end they still picked up the phrase, used of someone or something the speaker treasured: "sound as a good spindle's end".

But that was much later. While Aunt threw her spindle point into the fire, and prodded it into the heart of the flames, Katriona took off the amulet she was still wearing hidden under her clothing, and held it between her two hands. The disturbed fire flared up and the hot red light fell across the amulet, and it flared, too, and Katriona almost dropped it, as if it were a chain of embers and would burn her. She remembered the sense of it pulsing between her fingers on the princess's name-day; it had lain quietly since then, till this moment. The fire-coloured light flickered in the same rhythm as the vibration against her fingers, and the amulet sparkled along its whole length, even where the shadow of her fingers fell across it. "I think," she said slowly, "I think I will not wear you any more."

She raised her head and saw Aunt looking at her, the poker still in her hand. "I'll give you something to wrap it in," said Aunt, and

Katriona knew she meant something that would disguise it from magic-seeing eyes. There was a little iron cup that stood on its own three tiny legs, like a miniature cauldron, in a niche high in the stone chimney. It had held other small magics safe from prying eyes, but it was empty now. Katriona pulled a stool in front of the hearth and stood on it so she could reach the niche and the cup. The cloth Aunt handed her was white, and when Katriona laid the amulet on it, she half expected the whiteness to blacken and char; but it did not. She folded the cloth round it carefully, and curled her thin package twice around the inside of the cup, till it lay flat.

"Should I lid it with iron, too?" said Katriona.

Aunt thought. "No," she said after a moment. "I don't think there'll be enough leak to notice, not in this house. Let the poor thing breathe. Something like that – likely it'll be happier if it can keep its eye on us, too."

"On Rosie," said Katriona.

The local chief priest came calling to enquire self-importantly about Rosie's name-day and dedication. Aunt was ready for him, and polite to him, neither of which was true of Katriona, till Aunt sent her on an imaginary errand to rid herself of the distracting series of muffled objections, which were Katriona's only contribution to the conversation, stiff as it was already. Part of the vehemence of her feeling was based on the fact that the Gig's chief priest was a pompous ass (the Gig was too obscure to have its own bishop), although the sleekest and most worldly-wise priest, of which the chief priest of the Gig was neither, was never perfectly at ease with the meekest and least active professional fairy – of which Aunt was neither.

It was not an easy vocation, being a priest in that country, where magic was vibrantly everywhere, maddening and unquenchable, and the gods were assumed to be a kind of super-fairy except that you never saw them nor were offered any concrete proof of what the priests claimed they had done for you. Possibly because of the rampaging dailiness of the magic of that country, its natives could rarely be persuaded to spend any serious time or thought on questions of how the world began or what it was for, or why people were people instead of stick insects or pondweed, or any of the other standard varieties of religious enquiry. For the ethics restraining you from bashing your neighbour and stealing his land or his money or his daughter there were centuries of instilled belief that these were bad things to do, and a strong government that, for as many centuries, had agreed. And for ecstatic visions there was the illegal eating of fish.

Aunt's theory about priests was that religion had emigrated from some other, less magical country, and its missionaries, while of good stout disbeliever-thumping stock, had never really adapted to the peculiar conditions of this country, and therefore, while they had managed to rig a sort of clumsy administrative scaffolding, it had never, so to speak, had its walls and roof put on, and developed a vernacular architecture. The priests had gained some ground, over the generations, with certain cabals of magicians; but priests and fairies remained like oil and water.

Katriona returned from her errand to find Aunt alone, amusing Rosie by swinging on its thin coloured string the tiny god-charm the priest had blessed her with. Rosie sat on the floor and made snatches at it (falling over at intervals). "Fairy godparents might have been quite a good notion towards a truce between us," Aunt said thoughtfully. "It's a pity the possible precedent was such a disaster."

"He just wants the money!" Katriona said, outraged that Aunt had agreed to a second (abbreviated) name-day for Rosie – as if her first one had not been more than enough for anyone.

Aunt sighed. The priest was not a pleasant companion, and talking to him had given her a headache. "Yes, of course he does, but he'll use it to buy food and firewood for those who need it. Don't worry; I've already explained that my sister had Rosie dedicated before she died; she won't have the words spoken over her again." (You wanted to be careful about the super-fairies, just in case their magic was anything like the usual stuff, where doing the same spell twice could create serious havoc.) "But I couldn't afford to insist against it – what if he tried to trace my supposed sister's supposed priest to make sure the ceremony was done? Priests have more contacts than robins." Katriona subsided, but with an ill grace.

Foggy Bottom's priestling earned his title – and a certain grudging respect, even from Katriona – by nursing the sick and the indigent, but he was afraid of Aunt, as if religion and magic might ricochet off each other to the harm of innocent bystanders. While he was ready to do his duty by all his parishioners, even to the extent of rubbing the dedication herbs and oils into the potentially combustible foreheads of babies related to Aunt by blood, he was certainly not going to go out of his way to pursue her about it. After his chief's visit, he was only too visibly relieved to be let off the actual rite, and accepted the promised fee for adding Rosie to Foggy Bottom's church registry with a hand that shook only a little.

Rosie, who had to be present for this transaction, smiled at him benevolently, and would have pulled his priest's plait, except that he flicked it out of her way in time, and proffered the string of his hood as substitute. She pulled with glee and made happy little chirps at each tug. "She sounds like one of your robins," said the priest, thinking that she was a difficult baby not to like, whomever she might be related to.

"Not when she wants something and thinks it's not coming fast enough," said Aunt drily.

Rosie grew up square and strong and stubborn and inquisitive, with a limitlessness of both energy and persistence that meant she was a great trial to Aunt and Katriona while she was still young enough to require constant watching. "Mind you," said Aunt, "little children are like this" – Aunt was the eldest of eleven and spoke from long experience – "but I've never seen one that was Rosie's equal for sheer pigheadedness. With all due respect to pigs."

Katriona sighed. She wanted children of her own (even if it turned out that Aunt was right and she was wrong, and she was a real fairy herself), but the experience of raising Rosie was making her feel that perhaps she wanted fewer than she had previously imagined. Even when Aunt had one or two small boarders to stay, as she often did, till their baby-magic ran its course and they were safe to return to their families, Rosie was deflected from her purposes not a whit by prognosticating furniture, clothing that giggled and ran away when you tried to put it on, nor a ravening panther just outside the door apparently waiting to swallow the first person it saw. (It was something like a panther; manifestations of baby-magic are only as good as the imagination of the child, and this one's understanding of natural history was not so great as his desire for mayhem.)

This was convenient in one way, as a more nervous and dependent child would have been made miserable by baby-magic jokes and ruses; but Katriona sometimes thought it might have been worth it. Katriona had been officially sworn and contracted as Aunt's apprentice shortly after Rosie had come to live with them, which in theory meant that Katriona could be sent instead of Aunt to attend to any fairy task Aunt thought her capable of; but in fact Katriona found learning basic fairy craft something of a struggle, despite her zealous dedication. At first the only clear manifestation of her aptitude for any magic at all was her ability to throw (so to speak) cold water on the various conflagrations of baby-magic, and there was no plan or subtlety to that; it was just a reflex, like grabbing the milk jug before Rosie knocked it over or a boarder turned it into a wasps' nest. The early years of her apprenticeship felt like a kind of frantic juggling act, and the only real difference between handling magic and handling Rosie, she thought despairingly, was that there was no malice in Rosie.

Rosie hated her curly golden hair. When she was old enough to hold minimal conversations, the itsy-bitsy-cutesy-coo sort of grown-ups would pull the soft ringlets gently and tell her what a pretty little girl she was. She would stare at this sort of grown-up and say, "I am not pretty. I am intelligent. And brave." The grown-ups usually thought this was darling, which only made her angry, perhaps partly because she was speaking the truth, although it was tricky to differentiate between "brave" and "foolhardy" at three or four years old. (Fortunately her faith in grown-ups other than

Aunt and Katriona was founded on people like Barder. Barder had a ritual of picking her up, saying "Oof," followed by, "So, you're a strapping lass. Are you going to grow up to be a blacksmith like Narl or a wheelwright like me?" and tossing her in the air. She adored Barder from the beginning, and was magnanimous about the fact that as the years passed he threw her less and less high.) But aside from her hair, she was not pretty – all those fairy godmothers giving her lips like cherries and teeth like pearls and skin like silk and they forgot to make her pretty, thought Katriona – and she was intelligent.

She was intelligent enough, for example, to grasp that Aunt's prized scissors (the only pair in the village) were a much more precise cutting tool than a knife – neither of which, in theory, she was allowed access to. She nonetheless came indoors for tea one day with her hair lopped off to about half a hand's breadth all over her head. It stood out like the corolla of a ragged sunflower. Aunt and Katriona were initially so stunned that Rosie had time to put the scissors carefully back where they belonged, with an easy familiarity that proved she'd done it often before.

But the uproar this caused was nothing compared with the uproar when Katriona noticed she had also cut her eyelashes. Various negotiations (including, finally, such desperate measures as "supposing you ever want to eat again") eventually produced the grudging promise that, in return for Katriona keeping her hair cut short, she would leave her eyelashes alone.

Short hair rather suited Rosie. The bones of her square little face stood out with a clarity that seemed to reflect (or warn of) her personality. And without the distracting curls, Katriona found herself noticing more often the expressions flashing over that small candid face. . . When she was watching Rosie with only half her attention she was often startled into full heed by a turn of Rosie's head, a look in her eye, a tip of her chin, underscored, perhaps, by a gesture of her hand, a drop of one shoulder, a playful leap: and Katriona was reminded briefly but intensely of a fox, a badger, a wildcat, a doe. Not any fox or badger or wildcat or doe. Rosie had a humorous, wily, shrewd look Katriona remembered from a particularly kind and clever nanny goat they had met on their journey, and an earnest, ardent look that came from a sheepdog. Even Rosie's curious ability to mimic Aunt's robins – to the extent that the robins themselves went off into gales of good-natured robin-laughter about the nearness of her near misses – began to seem a little ominous. What, thought Katriona, did our princess drink in with the milk?

She refused to think about what she had said over the cradle during the wreck of the name-day: . . . *you can have my gift, it isn't very useful, I can talk to animals*. . . She had only been speaking to say something, to drive away the sound of the words Pernicia had spoken; what she said hadn't meant anything, any more than any words she or anyone else might have said could have driven off Pernicia's curse.

She mentioned the question of the milk quietly to Aunt one evening, and Aunt looked at Rosie for a while, her fingers, and foot on the treadle, continuing unfalteringly their business of spinning. Rosie was trying to feed her unwanted supper porridge to the left-hand fire-dog, which was her favourite. Katriona couldn't herself see the difference, but, knowing Narl, who had made the pair, there was one. Both bore hound faces, with flying-back ears lying along their necks as from a rush of wind, and open-mouthed, eager expressions. Rosie was murmuring to her friend; the only clear phrase, often repeated, was "It's good for you." Katriona, watching, saw the dog-aspect of Rosie more clearly than usual in the moving fire-shadows. There was that sheepdog, but there had been other sheepdogs; there had also been that gaunt, intense, solemn hound not unlike what must have been in Narl's mind when he made the fire-dogs; and a large, slow, thoughtful, heavy-coated dog rather like a small bear.

"I can't see it," said Aunt, later, when Rosie was in bed, "which is not to say it isn't there. I don't know, my dear. She's happy, she's healthy, she's growing . . . she is certainly growing . . . and we love her." Katriona could hear the tiny waver in Aunt's voice as she said "we love her", because they did – and she was the princess.

Small spider weave, thought Katriona. *And a poem is the most I can give her, my dear, my only darling*! When will she send word?

"It will have to be enough," said Aunt.

Mostly it was enough, except for the dreams when an assortment of terrifyingly grand or villainous-looking persons turned up on their threshold, quoting the rhyme, and demanding the princess' return. Katriona was grateful that Rosie got *into* life so enthusiastically; this made her seem, to Katriona, like a real member of the village. But then what did Katriona know of princesses? Maybe they were all like real members of villages, except that they were princesses.

That was the year Rosie was four. It was a few weeks after Rosie cut her hair that something more disturbing happened.

Chapter 7

After the princess' calamitous name-day four years ago, there had been a great upheaval at the palace, and the wife's cousin's sister-in-law of Aunt's robin friend found that she no longer lived outside the queen's quarters. And then, because the queen no longer had her chambers there, the robin found that the garden that was her territory and her delight was changed, in a robin's opinion, very much to its detriment; and so she and her young family moved house.

Indeed, they left the palace grounds altogether. There was a thick new sadness that hung round the royal residence, and this being the country it was, it was a chalky sort of sadness, and the air was dusty grey with it, and birds preferred to nest elsewhere. Aunt and Katriona found themselves, for the first time in Katriona's memory, depending on Cairngorm's pub for news of the royal family.

There they heard, a month or two after the visit from the second herald, that the queen and princess, immediately after the terrible name-day, had been smuggled away from the court in the royal city to a stronghold called Fordingbridge in the western mountains, and that three-quarters of the royal magicians and the two finest regiments of the army had gone with them. It was a good sign, everyone said, that the king and queen felt secure enough in their provisions for their daughter's protection to let it be known where she was held. The king had stayed in the royal city, where he could best rule his country; but he visited his family often. Sometimes the queen returned with him to the city for a little while, for her new sorrow and dignity made her husband's people love her more than they had when she had merely been a good listener to boring speeches; and they begged to see her. She was known not to be in the best of health, but everyone but Katriona and Aunt believed that she had her little daughter under her care.

Although there was a hiatus in Aunt's private sources of information, the animal kingdom was, in fact, keenly interested in what was happening to the royal family. There had been robins, and sparrows, and starlings, and rabbits, and mice, and beetles, and many other easily overlooked creatures, who had seen Pernicia's appearance at the princess' name-day, and they didn't have to understand human language to recognize very bad news for everybody when they saw it. The dog-fox Katriona first met had reached his own conclusions independently but most of the other animals that helped her and the princess on their long journey knew perfectly well whom they were helping and, even if they didn't know the human tale of the old enmity between Pernicia and a queen of long ago, why. Secrets were something animals were naturally good at (something humans had had to give up when they became humans, like a decent sense of smell). The fox was ashamed of himself later (as much as foxes are ever ashamed), when he heard the full story. He had known he was talking out of turn.

The princess' flight across the country was well concealed in the minds and memories of the animals before Katriona, wet and sneezing, arrived at Aunt's door with a baby in a sling. Even the robins had refrained, with heroic, unrobinlike discretion, from telling Aunt why Katriona was so long on the way, although they had kept her informed of her niece's curiously slow progress – and it had been obvious enough to Aunt from the explosive air of repressed excitement that some considerable mystery was involved.

Robins' endless discussion of infractions of their territorial boundaries are chiefly an excuse to exchange news and gossip. The communication line broken by the robins moving out of the palace garden was rearranged and reconnected. Via an uncle's third cousin twice removed, one of Aunt's robins, too young to have been involved in the baby princess's hair's breadth escape, innocently brought the news, shortly after Rosie first learned to walk, that there was something very odd about the way the stronghold where the princess was now living felt, and that when the king and queen returned there after some time away, even the thought of seeing their daughter again seemed unable to lift their spirits, and they rode through the fortress gate as bow-shouldered as they had ridden out.

The thought of the queen, in particular, hurt Katriona so badly she began to talk to her in her head. The king at least had his ruling to get on with; the queen was only his consort, when it came down to it, a foreigner in her husband's country, there to be his wife – and to bear and raise his children.

At first the things she thought of to say to the queen were no more than a kind of mental pushing-away of discomfort; she said them in the same crisp, no-nonsense way that one might say a charm to a water nymph of uncertain temper known to reside there before crossing her stream; you do it, and you go on. But that didn't work for long, and as Rosie grew older, and there were more things to tell, Katriona began to organize little stories about her, about how clever and charming and infuriating and darling she was, stories to give a mother's love somewhere to go, somewhere to live, something to do besides endlessly grieve. . .

Katriona fell into the habit of doing this at night, in bed, as she felt sleep creeping near her, because it comforted her to pretend to comfort the queen; and she had, over the years, built up a fantasy of the queen, whom she remembered a little from the fateful name-day, although she had not been anything like close enough to see that she had eyes just like Rosie's (although her eyelashes were not so long), and her nose had a tiny bump in it, and there was a small mole low on her left cheek, which was how she saw her now.

She imagined a bedroom for her, too, because she imagined the queen falling asleep as she was, and Katriona's drowsy words slipping into her mind in that cloudy gap between waking and sleep. The bedroom was not large, but it was tall and light, with big windows that would make it very bright by day, when the curtains were drawn back; even late at night, the few dim lamps that stood in niches between the windows lit up the whitewashed walls and the white hangings round the queen's bed. It was never fully dark in the queen's bedroom; whether that was the queen's choice or that of those who guarded her, Katriona had never decided. It was a surprisingly small and bare room for a queen, but Katriona thought that must be her own inability to imagine what a queen might have in her bedroom. It was just as small and bare when it was sometimes some other room, whitewashed still, and lit by small lamps in niches, but with small, high, barred windows, as if the queen were in some fastness, pretending to keep her daughter company.

Katriona snuggled down in her own bed, looking, behind her shut eyes, at the queen lying on her pillow, her long hair in a single plait and the neck of her nightgown as white and plain as her bed hangings. *Rosie was very busy watching the dragonflies today*, Katriona told the queen. *She loved the colours of them, and the darting way they moved, and the way they can stop in the air, as if they were looking back at you. I was glad of the excuse to do no more, for a moment, than stand there with her and watch dragonflies, too, as if I were another child.*

The queen had been smiling about Rosie and the dragonflies, but as Katriona said *I was glad of the excuse to do no more than stand there with her*, her face crumpled, and tears crept out from under her closed eyelids. "Oh, Queen," said Katriona in distress, and, in her mind, reached out to brush the tears away – and the queen opened her eyes, sat up in bed, and grasped Katriona's hand.

Katriona felt the queen's hand on hers, felt the strength of it, the reality of it – her own fingers a little pinched together, the queen's fingers across the back of her hand, and the bar of her thumb across Katriona's palm.

Katriona gave a little throttled squeak; she would have liked to say something, something like, Oh, help, what have I done? but her voice wouldn't come. The queen seized her other hand and leaned forward to look into her face, and whispered, "I know you.

I have seen you many nights since I lost my daughter, and you have told me of her. Sigil told me how she sent my daughter away to save her, and I remember Pernicia's face and I know Sigil was right; but oh – I miss my child so much! I feel as if the very strength of my longing for her must make me guilty of risking her life. I have thought – feared – believed I only dreamed you, for how could it be otherwise: My longing would have created you, if you had not come.

"Tell me you are real. I dare not ask nor hear your name, nor where you live, nor how you come here. But tell me, while my waking eyes are on you, and I can feel your blood beating under my fingers, that you are real, that it is you who have my daughter, that the stories you tell of her are true stories – for by them I know that you love her – that it is for love of her that you have the pity to come to me. Speak – you must speak – but keep your voice low, for my waiting-women are always near, because I do not sleep well, not any night since I lost my daughter. Speak words that I can remember – then it will be worth it to me to have lost you, too – for after this you cannot come again."

Katriona made a great effort, for however it was that she sat on the queen's bed, she was also lying in her own bed many leagues distant. Her heart was beating too fast, and she was having trouble breathing, as if her body were suddenly too big for her heart and lungs, and the pressure of the coverlet on the queen's bed against the backs of her legs made her feel queasy. She spoke as if each word were a new thing that had to be created out of chaos: "I – I took her away with me, your daughter, on her name-day. It was I. I am real. I took her home. I have her still, I and my aunt. We love her. The stories you have heard me tell over the last four years are true stories. She is as safe with us as . . . as ordinariness can make her. We will not give her up. . ."

And then the queen, and the queen's bedchamber, were gone, and she was gasping like a wood-spirit whose tree has just been cut down; and Aunt's arms were round her. When her breath steadied, Aunt said, "I want you thoroughly awake before you try again to sleep. Come downstairs; I will make up the fire and brew you a tisane."

Katriona came, shivering with shock, her head still pounding and her breast aching, as if she had had to hold her breath for a long time. She sat in her usual chair, with her head flung back, and her eyes were drawn to the niche where the little iron cauldron stood; and it seemed to glow red in the near-darkness, though it might only have been the firelight, which Aunt had stirred again to brightness. Katriona lowered her head, to watch Aunt move around, choosing a few leaves from a little basket and a drop from a little bottle, adding water from the big kettle that always sat over the fire; and she saw that Aunt looked grim and haggard.

When she handed Katriona the cup, Katriona drank it immediately, although it burned her mouth; but her head felt clearer. "I am sorry," she said. "I didn't know. . ." But then she thought of the queen's grief, and she said, "I didn't know. But I am not sure I am sorry."

Aunt was staring into the reviving flames. "I had no idea your magic was so strong yet," she said. "I knew – I knew since they brought you to me – such a little thing you were, small for your age, and being shaken to bits by what was in you. That is, if you want to know, why I wrestled you away from your other aunts and uncles, who wished to reclaim you after – after the fits stopped. I knew what was in you would come out for good or ill; and I wished it to be for good." She smiled a little. "I might have tried anyway, because I loved you, but I would have feared I was only being selfish."

Katriona's eyes filled with tears. "Aunt . . . my magic isn't really coming in. I have wanted you to be right, that I am a fairy like you – how I have wanted it—" The tears overflowed and fell down Katriona's face. "But you are wasting your time, teaching me things, and you should have a real apprentice, not a . . . not because I am your niece. The magic . . . I do feel it, sometimes. But it just drains through me – it doesn't stay. I can't even talk to animals as I used to – you know that—maybe I did give it away, somehow, on that awful name-day – I'm glad it lasted long enough to get us home. It's almost gone now, except for cats, and a fox, once or twice. I've thought that if a familiar found me . . . or like your robins . . . but no-one has, and doesn't that mean . . . for the rest, it's just a great dark emptiness with a few broken scraps I can use when I can find them. The things you teach me are still all easy, Aunt; you don't know yet that I can't go on; and I haven't had the courage to tell you."

"My darling, I am the one to apologize. I have wondered what your magic has been doing with itself, because I have felt its presence; but I have also known it was not available to you somehow. I thought only to leave you alone a little longer, not to press you, as one does not ask much work out of a child who has outgrown its strength. I had no idea. . . My fault. I should have been more suspicious. Kat, the things I teach you are *not* all easy.

"What you describe is how it happens to everyone: magic does slide through you, and disappear, and come back later looking like something else. And I'm sorry to tell you this, but where your magic lives will always be a great dark space with scraps you fumble for. You must learn to sniff them out in the dark.

"As for your beast-speech, I always suspected it was a form of baby-magic; not all baby-magic is chaotic, nor lasts only a few months or a year or two. That yours was both coherent and long-lasting – have I ever told you about my baby-magic? – told me again that I was right about you. But you became an adult, willy-nilly, when you broke through the boundary to rescue the princess, and so your baby-magic left you. It means nothing that you do not yet have your familiar; Cresitanova, one of the greatest fairies this country has ever had, did not find hers till she was forty-five.

"Tonight – this is a tremendous magic you've done. It is no wonder there has been so little for us to work with here. For this was not the first time you have talked with the queen, was it?"

Katriona shook her head miserably. "Almost from the beginning – more often later. But I thought I was just making it up. I thought I was just making it up. . . "

Aunt said, "It was generously meant, and where magic is concerned, well-intentioned mistakes are slightly less likely to catch you out later on. Did you tell her your name?"

"No. She told me not to, nor where I came from; and she said I must not come again."

Aunt, for the first time, relaxed a little. "That was wise of her — wiser than you could expect of a mother speaking to a stranger who has her child. Did you tell her Rosie lived with two fairies?"

"No. But she'll have to know there was magic involved, won't she?"

"It is not the queen we must worry about, but Pernicia. But Pernicia may underestimate the queen, and, should she come to learn of the magic that sat on the queen's bed tonight, she may guess it was some phantasm drawn up by some royal magician, to soothe the queen's fears. After all, it had no name and no home. It is for this we will hope."

They did not know what Pernicia learnt or guessed of that night, but it was barely six weeks later when the news reached Foggy Bottom that someone or something had broken into the deep place in the western mountains, and that while the princess had been successfully defended and taken unharmed away, Fordingbridge was understood to be no longer secure or securable.

"And," said Shon, the carter from Turanga, the nearest city outside the Gig, "they're not telling us where they're keeping her, this time. They're equipping and fortifying several strongholds, and they'll defend 'em all, and maybe they'll keep her at one or maybe they'll move her round from one to another in secret — or maybe they'll have other ones no-one knows about and keep her there. They're a-hiring more soldiers, and several of the biggest Academicians have left the Academy to work for the king, and they all figure it's all going to be worth it to 'em, dividing up their brains and muscle like that" — because foremost in everyone's minds was the fact that this first stronghold had been held by the the two best regiments of the army and the majority of the court magicians, and that this had not been enough.

There was an interested murmur among the listeners — Shon's appearance in the village always drew a few people, hopeful of news, to the pub — but it was Cairngorm's voice Katriona heard clearly: "She's safe *now*," Cairngorm repeated, loyal subject of their majesties and mother of two daughters. "She is safe *now*."

"Yes," said Shon positively. "The magicians saw what was

coming, and the soldiers got her away. She's fine."

This was said over the head of Rosie, who was making her determined way through furniture- and people-legs towards Cairngorm's big ginger cat, Corso, who, eyes half shut and watchful, permitted her approach. Katriona had come in for a jug of the pub's excellent cider. Flora had drawn it for her, and now, trying not to clutch it as if it were a baby in danger of kidnapping, Katriona gave Rosie a minute to say hello before she went after her. She felt at such a moment even saying Rosie's name aloud would draw the wrong sort of attention to her. (Rosie squatted down with her knees under her chin, peering, but courteously sidelong, into Corso's face. Corso turned his head just enough to make it easy for her but not too easy. Katriona had noticed before that Rosie, unlike most small children, did not make the mistake of trying to fondle an animal when it had given no indication of any desire to be fondled by a small child. It seemed to Katriona ironic that Rosie apparently had a better grasp of animal etiquette than human.)

Flora, who had taken Katriona's silence as politeness, laughed, as her friend sidled out of the door with the jug in one hand and a smaller, stickier hand in the other. "You're acting as if they could be interrupted," she said. "You could beat them all over the head with a stick, yelling 'fire!' and they wouldn't turn a hair. This is news, Kat. Don't you understand about news?"

" It's just so awful for the king and queen," muttered Katriona. "I keep thinking, if it were my – I used to dream about the queen, sometimes."

Flora sobered. "Yes, you're right. But the princess is alive and well and safe, Kat. Remember that. The queen is probably giving her an amazing high tea right now – has done every day since they escaped – just in relief that everything came out all right. All the jam scones she can eat, and three kinds of cake."

"Yes, probably," said Katriona.

Spear, returning from outdoor dog business, paused beside them and deigned to bow his head to be kissed on the nose: Rosie was only just tall enough. Still clinging to one of Spear's ears with her free hand, she said alertly, "Cake?"

"We're going home to tea now," Katriona told her.

"We're going to have cake," said Rosie. "Like the princess."

"You tell 'em," said Flora.

Rosie, sensing Katriona's mood (and with a mind to the possibility of cake), permitted her hand to be held for quite three minutes after they had left the pub. Once they were off the short village main street Katriona allowed her to drag herself free and run off to speak to a small huddle of village sheep, which had wandered to this edge of the common. Katriona could see a small boy with a stick who, she suspected, was fast asleep, but the sheepdog with him was awake and aware. Several of the sheep left their grazing long enough to butt gently against Rosie; some faces she petted, also gently, and some backs she scratched (her small arm disappearing nearly to the shoulder in the soon-for-shearing wool), as if she knew which each sheep would like best; and none of them baaed or stamped or defiantly urinated in the way of sheep wishing to see off an intruder. "Come on then," Katriona said, when Rosie had greeted all the sheep in the little group surrounding her. "Don't you want your tea?"

"Cake!" said Rosie happily, and came. "Don't frown," she said, looking up. "We can have a picnic, and pretend we're the king and the queen and the princess. You can be the princess. *I'm* going to be the king."

She is as safe with us as ordinariness can make her. What a pathetic defence!

Chapter 8

Katriona had always worried that some one of the fairy gifts she hadn't heard was a crucial one, and some day it would expose Rosie for what she was and that would be that: and that night, after Rosie was asleep (full of gingerbread, which she had accepted as a reasonable substitute for cake), she blurted this out to Aunt.

Aunt answered so quickly Katriona knew she had thought of this herself. "It is unlikely that any of the wishes you did not hear were substantially unlike those you did. But I think you should also have a little more faith in our Rosie. Look at how many of the wishes she has vitiated merely by being herself. Since she seems unable to carry a tune, the undoubted sweetness of her singing voice is irrelevant; that roar that serves her for a laugh might be bell-like if one could find a bell suitable for comparison purposes. What would it be made of, one wonders? Most of the village children before they're her age are already trying to learn the round dances on the feast days; you know Rosie's views on dancing."

("Stupid," were Rosie's views, and, if not bound by potent promises, she would disappear into the shadows at the edge of the feast-day bonfire, looking for better sport.)

"I feel certain she'll feel the same about flute playing. We can omit teaching her to embroider or to – to spin, which omission will please her; we will ask Barder to teach her to whittle instead, in a few more years. There are no golden ringlets, although I admit the eyelashes are a little conspicuous. That astonishing skin of hers only makes her moods transparent – which you have to admit is useful, although she will dislike it very much when she is older – and with that complexion I think she'd have the lips anyway. The teeth, I feel, are rather attractive."

Aunt was right, except perhaps about the teeth, which glowed in the dark very slightly; but by the time Rosie had a husband, who was likely to be the only other person in a position to notice, presumably she would be a princess again, and the teeth could be explained.

Aunt's robins had, of course, had their own version of the events at Fordingbridge, and their own guesses about what had caused them. (Most of the Gig fairies, whether they had animal familiars or not, consulted Aunt about what her robins had told her. Aunt said that this was only because her robins were more comprehensible than most, but Katriona thought it was that Aunt was the best translator.) Any animal with a fairy to talk to would bring her at once any apparent news of the princess who still lived with the king and queen, and any animal's news of that princess would be passed on till it reached an animal with a fairy to tell it to. Part of the secret of the princess' whereabouts (among those who knew and those who guessed something was up besides the strongholds and the magicians and the regiments) was that that tale of that other princess should continue to be believed. And furthermore, wherever the princess was, Pernicia was a problem belonging to the human world, and the humans were expected to sort it out.

But there never was any news of Pernicia. There was not even any news definitely of her in the tale of the breaking of Fordingbridge, just a horrid, murky, muzzy sense of bad magic. Many of the birds who had been close to Fordingbridge when it had happened – whatever, precisely, it was that had happened – were moulting out of season. (Nurgle's fish said that the water round Fordingbridge now tasted very nasty, and everything that lived underwater had left the area. Nurgle's fish was the worst-kept secret in Foggy Bottom, although, strictly speaking, the laws against contact with fish didn't specifically mention friendship.) What had Pernicia learnt during her self-imposed exile, that she could hide herself so completely when all the countryside was roused and looking for her?

Aunt and Katriona had celebrated Rosie's birthday the day after the princess' birthday from the first. This had been Katriona's idea, saying that it was one more detail making Rosie Rosie and not the princess; but both Katriona and her aunt knew that what it was they were celebrating was coming through one more of the princess' birthdays safely. Although Aunt had made a point of telling her niece-apprentice that Pernicia's additional last-minute spite – that the spell could kill the princess at any time that Pernicia chose – was almost certainly untrue.

"*Almost?*" said Katriona; but Aunt ignored her, carrying on in her dry, teachery voice, as if what she said was in the same category as the proportions of paregoric.

"She would have set it up for a birthday, because someone's birthday is always when they are most susceptible to magic, good or bad – a name-day is quite good too, but a birthday is best. If she said she'd set it up for the one-and-twentieth, then she almost certainly did—"

"*Almost,*" muttered Katriona.

"Especially because she had obviously set it up to connect somehow with the well-meant gifts already given, and that would be enough complexity to have to deal with on the day. Saying it aloud like that, however, especially with an audience, will have helped to settle it into place. Magic likes being announced. Of course that will also have given it added strength. . ."

During the latter half of the year that Katriona had once sat on the foot of the queen's bed and told her about her daughter, the queen was seen even less than she had been since her daughter disappeared. Everyone said that it was on account of the shock of discovering that Fordingbridge was penetrable, the shock of the possibility that even the king's best stronghold and best troops and best magicians – and fairies, although guardianship was not, generally speaking, considered the less biddable fairy magic's forte – were not enough to protect the princess against Pernicia. That it had, perhaps, only been luck that they had brought her away safely this time.

But ten months and eighteen days from the night Katriona had sat on the queen's bed, a royal herald on a tired horse trotted into

Foggy Bottom and announced that the queen had given birth to twin sons five weeks before.

"It's getting to be a habit with her, not letting on what's coming, ain't it?" said Grey, but Cairngorm said swiftly, "Can you blame her? She'd been fifteen years having the first, and look what happened."

"Yes, but that was the first, and a girl," said Bol, the barman.

"Lay your odds they'll have a private name-day, and no-one will know about it till it's over," said Gash eagerly, but there were no takers. Gash was right. Four months afterwards, Shon came with the news that the two little princes were called Colin and Terberus; and that there had been so few people invited to the very private name-day that the bishop had been insulted.

There were no fairy godparents for the little princes.

The queen had a third son the year Rosie was eight, and her brothers were three. The baby was named Osmer, and this time just enough people were invited to the name-day to satisfy the bishop. Colin and Terberus were there, and everyone spoke of what beautiful manners they had, and what quiet, self-possessed children they were, even at three and a half.

Katriona looked at Rosie and shook her head. "You aren't – er – doing anything, are you?" she said to her aunt.

Aunt had, she knew, cast a glamour over Rosie's arrival, so that everyone remembered Aunt going off to fetch Rosie about a week after Katriona's return from the princess' name-day. ("I have to," she had said. "I wish I didn't. I will make it as small and confusing a glamour as possible." When Katriona's magic had strengthened she had looked into this, and was impressed by her aunt's creative imagination. The glamour that obscured Rosie's arrival was so entangled in a fictitious bardic tale-spinning competition in Smoke River that what little of it you could make out, which wasn't much, seemed only to be one of the tales, about as likely as any of the rest, which included large silver carriages with long stiff wings that flew through the air like birds, long-distance speaking devices involving no magic, and a family of fire-wyrms asking the king for a permanent peace, and offering to live in the palace cellars and replace the central heating. The tale did not say what happened to all the human loggers and colliers and stokers this would put out of a job.)

Aunt shook her head. "No. Rosie's – er – strength of character is nothing to do with me. It's interesting, though. I wouldn't have expected it from that family. I thought they were bred for amenableness as much as for lack of magic."

They were outdoors, in the garden, setting out seedlings, Aunt's weather-guesser having promised faithfully that there would be no late frosts that spring. The cottage they lived in was a brisk quarter-hour's walk from the village, on its own little track just before the fork in the road that led, to the right, to Lord Prendergast's great spooky house Woodwold, and to the left, to Smoke River. It had its own garden, conveniently, rather than rights to one of the bits of common land beyond the cluster of village houses and outbuildings and barns. Aunt had done Lord Prendergast some particular favour, long ago, and permanent tenancy of this cottage, for so long as she wanted it, had been the reward.

That it had been this reward rather than some other may have been because Lord Prendergast, thoughtful liege lord that he was, knew that people generally preferred to have powerful fairies at a little distance. Neighbours of a professionally practising fairy have more than a usually severe dust problem, and their dja vines, supposing they have dja vines, grow about a league a year in all directions, and require severe and frequent pruning; and a well-grown dja vine has spines on it that make the thorns of a briar rose look like they're not trying. Fairies' residences also attract odd bits of weather – small wind-spouts and dust storms, funny-coloured fogs, and minor plagues of enchanted or half-enchanted creatures, drawn by the magic pulsing under their own skins, and who can behave in ways very disconcerting to ordinary people, who furthermore cannot disenchant them or make them go away. Of course the fairy can and does, in the interests of good relations, but it may not be quite soon enough for the neighbours.

"They can't – er – what do you mean, bred for amenableness?" Katriona said, her mind suddenly filled with a vision of councillors bent over parchment sheets of genealogies, like Lord Prendergast deciding which mares were worthy of his celebrated stallions' efforts. "You can't – you can't measure for amenableness, like you can for—"

"Height and weight and magic?" said Aunt. "True. But show me a committee of councillors anywhere who would choose a self-reliant, strong-willed spouse for their reigning monarch over a mild, biddable one, should the choice exist. I wonder if perhaps we got more in our queen than we realized."

Thinking about the queen always made Katriona irritable and unhappy. She began banging seedlings into the row she was creating so that the soil stood up in ridges round each tiny, startled-looking plant, and miniature battles seemed to have been fought between these redoubts. "Twenty-one of them!" Katriona burst out suddenly. "One-and-twenty of the most powerful and important fairies in the country! They could have made her invulnerable to curses! They could have made her invisible to anyone who wished her harm! They could have – they could – and they gave her golden *hair*!"

Aunt made no answer. They could hear Rosie singing – tunelessly – to herself, or possibly to Poppy and Fiend, their cows, pastured on the far side of the cottage. Fiend used to belong to Grey, but Grey had grown tired of calling Aunt, or, later, Katriona, out to his farm to re-spell her to be a nice cow and let down her milk and not knock milkmaids and farmers and buckets and stools over like spillikins. On a day that Katriona had had Rosie with her, and Grey had been a little long in pouring out his woes, possibly because Katriona had heard them less often than Aunt, when the two of them had gone at last into the barnyard they found six-year-old Rosie pulling mightily with both hands on one teat – she having first arranged Fiend over a convenient bucket, which was too heavy for her to move far – and producing a thin but respectable stream of milk.

Grey lost his temper and told Katriona to take the wretched cow home with her. Fortunately the cottage had a dairy and a larder; even magic would have had difficulty keeping up with Fiend when she was in a positive frame of mind. (Grey had softened enough to have her put to his bull, and to take in her daughters.) Meanwhile she was still called Fiend, because Rosie, under the impression that a fiend was a sort of flower, thought it was a pretty name.

Aunt and Katriona kept a few chickens, but the only other domestic animal they had — if either "domestic" or "had" was applicable — was Flinx, their not-a-house-cat. He was presently a fat tortoiseshell puddle sprawled in the sunlight a few rows over. Since he was only crushing a few nonessential greens, which would regrow anyway, they let him be.

Cats were often familiars to workers of magic because to anyone used to wrestling with self-willed, wayward, devious magic — which was what all magic was — it was rather soothing to have all the same qualities wrapped up in a small, furry, generally attractive bundle that looked more or less the same from day to day and might, if it were in a good mood, sit on your knee and purr. Magic never sat on anybody's knee and purred. Cats were the easiest of the beasts for humans to talk to, if you could call it talking, and most fairies could carry on some kind of colloquy with a cat. But conversations with cats were always more or less riddle games, and if you were getting the answer too quickly, the cat merely changed the ground on you. Katriona's theory was that cats were one of the few members of the animal kingdom who had a strong artistic sense, and that aggravated chaos was the chief feline art form, but she had never coaxed a straight enough answer out of a cat to be sure. It was the sort of thing a cat would like a human to think, particularly if it weren't true.

A few months before the birth of the princess, Katriona had woken before dawn on a sleety winter day to the sound of a kitten acknowledging to the world it was about to leave that it was dying, and had gone outdoors to rescue it. That was Flinx. Flinx had never decided if as a result he adored Katriona without qualification, or resented her for having heard him yielding up his final dignity that way and interrupted by saving him. He was never very far away from her when she was near the cottage or in the village (and he had been deeply offended by her five-month absence six years ago), but he wasn't a house cat, nor was he going to be mixed up with anything that might disrupt the regularity of his meals. The word *fairies* had just now caught his ear and he was ready to withdraw smoothly if the conversation was about to turn magical. He knew a few of the human words that applied to his least favourite subject, but what he knew better was the spiky, bristly, meditation-disturbing feeling that the results of those human words gave off. He had never understood why any cat would stoop to being a familiar.

The sun was warm and the smell of spring was sweet on the air (they were upwind of the muck heap which, even with magic to muffle it, was still discernably what it was) and Rosie was, for yet a few more minutes or weeks or years, safe. Katriona had decided that Aunt was going to let her outburst on the subject of fairy godparents pass as needing no response. Aunt often did on outbursts concerning Rosie. But now Aunt said: "Magic gifts are tricky. You stay connected with any magic you've ever performed." That's why no sensible person will have anything to do with bad magic, added Katriona silently, knowing that they were both thinking about Pernicia. "Furthermore, magic needs something to grip on to. It would find precious little purchase on any of the royals. If you want to give someone a piece of strong magic when they have no magic themselves, usually you invest a thing, like giving a spell-wrought sword to the fellow you want to win the battle." Aunt paused and looked a little wry. "Well, you'd wind your spell into the jewel on its hilt, perhaps. Evil magic will bind to cold iron better than good, but even so. . ." Aunt's voice trailed away, and Katriona knew they were both thinking of Pernicia again.

"Choosing a spindle was just . . . just showing off." Aunt spoke with a kind of forced resolve. The very antitheticalness of magic and cold iron meant that on the rare occasions when the two were successfully bound the weapon produced – since the only occasions anyone knew of had produced weapons – was almost inconceivably powerful.

There was another, longer pause, and then Aunt continued: "Babies are malleable as clay, and even foresight is almost useless till a child is at least a few years old." Katriona brought her mind back with an effort from the implications of Pernicia's choice of a spindle to contain her curse to the question of the fairy godmothers' gifts. "No-one wants to – to suggest anything that might bind a baby from growing into who she was meant to be.

"Your one-and-twenty godparents also had to come up with their gifts knowing there were twenty others doing the same. Some of the silliest gifts, you may be sure, were last-minute changes when what the poor fairy had planned was given by someone else first. It would have been impolite to ask anyone what they were giving the princess before they gave it, and last-minute changes are never satisfactory. That may be why some of the wishes seem to be going – er – a little wrong. Although given wishes stay given."

Given wishes stay given, thought Katriona. She remembered the queen's fairy, Sigil, saying, *My dear, do you have any idea what you have done?* But it was only baby-magic, Katriona pleaded in her mind. There was nothing there to give: clouds and confusion. She has no magic, and magic needs something to grip on to, just as Aunt said. Rosie just likes animals. That's all.

Magic makes any keeper of it more perceptible to any other keeper. Magic perceptions are a little different from the usual five senses most humans use to perceive the world around them. Magic is more likely to tell the perceiver who your parents are than what colour your hair is.

Pernicia knows about the royal family. She would never look for anyone bearing magic.

"'The fairest lady I ever did see,'" sang Rosie. "'Her golden crown she gave to me. . .'" Her voice both sweet and flat made a faintly eerie sound through the soft hush of wind in the trees that stood behind their house. The sharper sounds of birdsong might have been the harmony, if Rosie had been singing in tune. Katriona knew the ballad: the lady was giving her crown away in preparation for drowning herself, because her father was forcing her to marry a man she hated. The lady was a princess. Barder probably wouldn't have taught her the end of it, Katriona thought, but I don't think I can tell him not to teach her songs about princesses who come to a bad end. I'll teach her "The Fox Went Out on a Chilly Night". Why can't she just sing nonsense like other children?

The usual thing with fairies was that when they first began speaking in whole sentences that followed one from another in a way that grown-ups could sometimes understand, they spent a few months doing baby-magic, and if a nonmagical family were so unfortunate as to find their little one turning the cooking pots into elephants and making the time in that house never bedtime, they had to find a fairy to take it till the worst was over. (One of the many curiosities about this situation was that while grown-up practising fairies were almost all women, baby-magic was about equally distributed between little boys and little girls. Magicians, who themselves almost never suffered baby-magic although magicianry ran in families just as fairyhood did, had done complicated studies of this phenomenon but had reached no useful conclusions.) Sometimes a general sort of containment charm would do, but most often a three- or four-year-old fairy needed a grown-up fairy to prevent it from doing itself (or the unmagical members of its family) any actual harm. Aunt and Katriona were the fairies of choice for this task all over the Gig (somewhat to their dismay; a lot of other things don't get done when one is minding small children).

But Aunt had never lost her ascendency over even the severest attack of baby-magic, which had sometimes happened elsewhere. The pub gossips still told the story of Haveral, who hadn't practised in thirty years by the time Rosie was born, who lost control over a young fairy named Gobar. Gobar had turned herself into a giant stremcopus, which is a sort of tree-shaped creature that eats people, and Haveral into a small spotted terrier with only one ear. The first anyone knew about this was the stremcopus (which, fortunately, showed no sign of eating anyone) marching through Smoke River on its long rooty feet, roaring in a highly unstremcopus-like way, and waving its long branchy arms (most stremcopuses have at least six). Panting behind it came a small spotted terrier with only one ear, far too out of breath from trying to keep a pace more suited to eight-foot legs than eight-inch ones, to speak any counter-charms. As the ill-assorted pair disappeared down the road towards Foggy Bottom and Woodwold, another fairy blinked a few times and said wonderingly, "That was Haveral." "The stremcopus?" "No, of course not – the terrier." Versions differed, but it took Haveral several days, or possibly a week, to turn Gobar back into a small girl again, by which time they had passed through all the Gig's towns several times.

When Rosie had begun speaking in paragraphs everyone but Aunt and Katriona waited for some spectacular outbreak of baby-magic. None occurred. The villagers teased Katriona and her aunt about it, but teased them rather crossly, because they felt cheated of some good and deserved entertainment. Even with two experienced fairies watching her like hawks, Rosie, knowing Rosie, should have been able to get off at least one marvel before they bagged her. There were bets on it, and the odds were on Rosie. The two fairies smiled at anyone who brought the subject of Rosie's likely fairyhood up, Aunt placidly, Katriona nervously, because Katriona suspected Rosie was up to almost anything, even magic, even though she didn't have any.

Aunt was never forthcoming about her family but she let it be understood that the sister who was Rosie's mother had had no magic herself, and had married a man from an entirely magicless family, and that everyone's interest was misplaced. (Aunt wasn't from the Gig. The story was that there had been a terrible row with her parents when the young Sophronia had decided to apprentice herself to a professional fairy; she had been expected to satisfy herself with descaling kettles, and to get on with ordinary life. No-one knew if the story was true, although Katriona knew that the reason she herself had come to Aunt was that she had been thrown into so severe an irruption of baby-magic as a result of the shock of her parents' death that all the local fairies working together had been unable to cope with her, and had informed the reluctant family that someone of her own blood had the best chance of doing so.)

Many of the village households contained a minor, nonprofessional fairy who could tend the family water vessels and mild outbreaks of baby-magic in little fairies no more powerful than they were themselves; but it seemed to Foggy Bottom a bit rich that a family which had produced Aunt and Katriona could also have produced a little thug like Rosie if she wasn't a fairy, too. But Rosie did no baby-magic.

The nearest she came to it was befriending Narl, the village smith. Narl was odd even as smiths went, and most smiths were odd.

In a country as magic-ridden as that one, you had to be a particular kind of very tough egg to choose to go into smithery. Fairies could and did, of course, live with and handle cold iron every day, but no fairy would choose to be a smith. (It was suggested that the reason so many fairies burnt themselves on kettles they were clearing was because those kettles were so often made of iron, and contact with iron made fairies absentminded.) It was not only that even a drop of fairy blood in a smith could cripple him with rheumatism while he was still young; magic hated cold iron, and tended to hang around smithies for a chance to make trouble, which, though only rarely successful, made the atmosphere round a forge rather thick. Fairies who visited forges almost always found themselves flapping their hands sharply in front of their faces as if troubled by midges, and even ordinary people sometimes batted away invisible specks that weren't there. (Since Rosie's conversation was vigorously illustrated with hand gestures, in and out of the smith's yard, it was impossible to say if she was waving at invisible specks or not.)

There was another more intriguing bit of folklore that said that truth was truth in a smith's yard, but this had not been very rigorously tested, at least not for many years. There was an ancient story of the king, sixteen or eighteen generations ago, dragging his rival to a smith's yard to demonstrate that he was the true heir and the other an impostor, but the story didn't say what the demonstration had consisted of. And there was a tradition of moving deadlocked legal struggles to a smith's yard for the truth to be discovered that way; but this was not at all popular with the smith whose yard it was, since legal truths have a way of emerging with excruciating slowness.

There was a more dubious bit of folklore concerning fairy

smiths, but this was so manifestly nonsense that even children soon grew out of asking for tales of them, although the tales were good exciting ones full of adventures.

Smiths were also the only men who were not expected to keep themselves clean shaven. This wasn't precisely a law, as no contact with fish was a law, but it was rather more than a fashion, as it was rather more than a fashion to shave outdoors on the street (this was less strictly observed during hard winters), where anyone watching (although no-one did, because it was something that happened every day) could see that proper sharpened steel was being used. If a man habitually shaved indoors and in private, there might be a story that went round that he was a fairy, and using copper, in case of accidents; and there was just that unease about strange or unadmitted fairy powers that this would not be well thought of. Fairies were fine, more or less, and you wouldn't get through life in this country without their help; but you wanted to know when one was around. Wild magic and a bad heart, after all, had produced Pernicia.

A boy's first shave was an important rite of adulthood because it said that he put his baby-magic, if any, behind him permanently; and a man with a beard was as good as saying he was a fairy. Men with beards could expect to be asked for fairy aid, and to rouse anger if it were withheld, as if the man had lied or cheated. If you had a beard, you were a fairy – or a smith. And if you were a smith you wore an iron chain round your neck any time you were away from your own village, so that people recognized you.

But Narl was clean shaven. His nickname – never repeated in his hearing – was Ironface, because his expression rarely varied, and he never spoke more than he had to.

He was also notoriously resistant to children. This was hard luck on the young of Foggy Bottom, who would have hung round the forge to talk to the horses, if they could have. Rosie's befriending him was more like real magic than baby-magic, and the more inexplicable for that. Especially since Rosie was generally talking nineteen to the dozen when Aunt or Katriona, having mislaid her, knew to try the forge first, and came to rescue her – or rather, him. Katriona, red faced, tried to apologize, the first time.

"Don't," he said. "She's welcome here." There was a pause. Katriona could think of no suitable reply to this wholly uncharacteristic remark, and then Narl added, "I like her talk."

Katriona closed her hanging jaw with a snap, swallowed hard, said, "Oh – well – thank you," and took Rosie (still talking) away with her. "He didn't at all *look* like he was enjoying her company," she said to Aunt later. "Of course he never does look like he's enjoying anything. Or not enjoying anything, for that matter. But when he turns to you, with that great black apron and all that black hair, for a moment it's a shock, as if he's a bit of his own work come to life. You would think a small child would be afraid of him."

"Not Rosie," said Aunt.

"No," agreed Katriona, half proud and half perplexed. "Not Rosie." The soft thump of Aunt's treadle continued undisturbed for several minutes and then Katriona said, "You know – about truth in a smith's yard. You don't think—"

"No," said Aunt. "I think she is probably safer with Narl than anywhere else. If it had occurred to me that such a friendship were possible, I would probably have tried to help it happen – which almost certainly would have been a mistake."

Katriona gave a muffled laugh; it was hard to imagine anyone influencing Narl to do anything, even Aunt. And Rosie herself was about as influenceable as the waxing and waning of the moon.

After that first time, while Rosie was not exactly encouraged to run off and pester the smith, Katriona didn't immediately go after her when she headed purposefully in that direction. But, after a good deal of wrestling with her conscience, she went to their priestling, the one who had written Rosie on to the Foggy Bottom register, and paid him to pray for her safety while in the smith's yard: that she would not cut or bruise herself on cold iron, nor burn herself on hot, nor stand in just the wrong place when the fire, unbearably goaded by mischief-seeking magic, suddenly flared; nor any of the other things that can happen to a child in the way of grown-ups' work. Katriona would have preferred a nice straightforward charm, but nice straightforward charms rarely worked in a smith's yard. Any fairy who discovered how to build a charm that would reliably pump a smith's bellows, for example, would be set up for life; every smith in the country would want one. No-one had. A priest's prayers were better than nothing, and infinitely preferable to trying to dissuade Rosie from doing something she wanted to do. Prohibition was always a last resort in dealing with Rosie. Furthermore, Katriona had come to like the Foggy Bottom priest, because he was so obviously fond of Rosie; and the fact that she liked him, too, sweetened Katriona's attitude still more, although the truth was that Rosie liked almost everybody.

The betting on Rosie's baby-magic was eventually wound up, to the great grief and frustration of everyone involved, and villagers found other things to gossip about. But what few people realized for some time was that Rosie really was talking to animals. And that they were really talking back.

She had begun chattering to them as soon as she began talking, but she was a friendly little thing, and there were more animals than people round Aunt's cottage, with the forest on one side and some of Lord Prendergast's fields on the other. Although she spoke to animals no differently than she spoke to people, this was the sort of thing many children did, and if it was more marked in Rosie than in most children, there were many things about Rosie that were more marked than in most children.

Rosie, as she grew older, more and more evidently waited for the animals she addressed to answer her – her face, with its transparent complexion, told any watcher that she believed they did answer her. The oddest thing, however, to the villagers' minds, was that she slowly stopped speaking human language to animals. She would be found sitting or standing near Corso or Spear (the pub's tall majestic wolfhound and best peacekeeper) or any of her other many animal friends, often both silent and not doing anything. Everyone knew Rosie never spent any time silent and not doing anything.

Katriona came to fetch Rosie away from Narl's one afternoon and discovered her looking into the eyes of a sweating, shivering colt, whose nose rested in her cupped hands. Katriona could see her fingers gently stroking the little knob under its chin. Narl squatted beside her, his empty hands dangling between his knees, his head level with hers, looking into the colt's face as intently as she was.

Rosie let out her breath in a long sigh, sounding very much like a horse herself, with a *whuffle* on the end of it; and as she moved, she moved as a horse moves, and bowed her head as a horse bows its head, for all that she had only two legs and a short human neck. The colt turned its head, and tentatively reached its nose towards Narl, who turned his own face to lay his cheek against its cheek. "I've told him you're nice," said Rosie. "It's because you're clean shaven, you see. He's not going to stand around on three legs and let a clean shaven man do weird human things to his feet. Clean shaven men yell at you and yank your girth up too tight and flop on to your back as if they think they don't weigh anything, and jab you in the belly with their feet."

"He's not getting that handling from Pren's folk," murmured Narl, while the colt investigated his face with its lips. Its ears were easing, and beginning to prick forward.

"No, but he did at his first place," said Rosie, "and their blacksmith had a beard. Oh, hello, Kat. You'll be all right now," she said, as if to both Narl and the colt, and turned to Katriona. "I hope it's teatime," she said. "I'm hungry."

Chapter 9

"And it was nothing to Narl. They were just having a conversation. Aunt, it was baby-magic! And her family has no magic! I don't understand!"

"Nor do I," said Aunt, "but this has been going on under our noses for some time – probably from the beginning. Have you really not let yourself see?"

Katriona's eyes went involuntarily to the spinning wheel against the wall, with its blunt spindle. Barder had long ago made them a spindle end shaped like a little grinning gargoyle with wide-open and slightly popping eyes. It had a quite incredible number of teeth, but looking at it you had the impression it was a sort of watchdog, loyally protecting hearth and home. Katriona had laughed out loud with delight when Barder first handed it to her; since the little ashwood egret (which she wore round her neck on a bit of ribbon), Barder had been carving spoon and knife handles, but this was far more ambitious. Rosie had still been a baby, not quite crawling, in little danger yet of spindles and spindle ends. "It's lovely!" Katriona said.

"I've been practising," Barder said, obviously pleased. Barder's usual chair at their hearthside had a bit of rag hung over the back, to be unfolded and put on the floor under him the moment his pocket-knife appeared, to catch the shavings. "And Narl's been showing me some stuff about faces. I could see this little fellow staring out at me as soon as I picked up the wood burl."

She had stood, still smiling, turning it over and over in her hands; the spindle, the business end, was as sleek as the coat of a well-bred horse, and her fingers lingered over it appreciatively; the little face at the opposite end was so bright and alive it was hard not to expect it to blink and say something. "Thank you. I – I've been wondering if I could go on having a spinning wheel in the house."

Barder had glanced down at Rosie, who had, in the mysterious way of sitting up, not-quite-crawling babies, managed to move herself half across the long room to attach herself to his trouser leg. "Aaaah!" she said, which meant, "Pick me up and throw me in the air, please."

"I know," he had said, stooping to oblige. "That's why I made it. Half the farmers round here wouldn't know how to pay you if they couldn't give you fleece to spin."

Katriona now stood up restlessly and went over to run a finger down the gargoyle's small lumpy nose. This was a kind of semi-conscious good-luck charm for her, and the gargoyle's nose was shiny with stroking. She was aware that as the years passed it was slowly accreting all those bodiless wishes into a real charm, the way enough deposited silt will eventually become a peninsula, but she doubted it would keep Pernicia away.

Rosie's eleventh birthday was coming up soon. Katriona rubbed the gargoyle's nose harder. *Magic makes any keeper of it more perceptible to any other keeper. No-one looking for a member of the royal family would look for someone who bore magic. It isn't magic because it can't be.* Eleven: they were over halfway to one-and-twenty.

When the rest of Foggy Bottom caught on to the fact that Rosie really did have beast-speech (Narl had known from the beginning, but of course hadn't said anything about it), they enjoyed it very much. It was not as good as baby-magic – for one thing it was useful, which baby-magic rarely was – but it was something at last, something to make jokes about, and making jokes about your fairies is one of the ways ordinary people live with the magic they have to live with, and both the ordinary people and the fairies know it.

It distressed Katriona, because Rosie wasn't a fairy, and she shouldn't be treated like one; it wasn't fair. It wasn't her fault she lived with two fairies. Ordinary people didn't need to defend themselves against her by making jokes that turned her into something other than themselves. Well, thought Katriona, flinching away from the reality of Rosie's ordinariness, she isn't a *fairy*. Even the fact that her beast-speech proved to everyone's satisfaction that she was exactly who Aunt and Katriona claimed she was, because beast-speech was uncommon even among fairies and two unrelated examples of it in the same village were impossible, wasn't enough to comfort her.

But the recognition of Rosie's beast-speech also reawakened some old gossip from eleven years ago.

Ordinary people sometimes have a funny reaction to glamours, like the glamour Aunt had thrown over Rosie's arrival in Foggy Bottom, a persistent, fidgety feeling that something wasn't quite right. In this case it had produced a rumour that Rosie was Katriona's daughter.

The question Katriona had really feared was not whether Rosie was her daughter – which she would have denied very convincingly – but whether she was her cousin. Barder, who was the only person Katriona felt had the right to ask, had never asked, and the rumour had died a natural death years ago – so Katriona assumed. Eleven years later she would have had to make an effort to remember that it had ever existed at all.

She and Rosie were crossing the square from the forge to the pub, towards their road home again, late one afternoon. It was drizzling rain, and Katriona was tired. Since she had stopped visiting the queen, the strength of her magic had come into her with a thunderous crash, like swallowing an anvil. The dark empty confusing place where she went for scraps of magic she could use was no longer empty, but finding what she needed was perhaps more difficult than ever – in the first place because she knew it was probably there if she looked long enough, and second because it was like trying to locate one particular pebble in a boulder field, with a great storm wind rolling everything about, including you. Aunt said it eventually got easier. Katriona hoped so. She had performed a tricky exorcism that day – if they'd known how tricky, Aunt would have come with her – ridding a field of an old battle which had suddenly woken up again, and the reperformance of which was scaring Matthew's sheep.

It was Barder's half day today, and he usually came out to the cottage for the evening, and she was almost too tired to enjoy his company. A cup of tea will help, she thought. It might have been any voice she heard, or perhaps it was a voice that had made itself out of the air of Foggy Bottom and what some people said out of her hearing. As they passed the pub, Katriona waving briefly without looking up, the voice was saying, ". . . should have married her eleven years ago, or no reason to marry her at all."

In the first shock she thought she might have imagined it, but she hadn't imagined it, because there was Barder suddenly beside her, and she could see in his face that he had heard the voice, too. She saw that he was angry, and for all that she had known and loved him for most of her life, she did not dare ask why. The three of them walked to the cottage together, Rosie chattering about birds and horses and earthworms, and the other two silent, although Barder usually talked easily to Rosie, and as if nothing she said surprised him (like that earthworms have no eyes but see the earth they creep through in beautiful visions, like the sort of visions people hope to have from eating fish). Aunt met them at the garden gate, looked into their faces, and told Rosie to go and feed the cows and chickens. Rosie usually did this anyway, but she paused a moment, looking at the other three, knowing that she was about to miss something she would be interested in, and knowing also that it wouldn't happen if she hung around. She went off at a dragging, un-Rosie-like pace, her shoulders hunched and her head down.

"I don't understand," said Barder, as soon as the cottage door closed behind them. "It seems to me just meanness, and Foggy Bottom isn't usually mean without cause. I would have knocked that useless blockhead down" – by which Katriona guessed he had recognized the voice or the speaker – "but I thought you would not like it. Dear heart, I know you are not Rosie's mother. I remember the skinny little stick you were when you left for the princess' name-day, and you were the same skinny little stick when you came back with that enormous bundle of half-grown baby." He did not at first notice how still Aunt and Katriona became at his words. "I can't say I wouldn't have cared if you'd had a baby who – who wasn't mine; I would have cared a great deal. But – I would have asked – if I hadn't known she couldn't be."

"Aunt went to fetch her after I came back," Katriona said faintly.

Barder stared. "But – no she didn't – I saw you. You looked like you'd been dragged backwards through every hedge and spinney between here and the royal city. I heard you sneeze. I was coming back from Treelight, the short way, across Lord Pren's fields. It's not exactly the short way. I – I'm afraid I had a habit of finding an excuse to walk past your cottage while you were away, just to look, even though I knew I'd hear as soon as you got back. I saw the light when Aunt opened the door."

Aunt said sharply, "Did you tell anyone what you'd seen?"

Barder shook his head, slowly, bewilderedly. "No. My aunt – my mother's sister – was ill; that's why I'd been in Treelight. It was my half day. They only wanted to hear about her, at home, and by the next day I thought, what is there to tell? Kat's had a rough journey; let her recover in peace. We'll all hear about it soon enough. I waited till I'd seen Kat in town again, and then I came to see you, and there was Rosie. And then there was this story about how Aunt had gone to fetch her. I just thought people were remembering wrong – we were all mostly thinking about the princess then, and about Pernicia – it wasn't worth arguing about. Perhaps it was fairy business; you don't argue about fairy business. But *you* would remember. . ." He looked at the two of them, and his gaze settled on Aunt, and Katriona could see him working it out. Stop! she wanted to shout. Don't think about it!

" You laid it on us," he said to Aunt. "But why?" He smiled. "Anyone would think you'd stolen the princess."

The gargoyle spindle end blazed with sudden light, and three of Aunt's little bottles fell over – *ping, ping* – and the third one dropped off its shelf and shattered on the hearth. A sharp green smell invaded the room, and then all three of them were in a wild landscape, surrounded by irregular ranks of tall, wry, standing stones, bent and distorted in strange postures. Among the stones was a low, scrubby, creeping growth whose tiny pointed leaves gave off the harsh smell of Aunt's little bottle.

It was twilight, almost dark. To one side of them at a little distance trees began to mingle with the standing stones till – in the dimness they could not be sure – it seemed that the boles moved together into the darkness of a forest. There was a horrible feeling of unfriendly eyes watching. Opposite this wood, if it was a wood, on their other side, the standing stones and the low creeper grew sparser till the rough land was bare; but far away there was a tall bulk on the horizon, tall but narrow for its height – some immense standing stone? Or some bleak fortress built by human hands?

The sun had gone behind it, whatever it was, and the sky was still purple in the memory of the sunset, the sky and the castle. It was a castle. The castle, indeed, as Katriona stared at it, seemed to send up streaks of purple from its base, as she had once seen a cloak do. . .

"*No*," she said, and, somehow, she did not know how, flung herself and her two companions back into the cottage, where the fire still burnt on the hearth, and the gargoyle still gleamed honey-golden, as if it were a faceted gemstone instead of wood, and a light shone through it, and a dark sticky puddle, purple in the firelight, lay on the floor, glittering with shards of broken glass. Aunt was already picking up the ash bucket and throwing spadefuls on the puddle; by the time Katriona remembered to breathe, the green smell was almost gone, smothered in a fug of cold ash. Katriona coughed.

"P—" began Katriona.

"*Don't say her name*," said Aunt, and Katriona saw that Aunt's hands were shaking. Aunt turned her head as if looking for something and unable to remember where it was; she laid down the bucket and shovel and put her hands to her forehead as if her head ached. Katriona heard Barder sit heavily down; his chair legs bucked briefly against the floor. But she was already pulling the stool near the chimney and groping for the little iron cauldron that sat in a niche high up on its face. She felt its presence before her fingers found it, turning the cauldron on its side so it spilled into her hand. She climbed down, holding it still wrapped in its cloth, and then unrolled it and flung it quickly round the gargoyle's thick little neck, above the loop on the spinning wheel the spindle went through.

The translucent beads of the sabre-bearer's amulet gleamed like the gargoyle's face, only a creamy, swirly white, like fresh milk with the cream still on it, instead of the yellowy-coppery glow of wood; they swung gently against the frame of the spinning wheel. The cottage and the three people in it jolted back into normality, like the end of an earthquake, or the sudden departure of fever.

Aunt dropped her hands and Barder sat up. Katriona went behind Barder's chair and bent over him, wrapping her arms round his chest and putting her cheek to his; he crossed his own arms the better to seize hers, and pressed her to him. After a moment she kissed his cheek, and he released her; and then the three of them sat down near enough to each other that they could hold one another's hands.

"Thank the fates Rosie was outdoors," said Aunt.

"Then it's – true," said Barder.

"I'm afraid so," said Katriona. "But I didn't steal her; she was – er – given to me."

Barder nodded as if this were a perfectly reasonable explanation.

There was a little silence, and then Katriona said, "Is it because Barder saw me that the glamour didn't work, Aunt? Do we have to worry about anyone else who might have seen me? I had thought no-one had seen me – but I was so tired by then—"

"Don't blame yourself," said Aunt. "You did extraordinarily well. And I don't think that's why it didn't work. I'm afraid glamours work best where there are fewest connections – and Barder cared far too much. I imagine Flora might have a little difficulty deciding when Rosie arrived, too, if she had any reason to think about it, but she doesn't. Barder, I'm sorry. This really isn't the sort of thing that happens just because you're – er – a little fond of someone who's a fairy."

"I'm not just a little fond of her," said Barder in a voice that was very nearly normal. "Do you know – what happened just now, or don't you want me to ask?"

Aunt and Katriona exchanged a look. Aunt said, "No, I don't know. But I won't uncork bdeth juice in this cottage again."

"Bdeth juice?" said Katriona slowly. "But bdeth grows quite near here – where the Gig runs into the wasteland where no-one lives."

"Yes," said Aunt.

There was another little silence.

"Something was watching us from the wood," said Katriona.

"I don't think they saw us," said Aunt. "I think – I hope—they will not have seen us. I think I did that much. But that was all I could do. And they would have figured us out soon enough if you hadn't brought us away so quickly.

"Barder – you must have some protection, before you leave us tonight. I'm not sure . . . I could simply make you forget, I think. That's perhaps safest, and you'll sleep better. "

"I – I'd rather not forget," said Barder. "If you don't mind. And – Rosie matters to me, too. What – whoever she is."

Katriona said suddenly: "Touch your gargoyle's nose. The one you made for a spindle's end."

Barder had his back to the spinning wheel. He looked at Katriona in surprise, but he turned slowly round and saw the shining gargoyle and its necklace, which looked like woven fog strung with will-o'-the-wisp. "The fates of my ancestors," he said in wonder, but he stood up and moved towards it, holding out his hand. He hesitated just before his fingers touched the gargoyle's nose, but he leaned forward – for a moment his entire body lit up with the soft eerie light of the amulet; and Katriona caught her breath, thinking that she'd never realized how beautiful he was.

And then the light went out, and the gargoyle was just a spindle's end, with a nose shiny from rubbing, and the amulet was just an odd piece of jewellery; and the outside door banged open, and Rosie said plaintively, "Are you *through* talking yet? I've been as long as I can, and I'm hungry."

*

Five weeks after that the king's fortress of Flury was broken into, and the regiment which guarded it was found asleep at their posts, fallen any way across their spears and their swords; and their horses were asleep, and the horseflies on the horses were asleep, and, deeper inside, the magicians were asleep, and the fairies were asleep, and everyone else, from the courtiers to the kitchen maids, was asleep, too.

The carters who were bringing their weekly waggon loads of fresh food ran away in terror, and Shon had spoken to one of those carters, because Flury was not so very far from Turanga. "He says the same thing happened at Fordingbridge – everyone was found asleep – only it was a relieving regiment as found 'em, and that's why the story didn't come out, as it has this time. He says the sleep's a bad one, and everyone wakes up from nightmares, and some of 'em were sick, and some of 'em are still sick – especially the magicians."

"What about the princess?" said Cairngorm.

"The princess had been taken away a fortnight earlier, while the king was there to go with her, which must be nicer for her – she must hardly ever see her mum any more, the queen mostly stays in the royal city with the little boys," said Shon. "I've heard a rumour they smuggle her back to the city sometimes. . . "

"I hope so," said Cairngorm.

"Yuh," said Shon, childless himself and not very interested. "There's different stories about why the princess got shifted early this time. Some say the royal magicians set up a – a random pattern spell about when to move her, and some say some fairy seer got her knickers in a twist and insisted she be moved early. It don't matter which – just that she wasn't there."

"They'll beat Pernicia yet," said Dessy, Flora's younger sister.

"Love, we hope so," said Cairngorm. "But we won't know till the day after the princess' one-and-twentieth birthday, and that's some years off yet."

The single sentence every one of the princess' people remembered best about the curse Pernicia had laid upon her was *My disposition of her future may happen at any time.*

Meanwhile Rosie went on talking to animals. Since most of the people who had much to do with her liked her, and because Narl seemed to take her seriously, and because she was Aunt's niece and Katriona's cousin, the jokes made of it were rarely unkind. But because she would tell people about it, certainly if they asked, and sometimes if they didn't ("Dessy, it's no use flirting with that young thatcher from Waybreak, he won't have anything to do with you because he's afraid of your mother; his pony says so"), people heard a fair amount about it.

Occasionally the information was useful: she told Aunt that the reason why Jad, the baker's dog, was getting so thin was because the baker's hob didn't much like milk, but did like the table scraps that went into Jad's bowl. The hob was getting fat, because Jad was a big dog, and Jad was getting thin, because the hob's bowl of milk was small. "I'll see to that hob," said Aunt. "Poor Jad."

But it was evident that Rosie's range of acquaintance among the animal kingdom was not merely broad but voluble. People listened, and some smiled, and some asked questions – and the answers to some of those questions brought more fleeces to the cottage, and other trade goods, much to Rosie's astonishment and Katriona's bemused and secret delight. And some shook their heads. Especially fairies. This wasn't how talking to animals went. Except that it did, with Rosie. Katriona thought again of all the milk Rosie had drunk on her way between her old life and her new one, and wondered how Rosie might have grown up if she had drunk only magician-inspected, fairy-purified, royal domestic animal milk, once she had been weaned from her mother's breast. Perhaps the royal family's amenableness was more an inherited willingness to adapt to circumstance – and Rosie's circumstances were unusual. Katriona's own beast-speech had never been as fluent and comprehensive as Rosie's; Katriona might have given her something on her name-day, but it hadn't been a transfer of her own beast-speech, like a parcel changing hands.

There was an unusual silence (even allowing for Rosie's absence; she had special dispensation to stay late at the smith's that afternoon, and chat up some of Lord Pren's young stock) by Aunt's fireside after the news about Flury.

"I wish the queen's fairy – Sigil – would send us some word," said Katriona.

Aunt laid the charm she was mending in her lap. "She would if she could."

"I know," said Katriona. "That's what I mean."

They looked at each other, and each saw reflected in the other's eyes a tall castle standing alone in a barren landscape, with a smoky purple sky behind it.

Chapter 10

As the years passed and, it seemed, the king's folk must have searched every hand's breadth of the king's land, and the royal magicians had searched every thought's breadth of every dimension over and under the king's lands (by the time Rosie was thirteen, divisions of the royal cavalry accompanying royal magicians had swept through the Gig four times; but if they found anything mysterious at the edge of the wild lands where the bdeth grew, they gave no sign), and the royal fairies had touched or tasted or listened to every wisp of wild magic that sprang from the king's lands, and there was still no news of Pernicia – no sign, no trace, no trail, no clue – another sort of story began to be told. No-one could say where the first of these stories had come from, but that its purpose was to rally morale was perfectly clear.

The reports all agreed that the princes were growing up into fine boys, but they had an elder sister who was supposed to be queen, and no-one was going to forget this: not their parents, not their country, nor even themselves, who had, it seemed, never met her: the magicians had declared that it would be too dangerous. When the Princes Colin and Terberus made their first little public speeches on their eighth birthday, both of them mentioned her, and their hope that they would meet her soon. Everyone found this very moving, especially when Terberus had added suddenly, in his own voice, to what had obviously been a prepared speech, "I would *like* a sister." His people wanted his sister, too, and watching the little princes grow up and become young men who could give speeches only made that longing more acute.

And, if there is a powerful and wicked fairy somewhere around, you want to know where she is so you can stay out of her way. The possibility that she might jump out at you from any shadow is very unsettling.

So it was said that the princess had been turned into a lark or a peacock (or, blasphemously, a fish), so that she would have no finger to prick; that it had not been the real princess at the name-day, but only a magical doll, so the curse had not in fact been laid on the princess at all, and while the king and queen were keeping her tucked away somewhere while Pernicia was still at large, there wasn't really that much Pernicia could do to her but what she could do to anyone . . . which was likely to be nasty enough, and the king was very sensibly determined to drive her out of hiding and out of his country. There was even a story that Pernicia had been captured, but that this news was not allowed out because the king would not be satisfied till every one of her spies and helpers had been found and identified. Few people found this story very comforting: the idea of Pernicia no longer at liberty was outweighed by the idea that one's own friends and neighbours might be infiltrated by her confederates.

Almost everyone's favourite story was of the party planned for the princess's twenty-first birthday, which would beggar the descriptive abilities of all the bards in the country. The stories of the party grew more fantastic with every telling, and, of course, they all had blissfully happy endings.

These stories of the princess's prospective one-and-twentieth birthday party made Aunt snappish. "They're worse than castles in the air," she said to Katriona one afternoon after Gismo, one of Shon's alternate drivers, had been giving fantasy free rein at the pub about the latest schemes for wonders. "Or rather, they *are* castles in the air, and made out of big heavy stones that are going to fall on all our heads and squash us flat." Katriona let the confused provenance of this metaphor pass in silence.

The door crashed open, and a little gust of rain and Rosie walked in. Rosie was humming. Since her hums were all more or less tuneless, you never knew which song she had in mind if she didn't say any of the words. She looked at Aunt's and Katriona's faces and said, "What's wrong?" Katriona smiled at her, feeling at once better and worse for the sight of her, thinking, not for the first time, of what the king and queen had lost – not just their daughter, but Rosie.

" We were talking about the princess," said Aunt.

"Oh," said Rosie. She had some fellow feeling for the princess, since they were the same age, and she had grown up with the mystery of what had become of her, and of the grown-ups' interest in any tale purporting to have news of her.

Rosie had a notion that the only way grown-ups knew to protect you was to lock you up somehow – even protective spells usually had a locking-up quality about them, like the anti-drowning- in-a-bog one Aunt had laid on Rosie about eight months ago, after what Rosie still insisted indignantly was nothing *like* a near miss, and which simply prevented Rosie from walking in certain directions in certain places, although there were quite a few certain places round the damp and fenny Foggy Bottom. (There were serious disadvantages to being a fairy's niece. The bog spell took more upkeep than ordinary families could afford. Aunt had at least let the utterly humiliating spell that prevented her from being sat on by large animals lapse a couple of years ago; of course within a day or two a horse she was holding for Narl had stood on her foot, but he was the sort of horse who if he hadn't been able to stand on your foot would have bitten you instead, so she supposed it didn't count. Besides, it had happened at the forge, where even Aunt's charms became wandery and confused. She hadn't mentioned the episode at home.)

Suggestions about the princess' whereabouts nearly always included some reference to a fortress or stronghold, so Rosie always imagined the princess surrounded by a lot of stonework. At first she had seen her in a tiny tower room, but then she thought no, she's a princess, she can have a large room – and lots and lots of grim-visaged guards armed to the teeth with an assortment of deadly and terrifying weapons Rosie had never seen and could only pretend to imagine. It sounded like a pretty miserable life and Rosie felt sorry for her.

"Why don't we look for her?" said Rosie. "She could live with us. Aunt, you're the cleverest fairy in the Gig. Even Narl says so, and he's not trying to get a spell for free. If you found her, no-one would know where she'd gone, and so she'd be safe. She could have some fun here. I could show her where all the *bogs* are." Rosie had not come indoors in the best of tempers, as she had forgotten which way she had been headed till she found herself reheaded home, briskly carried by insurrectionist feet. The ballad she'd been humming as she came through the door – another one Barder had taught her – had a pleasingly bloodthirsty chorus which suited her mood: " 'I lighted down my sword to draw, and hacked him into pieces sma', and hacked him into pieces sma'. . . ' " Maybe she could be the princess' guard.

There was a little silence. "That's an interesting thought, dear," said Aunt, "but I'm afraid you have a rather inflated idea of my skills."

Katriona, fascinated, said, "What would we tell everyone about where she came from?"

Rosie shrugged. She had lived as long as she could remember with Aunt and Katriona; they seemed a fine sort of family to her. The only question she had yet been moved to ask about her parents was how tall they had been, as it was plain she was going to be taller than either Aunt or Katriona. (Her outlandish colouring, in mostly dark- or mouse-coloured Foggy Bottom, had been explained by a tow-headed father from the south.) "That Aunt has another niece, and us another cousin, of course."

"Of course," said Aunt. "How sensible you are, Rosie. What a pity we are unlikely ever to have reason to make use of your suggestion."

Rosie looked at her suspiciously – "sensible" was not a word she was accustomed to hearing applied to herself – but Aunt only gave her her usual serene smile, her temper quite recovered from Gismo's foolishness, as she went on with her spinning, the shiny nose of the gargoyle making a tiny bright blur as the spindle went round and round and round.

Sarkon, Barder's master, died as winter was closing in, on one of the shortest days of the year, when the cloud cover was so low and heavy the lamps in Cairngorm's pub had burned since morning. His pyre was lit the next day, and only Barder and Joeb, his Second Apprentice, asked for his ashes, for his wife had died years before, and they had no family. Because there was no-one else, Barder and Joeb agreed to hold the three months' mourning.

Cairngorm and Aunt and the wainwright's sister, Hroslinga – the wheelwright and the wainwright shared a yard across the square from the blacksmith – helped as they could. Mourning should not be borne by two young men alone, and this was just the sort of situation likeliest to bring the Gig's chief priest down upon Barder and Joeb and Foggy Bottom generally, with orations about proper respect and reverence and the importance of upheld tradition. Barder looked tired and preoccupied all that winter, and only twice came out to Aunt's cottage, where he promptly fell asleep in his chair.

Katriona already wondered, fearfully, if they hadn't been seeing less of him since the evening he had made the joke about Rosie being the princess; if he hadn't needed more of his half days to do something else in; if he wasn't less likely to stop for a moment if Katriona met him in town. There had never been, in the years they'd known each other, any specific words between them; neither of them could afford to get married and they both knew it, although Katriona had long believed he would have spoken if he could. He had made her the egret she still wore round her neck, and only she and Aunt and Rosie had spoons and knives with Barder-carved handles; but she couldn't help remembering that Barder had lately spent his spare time carving spindle ends, and that these were sent away for sale outside the Gig. Not that they needed another spindle end, she told herself, fiercely petting the gargoyle's nose.

Flora had told her comfortingly that Barder's mother had been heard on a number of occasions complaining about his attachment to "that fairy", saying that there wasn't any fairy blood in their family (which was manifestly untrue, since Barder's aunt in Treelight descaled half the village's kettles although she didn't otherwise practise) and that Barder himself had walked into the middle of one of her perorations at the pub one day and told her bluntly, if unfilially, to be either quiet or civil.

When Barder had befriended Rosie, Katriona had thought (pleased and gratified) that he did so initially for her, Katriona's, sake, but in the shadow cast by Sarkon's illness and death she began to wonder if he had befriended them both out of a more generally philanthropic feeling that they needed friends. Even the story of his confrontation with his mother could be read as natural chivalry.

On a day early the following spring, Katriona sniffed the air, looked at the clouds, consulted the weather-guesser, and decided that the rat-gnomes in Truga's henhouse could wait another day. She swept the floor as a sop to her conscience, finagling the chalky detritus of magic out of the corners with a few scouring charms, and then went out to dig in the garden. Aunt had gone to Crossroad Hill to meet Torg and Aileena, the chief fairies of Treelight and Moonshadow; Rosie was, as usual, with Narl.

She hummed while she dug and weeded – her own humming, she thought, under Rosie's influence, was much less melodic than it used to be – and thought about nothing in particular. She was still thinking about nothing in particular (except perhaps how it was that weeds grow so much more quickly than anything you've planted) when a human-shaped shadow fell across her. But when she looked up and saw Barder, looking uncommonly tidy and even more uncommonly nervous, she could not help her heart giving a great, voice-throttling leap, and tears prickling at the corners of her eyes.

She stood up, and went towards him, and then realized her

hands were filthy. She raised them, and looked at them in astonishment and dismay, as if she had never seen filthy hands before in her life, beginning to turn away to go towards the water butt where she could wash them . . . but he reached for her just before she moved, and seized her by the wrist.

They stood like that, their two arms extended almost full length between them, him leaning towards her, she half turned away to go to the water butt, but having turned her head back to look at him when he touched her – and their faces told each other all they needed to know, for he didn't seem able to talk either. They moved towards each other, she uncertainly, still not quite believing he had come to her after all, and he stepping forward eagerly. He kissed her, and she curled up her dirty hands so she could put her arms round his neck without spoiling his best collar.

"I would have sent for you if you hadn't come soon," said Aunt, returning an hour later. Barder and Katriona were kneeling side by side, companionably weeding; he had taken off his good coat and collar and rolled up his sleeves, but was ruining the knees of his good trousers. (Weeding had the attraction of novelty for Barder, besides the fact that he would have done anything Katriona asked after the important question had been answered the right way, first in silence and then in words. Weeding was one of those fairy eccentricities; no-one else did it; but fairies were always up to strange things, and no-one would want to take the chance that their balms, tonics and potions might be denatured by undesirable proximities in the fairy's garden.)

Barder laughed, but Katriona said, "You wouldn't."

"Perhaps I wouldn't've, but I would have thought of it. I have thought of it," her aunt replied, not the least discomposed.

"And you didn't know," said Katriona. "You didn't *know*."

"If you mean my magic didn't tell me, it didn't need to," said her aunt. "The entire village has been waiting. Possibly the entire Gig." Barder was growing as famous for the things he could do with wood, other than wheels, as Narl had been for some time for the things he could do with cold iron, besides buckles and horseshoes and ploughshares. The progress of such a prominent figure's romance was, of course, interesting. And everyone – except Katriona – had known perfectly well why Barder had been so absorbed recently in selling as many spindle ends for as high a price as possible; Sarkon's was a good house, but rather in need of the sort of repairs one wanted to have made before one brought one's new bride to it. Katriona now made a strangled noise, and Barder's ears, more visible than usual from the severity with which he had tied his hair back, were bright red. "I shall miss you, Kat," Aunt added, a little wistfully.

"Oh, but you're coming too!" said Katriona, climbing to her feet and taking her aunt's hands without, this time, considering the condition of her own. "We've just been talking about it. Lord Pren has agreed that Barder should have the house and yard and be called Master, since he is First Apprentice, and even Lord Pren knows that all the really interesting stuff Sarkon has been doing for years is really Barder –"

Barder made protesting noises.

"– And you know the house is big enough – big enough and to spare – and there is even a shed for the cows and chickens. You must come. What would we do about Rosie?"

Barder said shyly, "I've known all along that I could never have Kat if I didn't want you and Rosie, too. You can put in a garden like this one – in rows, and weeded. Joeb and I will break up the ground for you before you come, and put up the fence to keep the chickens out. Or in."

"You know you've been saying it's not good for Rosie to live outside the village with only two fairies, and it's more important as she gets older," said Katriona. "And I'll be *very* careful about the binding spells round the yard – you know I'm good at those. Our neighbours will barely know we're there."

"Hroslinga has a dja vine," said Aunt mildly.

"Oh – well – I'll think of something," said Katriona. "Oh, Aunt . . . "

Aunt had a preoccupied look. "I knew Rosie couldn't go far

from you, Kat – nor, I think, from Narl – but I was thinking of the house that Med left—"

"Because it's haunted," said Katriona, "with a particularly unpleasant mould spirit, who turns everything squashy and green, and moans all night."

"I could probably turn it out, you know," said Aunt.

"Is it – is it very distasteful to you, the thought of living in the wheelwright's house?" said Barder sadly.

"Aunt!" said Katriona.

"Oh my dear – my dears," said Aunt, "I will gladly accept your invitation to live in the wheelwright's house, if you are sure that you would like it." She looked at them and smiled, and then said with suspicious briskness, "I am going to make tea," but Katriona saw the tears in her eyes as she turned away.

"Then all that's left is to explain it to Rosie," said Katriona.

"Won't Rosie like the idea of living closer to Narl?" said Barder. "If Narl can stand it."

"Yes, she will, but she has a lot of – friends in the forest," said Katriona. Barder knew, of course, about Rosie talking to animals, but as he had watched her grow up thinking of her as Aunt's niece and Katriona's cousin, he had never found it surprising; and he had tried to put his memory of a certain evening some months back as far out of his ordinary daily thoughts as possible, to keep it safe and secret. He shook his head now, as the old view of Rosie collided with newer knowledge, and Katriona, guessing to what – or whom – the headshake referred, looked at him worriedly.

He saw the worry and, in his turn, guessed what it was about. "Don't fret," he said. "I took you for the good times and the bad ones in my mind years ago – and I've always known you were a fairy, even when you still thought you weren't. The rest of it doesn't matter." He paused. "I took you, and gave you me back – even if you didn't know it. What's happened to you has happened to me, too – even if I didn't know it."

Katriona put her forehead on his shoulder and sighed. Small spider weave, she thought. I wish it were as simple as that none of us speak aloud what we know. She still often heard the queen's voice in her mind: *I miss my child so much. . . Tell me you are real.* But she rarely remembered the small fairy's: *And a poem is all I can give her, my dear, my only darling!*

But at least I know one more thing – important thing – than I did this morning, thought Katriona. She smiled against Barder's shoulder, and raised her face to be kissed.

Rosie, to her dismay, found that she didn't know what she thought about the news that Katriona and Barder were to be married, and that they were all moving into town to live in the wheelwright's house with Barder and Joeb, who wished to stay on. That Katriona and Barder would marry she knew as well as everyone in the village (except Katriona) had known since Sarkon died; but she suddenly realized, now that the change was upon her, that she had never thought about what would happen afterwards.

I have been thinking like a *child*, she said to herself, in dismay and shame. She wanted to have thought about it before, so she would have those thoughts to help her know how to feel. Not knowing what she thought made her feel lost; and feeling lost made her feel suddenly as if she were somebody else, and that feeling set up echoes, deep down inside herself, and these scared her. These echoes told her that she really wasn't Rosie: and that she had never been. She was someone else; she had always been someone else. Someone who didn't belong to Aunt and Katriona, to Foggy Bottom. Who the someone else was the echoes didn't say. They only took things away – comfort, peace, security – they didn't give her anything to replace them. Almost she thought she could hear some strange voice saying some strange name, her name, her real name. She put her fingers in her ears, but it was not that kind of hearing.

For the first time in her life she woke up in the bed she'd slept in every night since she was old enough to sleep in a bed without rolling out, and didn't know where she was. She lay awake, listening to Katriona and Aunt breathing in their sleep – Katriona deep and low, Aunt with a little rustling noise – and didn't recognize them either; and she knew the noises of their sleeping and the shadowy shape of their bodies in their blankets as well as she knew anything, as well as she knew the shape of her own hand, her own name . . . but the shadows told her her name was not hers, and the shape of her hand was changing. She was fifteen, and she had grown four inches in the last year, and her body was evolving from square to lanky, and even her fingers were suddenly longer, the knuckles knobby, instead of dimpled like a child's .

She lay in the dark and listened, and heard the faint mumbles of the house mice, telling each other that Flinx was only just outside, and that one of the shutters was unlatched. She felt an owl wing silently overhead, its head full of wordless thoughts of dinner, loud enough nonetheless for Rosie to hear through rafters and deep thatch. And she heard other things, voiceless, thoughtless things: she heard the necklace that Katriona prized so highly sitting in its niche; she heard the gargoyle spindle end sitting in the wooden ring where it hung when the wheel stood idle, and they said to her: *Sleep, sleep, we will watch, and watch over you*. And then Rosie knew she was dreaming, and fell asleep smiling.

She didn't mention her confusion of feeling to Katriona and Aunt, partly fearing it might hurt them, especially Katriona, and partly fearing one of Aunt's foul-tasting tonics, but both Katriona and Aunt noticed. Katriona worried, because Katriona always worried, but also because she knew that what had started it was the news that they were all to move into the village and live with Barder; but Aunt said that Rosie was growing so fast she probably didn't know backwards from sideways while the rest of her tried to catch up.

She grew another inch in the ten weeks between Barder's formal visit to the cottage and the wedding, and Aunt basted another strip of material round the hem of the dress Rosie was wearing so that it still came to her ankles the way it was supposed to – and so that the scruffy third-hand boots that were the only shoes that fit her didn't show any more than they had to.

Rosie was unusually docile, which was convenient, but Katriona thought she would rather have had her banging doors and shouting that she didn't want to live in a town with everybody else's smoke and cooking smells and the dust from the road complicating the always complicated housekeeping in a fairy's home. But she didn't. She didn't even protest about wearing a skirt to the wedding, and she hated dresses almost as much as she hated her hair; she'd worn trousers since she could walk.

The best Katriona could think of to do was to ask Narl to keep an eye on her.

Katriona was well-versed in Narl's grunts by this time, and the grunt that answered this request told her that Narl had also noticed the change in Rosie, and had been thinking about it himself. Rosie came home a day or two after this and told them, looking and sounding more like herself than she had in several weeks, that Narl had begun to teach her horse doctoring.

Girls were less often apprenticed than boys, and no-one expected Rosie to need apprenticing away from home, since sooner or later she would turn out to be a fairy, and meanwhile there was always work for another pair of hands. Narl had had temporary apprentices occasionally – not the usual sort, for which he said, when pressed, that he had no time, but men (female smiths were rarer than male fairies) who already knew their business and were interested in learning to do fancy work, like Aunt's fire-dogs and Lord Prendergast's gates. But while Narl did a fair amount of horse doctoring, as all smiths did, and was good at it, as many smiths were not, he had never offered to teach anyone what he knew. Till Rosie.

Their unlikely alliance had intrigued the villagers for years, and the information that Narl was now teaching her horse doctoring only heightened this interest. Dessy, who was something of a romantic, once said to Flora that if you ever saw them talking to each other, Narl looked younger than usual (although no-one knew how old he was), and Rosie looked older. Flora knew what she meant – it was something about the way they looked at each other, as if they were not merely friends but old friends, partners, peers. But Dessy's tendency to daydream was a nuisance round the pub when there was always too much to be done, and so Flora said quellingly, "Talk to each other? You're thinking of somebody else. Rosie talks enough for six, and Narl doesn't talk at all."

It was also an odd thing that a smith should be teaching a future fairy a smith's pragmatic horse-leech skills because the reason smiths were popular as horse doctors was because most horses didn't respond well to magic – you laid a gentling charm over a skittish colt and he left off shying at leaves and rabbits and shadows and threw a proper tantrum about the charm. Blowing the fumes of mashed vizo root up his nostrils was easier, and more likely to work. Foggy Bottom, which by this time was rather accustomed to being frustrated by both Narl and Rosie, decided that the facts were merely that Narl and Rosie *were* odd, and let them get on with it. But Katriona wondered, grateful as she was for Narl's meddling, if Narl had any particular reason to believe that Rosie was not going to grow up to be a fairy.

By the day of the wedding Rosie was enough of her old self to protest violently at having flowers stuck in her hair. Aunt had the argument with her about it. Katriona was elsewhere, with Flora, twittering over the food, and worrying that there wasn't going to be enough (there was enough to feed everyone in the Gig three times over, as Flora was endeavouring to point out).

"I haven't got enough hair to stick flowers in anyway!" said Rosie passionately. This was perhaps not absolutely true; it was a little longer than it had been after her first self-inflicted haircut at the age of four. But not much. When she was excited about something, and had been running her hands through it, it was still short enough to stand out like a fuzzy halo. It was still markedly curly, too, but too short to twist itself into ringlets, as anyone could see it longed to do.

Aunt considered for a moment and said, "I'll make a bargain with you. You should wear a proper helmet of flowers – remember Soora at Garly's wedding last year? – but I'll weave you just a little, er, crown of them," thinking, this is just what I need, another last-minute job, I wish I had six hands, "will that do?"

Rosie, no fool, knowing she was being got round – and that Aunt had more than enough to do already – thought of Katriona, who probably would like her attendant to be wearing flowers in her hair. She remembered Soora's headdress; she had looked like a walking shrubbery, and Rosie had wanted to laugh. "Um." For Katriona, she reminded herself. "Um. I'll finish the gate ribbons for you."

Aunt sighed. "Thank you." Wedding gate ribbons were, in most parts of that country, a decorative detail only, but the Gig still took them seriously, possibly because the Gig, by its climate, was plagued by fog-sprites, which gate ribbons successfully confused. More solid spirits of mischief had to be kept out of important rites by brush and branches.

The crown suited Rosie – and crown it was. Katriona, having permitted herself to be reassured by the several tonnes of food distributed on tables both inside and outside the pub (the weather having been declared secure, without magical interference, by both Aunt and the weather-guesser), would have said she was wholly preoccupied with the immediate prospect of being wed to Barder. But she was struck by the sight of Rosie in her little crown of flowers, patched-on hemline, old boots and all. There was a dignity about her Katriona had not seen before, which was, although Katriona didn't know it, a combination of the newness of her increasing height and her first glimpse into the darker depths of what it means to be human, plus a resolution to bear herself well for the wedding of the person she loved best in the world, which – though she appreciated that Aunt had done her tactful best – included not snatching the stupid circlet off her head and stamping on it. This last was what was making her stand up quite so straight and proud. It looked like poise.

Rosie had her own room at the wheelwright's. At the cottage they had all slept upstairs at one end of the long cottage attic, while various stores, both magical and ordinary, took up the rest of the space, hanging from the roof, or neatly stacked and packaged on shelves and piled in corners. It was rather exciting to have a room of your own. But what did you do with it?

It was a small room, tucked in a corner of the ell that thrust out towards the common land that backed the village, and looking out over the shed that contained a bemused Poppy, a wary Fiend, and ten chickens in a sulk. Their sensibilities had been outraged by the move, and they were refusing to lay. Where Rosie knelt by her window she could see Flinx lying on the shed roof, a blobby sort of shadow against the flat darkness of the roof. She hadn't been sure that Flinx would come with them into town, although she had long ago figured out that any important situation containing Katriona would have Flinx somewhere lurking on the edges and pretending to be thinking about something else.

At present Flinx, having (briefly) met the wainwright's dog, Zogdob, was showing a preference for high places. There were several of the town cats with him on the roof, all of whom had attended the wedding, with unusual decorousness for cats, but then they were all fond of Katriona. (Cats hung round temples and priests' houses unless the priests positively drove them away. The priests' religion rather appealed to cats; they borrowed bits of it to work into their ideas of augury and metaphysics.) They were discussing the wedding in a desultory and solipsistic manner, but Rosie had the feeling that some of the sillier remarks were being made for her benefit, so she stopped listening.

She turned round and sat on the floor, leaning her shoulders against the sill, looking at her new room. All those freshly whitewashed walls seemed to expect something, as a waiting audience expects something, unlike the dark rough planking of the cottage attic (which you never got very near anyway because of the steep pitch of the roof), and Rosie had little personal gear to occupy space. She wondered who Lord Pren would give their cottage to. Who would sleep in that loft, cook over that fire? How long would it take them to learn the trick of making the pot hook swing smoothly when it had a laden pot on it,

without spraying the floor and the shins of the unhappy server
with boiling soup or scalding stew? Even Aunt hadn't come up
with a charm for it. "Iron against iron is too difficult," she said.
"If it were a matter of life and death I'd work something out, but
it isn't."

After Rosie had been introduced to her glistening, expectant
room she had briefly considered claiming to be afraid of the dark
so she didn't have to face occupying it alone, but she knew no-one
would believe her — and after the silent echoes of the last
few weeks which told her she wasn't who she'd always believed
she was she didn't have the heart for deliberate impersonation.
Besides, it wasn't exactly that she wanted to share a room
with Aunt; she was just worried about how everything was
changing.

Poppy had said comfortably that it would all turn out for the
best, but Poppy usually said that about everything, and she was
also heavily in calf which always made her sentimental. Fiend,
also in calf, was less sanguine; but she was at her most pessimistic
when she had a baby due, believing that wolves would be
conjured out of the air by the effort of her labour. The chickens
only said that the dust was all wrong and the bugs were all wrong
and the shape of their coop was all wrong and how could any
human think they could lay under these conditions?

Rosie turned round again, and looked back at the night. Even
the sky looked different from her new window, although (she
supposed) it was the same sky. The other cats had left, and Flinx
had moved a little nearer the window of the bedroom Katriona
now shared with Barder. The moon was full tonight — it was
supposed to be good luck to marry during a full moon — and the
sky was bright with stars. The usual Gig ground mist hadn't
risen above the first storey where Rosie leaned her elbows on
her windowsill.

All three of the humans from the cottage, Aunt, Katriona and
Rosie, were sleeping in the wheelwright's house for the first
time tonight — all three of them, who were now four because of
Barder (five really, for Joeb had another little room in the corner

between the house and the shop), and she guessed they would soon be more than that, because Barder and Katriona would have children. And there was a baby-magic boarder coming tomorrow; Aunt had been holding her family's frail control over her together with a series of charms, but had promised to take her in the moment the wedding was over. It was late, and Rosie was exhausted, but she wasn't ready to lie down and sleep, and risk waking up and not knowing where she was, now that she was somewhere she didn't know.

She wondered if she would like living in town. The air smelled so different here; the fields and woods and garden and animal smells she was used to were still there, but so were the chimney and cooking smells of houses other than their own, the slight whiff of lime that told of rigorously clean privies (the village council were adamant about this), the drift of strange and varied stable smells from the animal pens, and the dust and dung smells of the road. She could even hear a murmur of people talking, and there was a burst of not-so-distant laughter, where a few people who had outstayed the wedding party were still at the pub.

Feeling misplaced and astray had become familiar in the last ten weeks. At least this strangeness seemed friendly. She began telling over in her head some of the latest of Narl's teachings as something to ground herself with. This was only partially successful, since few of his recipes were exact; you added enough staggleroot to make the paste stick together, for example, except that the berries' stickiness varied from year to year on account of the weather, and if you added too many then when the paste dried on the horse's leg it wouldn't come off.

She knew it couldn't be accidental that Narl had chosen just now to start teaching her, and she only hoped he meant it, that it wasn't a sort of toy to distract a bewildered child. Even as she thought this she realized how offensive such a suggestion would be to Narl, and she almost laughed, but laughing was too difficult just now. Laughter would rattle her bones apart.

Maybe she'd ask Aunt for a few bunches of dried herbs to

hang in her bedroom – they'd make a nice smell, and would dim the awful whiteness of the walls. Barder had whitewashed the bedrooms himself, to make them light and cheerful; she couldn't say she preferred gloom. She'd get used to the sounds and smells, and a room of her own. She looked round the room once more, and pulled the shutters closed, ready to go to bed. At least it was her own bed, carted in from the cottage, and her own clothes hanging on pegs by the door. She might have had a candle, but if this was to be her room, she wanted to know her way in the dark.

PART THREE

Chapter 11

Rosie had an additional reason for being doubtful about the move to town. While Barder was offering them their own house, his shop shared a courtyard with the wainwright, and the wainwright had a niece, Peony. Rosie had thought after Flinx's dramatic meeting with Zogdob, *you're* the lucky one, you're allowed to run away.

Peony was nearly the same age as Rosie, and an only child in a house of adults not her parents, for she lived with her aunt and uncle. But there the similarity between them ended. Peony had long golden curls – although of a softer shade than Rosie's short defiant hair – and limpid blue eyes that smiled even when her face was solemn. Grown-ups had never patronized her; she was too graceful and too self-possessed, even as a baby, and as she grew older she was too sweet-natured. Condescension would have slid right off her, like snow on a warm roof. She was rarely disobedient, and when she was, it was generally to do with her lingering to give delight or some more practical aid by her presence, when her aunt and uncle expected her to perform some errand quickly.

She could sew, cook and clean; she wrote a good clear hand and did sums accurately. She could carry a tune, she could dance, and play upon what variety of musical instruments the village offered. She was also beautiful. (She had long curling golden eyelashes, although not so long as Rosie's.) It was all too much. Rosie had thought so for years, and avoided her.

Nonetheless, they met up occasionally. The village was too

small for everyone not to know each other, and furthermore, Peony was only seven months older than Rosie, and most grown-ups seemed to think that accidents of chronology should oblige children to get along. Rosie was too good-natured herself to hate anyone without serious cause, but in Peony's case she had considered it. Rosie had heard rather too much about Peony's manifold perfections from the village folk, especially after some one or another of Rosie's more tactless imbroglios. It was all the harder for poor Rosie because she and Peony were the only girls of their age in Foggy Bottom; everyone else was several years older or younger.

Rosie's good nature had been sorely tested when that particular implication of Barder's suit sank in. Since all three grown-ups, Aunt, Katriona, and Barder himself, were watching her anxiously, they saw her start, and heard her grunt, as if from a physical blow, a few moments after the initial announcement. What they did not know was that the grunt was a valiantly suppressed "Next door to *Peony*? I'd rather live in Med's old house, with the mould spirit. Maybe Lord Pren's new tenant will need a cowherd."

She'd managed to elude Peony during the busy weeks leading up to the wedding although Peony had often been underfoot, brightly offering to do anything she could do to help, and saying disgusting things to Rosie like, "Oh, I do hope we can be sisters." Rosie had been able to pretend she hadn't heard. She wouldn't be able to go on ignoring her now that she actually lived here.

But the confrontation didn't go as Rosie expected, although it had begun as unpromisingly as she could have desired. Everyone had slept late the day after the wedding (Rosie had staggered out to feed the cows and the chickens and then gone back to bed) and it was midmorning before Rosie ventured into the forecourt. She had been driven there by Aunt, who recognized Rosie's lurking about the kitchen for what it was, and knew that Peony was outside doing her own hopeful lurking. "My dear," said Aunt, with a sympathy Rosie couldn't help but hear, "you are going to have to come to some kind of terms with her. I know she is — she is not at all like you. But she is probably not all bad, even if she is a paragon."

Peony, of course, stopped whatever she had been doing, and came up to Rosie with her best, most winning smile, and said, "Well, now that all the fuss is over, perhaps we can begin to know each other."

Rosie, looking for allies, had glanced around hopefully for Zogdob, but Zogdob was curled up at the very back of the courtyard, pretending to be asleep. "Um," said Rosie unencouragingly, standing like a soldier on parade, back stiff and eyes straight ahead. She stood up as much as she could around Peony, because standing she was half a head taller than the older girl.

"You know," said Peony thoughtfully, looking up at Rosie, "you have the longest eyelashes I have ever seen—"

"Get *dead*," said Rosie furiously, abandoning her imitation of a statue: "I *hate* my eyelashes."

Peony stared at her with her mouth open, and then she burst out laughing. She put her hand on Rosie's arm, and to Rosie's own astonishment she did not resent the touch; she heard in Peony's laughter that Peony was as worried about her new neighbour as Rosie was about being her neighbour, and that Peony had been sure she would say the wrong thing to Rosie, and it was a great relief to have done so and got it over with. Rosie began to laugh, too.

Her chest felt tight from weeks of work and change and fear and resentment and hope, and the first laugh hurt; but then she pulled in a great deep breath that filled her right up, and she laughed with Peony till they both had to sit down, right where they were, in the middle of the forecourt, and Peony's uncle, Crantab, had to shout at them to move out of the way. When they finished laughing they were on their way to being not just friends, but the dearest of friends, the sort of friends whose lives are shaped by the friendship.

Aunt and Katriona's baby-magic boarders rose to an all-time high of seven within a month after the wedding and Peony's suddenly ubiquitous presence in their household was seized on with a slightly desperate gratitude – even two full-grown fairies at the height of their powers might blanch at the prospect of seven baby-magic boarders at the same time, and their other work did not ease off just because their home life was in an uproar.

Peony was (of course) good with small children, delighted to be of service, and happy to wear a charm that Katriona made her so that she could help maintain some semblance of order. Even if the charm did make everything she ate while she was wearing it taste like sheep's brains. She mentioned this, after about a fortnight, humbly, to Katriona, who said, "Oh, fates, I'm sorry, that happens sometimes." She made a new one, and watched Peony closely at their next noon meal, but Peony wouldn't catch her eye, busying herself with preventing Mona from scaring Tibby into bursting into tears by making goblin faces (complete with warty green skin and fangs) at her. When Tibby wept, the tears turned into all sorts of interesting things, most of which would make Tibby cry even harder.

The next midday Katriona drew Peony out into the courtyard, pulled the charm off over her head, and handed her a basket. "Go and have your meal with Rosie at the forge."

Peony blushed. "The new charm is better, really. It almost makes me like sheep's brains."

Katriona laughed. "I can cope alone for an hour. Go on or I'll put wings on your heels and fly you there."

Nearly three months after Peony began taking her noon meal at the forge, Rosie was returning home after a long day: determining whether Grey's wheelhorse's lameness behind was caused by sore back muscles (*I dunno*, said Kindeye, the horse: *It's me ankle what hurts, but it – it do echo a bit, now you ask me*) or a mild-mannered riding horse's head-shaking by a tooth abscess (*My head buzzes, I don't like it, make it* stop, said Yora distressfully) or if a mare visiting Lord Pren's stud wouldn't come into season because she didn't like the stallion her owner wanted her bred to (*Hmph* was all she would say to Rosie about it).

She found Katriona turning the several hundred spiders mobbing the kitchen ceiling back into the grains of barley they had been before Mona turned them into spiders. Katriona was returning them to their original shape very neatly, in clusters, so that they fell into the basin she was holding under them, *taptaptaptap*. Peony, for once looking a little tousled and harried, was sitting at the table mending knees in very short trousers. When the ceiling was spider-free (nearly: "Oops!" said Katriona at one point. "Sorry, I didn't realize you were a real one"), Katriona put the basin of barley on the table and sighed.

"Peony, love, you need some fresh air. Our little horrors are all asleep – or if they aren't I'm going to blow sleep-smoke over them, and professional scruples can go hang for one evening – Rosie, why don't you take Peony for a walk?"

They wandered down the road, away from the square, towards the crossroads where you had to choose either Woodwold or Smoke River. It was a hazy, damp night, and you could almost hear the fog-sprites giggling. It would rain by morning. Peony put her arm through Rosie's and sighed.

" You're in our house more than you're in your own," said Rosie, a little jealously.

Peony smiled. "I'm useful there."

" You're useful *everywhere*," said Rosie feelingly but without animosity. "Don't your uncle and aunt miss you?"

Peony was silent, and Rosie felt a sudden pang of doubt. "Peony?"

Peony sighed. "I'm so tired, I can't . . . Haven't you ever noticed the difference between your house and mine?"

"Yours is cleaner," Rosie said promptly. Rosie was very popular with Peony's aunt and uncle, because she had taken on the exasperating and painful job of bashing and lopping their suddenly riotous dja vine into some kind of order. This was an almost weekly job, and Rosie felt she now knew how warriors riding into battle against fire-wyrms must feel. Dja vines did not, it was true, breathe fire, but their temperament and their teeth were similar. Peony's aunt, Hroslinga, made a point of inviting Rosie in after each of these hazardous undertakings, and pressing samples of the baker's best cakes on her. Hroslinga was an earnest, anxious, fidgety woman who kept her house extravagantly clean (thanks to one of Katriona's charms, any venturesome magic dust fell off at the front step, although this did mean the front step required a good deal of sweeping) and did beautiful sewing; Rosie was unable to carry much conversation on either of these subjects, but liked the cakes.

Peony gave a sort of half laugh, half cough. "Yes, it is cleaner. And quieter. And . . . my aunt and uncle took me in when my parents died; they're brother and sister, you know that, don't you? And my mother's only relatives, and my father was from the south." Rosie knew all this. "It never occurred to them to . . . escape the responsibility; they're good people. They've raised me kindly and treat me well."

"They should!" said Rosie, unable to remain silent.

"Ye-es. I suppose. And I'm useful to them, so it's not as bad as it might be—"

"Oh, Peony," said Rosie sadly.

Peony said drearily, "They don't love me. Not the way Aunt and Katriona and Barder love you."

There was a little silence, and then Rosie said, "*I* love you."

Peony made the little half-laugh half-cough noise again, and in something more like her usual voice said: "Well, I told you we would be sisters, didn't I? Oh, Rosie, I was *terrified* of you! You're as tall as a man, and as strong, from all that time at the forge, and you were Narl's *friend*! Everybody is a little afraid of Narl! And your aunt and your cousin are the two best fairies in the Gig, and you talk to animals better than any fairy anyone has ever heard of. You were going to despise me, I knew it!"

"I wouldn't have dared. The whole village thinks you're perfect."

"Yes," said Peony, all the energy draining away from her again, and in that soft monosyllable Rosie heard what her friend was trying to tell her, and her heart ached.

"There'll be supper by the time we get back," said Rosie, and Peony nodded. They returned to the wrights' yard in silence, but Rosie had Peony firmly by the hand, and Peony did not resist when Rosie drew her indoors. A delicious steamy smell of meat and greens and boiled oats met them, and Katriona's voice.

"I've never seen anything like it. In the first place, *seven* of the little monsters at the same time? And this – er – lively with it? There isn't that much magic in Foggy Bottom – in the Gig – and Dackwith's family, you know, has never had any magic in it ever, not even a third cousin who could clear a kettle. And usually – you know how it goes – all you have to do is herd them, like a sheepdog with sheep. Kids are usually pretty willing to be herded, underneath the tricks; as often as not they're scared to death by what they can do and really want you to stop them even if they can't help trying to do it anyway. Not this lot. Some days I've actually thought they were going to get away from me – like today, right, Peony?" She was ladling as she spoke, and Rosie and Peony sat down next to Joeb and Barder, Peony's eyes lingering briefly on her charm, now hanging harmlessly on the wall, above Aunt's spinning wheel. The little gargoyle face grinned as if it understood the joke.

Joeb sneezed. No-one – including Joeb – had known he was allergic to magic dust till Aunt and Katriona had moved in. Aunt was providing him with free anti-dust charms, since it was her and Katriona's fault that the wheelwright's house was suddenly much fuller of dust than it had been, but finding precisely the right strength and proportions was proving difficult. Joeb was perfectly good-humoured about it, and they would get the charm right eventually. (Neither Aunt nor Katriona could think of anything to do about Barder's mother's habit of running a finger over some surface, whenever she came to visit, and then inspecting the inevitably dirty tip of it with the expression of a woman who has just found a toad in her soup.)

"And it's not only the children, is it, Aunt?" said Katriona. "I was rite-keeping Shon's new wheelhorse, and of course he's risking it by waiting till he can come to Foggy Bottom to have a new animal rited, but the worst has never happened yet, has it? But this time I could feel the – the texture of the keeping trying to twist out of my hands. I've never seen nor felt anything like that either."

There was a silence, but Aunt was frowning.

Joeb said hesitantly, "Er – there's a tale – a fairy tale—" And sneezed, harder this time.

" Ward and keep you," said Katriona quickly. You could lose all kinds of important bits if you sneezed too hard and one shot out, and there was something waiting to steal it. Not that she or Aunt couldn't get it back, but it was better not to lose it in the first place. "Yes?" she said. "You mean that might apply here?"

"Well, it might," said Joeb cautiously; he was still a little in awe of his master's new family. "It's just that sometimes when a fairy marries, there's more magic around for a little while after. "

Aunt said, "Yes, I know that one. It's supposed to be one of the reasons fairies marry less often than the rest of you. I think the tale came after the fact, but never mind."

"It's true then?" said Katriona.

"Perhaps," Aunt said neutrally. "Church ceremonies trouble the connection between the magical and the ordinary. A fairy in the middle of an important one could draw a kind of magical attention to it that pulls the balance out for a little while."

"Draw . . . attention?" said Katriona; and Rosie looked up from her plate, wondering why Katriona's voice had gone so odd.

"I wouldn't worry about it," said Aunt, still neutral. "It's only a little extra baby-magic – seven of them together are very likely to have had some cumulative potency as well – and Shon may have waited longer than usual." But Aunt's and Katriona's eyes turned to Rosie, and then, after a moment, Barder looked at her, too, thoughtfully.

"Don't look at me!" said Rosie. "It's nothing to do with me! All I did was stand around wearing that silly crown of flowers and being taller than everyone except Barder! I only talk to animals! I'm *not* a fairy!"

Three days after that conversation Rosie woke up in the middle of the night to a *crash* that shook the house. She lay for a moment trying to catch her breath, because she felt as if she personally had been thrown to the ground and the breath knocked out of her, though she was still in her bed. Her head swam. But as soon as she could she levered herself out of bed to look for the others. She still did not know the house well enough to walk through it confidently in the dark, and she felt her way down the stairs, towards the wavering light she could now see round the frame of the not-quite-closed kitchen door.

She pushed the door open with an effort and found Aunt bent over the fire, which should have been banked and dark at this time of night, rapidly throwing some reeking herb on to the flames, while Katriona knelt by the hearth muttering rhythmically, in what Rosie recognized as a spell-chant; but she had never heard her speak so quickly and desperately before. There were little flickering shadows on the walls, like robins' shadows, although Rosie could not see the robins themselves.

"Kat—" she said; but her voice was a croak; the pressure on her chest she had felt upstairs had returned. She thought she heard Katriona falter at the sound of her voice; but by then Rosie was sinking to her knees, her vision slowly clouding over: I'm fainting, she thought; I've never fainted before; how very odd this feels; I feel as if I am no longer quite *here*. There were strong streaks of colour across her vision – purpley grey, like a malevolent fog. And then she felt something round her neck, and it burned, it was burning her, no, it was burning the queer oily cloud she seemed to be suspended in, and then she felt a hand grasping her upper arm so hard it hurt, and she was back in the kitchen again – of course she had never left it – only she was lying on the floor, and it was Katriona's hand on her arm, and Katriona was kneeling beside her.

"Rosie?" said Katriona.

Rosie sat up cautiously. She could breathe again, but there was still a hot, almost-burning sensation round her neck and across her upper chest, as if she were wearing a fiery necklace; she put her hand up to it and found a little bit of charred string, which came apart in her hand. She looked at it, completely bewildered; the fragments smudged across her fingers and fell to her lap. "Oh, Kat," she said, "I'm sorry; I've ruined your magic for you, haven't I? I didn't know you ever did – did things – in the middle of the night like this. I woke up – there was this awful crash – and I couldn't breathe for a moment."

"It's not your fault," said Katriona; there was a lit candle at her elbow, and the hollows of her eyes looked huge. "If – if it was disturbing you, you were right to come and tell us. It's a very good thing came down. Rosie, if anything like that ever happens again, come and tell us *at once*. Do you hear me? Promise. Promise that you'll find Aunt or me *immediately*."

"Yes – yes, I promise," said Rosie, looking at her wonderingly. "Was – was it just me? Not Barder or Joeb or the littles?"

"Yes, it was just you," whispered Katriona, and she let go of Rosie's arm and sat down with a bump. "Different people – react differently. Like Joeb and dust. It's not your fault."

Rosie looked across the kitchen to where Aunt was still standing by the fire; but the herbs she threw in now she threw in pinches, not handfuls, and the tension had gone out of her. She looked at Rosie and smiled. "Go back to bed, dear heart. It's over now. Kat, you go to bed too. I can finish here. It's over."

The baby-magic wore off at last, and Katriona's seven little monsters were sent home, Tibby and Dackwith and Mona looking rather dazed, as if they couldn't quite remember what had been happening for the last four months. The weather was peculiar for the rest of that year (much to the farmers' dismay), with hailstorms in summer and warm heavy rain after the winter solstice when there should have been hard frosts and fairy rimes which might tell fairy seers something about the year to come. Katriona and Aunt were kept busier than usual disentangling sprite and spirit mischief, and even the good-natured domestic hobs and brownies showed a tendency to curdle milk and sour beer and throw shoes left out to be cleaned in the dung heap. But the year turned, and became another year, and things settled down to their usual level of business.

Katriona and Barder's first baby was born eighteen months after the wedding, shortly after Rosie turned sixteen. Rosie was steeling herself to feel superfluous and misplaced (she had spoken to Peony about this, but no-one else), and the afternoon Katriona's pains started and the midwife was put on alert, there being nothing at the forge that couldn't wait, Rosie went out for a long walk in the forest. She gave herself a very earnest talking-to, only half listening to all the birds and beasts giving her kindly messages for the mother-to-be – or at least only half listening till Fwab turned up. Fwab was a chaffinch who felt that his second-most-important role in life (the first being to raise as many little chaffinches as possible) was to educate the strange human who talked to animals.

He flew down and landed on Rosie's head, and gave her scalp several sharp pecks. "Ow!" said Rosie crossly, and brushed him away. He fluttered just out of reach and sat down on her head once again. *Pay attention*! he said, peck. *Babies are important*! Peck. *Babies are the most important*! Peck.

All right, said Rosie. *I hear you. Go away*.

You humans live too long; that's your problem, said Fwab, but he spread his wings and flew off.

It had already been arranged that Rosie should sleep with Peony if Katriona was still having her baby overnight; but that night Rosie couldn't sleep. The houses were close enough together that she could hear the bustle from the other side of the courtyard, and see the glow of the light cast from the upstairs window. Besides, she could hear the mice chatting away about it. Mice are terribly chatty. They will chat about anything, and if there is nothing to chat about, they will chat about having nothing to chat about. Compared with mice, robins are reserved. Rosie felt that if mice did less chatting they would be supper for cats and owls less often, but this was not her concern. The most important rule of the beast world was: You do not interfere.

So she lay next to Peony the night Katriona's first baby was born and listened to the mice, and so of course she knew when the baby's head was seen, and when the rest of him followed, and she wondered if Katriona had thought about the mice, and if she hadn't sent Rosie any farther away because it was all right with her that Rosie should know from them what was going on, or that there was nowhere else to send her . . . or that Katriona had forgotten about Rosie in the excitement of the baby. She remembered the dark wakeful nights in the cottage loft before the wedding, when she had listened to the echoes telling her she was not who she believed she was. She wished she had the gargoyle spindle end with her, tucked under her pillow; she had thought of asking if she could take it with her, but it seemed too childish, and she was too old to be childish. She had given up being childish during those last weeks at the cottage.

She was already tiptoeing round Peony's room and picking up

her clothes when she heard the first faint cry. She dressed slowly and carefully in the gentle darkness, as if she were preparing to meet a stranger she needed to make a good impression on. She stepped into the hallway, but then halfway down the stairs she stopped, and wasn't sure if she could go any farther. She put her hand against the wall, and finally went on, but as if this were an unknown staircase, and there might be ogres at the bottom.

She met the midwife, wrapping her cloak round her for her homeward journey, crossing the forecourt; Arnisa smiled at her, and patted her arm. "A fine big boy," she said. Rosie went in the kitchen door and exchanged a long look with Flinx, who was guarding the door from the kitchen to the rest of the house and, for once, failing to present himself as utterly indifferent to circumstances. She went slowly upstairs to Barder and Katriona's bedroom, making a wide circle round a bundle of stained bedding and soiled straw standing by the door.

"Come in," said Aunt's voice. "I thought you wouldn't be asleep."

"I knew the mice would tell you," said Katriona faintly, as Rosie timidly pushed the door open. "Come and see." Katriona looked exhausted, but her face had been washed and her hair combed. The bedclothes still smelled of the herbs in the linen cupboard, but there was another, stronger smell in the room. Barder stood up from Katriona's side and came towards Rosie, offering her the little bundle he carried. It took her a moment to realize that he was expecting her to take it in her arms, and not just peer at the little red squinched-up face at one end of it. "This is Jem," said Barder. "He's your – I'm not sure what the name of it is, but he's your family."

Chapter 12

Rosie wasn't so sure about babies, whatever Fwab said, but she didn't feel superfluous and displaced so much as suddenly one of the grown-ups who were all in this mess together. The empty, lost feeling that had troubled her before Katriona's wedding had been mostly filled up or pushed aside by her new life and new responsibilities – but Jem squashed the remains of it flat. Jem took up as much time as there *was* time. "Is it because he's a fairy?" said Rosie, baffled, to Aunt.

"No, dear, it's just because he's a baby," said Aunt, refraining, with heroic self-control, from remarking that Rosie had been a baby just like him (if not more so) not so very long ago. When Rosie was eighteen and Jem was two, and walking, and beginning to talk, and while he was a total little pest (thought Rosie) he was also almost recognizable as a future human being, Katriona had Gilly, and it started all over again.

One evening when Rosie was walking Gilly, who was going through an unfortunate phase when she would only consent to sleep if she was in some grown-up's arms and that grown-up was walking the floor with her, Rosie thought: We haven't heard any rumours about Pernicia in . . . in . . . since the wedding. Shon doesn't tell us stories about the king's magicians any more – and we haven't seen some poor cavalry lieutenant through here on a wild-goose chase in a long time. Rosie looked into Gilly's little sleeping face – she had gone all limp and squashy, like bread dough that has absorbed too much water – and tried to be pleased. But Rosie at eighteen was too old to believe that something out of sight was something safe; and from nowhere a cold tendril of fear touched her.

"Thank you, love," said Katriona, coming through the door yawning from her nap; "I'll take her now."

"Kat –" said Rosie, handing the baby over delicately, but not so delicately that she didn't grizzle and threaten to wake up and cry properly, "Kat, we haven't heard about Pernicia in years. Even Gismo doesn't have any stories about anybody but the three princes any more."

"No," said Katriona, beginning to walk round the kitchen as Rosie had walked. The kitchen was their biggest room, and well laid out for walking, with the long table down its centre and the spinning wheel in the corner by the door. "No, we haven't." Her eyes went to a little three-legged iron pot that now held a roll of charm string. Rosie had never found out what had happened to Katriona's necklace; only that its loss had distressed her greatly.

"But what about the poor princess?" said Rosie.

"I don't know," said Katriona, looking back at Rosie, and Rosie saw that she was sad and frightened and worried, and Rosie thought, how like Kat, to love someone she's never met because she has a curse hanging over her and it must be really awful for her. Poor princess. I wish I could tell her she has someone like Kat on her side. I hope the royal fairies are nice to her, but they can't be half as nice as Kat. "Maybe Pernicia's given up," she suggested, "and the princess will go home tomorrow."

Katriona tried to smile. "I wish." She went on, quietly, not to disturb the baby, but as if she had thought about it a long time: "Curses tend to wear out, of course; but she'd know that. She'd have set up something to bind over the passage of time before she came to the name-day. Sometimes crossing the threshold from child to adult may break even a powerful curse, as it did for Lord Curran many years ago" – Rosie nodded; Barder had taught her the ballad about it – "we hoped . . . but she must have found a way round that too. Aunt has always said it's been the twenty-first birthday from the beginning; the rest is just cruelty, as if the curse weren't cruel enough. . ."

"Maybe . . . maybe it is only cruelty," said Rosie hesitantly. "Maybe it is only that one birthday. Maybe the princess could go home tomorrow. Till the night before her twenty-first birthday."

"No," said Katriona. She was frowning slightly, and her eyes were focussed on something Rosie couldn't see – something that Rosie wouldn't have been able to see even if she'd turned round and looked. "No. Sig— The queen's fairy would know if it were safe." She blinked, and now she was looking at a spider letting itself down cautiously from a ceiling beam. Rosie looked at the spider, too. It swung back and forth indecisively, gleaming a tiny chitinous gleam in the lamplight, and then ran back up its invisible thread, and disappeared into the shadows.

Katriona rearranged Gilly slightly. "I'm only half awake, Rosie, don't listen to me maunder on."

"I wish I knew the princess would win out in the end," said Rosie.

"So do I," said Katriona.

By then Rosie was very absorbed with her work as a horse doctor – and occasionally cow, sheep, pig, goat, dog, bird, cat, and almost anything else that wasn't human doctor. Aunt and Katriona had tried to tease her about all the business she was taking away from them, but she was so distressed by this they stopped. (Barder still occasionally told her that she should stay at home more and whittle spindle ends, but since this was usually a lead-in to his showing her another deft little trick with knife and wood, she allowed this.) Often enough the answer to some ailment came from a joint consultation. Most animals, for example (unlike most humans), knew when they were being haunted; this saved diagnosis time, because Rosie could relay the information. But Rosie couldn't do anything about an earth sprite causing mud fever or a water imp causing rain scald, although once, on an occasion of the former, she discovered half by accident that the earth sprite was in a temper because all his best tunnels had been knocked through and redug by a mole, and managed to talk the mole into moving its efforts to the other side of the field.

She had seen the two grooms in Lord Pren's livery arrive at the wrights' yard across the square from the smith's one morning, and had guessed they were calling for Aunt and Katriona, and was a little intrigued at what sort of thing Lord Pren would feel required both of them; but when she saw Aunt coming across the square towards the smith's yard with the two grooms following, leading their horses, her heart sank, because she was afraid she was going to be asked to baby-sit.

"They want *me*?" she said.

"You," said Aunt, smiling.

"Told you," said Narl, through a mouthful of nails. "Been waiting till you turn eighteen." Eighteen was the official age when you could declare you weren't an apprentice any more, or at least that you could begin to take on work of your own, even if you stayed with your master, and if he or she did not object to it.

Rosie, for once speechless, climbed up behind the second groom, and juddered back to Woodwold at a cracking trot. She didn't much like riding horses; it seemed rude. *Pardon me*, she said to the horse. *My pleasure*, replied the horse, who fancied himself quite sophisticated in the customs of humans.

She had been to Woodwold before. Lord Pren invited the entire Gig to dinner on certain feast days every year (and the town councillors sat at the Prendergasts' own table), and then the park all round the vast conglomeration of buildings and towers and corners and crannies that was Woodwold was covered with stalls selling sweetmeats and charms and ribbons and weaving and toys and spindle ends (Barder's had fetched the best price now for several years, but Rosie's were beginning to come close), and there were always bards and mastersingers, and dancing, especially as the sun went down and the beer, ale and cider consumption went up. Even then, with hundreds of people around, you could feel the great bulk of Woodwold watching you, but Woodwold was the only really big building anywhere in the Gig and the only one therefore that most Gig citizens had ever seen; and while there were tales about Woodwold, well, there would be. It would be very disappointing if your lord didn't have tales spun round him and his family and his holdings; and the Prendergasts themselves had all been so tediously normal and solid and responsible for so many generations it was a good thing that Woodwold existed to give the bards something to work with. But if it loomed over you, well, presumably all large buildings loomed; they couldn't help it; and the *watchfulness* of it was probably just a surfeit of bards' tales (and possibly of beer).

But Rosie felt differently about Woodwold when she started coming out alone with Narl as part of her apprenticeship.

After the fork in the road out of Foggy Bottom the way broadened from a carriage width to twice that, and just before you got to the big gates it went twice its double width to a great round space like a courtyard, except there was nothing there but the gates and the stone wall, twelve foot high, stretching out on either side farther than your eyes could see. The gates themselves were twice as tall as the tallest carriage and wrought with an intricacy Rosie found amazing. (The Gig, and many of the Prendergasts' outside visitors, said of them that they were so beautiful they might have been magic, if magic could ever have stuck to cold iron, or a blacksmith work it.) When you crossed the invisible line from outside Woodwold's grounds to inside your stomach gave a tiny lurch as if you'd been briefly turned upside down and then right side up again, and your horse's hoofs and cart wheels, or even your own feet, threw up surprising clouds of dust, just for a few steps. (Lady Prendergast always ordered long chains of dust-laying spells before the feast days, which were draped gracefully over the open gates.)

Then the drive went on and on and on, because the park went on and on and on, and there were beautiful trees and small russet-coloured deer nothing like the large ordinary deer in the Gig forests (including the fact that they were half tame and looked forward to the days after the open feast days, when there were always excellent gleanings to be had round where the food stalls had stood) and sudden vistas with queer little buildings or statues at the ends of them. About the time you decided you'd wandered into some kind of enchantment and were beginning to wonder if you could get out again, there were the stables, on the outskirts of Woodwold.

Woodwold always seemed to stand against the sun whichever way you were facing as you looked at it, and wherever the sun was in the sky. It was built of both stone and wood, and both had darkened over the centuries and, seemingly, grown into each other, till it was impossible to tell where one left off and the other began. If you tried to analyse it, it was a very uneven house, with a wing here and an outbuilding there, an extra storey in this bit but not in that, six windows on this side of this door but seven on the other. But its impression was nonetheless of great centredness, of some profound organizing spirit or principle that informed it from the least and lowest scullery to the tip of the tallest tower, where the Prendergasts' standard flew.

Which is to say it felt alive. Or at least it felt alive to Rosie. She always half expected it to talk to her – she could half feel the sense, whatever it was she used to talk to animals, straining for some contact with it. The stone wall was the boundary; she would have known where she was as soon as she passed the gates if she'd come blindfolded. She would have felt Woodwold's presence.

It seemed bigger that day, without Narl. Narl was a greater neutralizer of unknown potencies even than Aunt.

She felt she was lucky, that first time by herself. Gorse, Lord Pren's favourite stallion, was off his feed. *They treat me like a parade saddle*, Gorse told her. *To be polished and polished and polished, and then hung on a hook until there's a parade*. Gorse was sixteen and a half hands tall and as golden as late-afternoon sunlight; just standing near him made you feel prouder and nobler.

Your manners are too good, said Rosie. *If you'd bite people occasionally, and throw tantrums, they'd get the idea.*

Gorse bowed his head so he could look into her face – if Gorse had a fault, it was that his sense of humour was a little stately – and she could look in his. The resigned sadness in his dark eye made her brusquer than she would have been if she'd remembered whom she was talking to, and that her future might depend on what she said next. "Take him hunting," Rosie said aloud. "Let him get sweaty and dirty and tired and frightened. He's gone all hollow inside; he needs something to *do*."

"He – he is put to the finest mares in the country," said the Master of the Horse, rattled and anxious. He thought of being angry, but the look on the horse's face – and on Rosie's – stopped him.

Rosie gave a little jerk of laughter. "That isn't what you *do*," she said. "Is it?" She liked Lord Pren's Master of the Horse, and, more important, he liked her. He'd always been very polite to her when she had been there with Narl, and even contracted apprentices, which she was not, were not necessarily treated with much regard. She now looked the Master full in the face, saw him take in what she had said, and then a reluctant smile relaxed his expression. "You're every bit as blunt as Narl," he said. "He seems to have trained you thoroughly. Very well, I shall tell Lord Prendergast that he should take the most valuable horse in his stables out hunting. There's a boar hunt soon, for the rogue that has been tearing up Mistweir; will that do?"

Woodwold's Master of the Horse began calling her "my Rosie" when talking about her to other horsefolk, and seemed to look on her as something between a protégeé and a daughter. But her particular gift was not merely that she could talk to the horses, but hear and be heard by them. She was called out one day when Fast, a big blood-bay racer, had developed his dislike of moving shadows to a point when he would throw himself over backwards rather than leave his stall – and then take his stall to bits because he felt restless and shut in.

You self-absorbed brat, she said, flinging his stall door open. *You try one of your melodramas on me and I'll hit you over the head with a* plank. *What is it you think you want? To be king of the world? That would get boring too, you know, making decisions about who's right and who's wrong when your citizens disagree, and trying to figure out who's plotting against you and what to do about it. Get it through your* thick head *that there are other creatures here who are* just as important as you are, *whatever you may think, and start behaving like it, or I'll tell the huntsman to turn you into a* hearth rug.

Fast, who had reared up as soon as the door opened, dropped back to earth again looking rather dazed. Rosie felt a very little bit guilty, because he was very young, and very, very fast, and his grooms and riders had all been taught to treat his every whim with great deference. It was not entirely his fault that he'd started stirring things up because he could. But he still had to be made to stop. Lord Pren would neither have a dangerous horse in his stables, nor sell a brute on. Rosie told herself she was saving Fast's life, crossed her arms, and scowled at him ferociously.

She could feel him thinking, but he gave her no words. After about a minute of tumultuous silence he bowed his neck and made small humble chewing noises, like a distressed foal. Rosie unfolded her arms and reached to rub his forehead. *Want to go for a walk?* she said. *It's a lovely afternoon.*

She told Narl about the confrontation with Fast while she watched him working on the new good-luck medallion to hang behind the bar at the pub. They'd had a silver one that had belonged to Cairngorm's grandmother, but it had exploded, a few weeks ago, which had unnerved everyone very much, especially Cairngorm, who didn't think she had any enemies that either disliked her that much or could afford to do anything so histrionic about it. But she decided to take no chances, and ordered its replacement in cold iron. Barder had lately been teaching Narl fancy knot-work, and the medallion looked like a great weave of black rope.

Rosie had taken Fast for his walk down the drive to the gates, and had stood staring at them for several minutes while Fast browsed for more interesting grasses than grew in Woodwold's flawlessly kept paddocks. At a distance you saw uprights with three crosspieces near the top and three more at the bottom, but when you stood close and peered, the framework disappeared in a seethe of plants and animals, all wound and folded together like a heap of sleeping puppies, so that lions' faces emerged from twists of clematis vines, a leaping hare arched its belly over a curl of snake, and pansies and roses grew like a mane down the backbone of a bear. She had reawoken to her surroundings when Fast came up behind her and nibbled at the nape of her neck.

"Narl. . ." she began, and he glanced up at her, and she thought, you wretch, you've *already* decided not to answer whatever it is I ask. "Is it true Lord Pren brought you here to make those gates?"

"No," said Narl, and returned to his medallion. Rosie sighed, and headed for home, to weed the herb garden.

She was still thinking about Woodwold when Aunt called her in to help get tea ready. She couldn't quite bring herself to say "I keep waiting for it to speak to me" so instead, "There's a funny . . . almost . . . *smell* to the place," she said. "Isn't there? Of course they've got some kind of barrier up at the gate, and the jolt of crossing it almost makes me think I'm smelling hot mead or cellar mould or something. But after you're well inside . . . it gets more distinct, not less, except that you can't think of anything it smells *like*. It's not even really a smell . . . I think."

Aunt looked at her with interest. "No, you're right. But it's as much like a smell as it is like anything else, and you might as well call it that. I wouldn't have expected you to pick it up. You have absorbed more living with Katriona and me than I thought."

" You mean it's a magic smell?" said Rosie, wrinkling her nose; but that may have been from the proximity of Jem, who had been outdoors rolling in something noxious, probably from watching Zogdob do it first. Flinx, following Rosie in from the garden, had already approached Jem in apparent disbelief, stuck out first his whiskers and then his tail, and stalked majestically from the room.

"Not exactly," said Aunt, "but it's a smell that is produced by the fact of having magic around."

Rosie laughed. "A typical fairy answer. Even if I had turned out a fairy, I would never have got my mind round it. You'd've had to make a charm for me – like Snick carrying a bit of hawthorn and rowan when he plays cards – or I'd've gone on doing a kind of horrible baby-magic till I died of old age."

Aunt got the look on her face that meant she was thinking about something else, and even if you asked her what it was she wouldn't tell you. "Not necessarily. Magic usually flows to the shape of its vessel. If you would be so kind as to divest that child of his clothing, I will upend him in the bath. In his present condition he will put us all off our tea."

When the initial force of Jem's protest was spent, and he had declared his intention to be a fish, in the hopes of getting a reaction for having used a bad word (disappointed, he began to splash water on the floor), Rosie said thoughtfully, "But I still don't understand. The Prendergasts aren't fairies or magicians. They barely have baby-magic —that really fine walking forest a few years ago was the butler's son, wasn't it? I remember you making that enormous charm so he could stay at home. They don't even keep fairies of their own – which is why they're always asking for you and Kat. So what is the – the smell?"

Aunt finished scrubbing Jem's hair and dipped some water over his head. "It's the house itself," she said briefly. "You've heard the stories."

This was not the answer Rosie wanted. The idea that something so powerful slept so lightly under the surface of the ordinary world – magic-pocked and -dishevelled as the ordinary world was – that even an ordinary person who happened to live with two fairies might notice its presence, made her very uneasy. Never mind that it always seemed to be on the brink of talking to her.

Aunt, looking at her, guessed some of this. "Think of it as a kind of watchdog," she said. "Think of Spear."

Rosie's mobile face immediately relaxed as visions of large, turreted watchdogs marched solemnly across her inner eye. She had taken her first steps clinging to Spear's tail, while Flora and Katriona washed platters and mugs and talked. While his dark coat was now almost white with age he was still the terror of rowdy drunks all over the Gig.

Chapter 13

What began with a minor charm gone slightly awry had set a pleasant precedent. Most noontimes Peony still came to the smith's yard with her and Rosie's meal hot from the fire at home or from the big communal oven between the pub and the baker's, and she and Rosie and Narl ate together, or rather Peony and Rosie ate together and talked (Peony was more sympathetic towards some of Lord Pren's spoilt beauties than Rosie was) while Narl wandered round the forge examining whatever he was doing or was planning to do today or this sennight or next year. Narl thought sitting down to eat was a waste of time (and hot food in the middle of a working day nearly indecent).

One day Peony was describing the collar she was embroidering for Dessy to wear at Flora's wedding, and broke off and began to laugh. "Rosie, your face. You would rather be bent into a curve, fried in the fire, and nailed to the bottom of some horse's foot than pick up a needle, wouldn't you?"

"Yes," said Rosie. Rosie had been taught basic hemming and mending from Aunt and Katriona, hated it, and while she was far too honest to try to get out of it by doing it badly, did it naturally so badly that she got out of it anyway.

"The problem is only that you've never learnt to like sewing. Embroidery is the way to do that," said Peony.

Rosie periodically fell into moods of gloom because she felt she was so little help to Aunt and Katriona, who would probably rather have had her time and a clever pair of hands than the coins

Woodwold's Master of the Horse gave her, and so she was willing (if reluctantly) to think that possibly needlework could help make up for her other failings. So, that evening, while they were alone in Rosie's kitchen, Peony brought out a few coloured threads and a bit of stiff cloth, thoughtfully chose a nice serene blue to begin with, and showed her friend two or three basic stitches.

But Rosie's fingers, once the needle and cloth had been turned over to them for practice, as if they each had minds of their own and been perfectly drilled in teamwork since birth, started flying across the little stretch of linen, dipping the needle in and out and producing, as if from out of the air, the most wonderful landscape of bright flowers and butterflies.

Rosie's fingers came to the end of the bit of material and turned it ninety degrees to begin the next row; but the rest of Rosie jerked violently back, like a person on a runaway horse might pull on the reins, and the little square of cloth fell to the floor, needle and thread trailing behind it. Rosie tucked her hands under her arms and sat, trembling and shoulders hunched, in her chair, while Peony bent down and picked up the scrap of cloth, and stretched it gently between her hands.

"But Rosie, it's beautiful," she said. "When did you learn to embroider like this? I thought you told me you didn't know how."

"I don't know how," said Rosie in a muffled tone.

"Well, it doesn't matter," said Peony, meaning to be soothing. "You do know how, and this is one of the prettiest bits of work I can remember seeing – far beyond anything I can do. I don't even understand one or two of the stitches you've used. Your work will be in terrific demand the moment I show this to anyone—"

"You can't," said Rosie, making half a snatch at it where Peony was holding it up, and pulling her hand back at the last moment as if she were unwilling to touch it. "You're not allowed to show it to anyone. I forbid it."

"But –" said poor Peony, bewildered. "But – aren't you going to do more? Don't you understand how good you are?"

"I'm not good at it!" shouted Rosie. "I don't know what happened! It's got nothing to do with me! Don't you dare tell anyone! I am never going to touch another needle as long as I live!" And she burst into tears and rushed out of the room, narrowly avoiding bumping into Aunt, who had come to see what the commotion was about.

In a little while Rosie, with her head under her pillow, felt, by the gentle flexing of the floorboards communicated through her bed frame, someone come into her room. A familiar hand touched her shoulder, and a familiar weight sat on the edge of her bed. Rosie, without taking her head from under the pillow, reached out one of her dangerous, traitorous hands, and grasped Katriona's hand.

Katriona could feel the fingers still trembling, and her professional fairy's mind noted the signs of aftershock. An old enchantment suddenly brought into use often made its subject tremble uncontrollably; it was another example of the force of Rosie's personality and will that she had managed to raise the latch on a door, thunder upstairs, put a pillow over her head, and reach out to cling to Katriona's hand as if that clasp was all that was saving her from falling into a chasm.

An old enchantment suddenly brought into use also left a trail in the air, like smoke from a fire, for anyone to see, if they were looking. No Gig fairy would think twice about it, coming from this house, any more than any passer-by would think twice about ordinary smoke from a house chimney. Aunt was, even now, hastily lighting a larger magical fire to obscure the faint trace of the accident that had befallen Rosie.

Just as their own relative poverty protected Rosie from learning how well she might make sweetmeats, so her loathing for needlework would, Aunt and Katriona had allowed themselves to think, protect her from her gift for embroidery. Who could have anticipated a loving, patient and domestic friend like Peony for Rosie? Katriona sighed. Would Peony want to show Rosie how to dance and play the flute next? They couldn't risk putting the tiniest charm against it on Peony; it would be impossible to make such a charm invisible without making its unseen presence even more obtrusive in other ways.

Katriona thought of several occasions earlier in Rosie's life and thought, This is such a *small* mistake. Surely we'll be lucky this time. We must be.

Katriona stroked Rosie's shoulder briefly with her free hand and then pulled a little tuft of herbs tied together with string out of her apron pocket. "This will help the shakes," she said to the head under the pillow. "If you will come out from under there and sniff it."

Rosie sat up and shed the pillow like a bear emerging from hibernation. She clamped her shaking hands together on the tuft that Katriona offered her, and sniffed. Her eyes were wet and red. When she spoke her voice was not quite steady. "There's something wrong with me, isn't there?" she said. "There's something I can't quite remember about – about before I lived with you. I know I was too young to remember anything, but I do. Well . . . it's not exactly a memory. It's just . . . knowing that something doesn't fit."

She stopped, because she wasn't going to tell Katriona about the time just before the wedding, when Katriona had been so happy, because it might take something away from the memory of that happiness to know that Rosie hadn't been. "It never bothered me. But . . . that was an enchantment, just now. Peony may not know it – she didn't grow up with two fairies – but I know it. Why did someone put a spell on *me*? A spell to do *embroidery*? What am I? What's the rest of the spell? Do you know?" What she wasn't saying was: Am I dangerous to you and Aunt, to Barder and Jem and Gilly – and Peony? What do you know about what I can't remember? Aunt always says that my mother had no magic and my father's entire family had never had any magic. Then why enchant *me*?

What she wasn't saying was: I *am* your cousin and Aunt's niece, aren't I?

Katriona was shaking her head, not because she wished to lie to Rosie any more explicitly than the last nineteen years had been a kind of lying to her, but because she had no idea what to say. If she had not been so preoccupied, she would have heard the unspoken questions, and would have known that a warm flood of reassurance would drown the awkward ones most effectively; but she didn't hear them.

Katriona still often dreamed of the princess' name-day, and about small spiders weaving grey webs on velvet sleeves, and woke up suddenly as if she'd heard the words spoken aloud, finding herself in her own bedroom with Barder's warm, gently snoring body lying comfortingly next to her. She didn't like remembering. She didn't see it couldn't mean that Rosie would, one day, be taken away from them; and – as Barder had said the night Jem was born – she didn't know what you called it, but they were her family. Rosie was theirs. But since Katriona had married, and especially since she had had children of her own, her dread of the memory of Rosie's origin became almost intolerable.

The three of them who knew never discussed it. Aunt and Katriona were rarely alone together any more, but even when they were, the subject of Rosie did not come up as it used to. Rosie was an adult: she had her work and a life of her own. Their old discussions of how to manage her were no longer necessary; and what else there was to discuss . . . did not bear discussion. Not with her twenty-first birthday now so near. Barder never mentioned it, although, Katriona thought sometimes, watching him tease Rosie, or teach her a new ballad, or a better way to arrive at the effect she wanted on something she was whittling, that he was restraining the same sort of fierce possessiveness about her that Katriona herself felt: Rosie was one of them. But as Rosie grew older, so grew nearer that inevitable parting, a parting so profound Katriona thought it would be like seeing her die. . .

And what if they could not, finally, defeat Pernicia? They had two years left: and still no word, no robin-borne whisper, nothing, from Sigil. Only two years. Katriona plunged into speech, to get away from that most appalling thought.

"I – we – it will only make things worse, to tell you now," she said. "I'm sorry – darling, I'm sorry – I'm not just being mysterious, you do believe me, don't you? We have been waiting for – for a sign. I do not know why it is so long in coming."

There was a silence. Rosie was still sniffing, half tearily, half dutifully, at the herbs in her hands. But her colour was better, and her hands no longer shook. She heard in Katriona's voice that they had been waiting years. Nineteen years? You are so *helpless* when things happen to you when you were a baby. You can't even remember what they were. You can only sort of half guess they were there. . . She thought of the echoes in the darkness, before the wedding, before Jem's birth, telling her that she was not who she believed herself to be, that she did not belong to these people she loved. "The Beast at least knew why he had been turned into a beast," she said finally, referring to a tale she had made Barder tell her over and over when she was very small, and Katriona, her nerves overstretched with sorrow and anxiety and indecision, gave a shout of laughter.

Rosie smiled reluctantly. "If it weren't fairy business, I'd fight you about it," she said. "But if I do, we'll both get cross, and then Aunt will have to make peace between us, and I still won't have learnt anything, so I won't." She handed the herb bundle back to Katriona. "Thank you."

She brooded. "This is the first time I can ever remember wanting – just a little – to be a fairy. So I could *know*."

"Darling, it doesn't work like that," Katriona said gently, trying not to start laughing again, because she knew it would hurt Rosie's feelings, when the laughter would be at herself, for her frustrated unknowing. Rosie was giving her a you're-just-saying-that-to-make-me-feel-better look, and Katriona added truthfully, "I'm still waiting for my familiar animal to find me, you know. I'm a fairy, and I *don't* know."

Rosie, who could only, barely, with the greatest effort of intellect, imagine what it was like for the rest of the human world not to talk to animals, and couldn't even begin to imagine what it was like for Katriona to have had beast-speech and lost it, gave a deep sigh, leaned forward, and kissed her on the cheek. "Thanks for the herbs. I have to go and find Peony, and apologize."

*

Peony had been so distressed at causing her friend pain that she barely heard the apology because she was so busy proffering her own; and that was the end of it, except that she tried never to mention embroidery in Rosie's hearing again. And when, months afterwards, she had offered to teach Rosie the steps of the commonest round dance that everyone (except Rosie, Narl, and old Penfaron, who had a wooden leg) danced on feast and festival days, and Aunt and Katriona who, this time, were in the room when the offer was made, said "No!" simultaneously and rather too loud, neither Peony nor Rosie asked for any explanation.

About a week after Peony had shown Rosie a few basic embroidery stitches, a hippogriff was seen flying over the Gig. Hippogriffs were generally creatures of ill repute, unless you were a magician, and it was bad news to have one in your neighbourhood. It might mean that the wrong sort of magic was about to follow it; and this one, certainly, seemed to be looking for something. People grew alarmed, and there was a run on aversion charms, which made you, more or less, depending on how good the fairy who made them was at the job, beneath the notice of any wandering magic looking for someone to seize on to. Aunt's and Katriona's were very good charms, and by the time the hippogriff had not been seen again for a fortnight and people were beginning to hope the Gig was to be spared after all, they had no more charms to sell, and no chance of making more till winter, when the deer's-foot vine turned red and the salia berries yellow. In the general unease it seemed surprising to no-one that Aunt and Katriona gave aversion charms to Rosie and Peony.

But the hippogriff did go away, and the only bad news the Gig heard that winter was of an invasion of taralians, which were large striped cats of fierce intelligence and fiercer appetite (a full-grown taralian could eat a horse in one go) and which the king himself had led the army against. The army had been victorious, and the remaining taralians had been driven back across the border into the wild wasteland of the south where they had come from, but the king had been wounded, and while the wound was slight, he was slow to recover his strength, and there were murmurs of a spell.

Why had the taralians come into human-settled areas in the first place? They were savage on their own ground, but they rarely left it, and the winter was not a hard one.

The king, it was said, had symptoms very like those of the soldiers and courtiers who had been thrown down by the enchanted sleep at Fordingbridge and Flury: headaches, lingering lethargy, inability to concentrate or to make decisions, insomnia, nightmares. It was all the more disturbing not only because he was the king, but because everyone knew this king to be a robust, phlegmatic man who ruled thoughtfully and kindly, and with a reassuring lack of imagination.

The danger to his daughter had sapped him at last, the whispers went. Too much of the king's resources had been spent to protect her; were still being spent to protect her – wherever she was. Too much more was spent looking for Pernicia: too much wasted. Pernicia had been not only wicked and powerful but clever; twenty years of helpless fear had worn the country down, the king most of all. When Pernicia sprang her trap at last he and his magicians and his armies would have no strength to resist her, and she would have not only the princess, but the country – just as the old tales of her had predicted. But she would not have done it this way if she had been able to seize all at once, which meant she was not so powerful as she pretended: let us, said these whispers, return to normal now, when there is still a little time left. Who has seen Pernicia since the name-day? She would not bide her time so if there were a faster way. Perhaps the curse on the princess is not what Pernicia declared it: it is, instead, that those around her will fall ill of some mysterious illness that bleeds off health and strength and will and courage. Bring her home now – and let her pass the crown to Prince Colin, whom the people know and love. Let them rally round him, this last year before the princess' twenty-first birthday, till there is no trap for Pernicia to spring. The curse never was that the princess should die of the prick of a spindle end; and there are no such spindle ends left anywhere in the country.

Let her come home. Let this farce be over with. Let us welcome the young king to be, and forget Pernicia. The curse on the face of it is nonsense – has always been nonsense – and we have been fools to believe it.

That is what she would want us to believe, said other whispers. That is also why she waited so long, for our nerve to break at the very last. Never has a queen of our country abdicated. Wait till the princess' one-and-twentieth birthday; it is only one more year now. Wait.

Spring in the Gig came that year with an unusual number of daffodils opening as cabbages or hollyhocks, and most of the lilacs were a rather distressing cerulean. The old cottage where Aunt and Katriona and Rosie had once lived was so infested by a species of bat, which not only left its droppings about in the way that bats do but snored thunderously, that a complete removal spell and purgation had to be done on it over the course of several days while its current tenant stayed at the pub and recovered her equanimity. The mould spirit in Med's old house was joined by several of its cousins who decided the house wasn't big enough for all of them, and began to colonize the houses on either side, and were fearfully rude to Katriona when she told them they either had to leave or she'd dry them to thistledown and blow them away on the wind. (After a few third cousins had bounced away as dandelion fluff, however, the rest decamped.) And the quantity of magic dust, both the chalky kind and the almost invisible twinkly kind, on the baskets of herbs Rosie brought to the smith's yard to be rendered into ointments and tonics for her horses, was so excessive, that sometimes, when it leaped out of the basket to run away, it took the herbs with it – much to the delight of the village cats, most of whom took to hanging round the forge more than the priestling's house, and batting at bits of nothing with their paws, which of course all cats did anyway, but the habit was much more disconcerting in a smith's yard, which pleased the cats even more.

Most years there was a new sort of fever that emerged from the Gig marshes as spring warmth awakened them from their cold winter dreams, but this year's were unusually widespread and persistent; Aunt's robins told her that it afflicted many birds and beasts as well as the human denizens of the Gig. Fwab and several other creatures both winged and earthbound told Rosie that there were far too many migrants, moving both in and out of the Gig, and that everyone was edgy and anxious for no cause they could name. Except, of course, that this was the beginning of the princess' twenty-first year, and that her twenty-first birthday was now less than twelve months away.

There were more reports of disturbances in the rest of the country than usual, too. Since things were always turning, or pretending to turn, into other things, or behaving disconcertingly, at least briefly, in that country, it was sometimes difficult to judge which reports needed investigating and which could be left alone. A large family of gripples was unearthed in Incorban, which explained why the civic water supply kept turning purple and then failing; the purple colour had seemed very alarming, and so the king had been applied to. "Oh, *gripples*," the mayor said, heaving a sigh of combined relief and dismay; at least it was only gripples, but then gripples were a terrific nuisance, and would be expensive to dislodge.

There was a sudden rash of sightings of merfolk in the great inland lake called Gilamdra. A merperson's touch is poisonous, but merfolk are so beautiful there is almost always someone, most often someone young and romantic, who will try it anyway. (Priests were curiously apt to this error. The priests – those that survived – insisted that they had been trying to convert them.) It wasn't just a question of staying away from the shore, however, because the merfolk sang, especially the women, and their singing was as beautiful as they were themselves, and as penetrating as a draught under the door. The king sent a troupe of magicians to Gilamdra, and the magicians hung an inaudibility veil round the lake, which made the lap and splash of the water weirdly silent as well, and created a kind of sticky boundary that birds flew through with a jolt and a gluey *pop* and a squawk of protest.

Also in that last year before the princess' twenty-first birthday an unusually high percentage of the first- and second-years at the Academy decided to return home and take up farming or politics;

several of the oldest Academicians decided to retire; and a number of village fairies had a change of heart and became midwives or dairymaids or married the fellows who'd told them they'd be happy to marry if they'd give up this magic thing.

Narl was still Foggy Bottom's official horse-leech but he now would only say "Ask Rosie" any time his opinion was sought. The occasions when this pronouncement brought a desperate cry of *Narl!* from Rosie herself became fewer and fewer, and one of the things that came to be said about her was that at least she'd tell you what was going on and what she was doing about it, which Narl never had. She went up to Woodwold so frequently that spring that most of Lord Prendergast's folk knew her by sight, and often, when the Master of the Horse was finished with her, she found the cowman or the shepherd, with a client on a string, waiting for her. She also spoke to the great bell-voiced hunting hounds, the swift silent sighthounds bred, it was said, from the queen's own fleethounds, and sometimes a terrier enduring, in that well-ordered estate, an insufficiency of frustrations to go terrier-mad over. She spoke to curly, soft-eyed spaniels, and she learnt to withstand the attentions of a particular spaniel named Sunflower, who loved people, all people, so much, she could not bear to miss any opportunity for hurling herself upon them, and was so utterly beside herself with joy at finding one that could *talk* to her that any attempt Rosie made to try to persuade her that restraint was a virtue was lost in the tumult. Sometimes Rosie spoke to lapdogs suffering from a surfeit of tit-bits; she did not care much for most of these – too many of them didn't have the sense they were born with – except for Lady Pren's own hairy palm-sized mite, Throstle. Throstle was a fides terrier, more commonly called a teacup terrier. Teacup terriers were supposed to be small enough to curl up in a teacup (they were also rather the colour of tea leaves, and their rough coats had something of the same texture), and were mostly to be found up a lady's sleeve or in her pocket, and were often rather crazed, for they had a vague racial memory that they had once been bigger. Throstle appeared to be totally unaware that he was too small to protect Lady Pren from anything larger than a medium-sized beetle, and took his position very seriously.

Rosie spoke to the half-wild birds in the mews, who answered in images as sharp as knives and flung as quickly as a falcon seizing a smaller bird out of the air. They spoke of death and of food, and of their handlers, whom they both hated and loved, for they were only half wild, and they knew it.

And one spring day when the sky was so bright and hard you felt you could rap on it with your knuckles and it would sing like beaten metal (a very rare sort of day in the misty, clammy Gig), she spoke for the first time to the great white merrel, with its ten-foot wingspan, which lived in the rafters of Woodwold's Great Hall where it shone from the darkness like a moon from a cloud; and it told her that the incomprehensible noise of banquets and their smothering smells, and the cheeping and scurrying of servants, were a poor trade for the freedom of its forest.

The Great Hall, even almost empty, as it was whenever Rosie had occasion to be in it, seemed to her nearly overwhelming. She did not come here often, and rarely lingered. It was so tall that the ceiling was lost in shadows with the shutters open and sunlight streaming in across the pale scrubbed planking of the floor; and it was large enough that you wouldn't be able to recognize the face of someone half its width away from you if the person were your dearest friend. Lord Prendergast held his judicial sittings here with an eye to intimidating miscreants.

Rosie thought she could have grown accustomed to the mere size of it. But the loomingness of Woodwold was especially acute here, and it seemed to her there was a kind of weight upon her as soon as she crossed its threshold, the weight, perhaps, of the long years of its existence, for this was the oldest part of Woodwold; but more, of its strange half-waking awareness. The pressure eased when she went further in, to Lady Prendergast and her ladies' rooms, to talk to lapdogs and canaries, or downstairs to the kitchens to negotiate an invasion of squirrels. (Squirrels did not, in fact, negotiate. They believed that they were too quick and too clever for anything ever to catch them, or to keep them away from anything they wanted, unless they were having a bad day, and it was up to Rosie to convince them that "having a bad day" is a flexible concept, especially if there were enough ferrets and tunnel-hounds involved.)

I am sorry, Rosie said to the merrel. *I do not think I can ask them to give you your freedom*.

I know you cannot, said the merrel. *But you asked and I have answered*.

She asked, humbly, half expecting the creature to break its chain and fall on her with its beak and talons in a fury of frustration: *Is there anything else I can do for you?*

There was a silence like the pit of winter, and then, as if from a very long way away, she heard a small voice like a fledgling's say wistfully, *Will you come and talk to me again some time?*

Yes, said Rosie. *Of course I will. I would be glad – honoured – to do so.*

She often thought of the imprisoned merrel, after that first conversation. She decided that she could go on not knowing what the spell on herself was, and why it was there, for as long as it took Katriona's sign to arrive. She thought of all the things she had done in twenty years that had not brought it on – whatever the spell was about. Enchanted embroidery, although it had felt very nasty at the time, as if her hands no longer belonged to her, was pretty negligible after all. Especially when you remembered the merrel.

She thought of the merrel stretching its wings, silently, in the dark peak of Lord Prendergast's Great Hall; she thought of how carefully it moved among its cage of rafters, so that the chain around its ankle did not clink; so carefully that any of Lord Prendergast's guests who did not know it was there would never look up to find it. (The floor beneath it was scrubbed twice a day; in moulting season it was swept three times.) She thought of the story the huntsman told her, of how it had been wounded – they guessed – by a dagger of falling ice, in the mountains where the source of the River Moan flowed, several days' ride from Woodwold; and how Lord Prendergast's hunting party had found it, but that he had stopped them from killing it. Even with a broken wing and half dead of starvation no-one liked to approach it. The huntsman threw a net to tangle its feet, and Lord Pren himself had hooded it with soft leather cut from his own hunting waistcoat, and then had it bound and brought home, and its wing set. But the wing had not healed as it should, and so it was given the vaulted height of the Great Hall to live in, where no-one dared trouble it, and it was fed by a falconer with a very long pole.

The merrel also knew its wing had not healed. *But I could reach a great height once more before it failed me,* it said. *And from there I would fold my wings and plummet to the earth as if a hare or a fawn had caught my eye; but it would be myself I stooped towards. It would be a good flight and a good death. And so I eat their dead things cut up on a pole, dreaming of my last flight.*

Chapter 14

That spring, too, Narl gained a new apprentice. Ordinarily such an arrival would be the focus of conversation and speculation for weeks: not only had Narl accepted him, which was unusual enough, but this one was a handsome young man, and as clean shaven as Narl.

But the run of odd fevers round the Gig, especially in Foggy Bottom, which neither Aunt's herbs nor the priest's arcane mutterings seemed able to cure, nor even, much, to ameliorate, distracted everybody; and those who were well enough for gossip had no time for it. The fevers were not severe, but their prevalency, lack of origin, and reluctance to depart were disturbing enough to take the edge off any interest in a good-looking, well-mannered young stranger.

Katriona had less to do with the sick that season than she might have had some other year, because she had four little wielders of baby-magic to look after, including their own Gilly, who had been set off, early and spectacularly, by the birth of her little brother, Gable. (Jem had recently slid through his own incursion of baby-magic without much more than the occasional manifestation of a black, red-eyed Thing that crouched in corners breathing stertorously. Jem had insisted that it was friendly, so they had left it alone, although everyone but Jem had circled its chosen corners somewhat warily.) Gable, fortunately, was a placid baby, and never interrupted his nursing while Katriona was frantically flicking counter-spells with the arm not holding him.

Peony was constantly in demand either as a nurse or to help keep order at the wheelwright's, and she missed her noontimes at the forge for some weeks. Rosie had told her of the new apprentice's arrival, his name, Rowland, and the fact that he had no beard. But Rosie was not very interested in him, and so Peony wasn't either.

Till the first day Peony returned for her usual noontime at the forge. Rosie, standing at the head of one of Lord Pren's horses, looked up just before Rowland's and Peony's eyes met. "You're here!" said Rosie. "I'm positively starving. Peony, meet Rowland. This one needs settling" – meaning the horse – "before I want to leave him. Don't eat everything."

By the time Narl and Rosie had left their charge with a little hay to keep him contented, Peony and Rowland had been trying to start a conversation for some while. Rosie was vaguely aware that her friend and the new apprentice were behaving out of character; Peony could talk to anyone, and Rowland had very pretty manners, much prettier than any smith's apprentice had any business having, which made him even more conspicuous than he was already for being tall and handsome and clean shaven. But here were these two social adepts standing staring at one another, Rowland with a hammer he kept passing from hand to hand, Peony clutching the basket in front of her as if she were warding off demons with it. Rosie was used to the effect Peony had on almost everyone at first meeting, especially young men; but Peony never behaved like this.

Something stirred at the back of Rosie's mind: surprise, curiosity, wonder. Dismay. And something else. "Narl," she said quietly. "Look. What is the matter with them?"

Narl straightened up from the wash bucket, drying his hands. He still had most of his attention on the horse they had been shoeing; it was just the sort of brilliantly athletic maniac Lord Pren's youngest son favoured – and, furthermore, it had terrible feet, with horn that wouldn't hold a nail. However often it came in to have a thrown shoe refitted, it would never believe that this wasn't the time that Narl was going to use the red-hot tongs and pokers on it, and not merely on its shoes. If he hadn't had Rosie to help him – she had told him she told the crazy ones stories, as you might do with a fractious child at bedtime – he probably wouldn't have been able to shoe it at all, however much mashed viso root he used. It looked half asleep now, musing over its hay with its ears flopping like an old pony's. He was half tempted to suggest that it was clever enough to know a good thing when it heard it, and merely liked Rosie's stories, but he also knew this wasn't true; the white round its eye as he approached it and the way it held the foot he was working on, told him better. It was always the crazy ones that hated being shod who most often threw shoes.

He gave his apprentice and the wainwright's niece a look while he passed his towel to Rosie, but he was more interested in the problem of where to put nails in a hoof already full of crumbling nail holes. His face was, as it usually was, expressionless. But Rosie was watching him as she washed her hands, and she had learnt to read his face in the years she had been hanging round the forge to a degree that perhaps Narl did not realize himself. And she saw awareness, or understanding, strike him as he looked, sharp as a knife, and where the invisible blade wounded him there bled hope and fear and longing – and something like resigned despair. This was so unexpected she almost put her hand on his arm, almost said to him, What is it? Can I help? I would do anything for you – when she realized, first, that he would not want her to have seen what she had seen, and second, that what she had barely stopped herself from saying was the truth.

She was wholly absorbed in giving her hands and forearms the scrubbing of their lives when Narl turned back to her, and she raised a carefully blank face to him. She could feel she was blushing, but she had splashed cold water on her face, too, which would do as an excuse. "They've just fallen in love," he said neutrally, and his face was again as calm and unreadable as it usually was.

His face was so tranquil and his tone so mild that Rosie almost believed she had imagined what she had seen. He was Narl, and nothing ever disturbed him, nor distracted him long from cold iron. She had drawn his attention away from its usual paths, but only briefly; Narl was about to take his noon meal standing up and looking at some half-finished project, or studying bits of waste iron that would no longer be waste when he was done with them.

But then the meaning of his words sank in. "They—?" she said, bewildered. "But—"

"It happens that way sometimes," said Narl. "Hard on them both, for he's promised elsewhere."

"P-promised?" said Rosie. "You mean, to wed?"

"Yes," said Narl, and got one of those even-more-than-usually-shut-in Narl looks on his face that meant he wouldn't say any more, and if Rosie had had her wits about her she would have wondered why he'd said anything at all; it wasn't the sort of thing Narl usually volunteered.

"I – I must tell her," she said, confused.

"You must not," said Narl. "He'll tell her. It's their business. Let them be. Rosie," he said, as she turned away, staring blindly into space, putting the towel down by feel and dropping it instead on to the unswept courtyard earth. "Rosie. She's still your friend."

And then he did put his hand on her arm, and she looked down at it, the big brown hand with the work-blackened fingers against her own sun-browned and -freckled skin. He removed his hand, and she looked up at his face again, and tried to smile, to nod. She thought she knew what she had seen in his face when he had first looked at Rowland and Peony: he was in love with Peony himself.

And Rosie had just learnt she was in love with him.

She blundered away, towards Peony and Peony's basket. She had been hungry, only a very few minutes ago. She concentrated on remembering that she was hungry. I am all right, she said to herself. I am all right. This was not easy, for dissembling was a skill foreign to her nature, but her wish not to cause distress to her friends was as strong as – stronger than – her own distress.

They all got through the meal somehow, Peony, Rowland and Rosie. Narl was invisible in the shadows under the roofed end of the forge; Rosie's eyes sought for him occasionally, looking for the shadow that moved, from where they sat in sunlight. The sunlight seemed unusually dazzling that day, full of little twinkly bits that got in your eyes and made you blink, or even made you flap your hand in front of your face, as if they were something you could brush away. She wondered how long . . . she wondered if Narl had ever thought of making his feelings known. Rosie thought she knew the reason for his silence; Peony was not in love with him, and Narl had none of the suitor about him to woo her.

None of the three ate much. Narl's meal disappeared, but whether he ate it or fed it to one of the town dogs, no-one knew but Narl.

"Narl said people do fall in love in an instant sometimes," said Rosie, her voice muffled, since she had her arms on the table and her head in her arms. Katriona and Aunt were making and binding charms together, and Rosie had just finished whittling a top for Jem, who would have it in the morning. Gable was asleep in the cradle Katriona rocked with one foot, and Jem and Gilly and the small boarders were asleep upstairs, and in the kitchen they were waiting for Barder and Joeb to come in to supper.

The shutters rattled. It was a cold summer, and there was a searching, prying wind that sniggled round houses, under closed doors, and down the backs of necks. The fog-sprites were in an unusually bad mood, hanging so much dew on spiderwebs that the webs broke, and making day-old bread soggy rather than stale. Even the mice, whose households were always plagued by draughts, complained of the cold.

"That's true," said Aunt. "I've never seen it happen, but it does."

"Nor have I seen it," said Katriona, "but I've always wondered if there isn't some fate in it. Not necessarily magic, like that poor queen who fell in love with her husband's best knight, but fate, something that happens to you, like being born one day rather than another in this village rather than that one."

Rosie stood up and moved restlessly round the kitchen, stopping at Aunt's spinning wheel to rub the nose of the gargoyle on the spindle end. She'd picked the habit up from Katriona so long ago she could remember steadying herself with one hand on the frame of the wheel while she stretched to reach the spindle end.

The little face always seemed to grin a fraction wider for a moment after you'd rubbed its nose.

"You aren't in love with Rowland yourself, are you?" said Katriona in a carefully bland tone – reasonably sure that the answer was no, but sure as well that there was something further troubling Rosie than Peony's romance. One of the many things Katriona had worried about as Rosie grew older was the likelihood of her falling in love with somebody; Katriona had known that she wanted Barder or no-one by the time she was twelve, and Flora had found her Gimmel at sixteen, though it had taken them another ten years to be able to afford to marry. Rosie had never shown any signs of falling in love, although Katriona had lately wondered a little about Woodwold's Master of the Horse, and what on earth and under sky she could say if he put his suit forward and Rosie was inclined to listen; but it hadn't happened, and . . . the princess' one-and-twentieth birthday was eight months away.

A kind of numb, dislocated bewilderment had settled down over Katriona with the turning of this last year towards that birthday. She found herself remembering the events of the year the princess was born with great – and obtrusive – vividness: this was when they had heard of the princess' birth, this was when the herald had come and made his announcement of the invitations to the name-day and she, Katriona, had drawn the long lot. . .

Three times in the last twenty years someone – some magic – had almost found Rosie, and three times Aunt and Katriona had deflected or confounded it. The fourth time had brought, not a tale of another assault on another of the king's strongholds, but a hippogriff flying over the Gig; and while the rest of the villagers relaxed as soon as there were no more sightings of it, the Gig fairies could feel that it had left something behind. Something it had, presumably, come here to leave. Something that might be causing the fevers and the weather. . . Small spider weave! thought Katriona angrily – not for the first time. It is not the *wearer* who is lost! Why have you never sent word! We are only two village fairies and she is your princess!

Eight months.

"In love with *Rowland*?" said Rosie with a little of her usual force. "No. He's nice enough, but he's . . . he's . . . oh, he's *boring*." Her voice was plainly telling the truth, but her thoughts were on something else, and she turned her lips in and bit down on them, as if preventing herself from saying anything further.

Barder came in just before the silence among the three women became sticky, threw himself into a chair, and sighed. "Joeb will be along as soon as he's washed," he said. "I'm sorry we're late again. Every wheeled vehicle in the Gig seems to be having the most extraordinary bad luck. Spokes break, rims pop, axles crack – I don't understand it. Crantab says the same. He has a waggon in for repair now that looks like it simply made up its mind to burst. We could both take on new apprentices now – there's plenty of work for them – but this isn't the way it should be, and it's not the sort of work you feel really happy doing. . ."

His voice tailed away because the suspicion had to arise that the unusual level of breakages was due to some kind of magic, and cleaning up magical messes was not considered wholesome or honest labour. "The only thing no-one has brought me for mending is a spindle's end," he said, trying to make a joke of it. He looked at the two fairies. "Usually you tell me when it's something that concerns me or my work," he said.

Joeb entered at that moment, looked round, took the plate Aunt offered him, but instead of sitting down as he usually did, said hastily that there was something he wanted another look at tonight, and went back outdoors. In the silence of the kitchen they heard his footsteps retreating on the hard-packed earth of the yard.

"Kat," said Barder.

"We don't know," she said, but as if the words were wrung out of her. "It feels like a searching spell. Something that knows it has been searching for the wrong thing for a long time." Too long a time, she thought. Searching spells don't last twenty years, but this one had. It was a gallimaufry, a patchwork, a bristling, ragged confusion of the shreds of many days, days stretching into years, worked and reworked and turned back on themselves, the frayed ends teased out and bound together again, every failure stitched into the body of the thing, so that it would not be repeated, till at last it would find what it wanted because there would be nowhere else left to look. And it was almost undetectable; it was the shaggy greyish fringe at the edge of your vision when you had gone too long without sleep. It was – probably – a senseless series of fevers and breakages. Katriona couldn't have made such a spell. She didn't know any fairy who could have. It was so outlandish neither Katriona nor Aunt could fully believe it existed; and they were the only two of the Gig fairies who could so much as guess at it.

She is as safe as ordinariness can make her. Ordinariness and beast-speech, that rare fairy talent.

Aunt said: "Your waggon probably did burst."

Barder picked up the bread knife and examined it as if deciding what it was for. "Do you know what it wants?" he said.

"No," said Katriona. "Yes," said Aunt. "Sort of," said Katriona, speaking so nearly simultaneously that the four words came out as a kind of burst: "Noyessortof."

There was another pause, and Barder said slowly, "I see," and then the three of them exchanged a look so fraught with unsaid understanding – a look that appeared to bind them not merely all together but also to prevent their looking at something else – that Rosie began to pay attention.

She was aware that all had not been well in the Gig this year. She knew about the fevers and the breakages, and the steady high run on minor squaring charms, which kept ordinary things what they were. It was only yesterday that Dessy, having had the third mug in a row turn into a frog when she tried to put beer in it, and despite her having murmured "mug, stay mug" over each as she took it down from the shelf, burst into tears and swore she was going to run away to Turanga and find a job in anything that wasn't a pub. Rosie had happened to enter the pub while Dessy was still weeping and threatening to leave, and had got down on her hands and knees to talk the beer-mug frogs out from under the bar, where they were huddling, confused and frightened, and longing for something, so far as Rosie could make out, that seemed to be a sort of swamp made of beer and sausages.

But her real attention was elsewhere. She'd never before had a problem she could neither forget nor do something about. She wanted never to have seen that look on Narl's face; she wanted never to have found out what that look meant to her. She wanted not to watch Peony moving through elation and misery a dozen times a minute. She had wanted to blame Rowland for everything, but found she couldn't, because he was a friend. He was patient and thoughtful and funny (in a way that as she'd got to know him better reminded her of Peony. It didn't surprise her that they'd fallen in love, but she wondered how they'd managed to do it in an instant). He was interested in animals, not only the horses and oxen a blacksmith shoes. He learnt the names of all the village dogs, even the medium-sized hairy brownish ones that all looked alike to most people, and he stopped to listen to birdsong. And the cats liked him. They called him Sweetbreath and Aroouua, which was a cat word indicating that you had supple joints. They rarely said aroouua of human beings. They called Narl Stone-Eye and Block.

He wasn't really boring. She just wasn't in love with him.

She'd been listening idly to the conversation, wrestling unwillingly with her own thoughts, and she looked up just in time to intercept the charged glance among the other three. If I'd held a stick between them at that moment, she thought, it would have sizzled.

Rosie said to Flinx, lying near the cradle so he could play a kind of dicing with death between his tail and the cradle rockers, *You could tell us something, couldn't you? You cats know something's up; even the priest's cats are worried.* She couldn't be sure, then, if he let his tail be pinched deliberately, or whether, stiffening all over in outrage at Rosie's question – a cat does not submit to interrogation – he merely forgot, and left it in a dangerous location; but pinched it was, and he bounded to his feet with a shriek and darted out of the room. "Oh, Flinx," sighed Katriona. "You could lie somewhere else."

"That cat doesn't come indoors to lie near the fire because he's getting old," said Aunt. "He does it to prove that he should never come indoors at all." The conversation was turned; but supper was a haunted meal that evening.

Like most lunches were at the forge now, Rosie thought the next day: haunted. Rowland and Peony seemed hardly to talk to each other, and when they did speak it was like Aunt and Katriona and Barder last night; as if what they were really saying was happening somewhere behind their words. Rosie had begun to imagine – she hoped she was imagining – that whatever irresistible force was drawing Rowland and Peony together, there seemed to be another, nearly as powerful, that was dragging them apart. Rosie half wanted to watch them, and half wanted never to look at them at all. She developed Narl's habit of wandering round the forge staring at things, although she was careful not to choose the same things to stare at that Narl himself did.

She wondered why the air between Rowland and Peony seemed to twinkle sometimes, and that when they were together they seemed more troubled by magic-midges than people who weren't fairies, sitting in a forge, ought to be; and she pretended that her own skin didn't seem to tingle and buzz if she sat long near them. She had never paid much attention to people in love before – except Katriona and Barder, but they'd been in love since before she was born, and presumably all the itchy unsettledness of it had worn out by the time Aunt had fetched her home to live with her and Kat. Maybe this is just what love – that first burst of mutual love – was like. Magic did tend to be drawn to excitements and upheavals. She thought of asking Aunt, but she didn't have the heart for it.

Of course the village found out about Rowland and Peony. Peony's beauty and sweetness had made her prospective marriage the liveliest odds at the pub since Rosie's disappointing show of baby-magic, and far more heatedly contested, since at least half the men (young and old, married and unmarried) laying their wagers were in love with her themselves.

"So, Narl, are you ready to take on another man permanently?" said Grey one day. Narl only grunted, but Grey would have been astonished if he had answered so frivolous a question. But Brinet, from whom Rowland rented a room and in whose kitchen he had his breakfast, asked Rosie one day if Peony's aunt had started measuring the family wedding dress against her niece's figure; and Rosie, expressionless, grunted, and walked away.

"Grunted at me just like Narl! Not a word! Not a nod or a smile!" said Brinet, much offended, to Cairngorm, later that day. "I don't think working with a man like Narl is good for a young woman, however clever she is with beasts!"

But Rosie felt herself to be at full stretch and had no slack for dealing with busybodies. A few days after she had declined to answer Brinet, she found Peony weeping into a pan of potatoes she was peeling, and sat down and put an arm round her. "I – I'm sorry," said Peony. "It's just – suddenly too much."

"Can't you marry him then?" said Rosie, remembering what Narl had said, and guessing what was suddenly too much.

"No," said Peony, and when the single syllable made her tears stop Rosie knew how hopeless it was – knew, perhaps, because of all the tears she herself had not shed into her own pillow recently. "No. He's pledged to – to someone else. Someone he's never met. She – she has a curse on her, and it makes her very lonely and sad."

Rosie's heart sank. "It's a family thing then?" What is a blacksmith doing with the kind of family that pledges its sons to other people's daughters sight unseen? Especially daughters with curses on them? That explains his manners, of course, if he comes from that kind of family, but then what is he doing as a blacksmith? Because he is a blacksmith. Even I can see he knows what he's doing, and Narl would never have taken him if he didn't. Couldn't he chuck it all over and *be* a blacksmith?

Magic, thought Rosie, and frowned. Was this part of what Aunt and Katriona were talking about the other night, when Barder was trying to squeeze some answers out of them? But if the searching spell wanted Rowland, wasn't he right there? Maybe not, surrounded by cold iron.

"Oh, Rosie," said Peony, picking up a potato. "I hope you never fall in love with the wrong man – the wrong man that you know is the right man.

"It isn't for much longer," she added, after a pause. "He must go home soon and – l-live up to his oath. They are to be married shortly after her – her birthday, which is in spring, when the crocuses come out. Like the princess, and you, Rosie."

Rosie grunted a Narl grunt. She was back that day from Woodwold. Lord Prendergast's hounds had broken away from the huntsman, which had never happened before in anyone's memory, and Lord Pren had had to forbid the man to quit his post, and set a spy on him that he couldn't creep off and disappear, so devastated was he. Rosie was called out to talk to the dogs, who were all deeply ashamed by their ignoble behaviour, and grovelled abjectly to the huntsman, whom they loved, at every opportunity.

I don't know, said Huwreer, one of the oldest and wisest hounds. *I've never felt anything like it. It was like being six months old again, but crazy. I've known crazy dogs. They can't learn and they don't care they can't learn, and that's worse, and if your huntsman doesn't know his job, one crazy dog can ruin the pack, because when we're running* – Huwreer paused. Rosie knew what she meant. When a dog's brain is full of prey-smell there isn't a lot of room for independent thinking.

Storm coming, the merrel had said, sitting in the darkness in the roof of Lord Prendergast's Hall. *Storm coming*. The weather, advancing towards autumn, was as restless and volatile as Lord Pren's youngest son's horses; but bad weather had never sent the dogs mad before.

Rosie felt she was surrounded by bad weather – her own and everyone else's. Rain and wind hardly came into it. Rowland couldn't really have anything to do with the princess, but it still seemed so very *odd* that her own private world should be trying its best to crack up during this last, tense, distracted year before the princess' one-and-twentieth birthday. If this is what it felt like in the Gig, it must be really dreadful where she was.

"I am thinking I will ask my aunt and uncle if I can go to Smoke River for a season. Perhaps I can learn a spinning charm." Peony gave Rosie a thin, watery smile, like sun trying to break through rain clouds. "You know it is a great frustration to me that I spin poorly."

Rosie did know. Peony was slow and clumsy about this as she was slow and clumsy about almost nothing else. It was a long-standing joke between them that Peony had been able to spin perfectly well until Rosie moved next door. Rosie had once offered to loan the gargoyle spindle end to Peony, explaining about the nose rubbing, but Peony declined, saying seriously that if it were a charm, it belonged to their family, and it would have its feelings hurt, or might go wrong, if loaned outside.

"I'll ask Barder to make you a spindle end as a coming-home present," said Rosie, stifling the urge to beg Peony not to go away and leave her alone, alone with Narl at the forge every day.

The sun broke through a little more credibly in Peony's smile this time. "I'd rather you made me one yourself," she said.

Chapter 15

Autumn was a season of storms, when the winds shouted bestiaries and the genealogies of kings and queens under doorsills and down chimneys, and chimney pots, after such storms, were found to have taken up residence on other roofs of their own choosing, and sometimes in trees, and several times at the bottom of the town well, which they did not want to leave, saying it was peaceful down there, the presiding element disinclined to air-frenzies like wind, and that fish were pleasanter companions than humans. There were too many storms, and people grew weary of them, and the dull fevers of the spring and summer became sticky, hacking coughs.

It had been raining off and on, cold, obdurate, needle-tipped rain, with often a hard frost overnight, weeks of this, till the ice got into the ground and discouraged the winter crops from growing, and the tracks were sloppy and rutted and treacherous, and the sky low and dark and menacing. Foggy Bottom was less foggy than usual, for the nervy winds that had blown all year were still blowing, in haphazard gusts from all the points of the compass; the strange fevers that troubled the Gig backed and blew and came and went like the disagreeable winds; the fog-sprites huddled under people's eaves and shrieked like banshees, especially in the middle of the night; and none of the fairies' weather-guessers worked.

And then the storm descended in a lash of sleet and hail. Rosie was soaked to the skin running across the square from the smith's and home to supper. There were only four of them that evening; Joeb was taking his day off at Grey's farm where he was courting the dairymaid in any and all weathers, and Peony was with her aunt and uncle. Jem, Gilly and Gable were all asleep upstairs; Katriona's last baby-magic boarder had gone home three days ago. "We won't hear if anyone howls, in this wind," said Katriona. "Jem will come and tell us if anyone does," replied Aunt.

They all listened, but for nothing they knew to expect, and started in their chairs when an especially savage wind-fist drove at the shutters. Rosie thought of Narl sitting over a small solitary fire, and wondered if he ever wished for company. Katriona had occasionally inveigled him across the square to supper; she said they owed the master of Rosie's livelihood something, and he had refused any other payment. "She's done me a favour," was his only explanation. He talked little more at the supper table than he did during the day at the forge, but he wasn't a difficult companion; and he and Barder were old friends. Barder could translate Narl's grunts better than anyone else in the village, save Rosie. But Narl had not come to supper in the last six months.

There was a bang on the kitchen door, the door to the yard. It was so substantial and purposeful a bang that while everyone wanted to assume it was only, once again, the wind, they all knew it was not. They stopped listening for nothing and instead wished for this something to go away. There was another bang.

Barder sighed, because he had barely sat down to supper.

"Is it a bad break?" he asked resignedly – because it always was, at suppertime, and it would be, in this weather, or whoever it was would have waited till morning. It might be so bad a break there were horses to cut free; in which case Rosie would have to come with him. . . He spoke before he had the door properly open. But the tone of his voice changed the question on the last word, as he opened the door fully.

A tall dripping figure stepped inside, invisible within a silvery cloak that glistened in many colours: This was finer cloth than even Smoke River could make. Invisible, that is, except for the bare feet. Rosie noticed the feet first – clean and smooth, despite the weather and the roads – and the way they seemed to feel the floor as a hand might feel a tool unfamiliar to it.

"Forgive me," said Barder, embarrassed and stiff with it. "Good evening to you. I am the wheelwright, as well as – well, I fix most things made with wood. The wainwright shares this yard with me, but the nearest carpenter is at Waybreak. When there is a knock on the door at this time of day in bad weather, it is usually because there is something to be mended."

The head, hidden inside the deep hood, nodded. But as it flung its sodden cloak back from its face, Katriona leaped to her feet with a little, terrible cry. "It is too late!" she said. "You cannot have her!" She moved sideways to stand behind Rosie's chair, and put her hands on Rosie's shoulders, and Rosie, bewildered, and frightened by the tone of Katriona's voice, could feel her hands trembling. There was a muscular ripple across the feet, like a hand testing the heft of sword or axe; Rosie found it difficult to raise her eyes to the face.

The wet figure shook its head, and raindrops flew; there was a puddle forming on the floor. "You cannot deny what she is, any more than I can deny that the last one-and-twenty years have also made her yours."

He turned to look at Barder, who had closed the door against the storm but stood staring, with his hand on the latch, at their unusual visitor. Under his cloak he wore clothing that seemed to be made entirely of long ribbons of fabric cunningly wrapped and tucked; and his hairless skin was the colour of deep water in shade, a kind of dark silky iridescence not unlike that of his cloak. His bald head gleamed like a jewel. Strangest of all, by his side hung a long curved blade like nothing the Gig had ever contained, fine metalwork curling over the hilt and lettering in a strange language written on the blade, for it wore no scabbard, picking up the light as the man moved so that it seemed as if it moved of itself, as if it shrugged its own skin free of the wet caress of the cloak. No-one ever wore anything so obviously a weapon in the Gig; even when the king's cavalry rode through their sabres were sheathed and hung like long thin luggage from their saddles.

The stranger looked at Barder first, and when he had finished looking at Barder, he looked slowly round the rest of the room as if he had every right to be there and to inspect it so closely. If Rosie had not been frightened by his assurance – and by the casualness with which he carried his long blade – she would have been angry at his presumption. When his eyes fell on her she was enough recovered from the shock of his appearance – and Katriona's reaction – to stare straight back at him, but the protest she would have liked to utter remained stuck in her throat.

He turned at last to Katriona, and Rosie, seated while the two of them stood, could not decide if he raised his chin to condescend to her or to recognize her as an equal. "Listen," he said to Katriona, and as he stretched out his hand towards her a spider dropped down from nowhere, from some fold of his glittering, ribbony sleeve. "These are the words you have waited long to hear: 'Small spider weave on a silver sleeve, Oh weave your grey web nearer. From a golden crown let your silk hang down, For lost, lost, lost is the wearer.'"

The spider fell about halfway to the floor from the man's outstretched arm; hesitated, and ran back up its silk, disappearing briefly there in the silvery folds, and then let itself briskly down again. Now it had two streamers to work from; busily it began to swing itself back and forth, spinning a web, in the wheelwright's kitchen in Foggy Bottom, hanging from a stranger's sleeve. But just as the web began to take shape – it was a crazy-quilt web, each loop at variance with its neighbours – the spider paused, as if dissatisfied, and ran round its gossamer network, tweaking corners as if, from the spider's perspective, they would not lie straight, like a person making a bed.

"I know who you are," said Katriona, and the anger in her voice was startling. "I know who you are. Is this – festival trick – of yours intended to amaze the country folk? I think we deserve better than your contempt."

The man said gently, "I did not know I carried a passenger till just now, when I held out my arm."

The spider rushed down to the bottom of its uncompleted web, and appeared to hurl itself off the edge, like a child taking a running leap into a swimming hole. It touched the floor, snapped itself free of its silken ladder as if impatiently, and set off across the floor. Towards Rosie.

Oh dear, thought Rosie. Spiders like all insects were very hard to talk to – with a slight exception for butterflies, who were all crazy in an almost human way, especially the ones who had spent most of their short lives enchanted. Talking to them was like trying to walk on your hands, or say all your words backwards, or kiss your elbow. In some cases it was just about possible (Rosie could have something pretty nearly resembling a conversation with a butterfly, if both she and the butterfly were trying) but sometimes it wasn't. Rosie had never picked up much but an irregular clicking that she guessed might be some sort of code, supposing she could figure it out, from any spider.

This one was clicking furiously as it came towards her across the floor – a tiny smith's hammer tapping away at an even tinier bit of iron. *Tickettytickettyticketty*. She didn't want to bend over with Katriona's hands still heavy on her shoulders, so she sat quietly as the spider came up to her, made its way over boot to trouser leg and up to lap, and crept to the back of her hand. It was so light she could only feel it on her by looking at it; then she could just sense the bend of a hair as it trod upon her skin.

The clicking stopped abruptly. *I'm sorry*, she said to it. *I don't understand. I can't . . . er . . . hear you.*

There was a pause. Then a click, a pause, another click, another pause, a click, pause, click. Then a longer pause, and repeated. Rosie realized on the third repeat that she could hear differences in each of the four clicks; and so she strained to listen. *All . . . will . . . be . . . well*, said the spider, and stroked the back of her hand with several feet; they felt like eyelashes. There was something familiar about its voice – except spiders don't have voices – something familiar about its words, no, its inflection, no, *something* that reminded her of something from a very long time ago, from those ancient days before she lived with Aunt and Katriona. Something about her parents? She had never wanted to know about her parents, as if knowing, somehow, would make her belong less to the family she loved.

But the people round her were talking. Katriona's voice no longer sounded angry, only tired and disheartened. "I have nothing to return to you, for it burnt to black ash, and then crumbled to dust so fine I could not hold it, although I tried," she said.

"Did it?" said their visitor, and they all saw that he was shaken. "Did it? I had not realized she was so strong. When, can you tell me when it happened?"

"Yes," said Katriona. "Six years ago, in late summer, about three and a half months after Barder and I were married."

"Six years ago," said the man, as if thinking aloud. "Yes, I remember, it was a season of storms at Caerleon. We feared then that she had drawn a true line on what she sought, for we knew we had yielded more than we could afford. But when nothing happened – when nothing seemed to happen – we thought we had held after all. Well! Old Nagilbran would be pleased to know what good use his amulet was put to; he was inclined to think me frivolous." And the man smiled a grim smile that was not frivolous at all.

Why didn't Katriona say, "What are you talking about? What has another battle at another royal stronghold have to do with us?" But she didn't. She said, "I think it did more than the work of that one night. Since then there have been no more . . . except . . . I wish I had it now. You said you would take it from me when I had no further use for it, but I have use for it now, by reason of your coming," and she caught her breath on a sob, and her fingers dug painfully into Rosie's shoulders.

That the stranger was a fairy was as obvious as his bare feet. Rosie had never met a magician – seeing an occasional one riding with a company of king's cavalry didn't count as meeting – but the wildness that hung round this man told her he had never gone to the Academy, never spent long hours indoors memorizing the pronouncements of his forebears, never earnestly debated the existence of fish. The room was thick with the possibilities of his power. It fanned her face like the heat of the fire; Rosie half believed she could reach out and pluck a miracle from the air, and it would take definition and solidity from the mere shape of her hand reaching for it. And yet she could read from the way he held himself, as if she might read a horse or a hawk, that this man would placate Katriona if he could; that for all he wore a sword and stared round the room like a wealthy buyer at a fair, he came as a friend – even as a supplicant.

What could anyone in the Gig – except possibly Lord Prendergast – have to do with a man like this man? Rosie glanced down at the back of her hand; the spider had disappeared.

He stood as if waiting or thinking; at last he said gently, "You knew this day would come; I cannot help it, any more than you, any more than she herself can."

"I had no choice!" cried Katriona.

"You could have let her die," said the man. "She would have died by now, else. Several times over. Or worse than died. Do you need me to tell you so?"

But Katriona had sunk down by Rosie's chair, her hands running down Rosie's arm, and then she laid her head against her hand resting on Rosie's knee, and cried like a baby. Rosie, not until that moment realizing she could, leaned over and picked up her cousin, her foster-sister, the only mother she could remember, and pulled her into her lap, as if Katriona were the child and Rosie the guardian, the protector, the champion. Rosie put her arms round her, and swept the damp hair off her forehead, and kissed her, and Katriona clung round her neck and wept.

"Fox," murmured the man. "Fox – badger – bear – otter. Doe and cow, mare and goat, bitch and wolf and. . . You had a journey, did you not, with the little one? Rosie, is that what you call her? Rosie?"

Rosie surged to her feet, Katriona still in her arms, fury giving her the necessary strength. "Stop it," she said to the strange man who had hurt Katriona and ruined their peace. "I do not know what you are saying to Katriona, but I do not like it. I like it even less that you should talk about me as if I am not here. Rosie is my name. And you have not yet told us yours."

Katriona made a tiny sound of embarrassment or thanks, and Rosie bent and let her gently down, keeping her own gaze fastened on the dark man. The rain had stopped, and the wind. In the sudden silence, if the humans in the room had not been so intent on each other, they might have noticed that Flinx had crept into the kitchen, and the house mice had crept in round him, as if they knew that for this evening of amazements they were safe from him. One of the kitchen shutters – the one that never fitted properly, and leaked when the wind was from the west – rattled briefly and swung open, and Fwab hopped in, followed by several robins and an owl. The door to the courtyard opened silently, for Spear was clever with latches, and he was followed by Zogdob and Ralf, the baker's half-grown puppy. Through the open door anyone who looked might have seen several deer walking quickly into the wrights' yard, ears wide and alert; and a hump on a pile of timber might have been discerned as a badger. Still slightly too far away for human ears was the sound of galloping hoofs; just audible, but not absolutely identifiable as anything other than the wind, was the long ecstatic bay of a hunting hound declaring that he had found his scent and was following it.

The stranger murmured, "But they have never told her; Sigil, they have never told her," and many expressions ran over his face like small sharp gusts of wind riffling the surface of a pool: astonishment, dismay, disbelief, disapproval darkening to condemnation; and the man stepped towards Rosie and, to her utter horror, dropped on his knees in front of her. From that position he gently drew up his beautiful and dangerous blade and laid it across his hands, holding it up toward her as if it were a gift. Rosie involuntarily put her hands behind her back.

"It is your name, yes," he said, looking up at her, the sheen of his skin opalescent in the soft lamplight, the blade in his hands bright as the moon. "But you, dear one, dearest one, you are our princess, the princess we have striven so anxiously to defend, Casta Albinia Allegra Dove Minerva Fidelia Aletta Blythe Domina Delicia Aurelia Grace Isabel Griselda Gwyneth Pearl Ruby Coral Lily Iris Briar-Rose. And I am your servant Ikor, among the least of your servants, but I was to be your one-and-twentieth godparent, and so I was sent by the queen's fairy, Sigil, to find you, and to tell you that your long concealment is at an end at last, and we must quickly plan what to do; for she who cursed you seeks you even as I have done – and she will – as I have done – find you, for we can no longer stop her. We have tried, these twenty years, but we have finally failed, and we know it. No fairy – no magician – should have been able to make a searching spell that endured twenty years, but Pernicia did it. It is a great shaggy thing by now, spiny as a holly tree with the errors of twenty years' looking; and we have teased and pestered and vexed it as we could – the guarded fortresses were not our only means of confusion – but it has gone on looking. When we found that the spell had settled here, in the Gig – we knew what this meant. And so the best we could do at the bitter end was hope to find you first – only a minute first, an hour, a day – or three months. I gladly offer my life to you, but that is not enough."

Rosie heard what the man said, but she did not – could not – would not – take it in. She seemed to be floating free from her body; her body remained standing in the fire- and lamp-lit kitchen, Katriona beside her and the rain-drenched stranger kneeling at her feet; but she, Rosie, the real Rosie, had gone away, gone away to a safe place where she couldn't be told horrible, frightening, devastating lies. Dreamily she looked round her; it was a foggy place she stood in – even foggier than Foggy Bottom – and at first she could see nothing clearly. But she heard voices: animals, her animals, her friends, talking, talking robin to fox and deer to badger and otter to vole. They were all talking, talking to each other, using human kinds of words as the swiftest means of communication, all talking together, for tonight all defences were down:

You here!

Yes, and you!

And you and you!

Why did you come?

And you?

It is in the air.

Yes, the air, and the water.

It fell with the rain.

I heard it in the wind.

I felt it in my feet upon the earth.

Something coming.

Someone coming.

Some great thing happening.

We know of the princess.

We know of – her who cursed her.

We know that this thing is coming at last.

My grandmother told me it would come in my time.

My father told me. He remembered the day.

I remember the day.

The princess and the bad one.

But this thing – this happens here.

Here.

Near to us all.

I thought of Rosie.

We thought of Rosie.

Something about Rosie.

Rosie, our Rosie.

Our friend.

Our speaker to-all.

So we came.

And I.

And you.

And all of us.

But the princess!

She cannot be!

She talks to us!

She is the princess. The humans would not get this wrong.

The wet black man would not get this wrong. Can you not smell it on him?

But here!

Her!

Rosie!

Our Rosie the princess!

I knew there was something wrong about all those strongholds! Did you ever hear of anyone who got a smell of her?

But here, right here—

With us in the wet lands!

Wait'll I tell the cousins!

The princess! She's alive!

You know the stories, of how we all fed her as she fled across country, away from the one who wished her ill—

We fed and hid her—

Fox and bear and badger and deer and cow and ewe and goat and bitch and wolf bitch and cat and wildcat, we all fed her—

The stories never said where she fled to! – this from a very young and foolish rabbit, who was instantly pinned to the ground by the weight of disapproval this thoughtless remark brought him. *Well, of course not,* said a goose, and gave a scornful hiss as she swayed past him and settled nearer the door to the wheelwright's , wriggling between two sheep and a beaver.

The princess!

Our *princess!*

I should have brought her a gift – I know where there are some apples –

– some sweet acorns–

– some beautiful roots–

– a squirrel that hasn't been dead very long –

Rosie laughed, from wherever she was, in the rolling grey fog, and the laughter stirred her from lethargy, and she looked down. She seemed to be wearing a long dress made out of something as grey as the fog, grey and twinkling, but the fog only glittered in the corners of her eyes, whichever way she looked, and the great sweep of skirt that fell round her glittered and winked all over. She could feel the weight of the dress, heavy as cold iron, which made her stiffen her back against it to hold herself straight, like a horse in its first shoes lifting its feet high in surprise.

She thought, this is the sort of dress a princess wears; but I am not a princess. I left all that behind, back in the kitchen, with the man holding his sword and dripping water on the floor. I left it behind. I am a horse-leech, and I wear trousers, not heavy clumsy skirts.

She didn't want to see the dress, and she put her hands over her eyes; but the weight of it would not go away. She dropped her arms again, already weary of the weight of the sleeves. I left you behind, she said to the dress. I left you behind. I am Rosie, niece and cousin to the two best fairies in the Gig, I live in the wheelwright's house, Barder's, who is my friend and my cousin's husband; I am the friend also of Peony and of – of Narl. I am a horse-leech.

In her mind she glanced once more at the wheelwright's kitchen, looked at the kneeling man with loathing, but then she looked away from him, at Barder's kind thoughtful face, Aunt's sharp clever one, and at last looked at Katriona, at the tearstains still visible on her face, something like the well-known look of love and anxiety there, but now harsh and bleak and almost despairing. I left you behind, Rosie thought wonderingly, and looked down once more at the dress she was involuntarily wearing.

Something, some individual twinkle, moved as she looked, and she reached out her hand, and the spider crept on to her extended finger. *All will be well*, it said, and Rosie said to it, *I know your voice. I know you. Who are you?*

The spider didn't answer.

Rosie closed her eyes and took a deep breath, and ducked out of the cold heavy dress and slipped back into her body, still standing in the wheelwright's kitchen, and instantly she felt the warmth of the fire at her back, and the poised, tingling tension in the room. The animals were still talking:

But – the princess – here – that means—

Yes.

Yes.

But if Rosie is anyone's princess, she is our princess, and we will keep her.

We will keep her safe.

Let the humans do what they can.

Against the bad one.

And they will. For she is theirs, too.

But we will do that which has also to be done.

As soon as we find out what it is.

We will find out.

Yes.

Ours, sighed many voices.

Ours to keep.

Rosie's eyes were still closed, and among the animals' voices she heard another voice, and against Rosie's closed eyelids there seemed to be streaks of lavender and purple and black forming patterns that made Rosie feel dizzy and sick; and then there was another voice, a human voice, a voice that spoke to her of her death and was glad of the prediction. *I have found you at last*, it said. *Found!*

But then the voice changed, faltered, lost its malice, and became familiar – familiar and loved and near at hand. It was Katriona's voice, and it was calling her name, the name she knew, the only name she knew. Rosie. Rosie, Rosie. She opened her eyes, having forgotten that they were shut. The man, Ikor, no longer knelt at her feet, Katriona had her arm round Rosie's waist, and Aunt stood next to her and held a cup out towards Rosie, saying, "Drink this. How steady is your hand? Shall I help you?"

Rosie fumbled back a step, found her chair again, and sat down. A dog head insinuated itself on to her knee – one of Lord Pren's tall sighthounds, she could almost remember his name, yes, Hroc – and a half-grown puppy, far too large for the job, plunged into her lap, Ralf. Several mice ran up her trouser leg. Flinx, as if it were an accident, sat on one foot (Rosie could feel him hooking his claws into her boot to stay on), and Fwab perched on her head. She took the cup with one hand and then decided to add the other hand to the other side of it, but she drank without assistance, and as the tonic – she recognized the smell from one of Aunt's little bottles – slid down her throat she thought of the terrible voice she had just heard, and in her mind it infiltrated the name the man Ikor had just spoken: Casta Albinia Allegra Dove Minerva Fidelia Aletta Blythe Domina Delicia Aurelia Grace Isabel Griselda Gwyneth Pearl Ruby Coral Lily Iris Briar-Rose. And, looking into Katriona's face, she understood that it was all true; and understood as well why she had not told her; and bitterly resented it, almost hated her for it, almost hated Katriona. And yet she also knew that she was grateful – humbly, shamingly grateful – to have been just Rosie for almost one-and-twenty years; and she felt that her gratitude was an obligation as heavy as the truth, as heavy as the iron dress.

It's true, murmured the animals.

It's true.

She looked at the four human faces looking at her, and stamped one leg, because the mice tickled; her other foot vibrated with Flinx's purring. She couldn't remember him ever purring for her before. She stared at Ikor, leaning now against one wall, an owl standing on a shelf just above him, shining white as he shone black and silver, his hand on the hilt of his great curved sword, compassion and wonder in his face. *What stories*, she said to her friends, *what stories about how you all fed the baby princess? What stories about how she fled across country after her name-day?*

Stories, said a number of voices, and Rosie forced herself to remember that animals do not tell stories as humans do. Things told were how to build nests and line dens, how to escape your enemies, how to find or catch your food, and how to do these things while not attracting the wrong sort of attention, which included all human attention. *Why?* said Rosie. *Why did you help her – them?* Katriona had brought her home – brought her here. Katriona had been the one from Foggy Bottom who had gone to the princess' name-day; Rosie knew how every village, every town, had been allowed to send one person. The others from the Gig – Osib from Treelight, Gleer from Mistweir, Zan from Waybreak, Milly from Smoke River – all of them were only too glad to tell stories of their journey, of the name-day, in spite of what had happened to the princess. Katriona never spoke of it at all; it was Flora who had told her that Foggy Bottom's representative had been Katriona. Rosie, well acquainted with Katriona's tenderheartedness and distress at the princess' plight, had thought she knew why she did not talk about her experience.

Why? she asked again. *I do not understand. Why did all of you help?*

There was a rustle of puzzlement through the animals, but the puzzlement was at her for her question. At last the owl said to her, *We do not know why. It was the thing to do. The bad one is bad; the sort of human-bad that . . . leaks, like an old bole in the rain. Those of us who saw this knew this; it was there. Our parents and grandparents, if they were there, knew this. You humans use "we" and "all of you" differently. We did not gather together. We gave the story of the bad human-gathering day to our neighbours, and our neighbours to their neighbours, and they and we did what there was to do. The story now is the way of things. It is done.*

You are our princess, said other voices. *It is now, not then.*

Aunt. Of course Aunt knew; for Katriona would have come home with the baby princess – with her, herself, Rosie – and told her what had happened; and Katriona had been barely more than a child herself, fifteen, five years younger than Rosie was now. Barder – she could see that Barder had known as well, and for a moment she had to struggle to forgive the three of them for this, that Barder had known, too, for he would not have learnt till later; they would have told him over her, Rosie's, head, her unknowing head. Barder must have read something of this in her eyes, for he gave her a funny, twisted little smile, weaker than usual, but the familiar smile the two of them had exchanged many times in the last years, as the two ordinary people in a house that held two fairies, a smile of equal parts love and exasperation.

She was glad she was sitting down, for she could feel tremendous forces shifting inside her, aligning this new, appalling knowledge with everything she knew about herself, and everything she didn't know: with her memories of cutting her hair when she was four, of falling into a bog when she was ten, of looking into the darkness of the cottage loft when she was fifteen, of finding out that she was in love with Narl when she was twenty; of growing up talking to animals as she talked to people, and not understanding for a surprisingly long time that not everyone did this. She felt as if when she stood up again this immense change would have expressed itself physically somehow; she would be taller or shorter or have six fingers on each hand – as people with fairy blood occasionally did – but no, she was the princess, and her family, her real family, had no magic in it.

And then her eyes filled with tears, and she threw herself forward into Katriona's arms (Ralf squeaked, but held his place), Katriona, dearest cousin, sister, mother – and none of these, for

Rosie was a princess, the daughter of the king and queen, and no blood at all to Katriona, to Aunt, to Jem and Gilly and Gable, and the loss was suddenly more than she could bear.

"Oh my dear, my dear," she heard Katriona saying, "you are still our own Rosie; never doubt it."

She cried for what felt like a long time, till her eyes were sandy and her mouth dry, and then she stopped. She wiped her eyes (and Ralf's back) with a towel that Aunt offered her, and Spear and Hroc licked the bits she missed. When she raised her face from the towel the first thing her eyes fell upon was the little grinning gargoyle that Barder had carved. She remembered the story of the blunted spindles, how the lost princess had been cursed to prick her finger on a spindle – an iron spindle, such as Rosie had never seen – on her birthday, and die of it; and she remembered Katriona's habit of rubbing her finger down the gargoyle's nose, for luck or reassurance, and how she, Rosie, had picked the habit up from her.

The room was very full of animals now: sheep and lambs; a fawn, its mum with her head through the door; several more cats – mostly on the table; rabbits and hares; a grizzled old badger and a smallish young pig; a shiny black cock sitting on the back of Barder's empty chair, pretending to ignore the glossy cock pheasant, whose tail was longer than his if not so iridescent, on the back of Katriona's. Birds perched almost everywhere that would hold two clutching bird feet, including the backs of the sheep. There were a few moles pretending to be small humped velvety shadows, and a stoat, looking stubborn, as if his friends and family had tried to talk him out of coming and he had come anyway. Lord Pren's stallion, Gorse, thrust his head through the window Fwab had opened, and Rosie heard Fast whinnying behind him; and she could hear the teem and seethe of the courtyard, as more beasts came, and more and more and more.

Water still dripped off the trees and trickled down the roof, but the only other noise was what the animals made. Rosie could hear the giggle of otters, and she heard the pattering thoughts of goats and the more laborious ones of cows, and not far away in the forest there was at least one bear. She looked up as another shadow fell across the doorway, and there was Peony, an expression of astonishment on her face, and a half-grown fox cub in her arms.

Rosie stood up again, tucking Ralf under one arm; there was now a sparrow sitting on one shoulder, and a grouse on the other; one of the sparrow's wings clapped against her ear as it kept its balance; Ralf was under that arm. But it was only the tiny prickle of Fwab's claws against her scalp that was making her eyes water. Two of the mice she had shaken out of her trouser leg had scampered up the outside, and dived into a pocket just before her standing would have shaken them loose a second time. Rosie ran her free hand through her short hair in her old familiar gesture – Fwab, very used to it, hopping in the air just long enough for it to sweep under him – but this time, to those looking on, the resulting fuzzy nimbus looked less like a sunflower and more like a soldier having just removed a battle helmet. Her voice was perfectly steady:

"We haven't much time to decide what we will say, for Lord Prendergast's people will be close behind Gorse and Fast, and the village will be close behind them, as soon as they look out their doors for a breath of air before bed this evening and see the menagerie at the wrights'. My one-and-twentieth birthday is upon us – that is what you are here to say, is it not, Ikor? – and my final doom comes with it, for good or ill. What is it that we must do?"

PART FOUR

Chapter 16

A gain Rosie found herself standing at the strange window of a strange new bedroom, staring out into darkness and a series of roofs, and wondering what was to become of her. But this bedroom was still strange to her after three months, whereas the wheelwright's house had been home in three weeks.

The window she stood at now was high up, much higher than any village house, higher indeed than any tree Rosie had ever climbed. Nor were the roofs she looked out on the friendly, ordinary muddle of sheds and outbuildings suitable to a house that had belonged to several generations of village craftspeople, and some rather untidy common land beyond, but a long rolling sea of wings and stableblocks and armouries and chapels and bakehouses and dairies and servants' quarters, and still more walls and roofs that she had no names for, surrounded by beautifully kept parkland and pasture and gardens and poultry runs.

She was at Woodwold .

She wished for a cat to be lying nearby, flicking its tail in the starlight and muttering indecipherably. But the tower room – chosen by Lord Prendergast and approved by Ikor – was very high indeed, and the confusion of roofs alarming, even for a cat that liked climbing. It was always quiet up here, but tonight not only did no owls hoot, no horses whinny from the stables, no dogs bark in the grounds: the mice behind the wainscoting and the pigeons under the elegant lacery of the overhanging roof were silent.

Waiting.

Tomorrow was the princess's twenty-first birthday. There was to be a grand ball, the grandest ball anyone had ever seen or heard of, and Rosie, as if from exile or through a wasting illness, remembered the old stories of what the princess's twenty-first birthday ball would be.

The courtiers, including (so far) forty-four magicians and twenty-six fairies, had been arriving for the last two months. Ikor, the queen's fairy's special emissary, greeted them, and told them what they needed to know; and if any of them doubted him (as the magicians surely did, on principle), none of them challenged him. For the story – the story that was given out by Ikor – was that it had been the queen's fairy, Sigil, who had saved the princess on her name-day, and who had repulsed Pernicia and devised the princess's sanctuary. (As a result, fairies all over the country were being treated with a reverence they were quite unaccustomed to, and which the more practical among them found rather a nuisance.)

Sigil herself had not only refused to come forward and be made a proper fuss over; she faded to a vague colourless presence at the queen's elbow no-one was absolutely sure, a moment later, that they had seen at all. But the other courtiers, grand and strange, poured into the Gig, complaining about the roads, speaking with the accent of the royal city; and with them they brought exquisite gifts, for the Prendergasts, and for the princess.

The king and queen and their three sons had set out for the Gig as soon as possible after the announcement of the princess's whereabouts was made – an announcement that had flown on spell-wings from the Gig to the royal city – but they were taking a long passage through their country, meeting their people, letting them see from the joy in their faces that the news was true, and assuring them that they would take an even longer passage back to the royal city, and introduce everyone who wanted to meet her to the princess, who would be imprisoned no more.

There was no mention of the fact that Sigil had told the king and queen that they must not arrive at Woodwold before the very day of the ball.

There were people all over the country saying, Woodwold!

How very extraordinary! We never thought of Woodwold! And others who said, Lord Prendergast is a deep one, keeping to himself as he does; and yet the Prendergasts have always been like that, staying away from court to bury themselves in their own lands, notoriously loyal when they might have been kings and queens themselves, almost as if fate were laying something up for the future.

The entire country felt as if it were on holiday, as if all the feast days of the year – of the last one-and-twenty years – were being rolled together to make one immense, joyous, irresistible celebration. Because the princess's ball was Pernicia's final rout – this too was explicit in the story Ikor was telling. Pernicia had failed. She had had her twenty-one years, and she had failed. They had kept their princess safe. On her twenty-first birthday they would not be looking anxiously over their shoulders for black and purple shadows where no honest shadows could lie; they would be celebrating the end of darkness.

For this was a part of the great magic Sigil and Ikor and Aunt and Katriona had created. This was a part of their last, desperate throw against the fate that had caged the princess on her name-day: that the people should believe that Pernicia had already lost, and that the princess's birthday was a time of rejoicing; that they might freely love their restored princess so much that the love itself was protection and defence – and that behind that defence other, secret defences could be devised.

People forgot; it was in the nature of people to forget, to blur boundaries, to retell stories to come out the way they wanted them to come out, to remember things as how they ought to be instead of how they were. And Aunt and Katriona and Ikor and Sigil had arranged to help the people forget, to remember just a little – just a crucially little – awry.

Pernicia could not be defeated by any of the usual means of straightforward feats of magic and of arms. And so they had had to come up with an alternative.

It was a deceiving magic so vast that the four fairies walked half in the spell-world all their waking hours, and their dreams were troubled by it even when they slept, which was little enough, and restlessly. Katriona felt as if she and Aunt and Ikor and Sigil had unravelled themselves from their human shapes and reknitted the thread into a world-shape: the shape of a world where Pernicia had lost, and the one-and-twentieth birthday of the once-cursed princess was a joyful and carefree occasion, where the only concern would be that you didn't miss anything particularly good to eat, and that you shouted loudly enough when the princess's health was drunk. She knew Aunt and Ikor felt the same by the expressions on their faces: the faces of people whose bodies could barely hold their clothes out in the right dimensions of height, width and depth, because there was so little of them left, beyond the magic they maintained and endured.

She wondered, now that she felt a tattered, shambling thing herself, if the tattered, shambling, persistent searching spell had once been a human being. She and Aunt had not seen it again since Ikor had arrived in Foggy Bottom. She did not know if it had disintegrated, or gone home, or. . .

The conspirators all wondered why Pernicia remained silent. Ikor had won their second-to-last throw – he had found the princess before she did; but the news of the princess's discovery was not only no secret; it had caused a tremendous thunderclap in all the ethereal layers, from the darkest underground chambers of the gnomes and earth-sprites and rock-witches to the high cold realms of the cloud-swallowers and the star-dancers. Pernicia knew. Pernicia also must know that some enchantment was making the people of the country she planned to destroy believe that her design had already foundered. But she was biding her time, as the last days ran out before the princess's one-and-twentieth birthday – when Pernicia would be at her strongest. The birthday, and their final contest. And Katriona found herself grotesquely grateful for her enemy's silence, for she did not think the conspirators' precarious delusion could have held against even so much as one gust of Pernicia's laughter, the demon laughter that had pulled the banners down on the princess's name-day.

Katriona often thought she could not have done it at all without

Sigil. It was not just a matter of four of them instead of three; it was the clear patient lines of the magic Sigil worked, which never sagged nor snarled and were never overwhelmed or confused. She never saw Sigil's face, although when she heard her voice, she sounded as nearby as if she stood next to her, with her arm round her waist again, and Katriona holding a baby princess. None of the three of them in Foggy Bottom knew where Sigil was, not even Ikor; she had not remained in the royal city, nor had she gone on the royal progress with the king and the queen and the princes. But the three other fairy conspirators often heard her voice, and constantly felt her presence, and her strength, and her love for the princess she had not seen in more than twenty years.

Rosie rested her chin on her hands, listening to the waiting silence. This is the only way, she told herself. We went over it and over it and over it – Kat and Aunt both said Ikor was right, it is the only way, and it gives us hope when there was none: because Pernicia had not been baffled or defeated, and all there really was to set against her, here at the final confrontation, was Rosie herself. Which was all there had been twenty-one years ago; all that Katriona and Aunt and Sigil and Ikor had been able to do was give her time to grow up.

It had been Ikor's idea, of course. It took an outsider to see it, to suggest it; Ikor, who had been chosen by Sigil not only because he had been the twenty-first godparent and the bestower of the amulet, but also because he was the sort of person who saw what there was to see and the sort of fairy to shape it best to his purpose. Yet he had almost been undone by the knowledge of Rosie's beast-speech; "It cannot be," he said, over and over. "It cannot be." This was the only time during that long night that Katriona laughed. "But it is," she said. "Don't you think – I have often thought – it is one of the things that has saved her this long? She has been as safe as ordinariness could make her: ordinariness, and that she talks to animals like a fairy. Better than a fairy. "

These had also been the only moments during that long night that Ikor had lost his ascendency over them, as he repeated, "It cannot be." They were, for another little while, a family, united against an invader. But Rosie could not hold to that memory, not sitting in a tower room in Woodwold the night before the princess' birthday. What she remembered was the look on Kat's face when she agreed to Ikor's plan.

Often in the last three months Rosie recalled the voice she had heard the night of Ikor's arrival: *I have found you at last! Found!* That she had not heard it again gave her no comfort; for she knew the truth behind the conspiracy. And tomorrow was the princess' birthday.

Rosie remembered the look on Peony's face as she stood in the doorway on that evening, the fox cub in her arms, contemplating them all – the animals wrapped round and flowing from the figure on the chair, the figure of Katriona's cousin and Aunt's niece and Peony's best friend, who had just found out that she was a princess, a princess with a curse on her.

Everyone had fallen silent, and looked at the newcomer, framed by the wet twilight; there was a peevish mutter of wind. The firelight touched her worried face with gold, and set fire to her bright hair and the fox cub's fur.

"I – I saw – from my window, and I came down. . . He just – just jumped," said Peony. The fox cub had turned over on his back, the better to bat at one of Peony's long ringlets, fallen gracefully over her shoulder, with his forepaws, and looked perfectly content and at ease. "I – I thought he must have mistaken me for you, somehow, so I then had the excuse of bringing him to you. Rosie, are you all right? You look strange. Why are so many of your friends here? Is something wrong?"

"Mistaken you for her?" said Ikor. "Mistaken you for her. . ."

Peony turned to look at him, astonished. "I am Ikor," he said, and bowed. He had not bowed before; he had spoken to the others directly, and had knelt to his princess. But to Peony he bowed, a beautiful bow, no less graceful for the swing of the curved blade at his side. That will be how courtiers bow, thought Rosie, and, as Peony gave him a bemused little curtsy in return, she thought, and Peony curtsies like a lady, even if she's the niece of the wainwright.

And then Ikor had said, gesturing with the hand that did not rest on his sword hilt, "And this is Casta Albinia Allegra Dove Minerva Fidelia Aletta Blythe Domina Delicia Aurelia Grace Isabel Griselda Gwyneth Pearl Ruby Coral Lily Iris Briar-Rose . . . your princess."

Peony had gone pink and then white, and Rosie, both at the time and later in memory, had never understood why there had never been the least flicker of disbelief in her face. Peony heard and believed, and with a tiny "oh" she made her way through the seethe of animals and dropped down at Rosie's side; but poor Rosie slid off her chair and sat on the floor, her free hand clutching at Peony's free hand – the fox cub and Ralf showed signs of disagreeing with each other, and had to be held back – saying, "Don't kneel! Kind fates, Peony, Peony, *please* don't kneel!"

There was a clatter of hoofs outside, a heavy, purposeful clatter of ridden horses, and voices. Rosie knew one of the voices, one of the grooms from Woodwold. "They've come for Gorse and Fast," she said, and Ikor nodded, and the owl that had been sitting on a shelf over his head stepped off it on to his shoulder. Rosie could feel Ikor asking for volunteers among the other birds – he didn't exactly have beast-speech, but he was getting his point across – and there was a general rustle of reluctance among the smaller birds, and they were all smaller than the owl. *Fwab, you go*, said Rosie. *I'll watch out for you.*

Watch what out for me? said Fwab. From where you're standing you can just about watch my tail feathers disappearing down someone's gullet. But he gave his wings a flap, sat down again long enough to peck her scalp sharply for old time's sake, and flew to Ikor's shoulder, stuffing himself as well as he could under Ikor's ear.

Truce, said Rosie to the owl.

Truce, said the owl, amused. *I would not have come here were I looking for breakfast.*

There was an inaudible mutter from Fwab, but he poked his head a little further out from under Ikor's ear, so he could get a good view of whatever was going to happen next.

The owl swivelled his head, and looked straight at Rosie with his wild yellow eyes. *I stay to do you honour, princess. I sit on this man's shoulder because he says this will help you. You have a terrible enemy, princess. We feel her with this man, though he comes for good.*

"Forgive me, small one," said Ikor, "but an owl is so impressive," and between his thumb and forefinger appeared a small seed, which Fwab, after giving it a dubious look with his left eye and a brighter one with his right, plucked up delicately and swallowed. He was just swallowing his second seed when the groom Rosie knew appeared at the doorway, shaking a dripping hat.

"His lordship's compliments, but two of his lordship's horses have seen fit to bolt off here – Rosie, what on earth's up?" the groom added, gawping at the multitude; and then Ikor moved so as to catch his eye. The owl was very impressive, towering over him from its perch on his shoulder, the crown of its head brushing the ceiling; its pale tawny-grey colouring seemed meant to complement Ikor's own. "Forgive me," said Ikor. "I fear it is my fault." He said nothing more, but the groom looked at the owl, and watched Fwab accepting several more seeds from Ikor's fingers, and assumed – what Ikor meant him to assume.

Most of the rest of the mice had crawled up Rosie's trouser legs, and two or three down her waistcoat, now that she was so conveniently sitting on the floor (and she had her arm so firmly round Ralf's neck). Flinx was still purring, now pressed against Rosie's side (having quelled Ralf with one look), but there was another owl, two kestrels and a merlin, and other cats; and mice were always happiest in the dark, with a low ceiling. Rosie had to stifle a growing compulsion to laugh, mostly at the terrifying absurdity of her situation, but as if the small scritchiness of mouse feet and whiskers were the last straw; and she clung to Peony's hand (Peony, too, seemed to be having trouble with her breathing) and gulped at the bubbles of laughter.

"Indeed I was on my way to – hmm – ask an audience of his lordship when I was – hmm – when I chose to come here first. Perhaps you would be so kind as to give him a message that I will wait upon his convenience tomorrow morning?"

The groom had slapped his wet hat on his head again to answer this imposing stranger politely. A raindrop fell off the brim and ran down his nose; he sniffed involuntarily. "What name shall I say?"

"Ikor, Queen's Messenger."

Queen's Messenger. The animals murmured among themselves, and Rosie felt it against her skin like a draught, raising gooseflesh. She swallowed another bubble of frightened laughter, and hiccupped instead.

The groom's glance brightened at once, and he gave a crisp bow. "Sir," he said, and then the other groom appeared at his elbow and said aggrievedly, "They won't *budge*. I've got their bridles on and everything and they just clamp their jaws and stand there."

Rosie said hastily, *Go on, my friends. I'll see you tomorrow. I think.*

But the horses did not move; Rosie heard the groom muttering and wheedling. Gorse said, *There is something very wrong, Rosie, princess. We have tasted it on the air, long time past, we have smelt it coming closer, looking, looking for something, like a bully his lost whip, like a wolf his dinner, not just looking but desiring, craving, must-having. Long before this short now, when this strange man comes, and says that it is you it looks for, because of this thing you are, and it will become the whip in the hand of the bully when it touches you. We all fear this hand. We fear this man, who brings the smell, and the desiring, with him, although it is not in him; he carries it, like harness, and that which laid the harness on him is not far behind him.*

But you are ours, princess, you have been our friend, you have been our friend since before you learnt to speak to us, and – we may not like it, but we need human friends, because we have human enemies whether we will or nay. Now we hear what this man says as his words strike you like blows from a whip. You are the thing that brings the bully, the wickedness, here, but so also are you the thing that will drive this wickedness from our land. We understand this now, beyond his human words, for we have our own legends and our own losses. This man, with his fear and his wounds where the harness has rubbed him, cannot save you alone. We will not give you up to him, to humans. That is why we are here – why so many of us are here. We came before we heard what this man told you; we heard a thing coming – a big thing and a strong thing. And more of us come now that we hear the tale he is telling. Do you not understand?

Rosie said bemusedly, *Perhaps you understand better than I do. Humans talk so much. We do not see or hear or taste or feel or touch nearly so much as we talk. I am deaf and blind and dull with it, I think.*

The bigger the herd the safer, said Gorse. *We do not wish to go. Sip and Mally – those who carried the grooms here – will join us if we ask them. I can call every horse from my lord's lands, if you ask. There is not just one owl or one hawk in your big room – and they hunt alone – and there are mice and rabbits and small birds, in spite of them, who come also to you.*

No, said Rosie. *Go home. In this case the big herd only makes us visible, and we do not want to be visible. Go home. Please.*

Gorse tossed his head in irritation, and Fast bit a piece off the warped shutter and chewed it, clanking his bit and throwing splintery foam. There was a yelp of protest from one of the grooms. After a moment Gorse said, You are the princess. *We know what this means. You should have the biggest herd of all.*

Rosie said, *I don't want to be the princess*, and she could feel laughter and more tears both struggling to get out, and she hiccupped again.

Gorse said gently, *I did not want to be my lord's best stallion, to be led in front of men with cold eyes, to waste my time indoors so that I do not ruin the gloss of my coat, to be put to mares who do not know me nor I them. Fast did not wish to be able to run so that madmen would ask him to do it again and again and again. We are what we are. Some day I will no longer be able to mount the mares, and then I will have a little green paddock of my own with a few of my old mares who will no longer have foals, and I will stand in the sun till every hair of my coat is burnt dull dun. Some day Fast will no longer be able to run. We are what we are, princess.*

Rosie said at random, because she did not want to listen to what he was telling her, *Horses do not speak as you are speaking to me. You sound like the merrel.*

Gorse said, *We animals talk when we have need. This, now, what is happening, this is need for all of us. You do not expect a colt afraid of the blacksmith to tell you everything he knows; what need have you of it? It is only one colt, one fear, one blacksmith.*

Rosie said slowly, *Fwab told me once that we humans live too long.*

I do not know. Humans talk. It is the way humans are. Perhaps the talking fills the years; perhaps the years stretch to hold the talking. In winter I like the warmth of the barn humans have built us with some of the things they talk about, and the sweet hay, and the corn. The merrel tells stories because it is alone and lonely, and talk is all it has left, talk and memory. Come to me in my paddock, when I am old, and we will talk.

I – said Rosie, but she had nothing to say.

Tell us again to go, and we will go, said Gorse. *But remember who you are. And that if you have need of us, you must ask.*

I will remember, said Rosie. Her hiccups were gone. *Go. And I will come to you in your paddock, when you are old. We will come through this time, because I want to see you sunburnt and dusty.*

She stirred, and found Ikor watching her. "I believe your horses will go with you now," he said, and Rosie smiled faintly as the grooms bowed to him respectfully and disappeared from the doorway. There was a subdued tap of hoofs, and a faint smoky trail of disappointment from Fast, who had hoped for action, hoped for an enemy to trample or to outrun. *I will remember what Gorse says,* she said to his fading presence. *Remember I am not old yet!* Fast replied.

"Quickly now," said Ikor. "Close the doors and windows!"

Rosie, looking round, realized that she had been half aware that the beasts had been spreading through the house and finding places to settle down, for the night, for the companionship, for the news, to be near her, and (in many cases) out of sight of the villagers; and somehow Ikor had put this to them as well, that there was some last virtue in secrecy till they decided what they would do; this night, they were going to decide. And so there was a kind of patchwork quilt or carpet or drugget of animals upstairs and down, several sheep and a badger in Jem and Gilly and Gable's room and a goat and twin kids in Katriona and Barder's with a few geese; a small heifer and six otters, two hedgehogs and a dozen voles in Rosie's; a fawn and its mum at the top of the stairs, and a stag, antlers conveniently shed only a few days before, at the bottom, rabbits on the landing, and a small bear in the shed with Poppy and Fiend and the chickens; and birds and mice (including a few sleepy dormice tucked behind the shutters) and cats and three dogs, several half-grown piglets, and a fox cub in the kitchen. Most of the robins were in Aunt's lap, and Flinx was now in Katriona's. The owl on Ikor's shoulder had returned to its shelf, but Fwab had half tucked his head under his wing and was pretending to doze on Ikor's shoulder, a pretence belied by the quiver that went through him every time Ikor gestured with the seed-producing hand.

They had talked all night. Rosie could remember how long a night it had been, and yet how surprised she was when she saw dawn leaking through the cracks in the shutters, as if dawn was not going to come again until they had met Pernicia and defeated her, or she them. Rosie had to keep jerking herself back from thinking it was all a long pitiless dream: Ikor, the news he brought, the news that Pernicia was not merely their country's problem, like a drought or an invasion of taralians, but their problem, *her* problem, her own particular enemy who knew her name and sought her life – her, hers, Rosie's, because she was a princess and not Katriona's cousin and Aunt's niece, which she could not forget, because Pernicia would not, and because she had promised Gorse she would remember who she was.

Nor had she ever been surrounded by so many and different animals all intent on the same business – her business – before; and the churn and roil of remarks and opinions (and requests for repeats of what had just been said: Rosie was by far the best human translator, or conduit, and Aunt's robins, who were fluent with Aunt, tended all to talk at once) made Rosie dizzy. And so she missed some of Ikor's description of the last year, of how everyone close to the king and queen sensed that what they had been waiting for, and dreading, and hoping to avert, had not been averted at all (unless they could take some credit for the last twenty-one years) and was approaching the culmination it had always been moving towards.

"The magicians and we fairies had it the strongest, of course, but even the scullery maids and the stable lads could feel it advancing, like a bad storm makes the hair on the back of your neck prickle.

"And so we had to find you first, for if she met you, touched you, grasped you, before we did – well – there would have been nothing left we could have done to stop her. "

Rosie remembered the voice in her head: *Found!* But she did not want to tell anyone about it – especially not Ikor; and she had a fuzzy sense that describing it aloud would make it more real, and she did not want it to be real.

" You truly didn't know where we were," said Katriona.

"No," said Ikor. "That was Sigil's decision, although I agreed with it. Knowing leaves marks, however faint. We would have liked no marks at all, but Sigil had to speak to you, and you had to take the princess away from the place where . . . from the name-day. But at least those were the faintest of traces, and we did what we could to confuse them. If we had known in what direction to channel our thoughts – or even what direction *not* to channel them – No. That would have brought disaster, not safety. The royal magicians, of course, did not agree, but they could do nothing about it." He made a faint dry huffing noise that was almost a laugh. "Sigil had made up her mind." He paused and the humour left him. "There has never been any consensus among us on whether the curse could have been . . . brought off . . . early; Sigil and I both believe that even if it could not, Pernicia would have enjoyed . . . having the princess under her hand . . . before she closed her fist."

"How did you find us?" said Aunt.

"I followed the track my amulet had left, one-and-twenty years ago. Oh yes, it was a very pale and faded track indeed! But I could follow it, and perhaps, no-one else could, since Pernicia never found you. It was why I was chosen for the journey, although" — there was another brief pause — "I would have vied to be chosen anyway. But my . . . situation . . . was also uniquely persuasive; the forgotten godparent who had nonetheless inadvertently given . . . something."

Rosie could feel his eyes on her, but she kept hers resolutely on the floor. She was still periodically shaken by deep tremors, and had chosen to sit on the hearth, with her back to the fire; her shirt was so hot that sometimes when she moved and it touched her skin it burned, and she jerked where she sat, but she did not move away. Some of the younger animals were falling asleep. The fawn on the landing had stopped saying *But I don't understand*, and the kids in Katriona's bedroom had stopped saying *But why would anyone want to do that?* and various other little ones had stopped saying *But that's so mean. Why is she so mean?* Ralf had curled up, nose under tail, and gone to sleep in her lap; Peony sat next to her, a little way along from the intensest heat of the fire, but they were still holding hands. The fox cub, also asleep, had his nose under Peony's elbow, and his long fuzzy cub's brush drooped over her knees. Katriona kept glancing at them, as if to reassure herself that they — or at least Rosie — was still there; Rosie would meet her eyes when she felt her looking, but not Ikor's .

Her mind wandered again, thinking of the embroidery spell. It would have been one of the gifts from her fairy godmothers, she thought. She remembered that there had been fairy godmothers, and that Katriona had not thought highly of them, although she couldn't remember ever having heard what the gifts were. If they were things like embroidery, no wonder Katriona hadn't been very impressed. What else could she do? Darn like the wind? Spin straw into gold? She caught her breath suddenly: My awful, horrible hair. princess's hair! Golden curls! I wonder – ? She glanced sidelong at Peony's long golden waves; yes, but they suit her, she thought. She put one hand up to her head and gave her hated hair a yank. It was quite firmly hers, whether it should have been or not.

I wonder what Ikor would have given the prin— me?

"— when Rowland disappeared, that's when we really began to

worry," Ikor was saying, and Rosie felt the shiver run through Peony at his name. Rosie saw "Rowland" shape itself on her lips, but she did not speak aloud. What had a blacksmith's apprentice to do with anything – even a good blacksmith's apprentice? It couldn't be the same Rowland. Even a good blacksmith's apprentice with a funny vow in his family that would stop him marrying the girl he loved. . .

"Cold iron," said Aunt thoughtfully. "I have thought there was something odd about that boy, but I was so sure there was nothing wrong with him I was willing to let it – and him – be. There has been so much going on this year. . . "

" Yes," said Ikor. "Cold iron. We knew when he disappeared that he must have gone as a blacksmith – the irony of it (if you will forgive the term) is that it had been my suggestion that he take up smithing, because of the vow. He was of apprenticeable age, and his father came to us for advice. You know that every heir-prince of Erlion makes a vow on his tenth birthday? Of course he knew the story of our princess, but there was no guessing. . . The vows usually run along the same lines, dedication to the princedom and to the realm, and so on and on. It's been more of a form than a vow for generations – but the power's still there, which is one of the reasons that the Erlion princes are such good friends to our monarchs. Young Rowland thought he would do something a bit grand; although my impression of the boy was that he wasn't thinking about the grandness of it so much as of the poor lonely princess with no friends, and no-one, presumably, willing to marry her, which would be a terrible thing for a future queen.

"Rowland shouted it right out at the ceremony. No-one had thought to ask him what he was going to say because they assumed he would say what his father and his grandfather and his great-grandfather had said. His poor father, when he came to us, said that he had remembered to ask Rowland if he had got the words of his vow by heart, and Rowland had said that he had, but his father hadn't asked what those words were: he wanted Rowland to know that his father trusted him not to make a mess of it. And there we were.

"So, since the Erlions always apprentice their children – they think it builds character – I suggested that he learn to work iron. By the time old Erlion got back to his palace, there'd been a hippogriff seen, and he'd set out to us the day after the ceremony which was, for a mercy, private, so at least we managed to block up most of the gossip. He found a smith to accept the boy at once; and fortunately Rowland took to the work. All that iron was the best warding charm we could have come up with, and – it left no track to follow. Including, of course, for us, when he disappeared, most of a year ago. Didn't that cause an uproar! Maybe worse even than the ceremony of the heir's vow. Because we all knew that the likelihood was that wherever he thought he was going, and for whatever reason, the power of the vow would pull him to the princess."

Peony was shivering uncontrollably now. Rosie, half stupid with her own troubles and half grateful for the distraction of someone whose troubles might be even more oppressive than her own, put an arm round her. Ralf grunted and stretched in his sleep, laying his head on the fox cub's back as if there had never been any thought of dispute between them. The fox cub opened one eye and closed it again. Peony put her face against Rosie's shoulder, and Rosie felt a few tears damp through the cloth to her skin.

". . .so I wasn't very surprised when I picked up Rowland's trace, too, the moment I reached Foggy Bottom. My princess," he said, turning to Rosie, and obviously having to make an effort not to drag her up off the low hearth or prostrate himself at her feet, "I suppose you have met Rowland?"

A brief desire to laugh washed through Rosie again, making her feel rather sick. She had felt too many things in too short a space of time. "I know him," she said. "I suppose I know him rather well, since I often work with him. I'm the horse-leech here. The blacksmith, Narl, that Rowland has apprenticed himself to, is – was also my master, and is one of my best friends."

Ikor looked at her, and Rosie could guess that he was trying to decide how to phrase his next question. "Are you aware of any – connection between you?"

Peony was holding herself so rigidly she felt like iron herself, except she was warm. Rosie tightened her arm round her and said, firmly and truthfully, "No. I – er – we have nothing to say to each other. He likes – pays attention to animals, and his manners are very nice. That's all." She tried to think of something to say that would comfort Peony, but nothing came to her. "He is very clever with iron. Narl enjoys teaching him."

"You need not marry him if you do not wish to," said Ikor. "We've studied that for the last eleven years and – with both of you present and willing – we can dismantle the bond."

"Well isn't that grand news," spat Katriona. "Better than strawberries in January. That's the sort of announcement I would expect out of a magician, not a fairy. Ikor, what are we going to do *now*?"

There was a silence, and it grew upon Rosie that she knew what Ikor was going to say, knew what was in Ikor's mind, what had been forming in his mind since Peony had first looked through the door with the fox cub in her arms.

No, she thought. No. I'll run away first. If I run away, it – they – she – will come after me, and it'll leave everybody else alone. But even as she thought this she knew it wasn't true. She knew it was not just the princess's life – her life – at stake. She'd known that when she was still just Rosie, village horse-leech, who, when she thought of the princess, pitied her, for carrying a doom that stretched over her entire country.

Peony sat up, and released her grip on Rosie's free hand. "Yes," she said. "Yes, of course I will."

"You will what?" said Ikor softly.

"Ikor—" began Rosie, furiously.

"Rosie, no," said Peony. "It's my idea. I don't say he wouldn't have tried to give it to me if it weren't, but he didn't have to." She turned back to Ikor. "I'll be your princess for you. I'll be the princess everyone looks at while you and Rosie do – do whatever it is you have to do. That's what you want to ask me, isn't it? But you will have to teach me how. I don't know any more about being a princess than – than Rosie does."

"Peony—" began Rosie again.

Peony turned to her swiftly. "It's all right," she said, patting Rosie's hand. "It's all right."

They looked into each other's eyes for a moment. Peony's were blue and clear and steady, as they always were. Rosie groped for some concept of how Peony could accept such a burden. "Can you – can you do it for Rowland?" she said at last.

"For your country and your queen," said Ikor.

Peony gave a squeak, halfway between a laugh and the sound someone makes when they've closed their fingers in a door. "No, I can't do it for Rowland, or – or for my country and my – my queen. But I'll do it for you, Rosie."

Chapter 17

Ikor returned from his interview with the Gig's lord, on the day after his storm-escorted arrival in Foggy Bottom, with the information that the princess and her lady would remove, and welcome, to Woodwold, and the sooner the better; let us say – tomorrow. Lord Prendergast was insisting on sending his best travelling carriage.

The news went like wildfire round the Gig; Ikor made no attempt to disguise himself, nor his presence at the wrights' yard, nor the reason for it. "We have nothing to spare for such minor glamours," he said, grimly, when he set off the morning after his arrival for his appointment with Lord Prendergast. "It is better to say – what we are saying – at once." And so – according to the story that flew back to Cairngorm's pub faster than Ikor's feet could bring him – when the Queen's Messenger had been formally announced at the door of Woodwold's Great Hall, he gave his business in a cool voice that was nonetheless heard by everyone in the huge room: "I come, Lord Prendergast, to crave the favour of your hospitality for our princess, the king's heir, who is free at last from her long concealment." In the hush that followed, Lord Prendergast was the first to move, stepping forward to indicate to the Messenger a smaller room where they could speak privately. He had a dazed expression on his face, but his manners, and his loyalty to the king and the king's heir, were perfectly in place.

There was a crowd gathered round the wrights' yard by the time Ikor returned (having refused the lord's carriage for himself), to congratulate, to stare, to wonder, to question. Barder and Joeb and Cantrab were trying to get on with business, though their hands were slow, and they shook their heads a lot – not only in response to their neighbours' remarks.

The women were in the wheelwright's kitchen. Aunt was spinning, soft *thump thump thump* and even softer *whrrrrr*, as if it might have been any morning of any day. Katriona was brewing a serenity-restoring tisane. Peony, her colour very high, was trying to comfort her aunt, who was weeping, Rosie thought, in bewilderment, because she didn't know what she should be doing; Rosie recognized this in another because she felt that way herself, although she shed no tears. But Rosie felt something beyond bewilderment: she felt trapped. Trapped, suddenly, by the people she had known all her life. But now they were the audience, and she – she and Peony – were the spectacle.

Jem and Gilly were trying to play on the kitchen floor, but their hearts weren't in it. Gable, the most equable of babies, was inclined to fuss; Rosie picked him up and began to play pat-a-cake with him, less to soothe him than herself. She went on playing pat-a-cake even as Ikor told them they were leaving the next day; but still the message passed through her, and she heard the mice in the walls taking it up, and a few minutes later Zogdob howled, a long, despairing wail: only Rosie really understood about scratching a dog's spine properly, and she was going away. I wish I could howl, Rosie thought.

It was Peony who managed to laugh a little, to say "I don't know – I don't know anything," to kiss proffered cheeks and squeeze proffered hands, when the princess and her lady were briskly escorted from the smaller prison of the wrights' yard into the travelling carriage that would take them to the larger prison of Woodwold. Rosie stared round dumbly, registering both curiosity and a sort of shocked reverence – and, on a few faces, pity – in those who had come to see them off; only Flora came boldly up to her and gave her an immense hug and then a shake, murmuring, as if to a small child, "It's all right. Rosie, it's *all right*," and Rosie willed herself to smile. Even Fwab, materializing from nowhere, pecking her scalp and tweaking her ears, could rouse only a minimal hand flap to dislodge him.

Rosie had never ridden in a carriage before; she didn't like it. It had a roof, and a closed door, and it was a prison, too, and the wheels and the horses' hoofs said *gone gone gone* and *lost lost lost*. It was a low, foggy, overcast day, and cloud-streamers drifted by the carriage window – Lord Pren's best carriage had windows made of clear glass. Rosie tapped her finger on it: it was cold and damp.

She was accustomed to the tiny, disturbing jolt as you passed the iron gates into Woodwold's lands, but it was much stronger the day that the princess and her lady arrived, and Peony, who only knew Woodwold from feast days, had a little "Oh!" of vertigo startled out of her. Rosie thought she felt Woodwold stir; and she felt it stir again, more urgently, when they crossed the threshold of the Great Hall. Rosie, without meaning to, in a gesture rather like rubbing the nose of the gargoyle spindle end, or picking up a baby to play pat-a-cake with, called out, *Merrel?*

Princess, it replied, in a way that gave and included the name she thought of as her own, *Rosie*, and Woodwold, somehow, heard it, took it in, grasped it or swallowed it. Felt it. And responded. *Prinnncessss*, it said. *Rooosie*.

It was a hearing like no other Rosie had ever experienced, as if trees and stones had spoken. For a moment she could not move, as if, by hearing something speak that did not breathe nor have voice nor move, she herself was robbed of all these things; and another world blossomed round her, a world in which a human could not live. But then the floor rippled under her feet, a tiny ripple, no more than the lightest suggestion of motion, and she staggered on her two human legs, and came to herself again, and she looked round, and thought no-one had heard what she heard, nor, perhaps, felt what she had felt.

And then Lord Prendergast himself was coming towards them, and she and Peony both swept into their best curtsies (Rosie's much more like a bow with a little angular twitch of skirts), and were horrified to find the lord's hands on their wrists, drawing them upright. "It is I who must bow to you," he said, and did so, and then he looked into their white faces and said, both solemn and teasing, as if they were merely two more of his daughters, "You must learn now, you know. It will not do if you bow to your own courtiers."

"Yes, my lord," said Peony faintly, and then Lord Pren turned to introduce them to his wife, seizing them again by their wrists while she made her curtsy. But Rosie was preoccupied with a deep, deep note, like the last resonance of a drum, which you cannot hear, but only feel in your body, which was Woodwold repeating, *Rosie. Princess.* The floor shivered again, not quite imperceptibly.

"I apologize for the—er—floor," said Lord Pren, looking awkward for the first time. "This house has sheltered my family for all the centuries it has stood here, and its loyalty is perhaps – er – tangible. We do most sincerely welcome you here, and we will do all in our power to make you comfortable, but – and – I suppose it has been over a hundred years since we have greeted royalty in this Hall, and perhaps – er – the house is remembering that you – er – merit a special respect – greater than your humble servants the Prendergasts. But – I have to say – Woodwold itself is a trifle – er – inscrutable – if that's a word you can use on a – er – house."

He fell silent, and they all heard the guest cups rattling on the table, and Lady Pren made a graceful pounce at the wine ewer, which was standing a little too near the edge. "It – er – its reactions are not generally this pronounced," he added, frowning slightly, in puzzlement or wonder, and Rosie recollected a favourite Gig rumour that the Prendergasts never went to court because if they left Woodwold for any time greater than the length of a hunting trip into the mountains beyond the river, it would pull itself out of the ground and go striding over the countryside after them. "But then perhaps it has never had the glorious opportunity to be the first to greet an heir-princess taking her proper station after long concealment," and again he bowed. Peony drew closer to Rosie, and tucked her hand under her arm.

But Woodwold quieted at his words, as if they had been the acknowledgement it wished or needed; and after a minute or two

Lady Pren began to pour. But Rosie, as she sipped the weak sweetened wine, felt an alertness round her that had not been here any of the times she had come before, and she went on feeling it, some not-quite-inanimate something watching for some enemy, fretfully aware, as no human in the house seemed to be, of some deception performed under its roof, even if the floor no longer shuddered. Rosie hoped that no-one else heard its abyssal whispers, *Princess. Rosie.* Or that if anyone did, they would not realize that only one person was being named.

The princess and her unlikely lady-in-waiting were installed at Woodwold at the top of a tower that stood at the peak of a kind of culminating swirl – you couldn't call it a corner, Rosie thought – of wall. Woodwold's many ells and additions followed their own logic through half or one-and-a-half flights up and down and precipitate twists and confusing passages and unexpected alcoves, and ceilings that swooped towards you and then just as suddenly flew up into domes and peaks. Their tower rooms, two above and two below with a stair between, were small by Woodwold's standards but big by Foggy Bottom's; their bedroom, one of the upper two rooms, was as big as any of the village cottages' entire downstairs floor. The room opposite was a parlour, and below there was an honest-to-goodness bathroom, with shining, well-rubbed piping Rosie might have found fascinating in other circumstances, and a dressing room; and opposite it (over a little hallway for privacy) was a room for guards and chaperones and the kind of paraphernalia they accrued. From the lower pair of rooms a wriggle of wedge-shaped stairs led down into the main body of the house.

Ikor hung his sabre, Eskwa, over the lintel of the door frame into their bedroom. "Eskwa both binds and cuts," Ikor told Rosie. "If you have need of either, he will answer to your hand."

The Prendergasts had been told that the princess and her lady would prefer to share a room for the sake of their own comfort and reassurance; and the Prendergasts, who had six children of their own and were very tender to the young women suddenly thrust upon them, found this not in the least odd. "After a shock like that poor girl has had, I should think she'd want her best friend by her side," said Lady Pren. That was true enough, even if not as Lady Pren understood it.

"I'm sorry, R – my princess," Ikor had said, upon returning from that first interview with the lord and his lady, and who, after less than a day in Rosie's blunt and matter-of-fact company, was showing signs of finding it as impossible to call her by her title as she found accepting it. "And Peony. But you must be bound together as tightly as we can bind you; and you cannot leave Woodwold till after the princess' birthday. Do you understand?"

They understood. They had understood even before Katriona told them it would not work if they weren't friends already. "Not just friends: if you hadn't already left deep marks on each other's lives. Peony, do you know that you have Rosie's gesture of running your hand through your hair? You didn't when we first moved here. And Rosie, you've picked up the head shake Peony uses to settle her hair back into place again, which you never used to do when we lived in the cottage – and when you haven't got hair to settle in place besides. You finish each other's sentences half the time – or sometimes, if you think no-one else is listening, you don't bother to finish them because you both know what you were going to say. If one of the rest of us needs to know, we have to ask. That fox cub wasn't so far wrong when he jumped into your arms, Peony, instead of braving the menagerie in our house. He knew you were – you were part of the same thing." They had been sitting at the hearth in the wheelwright's kitchen; it was evening. The name-day ribbons and rosettes were spread out on the table; they were still crumpled from their twenty-year-old journey at the bottom of Katriona's pocket, but were only a little faded, and they looked like what they were: ornamental badges from some royal rite. Rosie and Peony were to be escorted to Woodwold the following morning.

And Rosie and Peony knew, in a way they discussed with no-one else and did not need to discuss with each other, that the deception would not have worked if they had not already been such friends, if they had not already known so much about each other that each fitted instinctively to the shape of the other's habits, customs, life. They would not have been able to bear the further binding that Ikor now settled round them, that Eskwa oversaw from the lintel of their bedroom at Woodwold. It was not merely that they were rarely out of each other's sight now, never further than a room or a dividing wall distant; it was that they could feel the – the – the whatever it was, the magic, the magic that had drawn Rowland to Foggy Bottom and Ikor after him, the magic that was now rushing them all towards the princess' one-and-twentieth birthday.

They could feel Ikor plucking at the bond between them, taking tucks in it as one might take tucks in a dress passed from a bigger owner to a smaller, or as one pulls the unworn edges of sheet together and creates a new centre seam. Rosie began to feel that neither she nor Peony alone was quite real. When Peony smiled, her own lips turned up; when Peony waved her arm in the air, a ghost-shadow flew between her arm and Rosie's. As the weeks passed, Rosie saw more and more of these ghost-shadows; and she felt some kind of resonance between them and the heavy inaudible mutter of the house that sheltered and shadowed them. She felt as if her flesh, her self, were thinning, dissolving, like honey stirred into water, dissolving into the strange air of Woodwold, and into the passionate awareness of the presence of the princess in the people round the two of them.

It did not try their friendship; curiously, it made them cling to each other, for the knowledge of each other's solidity was the greatest comfort against ghosts. Katriona and Aunt spent as much time as either could spare with them, for the companionship of a third broke up the ghost-shadows as sunlight breaks up real ones, and Aunt and Katriona had long been known and welcome at Woodwold. Ikor, seemingly, could not find a way to settle in their company – perhaps since, once they had removed to Woodwold, he was very careful to address Peony as "princess" and Rosie as "lady" – and he was mostly as reticent as any of the awestruck servants of Woodwold were. But Katriona and Aunt and Ikor really had no time to spare, and mostly Rosie and Peony were alone together in the consciousness of what they did and who they were.

During those three months of zealous human preparation Woodwold remained restlessly half roused; Rosie felt its awareness following her through the corridors, up and down the stairs; sometimes she felt a quiver like an animal's skin when she touched a wall or a latch with her bare hand. She tried to say to it, *Sleep, sleep. I am nothing to you*, but she knew it did not heed her. And, on the night before the princess' birthday, with all the animals silent, Rosie could hear the murmur of Woodwold in the creaks of great beams and vast rock-slabs infinitesimally shifting against each other, and the nearly noiseless accumulation of dust: *Rosie*, it said. *Rosie*.

It's only the last name of the princess, Rosie said to herself. It's a house, even if it is big enough to be its own country. Houses don't memorize long human names – any more than I do, she thought, a little wistfully. Peony can remember it all, but I can't. The – the syllables I seem to hear are nothing but – a sort of draught, with a puff at the end that sounds like the name of – the name of a flower, or of a princess. It's nothing. It's a current of air.

She stared out at the clouded landscape, drawing swirls with her finger through the faint haze of chalky powder on the windowsill. The room was swept and dusted twice a day, but nothing could keep the princess' bedroom clean – although no-one but the conspirators thought this was anything more ominous than every fairy and magician in the country sending her their best wishes. And perhaps the persistence of the spiderweb in the upper left corner of Rosie's favourite window had something to do with the room being the top of a tower, and, until three months ago, little used. Rosie saw the spider often; it usually emerged from its corner when Rosie curled up on the seat and put her elbows on the sill to look out. In the absence of her usual animal companions, she had come to think of it as company, though it never spoke to her.

Rosie , muttered the rafters. *Rosie*, whispered the roof tiles.

The stories about Woodwold, which for many generations had

interested no-one but scholars and the citizens of the Gig, had been brought out of the backs of people's minds; except that there were so many gaps there was very little story after all (discounting, in the cause of temperate truth, the more elaborate flights of the Gig's bards), except that it was an odd old house, one of the largest and oldest and perhaps the oddest in the entire country, and it lay very near the edge of nowhere, on the bank of the River Moan. Some tales could be told of the Prendergasts: that they were even older than their house, that their forefathers and foremothers, fore-aunts and fore-uncles, had come to their ruler's call whenever their ruler had had need of them; they had stood by the queen when she foiled Pernicia the first time; they had fought at the side of the king when he drove the fire-wyrms out of the Gig. It was half remembered, half believed that it was at that time that the Prendergasts had fallen in love with the Gig and had decided to stay there, and that it was in thanks for their valour against the fire-wyrms that the king had deeded it to them.

There was a crumb of a story about why Woodwold had been founded where it had; something to do with a seer's vision. Forecasters' visions were the least reliable of the practical magics, and the longer-term a forecast the less reliable; few people would choose to build a house from something a seer had said. But the crumb of story insisted that the seer had been a member of the Prendergasts himself, which was curious, since seeing, however useless, required very strong magic, and the Prendergasts were not a magical family. Perhaps they had been, and it had left them over the generations.

There were no recent stories of the Prendergasts, unless you were horse-mad. The odd, damp little bit of country under their stewardship did, it was true, prosper, but fine hides and wool and weaving and ironmongery and carved spindle ends – and horses – did not make interesting stories.

People said, I wonder what the princes will make of their elder sister?

Everyone said, What shall we make of our future queen?

*

Ikor had removed to Woodwold with the princess; as a stranger to the Gig and a member of the royal court (and, perhaps, as a negligent wearer of naked sabres) he had an authority that the humans of Woodwold were glad to rely on (the animals were less impressed, and, Rosie feared, the house failed to notice at all). Aunt and Katriona remained – except for too-infrequent visits – in Foggy Bottom, and tried to seem no more and no differently distressed than Peony's aunt and uncle.

Peony's aunt and uncle were in considerable confusion of mind, waking, as they now believed themselves to be, from a long dream, in which Peony had been their niece. Their only sorrow now was that they could not quite remember how it had come about that they had been so astonishingly chosen to raise the secret princess. They felt they had the vaguest wisp of memory of someone, a fairy or a magician ("magician, I think," said Hroslinga. "Wasn't he tall, solemn, and dressed all in black?"), giving them a child to be raised as their niece: ("I remember him telling us he had to make us forget his visit," said Hroslinga. "I remember his hand coming towards my forehead to rub out the memory. I *do*.") "We always knew we were ordinary," said Crantab, "but we didn't know we were *perfectly* ordinary!" He loved his joke so much he had to tell it several times a day, but people were inclined to be indulgent to the man who had raised the princess, and went on laughing at it to please him. Crantab and Hroslinga were happy not to be called up to Woodwold; they were happy to leave all that to Katriona and Aunt, and to the mesmerizing and rather scary Ikor.

But Hroslinga, one day, having told the story of the black-robed magician all over again for the dozenth time to Katriona (the story, with a little help, was becoming ever more interestingly detailed – "Although, by the fates, she doesn't need much help," Katriona said to Aunt), said something else. They had been folding sheets together, and remembering that this had been one of the jobs Rosie and Peony had done. A silence had fallen as Katriona tucked little sprigs of lavender between the folds, and gathered up Hroslinga's sheets to hand to her, and Hroslinga, musingly, as she accepted the bundle, said, "It is a great relief to me now, to know that she isn't my own kin. I was never as fond of her as I knew I should be; and this has troubled me all her life."

She was too deep in her own thoughts to see how Katriona's hands shook as Hroslinga accepted the weight of the sheets; and she had no way of knowing that Katriona shut herself up as soon as she left, so she could burst into tears without anyone knowing. When she came out again a few minutes later, wiping her eyes, she went out into the yard, where her three children were playing under Barder's preoccupied but probably watchful enough eye, and hugged them all fiercely in turn ("Oh, *Mum*," said Jem disgustedly). She never told anyone what Hroslinga had said, not even Aunt or Barder, and, contrary to all her usual scruples, laid a mild enchantment on Hroslinga, that she might never say it again.

The other Gig fairies were pressed into service to the princess, too, but theirs was a different sort of service; they were to keep the bounds beaten, the bounds of the Gig, against . . . whatever might seek entry that was not welcome. Such was the disturbance round the revealing of the princess that there was a terrific amount of magical activity all over the Gig, and bounds-beating under these conditions was more than plenty to prevent any fairy having time or energy to be inquisitive about what another was up to, or to wonder if the two best fairies in the Gig didn't seem a little too weary and anxious and preoccupied when all they should be doing that was any different from what any of the rest of the Gig fairies were doing was missing their cousin-niece who was being well taken care of by that very odd but unmistakably magisterial Ikor, up at Woodwold with the princess.

It wasn't as though the bounds had to be held against anything – or anyone – in particular; it was just a general policing activity, although very trying. The entire Gig was drawing the sort of mostly minor but vexing magical disruptions that fairy houses did, but expanded for its greater dimensions: dja vines, instead of growing the length of an arm, grew the height of a tall man overnight; there were clouds of butterflies, wearing little frilly dresses made of primroses and hats of lily-of-the-valley (which was disconcerting in midwinter); door latches became oracular, so you could not go in and out of your own front door without being told (in sepulchral tones) what your next sennight was going to be like (fortunately the predictions were usually wrong); and three stremcopuses had been seen. Stremcopuses rarely came so far north, and never at this time of year; the winter winds made their twiggy arms die back at the tips.

Rowland had been the princess' first visitor, the very afternoon of the princess's arrival at Woodwold. He had appeared dressed like a blacksmith – if an unusually clean blacksmith – but he was unintimidated by the Great Hall as no blacksmith should be, and he carried himself not at all like a blacksmith. He also obviously assumed that he would see the princess. These things gave him away at once. The news of what, precisely, they gave him away as, tarried only a little behind the central tidings of the revelation of the princess herself. The story was, of course, exceedingly popular with everyone who heard it: the heir of Erlion who had vowed to marry the princess, and who, disguised as a blacksmith's apprentice, fell in love with the princess disguised as the niece of a wainwright. . .

Poor Peony had had only one caveat about her impersonation: "You cannot tell Rowland that I am the princess, that it is happily ever after for us," she had said, savagely: Peony who was never savage about anything. "For I am still the niece of a village wainwright, and he is the Heir-Prince of Erlion." Rowland, loyal subject of the king as well as Erlion's prince, kept whatever Ikor told him to himself; and perhaps only those who knew him well – Rosie among them – could read in his carefully composed face that happily ever after was not guaranteed.

Ikor, as tired and drawn as Aunt and Katriona and much more dour, once said to Rosie, "If he had met you anywhere but a smith's yard. . ."

He said it because his exhaustion was bearing him down till he hardly thought to remain standing beneath its weight till the princess' birthday; and the vow of the ten-year-old prince might have been another post to thrust under the sagging roof-tree of their artifice. But Rosie had her own fears and sorrows, and she could not stop herself from biting back at him: "Then he would have fallen in love with me? But he would not, you know. He might have found himself bound to me, yoked to me, like oxen in harness, but it would not have been love. Let them have what they have, because at least it is real, in all this . . . all this. . ."

Ikor fell on his knees beside her, which he never did now, not now that they were at Woodwold and Peony was the princess. "Forgive me," he said. "Forgive me."

"Don't be stupid," said Rosie; "if you don't get up at once I shall pull your ears. Hard. That's better. Look, doesn't it make – what you're doing – easier that Rowland is – is tied to Peony, not to me?"

Ikor rubbed his sleek and hairless head, as if checking that his ears remained unpulled. "Perhaps it does. Perhaps it does. It's just that all of this . . . all of this is wrong."

Rosie smiled a little. "I'm glad you think so, too," she said, daring him to protest that the wrongness that troubled him was not the same as that which troubled her. But he knew Rosie a little by now, and did not rise to the bait. "Yes," she went on, "like nobbling a horse, so he will lose a race he should have won; or possibly to put the buyer off, because you've decided you want to keep him."

Ikor gave her what Rosie called his not-the-princess look. "We want very much to – er – put this buyer off."

"We shall," said Rosie, trying to be encouraging. "We shall because we must. And I'm very stubborn, you know." But the not-the- princess look metamorphosed into another look, one that she liked much less, and might have called the yes-the-princess look, except that she didn't want to call it anything. She looked thoughtfully at Ikor's ears.

Rosie had been sitting in the window embrasure in their bedroom during that conversation with Ikor, while Rowland was visiting his supposed betrothed in the tower parlour. The duty or the honour of chaperonage was left to Lady Prendergast. Mostly Rosie was alone during Rowland's visits, listening to the murmur of voices through the wall. And what she mostly did was think of Narl. She had never told Peony her feelings about Narl, even before Ikor had come; it was the first secret she had ever had from her. She did not weep – she had not wept since Ikor's first evening at Foggy Bottom – but when she remembered Narl her dry eyes burned, and her eyelids seemed to blink open and closed in hinged sections, like shutters. Narl had not come to Woodwold once in all the time the princess had been there; any smith's business had to be taken to him at the Foggy Bottom forge. Even Lord Pren's own personal request could not bring him. People shook their heads, but those who knew him were not surprised; Narl would hate the commotion that hung round everything to do with the princess, and the commotion began at Woodwold's gates.

Rosie had not seen him since the day of the storm. Her last words to him had been "Oh, bother, it's *sheeting*," as she prepared to run across the square to home and supper; she had not even said goodbye. And the last day and a half at what she still thought of as her home had been busy, horribly, chaotically busy. But he had not tried to see her either. Or Peony.

Rosie felt sometimes that her entire experience of Woodwold was contained in her favourite window-seat, with the friendly spider in the corner. She sat there so often: when Rowland and Peony were together, in the middle of the night when the dreams were particularly bad and Rosie feared to wake Peony with her thrashings and mumblings, when the two of them were allowed an interval of quiet before the next meeting with the most recently arrived courtiers (the trickle rising to a deluge as the princess's birthday approached, till even Woodwold grew nearly full), the next dinner party, the next fitting of the princess's ball gown. It was, perhaps, the only place in Woodwold where she could draw herself together and remember herself, think of herself, as Rosie; it was therefore the only time she felt quite real.

The people round the princess and her lady cosseted them as best they could; they were often sent back up to their tower for a rest (one of the Prendergast daughters, who tended to forget to be daunted by royalty, said that if they didn't spend half their lives climbing all those stairs they probably wouldn't be so tired in the first place), but neither of them had any gift for ladylike resting.

Peony sewed, asking for anything that needed hemming or mending to be sent up to her; there was outrage at this request at first, but, as Peony explained, she had been a country girl all her life, and she had learnt to like having something to do with her hands; and (untruthfully) that she did not care for the fussy work of embroidery. And so it was arranged, with Lady Pren, in distress, patting her collarbones with rapid little blows like a bird's wings fanning, and, when this was not enough to relieve her feelings, twisting her necklaces till Peony gently took her hands in her own, and said, "Dear Lady Pren" (no-one, to Rosie's knowledge, had ever called either the lord or the lady "Pren" to their faces, although everyone in the Gig used the nickname out of their hearing), "you will do this to please me, will you not?" And Lady Pren would.

Peony was good at moments like that. Under Peony's gentle despotism, the Prendergasts' housekeeper forebore to cast herself as the victim in a melodrama over the fact that it was impossible to keep the princess's rooms dust-free (and, even more important, did not take it out on her housemaids). The horribly snooty majordomo smiled when he saw her, and, after the first sennight, did so even before Peony smiled at him. The nasty old earl from Scarent, who had obviously come early for the princess's birthday so that he could work up a really thorough dislike of her first, had been won round in a few days. And the Prendergasts' first grandson, who was three years old and a monster, could be wheedled into good humour with the same tricks Peony had used on Katriona's children and all her little baby-magic boarders.

So Peony sewed, when they were in their bedroom alone together and it was not time to sleep (or to pretend to). At first Rosie sat with her hands pressed between her knees as if they might do something awful if she released them, even in the absence of embroidery silk. But one day when she was feeling as if she might burst from her own idleness, Barder arrived with a large lumpy parcel, which upon opening was half a dozen knobs of good cured wood, perfectly suited to the whittling of spindle ends.

"It wasn't me," he said. "I've been thinking you have enough on your plate. Narl sent them. He said you'd be getting bored." Barder accompanied Katriona to Woodwold when he could, "to see how you're getting on. We don't grow accustomed to your being gone from us, love, and nor do the littles, and specially not your creatures."

Rosie sighed. There were many worsts about life at Woodwold ; one of them was that it was, somehow, harder to talk to animals from the princess's tower than it had ever been from the wheelwright's yard or the smith's forge. Almost everyone in the animal world that Rosie knew was now strangely inarticulate, and creatures she had not met before were even worse. She also had the uncanny sense that everyone was deeply preoccupied with something else, so preoccupied that this was at least part explanation for why she found it difficult to have a conversation with them. It was the sort of preoccupation she was accustomed to when there were new babies at home; but she had always before known when it was that, and besides, for most everybody, it was the wrong time of year. But no-one would tell her what it was about, and grew even more inarticulate if she enquired.

There was the additional fact that the housekeeper had hysterics any time she found dog hair on the cushions or cat hair on the coverlet or the odd pinfeather on the carpet in their bedroom or parlour. Years ago Katriona had invented a charm that made animal hair leap off fabric as if stung and stick to the charm-bearer's brush, but Rosie couldn't ask her to make one now.

"I can tell Fwab from any other chaffinch, however far away he sits, for the drooping of him; and Flinx is hardly half the cat he was," Barder continued.

"*Flinx?*" said Rosie, astonished. "I'd've thought he'd be glad to be shut of me."

"You know cats better than that," said Katriona.

"Well. . ." said Rosie. "Flinx was so, you know, consistent."

"Consistency is the first thing you should be suspicious of in a cat," said Katriona, and was rewarded with one of Rosie's now-rare smiles, and felt her own face creak with weariness and worry as she smiled in response.

Fwab had tried to fly up to their tower window, and had succeeded, once or twice, but had had to admit that the protective spells were like a very bad headwind, and after the first week he did not try again. Rosie missed Fwab and Zogdob and Spear – and Flinx – nearly as much as she missed Narl; and perhaps Peony guessed this, for it was Peony, in the first days of their imprisonment, who had insisted on a tour through the stables every morning after breakfast. The Master of the Horse, although far more hesitantly and deferentially than before, still occasionally asked Rosie questions about this or that horse's mood or health, and she would have welcomed more such questions, but he did not seem to believe her when she told him this. But she did stop to rest her head against the head or shoulder of Gorse and of Fast every day. Gorse did not speak to her again as he had spoken the night that Ikor had come, but she felt a great warm solid understanding strength radiating from him, and she found herself relying on that minute every day when she stood next to him and felt it.

Fast showed her horse-pictures of vicious-faced women with teeth like wolves and claws like taralians falling under the trampling hoofs of valiant steeds who looked a lot like Fast, and whuffled the drooly remains of his breakfast down her lady-in-waiting frocks.

"How is Narl?" Rosie said, looking down, fondling a burl.

Barder gave a short laugh. "Who knows? He's still smithing. I hadn't realized that he'd got chatty with you around, Rosie, till you're no longer around and he's stopped. I don't think he says a word from one end of a sennight to the other; there's a joke that he won't take a stranger's horse because he'd have to tell 'em what the fee is." He paused. "Last time I spoke to him – I mean last time he spoke to me – was to ask if I had any burls to spare, that I should bring you a few to keep your hands busy."

The weeks crawled by. Astonishing numbers of sheets had been hemmed, or taken ends-to-middles and resewn; table linens had never been in such order since the Prendergasts had first swept the reeds off the floors and bought plates instead of trenchers and began using table linen. And a great many tiny rents and puckers and misdone previous patches in all the Prendergast daughters' wardrobes had been mended, because Peony had become friends with Callin, the Prendergast daughter who had made the remark about the number of stairs to the tower.

" You would think that the princess would have more to do than anyone; and yet all it is is waiting and *waiting*," said Rosie. She was down to her last spindle end. This one was her favourite. She had recognized it at once, as she rubbed her fingers over each of them in turn, deciding which one to do first; and so she had saved it till last.

But the spindle end, her best spindle end, was not going well. It was not that Rosie's knife slipped, nor that she could not see what her line was; but that the line, once seen, was not what it should be; and she kept turning the wood over in her hands, looking for the real way in to the spindle end she was sure she saw there. To give herself more time to think she had already finished the spindle itself; in her frustration she had cut it almost too thin – almost thinner than the finger of a three-month-old baby. Delicately she touched the tip of it with her forefinger. Nothing happened.

Rosie held the half-shaped wood in her hands for a moment and then looked up, across to Peony still bent over her needle, and let her eyes drift out of focus, trying to see the real princess. She hung between them murkily, not there but not quite not-there; and then Rosie picked up her knife again and began to chip at a fresh surface. This would be the princess' own spindle end. It would be an oval human face with a wide forehead and a round chin, like both Rosie's and Peony's, and curling hair, longer than Rosie's but shorter than Peony's, and a faintly smiling mouth wider than Peony's but narrower than Rosie's, a nose less delicate than Peony's but less blocky than Rosie's .

The princess' face had seemed to leap out of the wood at her, once she had seen her, and she had found it difficult to tear herself away from it, as if making it was important, and not merely a way of getting through some empty hours.

*

She turned away from the window now, and the comfortless, catless view, and picked up that last spindle end. It was too dark to see it, and Rosie did not wish to light a lamp; there would be lit lamps enough tomorrow night, during the ball, and she wanted to remember the darkness. She wanted to remember herself standing in quiet darkness, alone, with nothing but her thoughts for company, and the soft sound of Peony's sleeping breath.

The spindle end felt heavy, cupped in her hands; her thumbs found the wide-open, long-lashed eyes, the gentle rise of the nose, the smiling mouth, the tiny ridged roughness of the coiling hair. She had only just finished it that afternoon; every time she had looked at it, there had been one more detail to put right, and one more and one more. It had drawn her on till she had done all she knew or could guess to do; and she thought, This is the spindle end I would have given Peony when she came back from her season in Smoke River. I wonder what I would have told her it was?

Whatever happened, tomorrow night, her world would be changed utterly and for ever. During these last three months . . . at any moment, she almost felt, she might still have thrown off the frocks she had now to wear as the princess' lady-in-waiting, and run back to Foggy Bottom, and begged Narl to take her back. That she knew this was an illusion didn't make it any less alluring, because at some level it was still a tiny bit true – and her bound and caged will yearned at the crack between those bars that would not let it free. These three months were merely preparation, however tense and troubling; tomorrow was the day when the irrevocable change came. Tomorrow. The princess' birthday. Her birthday.

She knew what was supposed to happen. There would be – despite all the protective spells to the contrary – a spinning wheel and a sharp spindle end that the princess would be impelled to touch; but it would be Peony, as the princess, folded in spells and counterspells, who would touch it, either because the curse was tricked into recognizing her as the princess, or because Sigil and Ikor and Aunt and Katriona's conscious interference, buttressed and bolstered by the belief of everyone around them, would make it so.

But she would not die, because she was not the princess, and the curse, at the moment of consummation, would reject her, as the wrong end of a magnet tosses away iron filings. But the magic would by then have gone too far to turn back, like a bottle falling off the edge of a mantelpiece; and Peony would fall into an enchanted sleep, and every guardian enchantment of every fairy and every magician present – and there would be many present – would be wrapped round her at once, to hold her safe.

Magic gone wrong produces a perilous uproar, a perilous and unpredictable uproar, the greater for the greater magic. The only thing they could well guess about this uproar was that it would be powerful, as Pernicia's spell was powerful; powerful and wicked and still deadly dangerous, not least because all the fairies and magicians who would be there for the party could not be told what they were really doing. They would believe it was the princess whose enchanted sleep they were watching over. It would be up to Aunt and Ikor, and Sigil . . . because Rosie would be flung, in the recoil of magic gone wrong – somewhere; and Katriona was to go with her.

There would be much magic to counteract, to defy or deflect, and Rosie would not be able to do it. Katriona's part was to see that Rosie arrived at the final confrontation – whatever it was. But it was all horribly, incomprehensibly dangerous. Aunt and Ikor might have managed to lie to her about just how much they could not do and could not control; but one look at Katriona's face told Rosie the truth.

Rosie recalled some of the tales and ballads Barder had taught her: the hopeless causes, the outnumbered gallantry, the one-faint-chance against despair. She thought of her favourite stories: the magician Merlin, sired by a dragon, creating a great circle of standing stones to hold the light of midsummer to protect the ordinary people he loved against the wild magic of the strong young land they lived in; the harpist who loved his singing wife so much that he followed her to the land of the dead where between them they persuaded the god of that place to give her back, and when they died together, many years later, they were a legend more for their continued devotion to each other than the adventure of their youth; many of the tales of Damar against the North, especially of Harimad-sol at the Madamer Gate, and the holding of the way at Ullen. And she remembered King Harald of this, her own country, against the fire-wyrms – and her own progenitrix against Pernicia, although no-one knew much about that tale. This was another of those occasions, and she hoped that someone would be telling this story, too, some day, as the one faint chance that succeeded.

It was the best they could do. It was the only chance they had.

At dinner in the Great Hall, where all dinners had been held since the arrival of the princess, Rosie's consciousness flew up into the rafters to talk to the merrel. At first they could not make each other out through the great noise of many people eating and drinking and talking together, and through the many penetrating and single-minded thoughts of dogs and mice intent on anything that fell under the tables and off platters, and of cats trying to decide between nice fresh mice and unpredictable but always interesting human leavings. (The dogs kept Woodwold free of rats and – usually – squirrels and the occasional venturesome weasel, but mice were below their notice.) But Rosie and the merrel had persisted, or Rosie had, feeling almost as if the merrel were lifting her up, as if she did not merely sit but flew over the heads of the people – above the roof of the Great Hall, above the thick fogs of Gig winter and damp clouds of magic dust, to where the sun shone. . . However it was, they learnt to talk to each other, and Rosie mostly chose the merrel's company, except when someone, disturbed or intrigued by the intense, inturned look on Rosie's face, shook her shoulder or her elbow until she returned to her place at the table and answered whatever question had been put to her in a human voice. "I was just thinking," was all she usually said, and a small admiring rumour began to circulate about the princess' lady-in-waiting, that the girl who had once been a horse-leech had become a philosopher. The merrel, who after so many years of living above the Great Hall with nothing to do but think and listen, assisted in recent years by conversations with Rosie, had learnt human language almost as well as another human. It was the merrel who told her about the rumour. Under other circumstances Rosie would have found this funny.

I was just thinking, she said to herself now, in the darkness of the night before her twenty-first birthday. Once upon a time I walked where I wanted, and talked to whom I wanted, and . . . now all I do is sit and think as if I were chained by my ankle to a rafter. I don't suppose Narl will even come to the ball. Why should he?

Rosie could feel the mesh of thickening spells round her now, sticky as cobweb; the touch of it made her shiver as she moved, and in the corners of her eyes she could see it trailing behind her, like threads of dust shaken from an old curtain. The silent spider in the corner of her window had not come into the centre of her web and swung back and forth in a friendly fashion tonight; she huddled in her corner as if her own web imprisoned her.

It had been several weeks now that Rosie and Peony had breathed in exact unison. Rosie's breath caught in her throat often when Peony was with Rowland, but Peony had stopped letting herself weep – as at first she often had, with the bedroom door shut safely behind her, after saying a smiling farewell to Rowland and thanking Lady Pren for her attendance – when she realized that Rosie had to weep, too. The only time she and Peony could breathe to their own rhythm, these last few weeks, was when they slept. Rosie knew this from the many dark hours she sat awake in the window embrasure, listening to the slower sound of Peony's sleeping.

The entire Gig had been invited to the ball, and nearly everyone would come, except perhaps solitary blacksmiths. There were pavilions going up in the park, between the iron gates and the Great Hall, so that all those who came could be accommodated; and the great central doors to the Hall, which had not been used in over a century, had been unlocked – and unstuck – and would be left open that night; and a promise had been made, although no-one knew who by, that the princess and her parents would walk the full length of the way between the gate and the Great Hall several times that night, so that anyone who wished to see – and even speak – to them would have their opportunity.

The princess and her parents. My parents, thought Rosie. She had never said the words aloud, *my parents*, after she had learnt that they were the king and queen. This was nothing to do with the care of the conspirators about what words they used; the ban began much deeper than that. It began where the echoes had come from during the weeks before Katriona's wedding, the echoes that said she was not who she believed she was. But that was when she had first understood that she would grow up – that she was already no longer a child. She had thought since then – till Ikor came – that the echoes had only spoken about the loss of childhood, that inevitable loss. She had never guessed they were telling her she would lose everything. Even the embroidery spell, she had believed, would finally have a simple explanation – as simple an explanation as fairy business ever had. She had thought of the merrel, and the embroidery spell had become small and ridiculous; now she thought of the merrel and wondered how it bore the years.

Katriona had told her, quietly, during the last day in Foggy Bottom, of how Katriona, when Rosie was very young, had told the queen tales of her daughter, and how the queen had sent her away, and the words she had used when she did so. My mother, thought Rosie, deeply troubled; for it was Katriona and Aunt whom Rosie loved; and yet, to her own dismay, she found she wanted to meet her mother. . . Ikor had told her that they dared not strain the imposture by the presence of the princess' family till the very last; and so Rosie had pushed all questions about her parents to the bottom of the list of things to worry about, and she had been grateful for the excuse.

That excuse, like all other excuses, ended tomorrow.

Rosie felt her breathing falter and change, and knew that Peony had woken up. In a moment she had crept into the window embrasure next to Rosie, and they stared out at the darkness, which was no longer so dark. The dawn of the princess' one-and-twentieth birthday was breaking over the distant forest, and picking out the sweep of roofs and parkland below them that was Woodwold; far off, to their right, was a misty silver glitter of the river.

Chapter 18

The morning began as every other morning at Woodwold had begun for the princess and her lady-in-waiting. They took turns in the bathroom and the steaming cauldron of the bath; and then they fled into the dressing room where each helped the other with her laces and ribbons. Rosie, as a point of pride, had learnt to perform her lady's-maid tasks as neatly as any princess could ask – although she muttered to herself while she did them.

The maid who brought them their breakfast looked as if she had already been up and busy several long hours. She hardly lingered to look reverently at Peony – as the maids who brought them breakfast always did – and asked almost perfunctorily how the princess had slept. Rosie and Peony could feel the stir and bustle and excitement below them, even though in the magic-defended rooms set aside for the princess, they could not hear it. Rosie half wished they could just stay where they were until . . . well . . . maybe if they stayed here the spinning wheel with the deadly spindle would appear here, and they could at least do whatever they had to do in private.

But she knew this wasn't possible; and she knew as well that she would not be able to stay in two small rooms, however comfortable, all day, all this particular day, without going mad before noon. She sighed, and Peony sighed, too.

There was a discreet knock on the door; their escort downstairs to the public rooms had arrived. These were guards, a magician or two, and six or eight or it might have been ten ladies-in-waiting.

The ladies-in-waiting had rushed on to Woodwold from wherever they lived as soon as their fortunate preferment had been made known to them. Most of them would have cultivated Rosie as the known best friend of the princess, except that Rosie was half afraid of them, partly because they wore all their flounces and under-petticoats so easily, and partly because she couldn't manage to get their names straight: they seemed all to be called things like Claralinda and Dulcibella and Sacharissa. Even Peony had a little trouble finding things to say to them; not a one of them had ever baby-sat or collected eggs or carried water from the town well for a season after something disgusting drowned in their own.

Today at last the king and queen and the three princes would arrive. Their outriders were blowing in already, declaring they were only a few hours away. The first of these came and flung himself at Peony's feet, looking up at her hungrily in a way that had become very familiar in the last three months. Peony always glanced down, or away from that look; Rosie, because she was not the object of it, could watch her fill: her fill of knowing that she could not be the princess, she *could not be*, she didn't care who her parents were, where Katriona had found her twenty-one years ago, what Ikor said.

And today was the day she had used, for the last three months, as the excuse for not having to think about that yet.

After today, it would not matter what she thought.

If she was still alive to think anything.

After the man left, Peony and Rosie stared at each other. The meeting he proclaimed was the meeting they both dreaded most, even more than the prospect of Pernicia's spinning wheel with its wicked spindle, perhaps because Pernicia was unimaginable, while the king and queen were people, were the princess' mother and father, were the mother and father of a daughter they had not seen since she was three months old, over twenty years ago.

Everyone else was thinking about that, too, and staring at Peony.

"I – I wonder what the princes will be like?" quavered Peony, to say something, to acknowledge what was in everyone's minds, but unable to bring herself to mention the king or the queen.

"Little brothers!" said Callin, who had two little brothers of her own. She made her way through the flock of Claralindas and Dulcibellas, and now took Rosie and Peony by the arm. She was nearest in age to them of any of the Prendergasts, due to celebrate her own twenty-first birthday in six months, when she would be married to one of her father's liegemen. She looked sharply at them both, dispersed the ladies-in-waiting with a few brisk words that several of them would have liked to defy but did not quite dare (it would be different after this evening, when the princess had been properly reinstalled among her family, and the airs of the daughters of rustic lordships could be safely dispensed with), and then sent a boy off with a message to her betrothed that he was needed urgently, and, still holding the princess and her first lady-in-waiting by one arm each, marched them off for a walk in the park.

When her young man caught up with them, white faced and babbling protestations – the princess was not allowed to put her nose out of the front door without a distinguished and extensive retinue – Callin put her own nose in the air and ignored him. And because everyone was concentrating so mightily on the immediate business of the king and queen's arrival and the ball that evening, the little party reached the orchard without anyone challenging them.

It was Rosie who suggested they walk towards the great iron gates. She said they would turn round well before they came to the wall; and Callin's young man, nearly in a trance of despair, fatalistically agreed. Callin, having got her own way, was trying to cheer her young man up by whispering things in his ear; Rosie tucked her hand under Peony's arm, trying to ignore the fact that this was as much for her own balance as for mutual comfort. She wondered if Peony felt the queer erratic pull, too, or whether it was something to do with how the magic tugged at her, Rosie, who should have been the princess, and wasn't, or because she was anyway. It was a sensation she had felt often in the last three months, but not one she had felt outdoors and in daylight before; it was something that often accompanied her late-night watches in the window seat, a sort of prowling thing, there and gone and there again, restless and inquisitive. She half imagined a corporeal body for it: a tatterdemalion, shambling and shaggy, dumb but dogged. Its presence today should have unsettled her more, but being under a blue sky with birds singing in the trees of the park (and the occasional glimpse of hopeful park deer, alerted by the tents that something probably involving interesting human food was happening soon), lifted her spirits despite everything.

And that was how it was they met the royal party riding in through the gates, while a frantic cry had gone up behind them indoors at Woodwold, while they had been wandering in the park: "Where is the princess? They are coming – they have passed the gates – *where is the princess?*"

Rosie saw her parents at once, although they were not immediately different from those riding round them; everyone wore plain travelling clothes, and everyone sat their horses as if sitting their horses was what they had chiefly been doing for many weeks. Perhaps the king and queen rode in the centre, and perhaps those who rode immediately next to them had a look, while not aggressively watchful, somehow high-strung, alert, guardlike; and then Rosie saw the three littler figures on their horses just behind their parents, and knew they were the princes.

The queen saw the party on foot first, though they were far enough off the drive to have been missed by the messengers. Nor should they have been immediately recognizable as anyone but a little group of young Prendergasts or courtiers and their friends, although it was true that one young woman was rather more grandly dressed than the other three. But the queen urged her horse forward, through the encircling convoy, before anyone had time to react: they were looking for threats from without, not rebellion from within. The guard pulled their horses to a halt, and then other horses ran into them, and the youngest prince almost fell off his pony, and the queen by then had flung herself off her own horse and was running towards them. Rosie didn't know if Peony had said it aloud or not: *I can't – I can't*; but she felt her, both rigid and trembling, under her arm, as she had been on the night that Ikor had first come to Foggy Bottom.

Callin and her young man moved a little away from the other two. Rosie knew that she should have moved away, too, but she could not leave Peony to face this alone; she was half holding her up as it was. The unstable drag of the magic further confused her; she told herself that no-one would be looking at the lady-in-waiting while the princess and her mother met for the first time in twenty-one years, and that it didn't matter what she did or didn't do. But as the royal group had approached them she could feel the added protection that all those magicians and fairies had thrown round the royal family, and the sense of it was as if she were being rolled up in a carpet.

Time, in this strange space they were in, Rosie and Peony and the approaching queen, seemed to pause. The milling horses and gesticulating people were a tableau; even the birds had fallen quiet. The queen's eyes were on Peony, and Rosie's eyes were on the queen, so she saw the expression on her mother's face falter, although her foot stepping forward was still poised to strike the ground. And then the queen's gaze moved to Rosie.

Time began again. Between one step and another, one eyeblink, while the small uproar of the queen's horse thrusting its way out of its party was still going on and before the king and several of the guard had turned their horses to follow, before the queen's freed horse had finished shaking itself and put its head down to graze, a long look passed between Rosie and her mother; and Rosie suddenly thought: *She knows. How can she know? But she does know.* The queen gave her the tiniest of smiles, the tiniest acknowledgement, and Rosie, in that moment, saw a great love and a yearning just as great, but long endured and once again deferred.

The queen turned to Peony, and Peony, as if sleepwalking, moved into the queen's outstretched arms. "It's all right," were the first words Rosie heard her mother speak; "it's all right." Peony stiffened in her arms, and looked into her face, and perhaps what she saw there told her what the queen's look had already told Rosie, for she heaved a great sigh (Rosie's breath hurled itself in and out of her breast in echo) and returned the queen's embrace, just as if everything was and would be all right.

It was, perhaps, again something to do with the magic that was drawing them all towards what would happen some time that day, some time that night, when the ball to celebrate the princess's twenty-first birthday was at its height. Peony seemed to draw strength into herself after that first meeting with the queen, and she was as royal as any princess had ever been for the rest of the day. She seemed to know instinctively how to speak and what to do, and Rosie could see, through a fog that seemed to be thickening about herself, that almost everyone loved her immediately, even her eldest brother, who would not be king – even her youngest brother, rather against his will, who was used to being the centre of attention, and wasn't best pleased at being displaced.

As lady-in-waiting Rosie heard a few of the whispered asides from the Prendergasts' folk, about how kind and charming and wise Peony was, how despite the tensions and fears of the last three months she had grown no less kind or charming or wise; if anything, more, as if what she had been all along was merely being allowed to come to the surface at last.

She will make us a great queen, the murmurs went.

Rosie was growing dizzy. She put her hand behind her, to find a chair to steady herself against. It was some time in the afternoon, she thought, looking at the sunlight slanting in through the windows of the Great Hall; somehow she could not remember much very distinctly since the royal party had arrived. It's just the noise and confusion, Rosie said to herself. Even the merrel had withdrawn from her. But as she felt for a chair, or a table, or any steady, unmagical piece of furniture to grip, she felt someone take her arm, and she blinked her eyes hard till she could focus them: Ikor.

She hadn't let herself notice – or perhaps he had thrown some glamour over himself which today he had discarded – how haggard he had become; his skin was as grey as charcoal, and his cheeks were hollow; his purple-shadowed eyes seemed to stare at her from a great distance, but the look in them was as sharp as ever.

"Pardon me," said Rosie faintly. "Am I too far away from Peony?" She turned her head to look; but Ikor shook his head, and muttered a few words at her. The fog cleared a little; she could stand up again, but she could feel it waiting to re-engulf her, and she knew that whatever held it off now would not hold it long.

Ikor nodded and moved away from her. Rosie lost him for a moment or two, and then someone moved, and she saw him bending over Peony, whispering a few words in her ear; Peony smiled and nodded, courteous and agreeable as ever; and Ikor then left the Hall. But not long after, Peony put a hand to her forehead; recovered herself; lolled back in her chair; recovered herself not quite so quickly – and then her favourite lady-in-waiting was at her side, asking her what she could do for her, and the king was saying that it was not at all surprising that this was all a little too much, and that she should go upstairs and rest until the evening; and he drew her to him tenderly and kissed her forehead. The queen kissed her, too, but again the queen's eyes strayed to the lady-in-waiting who hovered at the princess's elbow, ready to assist her upstairs.

They did not go alone, of course, and Rosie fought the returning fog, so that she could be the one that Peony leaned on; and when they finally entered their room, she made her voice strong enough to dismiss everyone else, saying that she would look after Peony herself. Everyone left, although Rosie knew there would be more than the usual number of soldiers and magicians posted outside their door. She wondered if any of them knew why they were there, or if they believed they were only doing honour to the princess, who would be crowned heir by the king this evening. She thought of Eskwa over the lintel, and for the first time she was grateful for his presence. *Eskwa both binds and cuts; if you have need of either, he will answer to your hand.* Supposing she could make her hand work to grasp; supposing she knew what to do with a sabre, even one heavy and self-willed with magic. She was just beginning to unlace Peony's skirt, so she could lie down, when she felt her fingers growing clumsy from the numbing, stifling fog; and then she felt Peony turning round and catching her, Rosie, and giving her a shoulder to lean on as she drew her to the bed.

"I'm perfectly all right," said Peony. "Well – perhaps not perfectly. This is a terrible day, and I wish it were over. But Ikor told me you had to get away, and so I pretended to be fainting. I was not sorry for the excuse. We'll both lie down, in case anyone comes to check on us, but if you need anything, ask me. I'm right here." She gave a dry little laugh. "I'm right here, just as I have been, these last three months. Oh, Rosie, it is a terrible day, but think of it, tonight it will be over. It will all, all, be *over*."

"Yes," whispered Rosie from the fog, knowing that it would not be, not for her. There were nasty little hairy things nibbling at the edges of the fog and squeaking. They were a little like rats, but their bodies were snakier.

Peony took her hands. "You and Kat and Aunt and Ikor and Sigil *must* win. You *must*."

Rosie looked up at Peony's loving, anxious, hopeful face, and said, "Of course we must. Of course. And the princess' first royal decree will be a dowry to the Foggy Bottom wainwright's niece, so she can marry the son of the prince of Erlion." She fell asleep so quickly she did not see the expression on Peony's face.

She woke knowing that someone was sitting in a chair next to her bed; knowing who it was before she opened her eyes. "*Kat*," she said, almost falling out of bed in her haste to put her arms round her. "Kat, I haven't seen you in *forever*."

"I know, dear, I haven't liked it either. But both Aunt and Ikor thought it for the best. We couldn't risk my binding to you confusing or lessening the connection between you and Peony as we came near this day and – and – this evening. If we've got the bond between you and Peony wrong, nothing else matters."

"We breathe together," said Rosie. "And if we stand next to each other we only cast one shadow. A few weeks ago we had to start being careful not to walk in meadows – away from trees or something tall – when the sun is low, for fear someone would notice." The fog was much thinner than it had been that afternoon; this must be from Katriona's presence. But it meant she could see only too clearly the marks of strain in Kat's face, as harsh as they were on Ikor's .

Katriona patted her hand. "It'll be over soon now. "

"Tonight," said Rosie. "Tonight." She closed her eyes. She could still see the hairy, snaky things, but she could not hear them squeaking. She opened her eyes again.

"I don't like this fog round you, Rosie," said Katriona.

"It's better now," said Rosie. "It was bad earlier, when we came upstairs."

"It's better because I'm holding it off – as Ikor did. But if there's a fog, I should need to be holding it off both of you, not one of you – especially not you, Rosie." She paused, and then said, in a tone she tried hard to make light, "I brought you something. I don't really know why. It just seemed like a good idea, in the middle of all our strict plotting and planning, to allow a small harmless whim; and I remembered what you told me afterwards about wishing you'd had it the night Jem was born." And she held out the shiny-nosed gargoyle spindle end.

Rosie took it and held it a moment cupped in her hands, and then tucked the spindle between her knees, and rubbed her thumbs over the little thing's cheeks, its slightly protruberant teeth and eyes, and finally its shiny nose. For a moment she was in the kitchen of the wheelwright's house in Foggy Bottom – for a moment she was home.

And then she was back in the princess' tower room at Woodwold on the night of the princess' twenty-first birthday. She was silent a moment longer, staring at the familiar, friendly, ugly, spindle's-end face, and then she said: "The queen knows. I don't know why, but she looked at us, and she knew." She hesitated, and then added: "It was right after that that the fog began."

Katriona shivered. "That's probably my fault," she said. "I told you – when you were little, it hurt me to think about the queen, so I . . . And if she remembers . . . of course she remembers . . . the stories don't match. I told her her daughter lived with me and my aunt. We knew that I mustn't meet the queen now, but. . . It's going wrong. It's already going wrong. Oh, why does compassion *weaken* us?"

"It doesn't really," said Rosie, not because she had any idea about it, but because she refused to let it be true. "It doesn't really. Somewhere where it all balances out – don't the philosophers have a name for it, the perfect place, the place where the answers live? – if we could go there, you could see it doesn't. It only looks, a little bit, like it does, from here, like an ant at the foot of an oak tree. He doesn't have a clue that it's a tree; it's the beginning of the wall round the world, to him. And besides – doesn't Aunt keep saying that mistakes made in good faith are less likely to catch you out?"

But then Peony slipped through the door, and Rosie fell silent.

Peony sat on the bed next to Rosie and squeezed her hand. They sat for a moment in silence, and then there was a tap on the door. Rosie sat up hastily, pretending that she had not been asleep till a few minutes before, and Peony said, "Come in."

"King's, queen's, princes', Lord and Lady Prendergast's, and, oh, *hundreds* of people's compliments, Princess," said one of the Claralindas or Dulcibellas or Sacharissas, "and it's time to dress for the ball."

Chapter 19

Katriona had a grand dress to wear, too, emerald and sage green, and she liked it almost as little as Rosie liked hers, which was grey and silver and twinkly, and far too like the gown she had found herself in on the night that Ikor had told her her name, and she had wanted to run away. But this wasn't anything she could explain to the royal dressmakers, who were very proud of their work.

Several of the Claralindas shook the green dress out carefully from the bundle Katriona had brought it in and "oohed" and "aahed," admiring, if a little dumbfounded. (Some of the Claralindas who had been at Woodwold the longest were beginning to get used to the surprising things the yokels could do. Make ball gowns, for example. The Prendergasts had bought out Turanga's entire stock of fine cloth and leather and thread and trimmings, and made it available to any Gig resident who wanted it. The local plain tailors and seamstresses, accustomed to the needs of ordinary Gig life and work, would never quite recover from the fevered glory of those few months of sewing for the princess's ball.) "Hroslinga did most of it," said Katriona; there was a look on her face Rosie couldn't read, and, amid the Claralindas, couldn't ask. "She seems to think she owes our family some tremendous debt. But indeed I haven't had time to do it myself, and holding it together with magic seemed like a bad idea under the circumstances."

Barder would be on his way as soon as he finished taking the children to the pub, where they would sleep upstairs with Flora's two, and Cairngorm would look after them – Flora and her husband were going to the ball. "There'll be a few people who'll want a quiet drink at the pub," said Cairngorm, "instead of a princess and a lot of noise; and there should be someone here to give it to them." She had granted Bol, the usual barkeep, the night off; in his quiet, methodical way he was looking forward to the noise and the princess, even though she was only Peony, whom he'd known from a baby. Dessy, on the other hand, had been useless for weeks, dreaming of the great party, and incapable of talking about anything else. (Jem and Gilly had some idea they were missing something, but they did not mourn the ball once Barder had explained they would have had to go dressed in good clothes, and stay clean and tidy for several hours.) Katriona didn't mention Narl; the fact that she didn't seemed to Rosie to be the answer to the question she didn't want to ask.

One of the Claralindas was combing Rosie's hair, making tiny sighs of exasperation. "Look," said Rosie. "It *is* short, there isn't anything to do with it, so why don't you give it up and go and join the others?"

Rosie ran her hands through her hair once or twice (pulling out and glaring at a jewelled clasp the Claralinda had resourcefully managed to find enough hair to hold in place), and went over to her window embrasure for one last look at the landscape before it disappeared in the darkness of the night of her twenty-first birthday. The spider crept slowly to the centre of the web, moving its legs one at a time, seemingly with enormous effort, as if it were very tired; but once arrived, it gave a gallant little swing like a salute. In its weariness it seemed like another one of the conspirators; if spiders had faces, no doubt this one's would be haggard and hollow-eyed.

Rosie thought that with the enormous dislocations of this birthday was one tiny one: that it was a day earlier than all her other birthdays they had welcomed in all the other years. It is the princess' birthday, she thought, not mine. My birthday is tomorrow. Her fingers strayed to a pocket hidden in the sweep of her ball-gown skirt, and found the gargoyle's nose.

Princess, murmured the windowsill. *Rosie*, whispered the thickness of the wall. Some great diffuse understanding seemed to flow down, like a cloud from a mountaintop, or up, like mist from a bog; some tremendous effort of insight struggled to gather itself together into a definable shape. It could not quite find itself words, but Rosie knew what it searched for: *Soon. Immediately. Tonight. Now.*

She suddenly knelt and flung back the lid of the wooden step that let you mount to the stone seat, and gave you somewhere to put your feet while you sat there. Inside were the spindle ends she had carved in the last weeks, and on the top was the one she wanted, the one of the princess, the one of herself-and-Peony as one face, one human face smiling quietly to itself over some secret. She held it cupped in her hand for a moment, and then waited for a pause in the bustle around Peony.

"Put it in your pocket," she said. "They've left you a pocket, haven't they? It's probably silly of me, but Kat just gave me our old spindle end, you remember, the gargoyle, and it feels like a little bit of good luck, and I thought you should have one, too. I'm sorry it's only new. "

"I've always wanted you to make me a spindle end, Rosie," said Peony; "I've had this fancy I might finally learn to spin, if you did, but it seemed too silly to ask; and after I – I tried to teach you to embroider, I didn't dare." She tried to smile. "I – I guess I won't have time to start practising tonight. . ."

There was another tap on the door, and Aunt walked in, dazzling in dark red and gold, which set off her white hair, and with a gold chain round her neck, which was a present from the queen; she was carrying another similar one for Katriona. The four of them stood looking at one another, princess, her best friend from her country childhood, and the friend's aunt and cousin who were important fairies in spite of where they lived, and tonight looked it; and the Claralindas fell silent. Aunt opened the door again and curtsied, and Peony, her cheeks bright from having Aunt curtsy to her, raised her chin and swept out, followed by Rosie, Katriona, and then Aunt herself, and last the subdued Claralindas.

The guards upon the stairs stood to attention, and at the foot of the princess's tower were various other courtiers, and more ladies-in-waiting, bright as butterflies, both gay and solemn at being chosen to be in the princess's train on this night of all nights; and as the princess went lightly and gracefully downstairs she had a smile and a wave or a word for everyone who peeped out of a side corridor at her (including the Prendergasts' eldest grandson, who should have been in bed, and his perspiring nanny). Six footmen and twelve buglers announced her arrival in the Great Hall; but the princess drew all eyes by the simple fact of who she was, and that she was lovely and brave and clear minded, and her people had fallen in love with her; and many ordinary citizens at the ball that evening took private vows with themselves to protect her with their own lives, if it came to that; though there was nothing to protect her from, any more. That was all over; that was all in the past.

The Great Hall, busier in the last three months than it had been in centuries, had become more splendid every day as more visitors came with gifts for the princess, all of which Lady Prendergast scrupulously displayed in the public rooms. Peony had refused to wear any of the jewellery, and, after attempting to remonstrate with her, Lady Pren had decided that the many soldiers sent to Woodwold out of respect for the presence of the princess could perform a useful function (as opposed to eating their heads off and flirting with the younger and prettier maidservants, which seemed to be their chief occupations) and guard the necklaces and earrings and brooches and bracelets that she hung on the walls like tapestries. Even so, the Hall's decorations for the princess' ball were a revelation. The Hall seemed almost small, for the number of people and objects it now contained; and yet it also seemed bigger than it ever had, and, as Rosie made her entrance behind Peony's shoulder, the opposite wall – above which the merrel sat concealed – was too far to see, as if it lay in another country. If Woodwold trembled underfoot, it was only the weight of many feet; and if its walls whispered *Rosie*, no-one heard.

For the first few hours of the ball, Rosie felt more or less herself

– as much as she had ever felt herself as the princess's lady-in-waiting. Surely it wasn't surprising to feel a little dazed and isolated at your first royal ball, especially when you were pretending that it wasn't in your honour when it was, and when you were one of only half a dozen people out of hundreds who knew that there was someone lurking in the shadows somewhere waiting to kill you. She watched the people watching Peony and saw in many of their eyes that private vow they had sworn, and wondered if any of them had any inkling of the darkness round them, round the princess' birthday ball. She spoke to the Master of the Horse, whose face shone with dedication to his future sovereign; she spoke to Lady Prendergast, who could hardly take her eyes off her protégée. She spoke to Callin, who said, in her forthright way, "Horrid for her, everybody gloating over her like this. I think I'll go and push that icky little man's face in" – the icky little man was the Duke of Iraminon's ambassador. Rosie watched, amused, as Callin sidled up to the ambassador, and, looking at him through her eyelashes, asked him some question he was obviously only too willing to answer at length – securing Peony's escape.

While she was watching, Rowland came up to her and spoke her name. She had to prevent herself from starting away from him, and she knew, when she met his eyes, that she hadn't quite succeeded. She smiled at him, a little tentatively; her mouth didn't want to turn upward. She knew he was both aware of and hurt by her avoidance of him – she had said barely three words together to him in the last three months – but then he didn't know the truth of their situation.

"Rosie," he said, and then, in a rush, as if he had meant to say something else entirely, "can we not be friends? I must value a – a relationship between us, because you are Peo—the princess' friend; but beyond that I – I like you. Once I – I thought you liked me. I have not forgotten that it was you who taught me the names of the Foggy Bottom dogs, especially the medium-sized brown ones that all look alike, and to recognize birds from the songs they sing. I miss our days together at the smith's."

Rosie's eyes filled with tears before she could stop them. "Oh!"

said Rowland, horrified, groping for his handkerchief, "I beg your pardon!" Rosie remembered just in time not to blot her eyes on her sleeve, and fumbled for her own handkerchief, rolling the little gargoyle in her pocket as she did so. She blew her nose on her own but accepted and used Rowland's to mop her face, as a kind of answer to his question, because she couldn't think what to say to him. Presumably he would know soon enough, and then perhaps he would understand why she had avoided him.

But she had not answered his question, and he hesitated to put it again. He took his slightly damp handkerchief back, and folded it slowly, as if each corner squaring with the other corners was crucially important, while he tried to think of something else to say to her. "Narl sends his best wishes," he offered at last.

Rosie grunted, a Narl-like grunt. She could think of few things less likely than Narl sending anyone his best wishes; and as far as she knew, Rowland was now spending most of his time at Woodwold. He had asked and been granted a place in the rota of the princess' guard. But his remark did confirm her guess that Narl would not come to the ball. She had known he wouldn't, but her heart nonetheless sank further.

Rowland still showed no sign of leaving her, and the crush of people was willing to let them alone for a little while; it seemed fitting that the man the princess loved and the woman who was the princess' best friend should have a word or two to say quietly to each other. Rosie hugged to her the thought of the princess' first royal command. With a dowry such as the princess might bestow on her best friend, would the prince of Erlion allow his heir to marry a wainwright's niece? But even if she had known the answer was yes, this could not comfort her much. Ikor was quite capable of lying about the dissolution of the bond made by the Erlion heir's vow – or at least of refusing to do it, even if it were possible, if his magic or his understanding of his sovereign's subjects told him that it would be better for the country, and the country's head of state, if it remained intact. "What will you do," she said at last, "if you cannot marry Peony?"

"I don't know," he said, the words spaced out one from another.

"I know I must think of this. The people – the princess' people – look at us and smile and want it to be a happy ending. The story is a very satisfactory one, is it not? My childhood vow, and then falling in love with a girl I meet at a country smith's, when I, too, am in disguise, and she turns out to be the princess.

"But it is not a story, with the happy ending already written and waiting for us to turn the pages. The people I know – it seems to me they believe that the refusal to announce our betrothal is some kind of whim, to make the suspense more exciting. I know it is not. Ikor – Ikor told me very little, only that there is no betrothal, and – he could not hide from me that there is something else to tell; and I look in Peony's face, and I know there is something she is not telling me – something that hurts her – something that hurts us. I know there is something she is not telling me as clearly as I know she loves me. I – I spend my duty hours wondering what it is, while I walk up and down, or check that the emeralds or the rubies or the amethysts are still hanging where they were a quarter of an hour ago. What I find myself wondering about most often is the curse – the curse that we are supposed to believe has failed. I would like to believe that it has failed, quietly, with no sign of she who cast it, despite the fact that the entire country has lived under the shadow of that curse for twenty years.

"It is not only Peony's face that tells me there is something I do not know. It is Ikor's face, Ikor who came here first and arranged us all into this new order, this new story. Do you know that Ikor would not meet my eyes when he told me there was no betrothal? Ikor is not a man who does not meet the eyes of those he speaks to. And there is something in your Aunt's face, and your cousin Katriona's, and in yours, too, Rosie. There is a great and terrible weight upon all of you. This is what I fear – this is what I think: that the curse has not failed. Perhaps that is what the ball is for: to make most of the people believe, so that . . . so that what?"

He paused. They were both looking at Peony, who was now talking to Terberus. They were both fair and graceful, with quick, attractive smiles, and Terberus was only middling tall. They could be brother and sister, thought Rosie. She remembered something else that Katriona had told her on the last day in Foggy Bottom: how a glamour worked least well over the people who had the most connections with the truth. Love was a very strong connection.

"Rosie," said Rowland. "I'm not asking you to tell me what it is, because Peony would have told me if it would not do some harm for me to hear it. But – do you know what I do not know?"

Rosie looked at him. "Yes," she said. "I do know. And so I know why she cannot tell you."

She saw that, however much he thought he had accepted the existence of that hidden thing, the confirmation of it was a blow to him; and she was sorry for this, sorry for having dealt him such a blow on top of the last three months of denying their friendship. The few of them who knew – even if Rowland didn't quite know what he knew – should be able to stick together.

Perhaps it was the strain of knowing that whatever would happen would happen tonight, perhaps it was the magic-fog muddling her thinking, perhaps it was the hopelessness of her own love making her foolish, but she added impetuously: "But I think I can tell you that it means – it means Peony will not die tonight, whatever P-Pernicia does." As she realized what she had said, she saw a little flicker of understanding run across Rowland's face – an understanding too near the truth. He had no guess that Peony was not the princess, but he glimpsed a reason why two young women, one of them dreadfully cursed, might be bound so closely together as to confuse the curse into choosing the wrong one. . .

Rosie admired him for his immediate look of horror and dismay at the same time she was appalled at the slip she had made. "No, no," she said hastily. "It's not what you—" But at that moment Lady Pren decided that the two of them had talked only to each other long enough, and, important guests that they were, they had to spread themselves more liberally among the others.

Rosie found the young lord Lady Pren bestowed upon her rather hard going (as doubtless he found her). Perhaps as a result of her conversation with Rowland, she felt the fog pressing round her again, and the passage of time began to confuse and disorient her, as if she were standing precariously on the limb of a tree and time was the wind now lashing its branches. She came to herself standing alone – she didn't remember the young lord leaving – but there was a fleethound head suddenly under her hand, and so she stroked it, while it – Hroc – looked up at her and sent loving thoughts.

She looked down and saw that there was quite a little party of hounds following her – and getting under people's feet. Lord Pren allowed his favourite dogs indoors (as well as the ladies' lapdogs, which rarely, Throstle excepted, went outside), but under most conditions they stayed out of the humans' way for fear of being banished to the kennels after all.

If you want to hang around someone, you should go and hang around Peony. She's the princess here.

No, said Hroc. *She isn't.*

Rosie sighed – and caught a quick look from Peony, as ever not far away, feeling the sigh, and wondering if there were anything wrong she should pay attention to. Rosie shook her head, and returned her attention to Hroc.

Animals knew what they had to know about magic, that it was liable to turn them into brambles or thunderclouds at any moment and, if they were lucky, back again; but it was always there, like thickets and weather, and, like thickets and weather, to be borne as stoically as possible. Domestic animals (and the brighter or more inquisitive wild ones) knew that humans meddled in it, but then houses and barns and preserved foods over the winter were another sort of meddling, and on the whole domestic animals (and a few wild ones) approved of houses and barns and preserved foods. Coming up with ideas like houses and barns and preserved foods and then building or storing them (and, unlike squirrels, finding them again) was the sort of thing humans did, but there were limits. A fire in the fireplace was lovely, but it didn't change the fact that there was a snowstorm outside. The idea of what Rosie and the other conspirators were doing was, in animal terms, like trying to convince a snowstorm to fall on one house instead of the one next door.

Hroc had been there that first evening in Foggy Bottom, when Ikor had told them what they were going to do, when the necessity of some scheme against Pernicia was as plain to Hroc and the others as a flung rock in the ribs – even if the manner of it seemed like one of those strange human designs that get you ultimately into more trouble than they get you out of. But Hroc had shrugged a dog-shrug, as most of the other animals had shrugged their kinds of shrugs. Human business was human business, with which they would not interfere; and there were other matters to attend to. Rosie was still wondering about those other matters, about whether the sense of preoccupation she felt in her animal friends was something more ominous than that they had little to say to a woman who was spending all her time indoors, playing at being a lady-in-waiting, and doing no useful work. The thought that it was only this, that they had nothing to say to her any more, was so bitter that it was hard for her not to want the preoccupation to go ahead and be something ominous.

But the last thing the conspirators needed right now was Rosie's friends making it obvious that Rosie seemed ill and distracted on the princess's birthday.

Well, so pretend *she is the princess*, said Rosie, and Hroc gave her a weary look. *Pretend* was one of those human words. The only equivalents, and they were not helpful ones, were the deception of the hiding predator, and the playing-to-learn-skills that all animal children did to a greater or lesser extent. Hroc knew perfectly well what "pretend" meant when Rosie said it to him; he just believed it to be piffle, as if she had told him grass was pink and water was not for drinking.

She looked into his patient, intelligent eyes and thought, with a sudden bubble of panic: This isn't just a loophole, a gap for a nimble enemy archer to shoot through; this is an entire wall that isn't there: that the animals *know*. That they're waiting for something to happen – something besides the euphoric celebration of the princess's one-and-twentieth birthday. And that the something would happen to Rosie.

Why hadn't Aunt and Katriona *seen*? Never mind Ikor, who had a tendency to see only what he was looking for. And she felt the deep subterranean grumble of Woodwold agreeing with her, and knew, then, that some of why Woodwold had lain so wakeful these last three months was because of the perilously incompatible difference in the stories it heard through the footfalls of those who went loose upon the earth.

However deadly a mistake they had made, it was too late to change it now.

Hroc, sensing her distress, dug his nose into her leg a little harder. *At least tell the others to go away*, she said. *I do not want attention called to me this way*.

The other dogs stretched or shook themselves and began to wander away as if they had never been clustered round Rosie in the first place. And you say you do not believe in pretend, said Rosie, and Hroc smiled a dog-smile, with his eyes and ears.

The fog was returning in earnest. Rosie saw the king place the crown of inheritance on Peony's head, and the king's bishop bless her; heard the first official cheers led by her brothers; and she saw that the queen kept her eyes too carefully on Peony, and did not once look at Rosie, though she was always near at hand, and whom everyone else, in the knowledge that she was the princess' best friend, made a point of smiling at and speaking a word to. It was noted that the princess' best friend was pale and preoccupied (and that one of Lord Pren's fleethounds was shadowing her as if waiting to be a sort of self-motile sofa, should she need to sit down suddenly: the courtiers by now all knew about her talking to animals), but then who could blame her? My lord Rowland was almost as distracted, but he had his noble upbringing to fall back on, and he could (as the saying went) make conversation with an enchanted chamber pot. My lady Rosie was only a village girl after all. How lucky they were that the princess, although she, too, had been raised as a village girl, was so poised and gay on this splendid and historic occasion, and effortlessly seemed to take up her proper position.

Rosie heard the long speech the king's bishop made, and could hear by the way his voice soared and fell, and hastened forward and drew back to mark each word, that it was a speech full of erudition and noble sentiments, but she understood nothing of it. She made herself watch, and so noticed the Gig's Chief Priest looking both sulky and gratified as a member of the king's bishop's train, and the Foggy Bottom priestling looking thrilled and daunted (and almost unrecognizable in a shiny new hood) several tiers back in the same train. When, after the bishop, Lord Prendergast stood up and gave a much shorter speech, she only saw that he was smiling as he spoke. She must have lost a few moments, because a plate loaded with food was suddenly lying before her, and she discovered that she was sitting at a grand table with Katriona on one side and Barder beyond her, and Callin on Rosie's other side, and the princess' other ladies beyond. There was a reaccumulating drift of hounds and a spaniel or two over her feet and under and behind her chair, and Throstle, who had made a study of this kind of behaviour so he could perform it so charmingly that even people who didn't like dogs failed to protest, trotted along the table among the goblets and platters and epergnes, and jumped into Rosie's lap. Throstle adored Rosie, who had rescued him in the last three months from a life of uninterrupted lapdoggery by bringing him on her stable rounds every morning, telling Lady Pren it was therapeutic, which was true enough. (The new system had almost broken down after Throstle tackled a rat bigger than he was; he had it by the neck in the prescribed terrier manner, but it was going to beat him to death before it died. Fortunately Milo, Hroc's brother and best friend, had been there to finish it off.)

Peony sat between the king and the queen, with the princes on either side of them; and the youngest prince, who was the furthest away from her, on his elder brother's right hand, kept slipping out of his chair to stand by hers, holding on to the back of it and half climbing it, as boys, even princes, will do, as he spoke to her.

Rosie put her hand in her pocket, and touched the round butt of the spindle end, seeking the face of the little gargoyle, her finger finding its nose by the silkiness of the tiny well-polished slope; and the fog, while no lighter, for a time seemed a little easier to bear, although she had no appetite for supper. She looked round the table for other familiar faces, and caught Rowland watching her worriedly, and she did not have the strength to smile at him. She looked – not at, but round the queen, hoping for some glimpse of Sigil, who must, surely, have arrived in or with or somehow simultaneous to the royal train, even if she did not wish to attend the ball, and once or twice she thought she saw a small drab person bending near the queen as no servant but only a beloved friend could do; but Rosie could never see her clearly.

After dinner the dancing began, but Rosie did not dance. She would not have dared, because dancing was one of the name-day fairy gifts; but she had been able to say, truthfully, and with most of the Gig as witnesses, that she had never danced. Ikor claimed to have tried to teach her, and that even magic was in this case unavailing. (If there had been any jokes about clodhoppers behind her back, Rosie had never heard them. She was, although she was unaware of it, an imposing figure, not only on account of her height and the princess's fondness for her.) Fortunately Peony danced as well as if she were enchanted, and Rosie guessed which fairy had been the giver of that particular bounty by a look of such maudlin fatuity on her face that it caught even Rosie's cloudy eye. All the godmothers were, of course, present; and if one or two of them had some impression that their gifts had not gone quite as they had expected, they were too public-spirited to mope.

Katriona sat with her on a padded bench against the wall, and Rosie sent most of the dogs away again when they tried to follow her. Katriona held her hand as if feeling her pulse for fever, which perhaps she was; and Rosie leaned back against Woodwold's wall and half thought she felt it twitch. Through the fog she thought, I am still waiting to go home. I am not waiting for my birthday to be over so I can go – so that I can go to the royal city and become a princess, and – and let Peony be herself again; I am waiting for a few months of sham to be over so I can go home, and live in the wheelwright's house, and work as a horse-leech. She made an effort to keep her head up, not only so that she might be seen as sitting with dignity, instead of lolling feebly, but because looking down at her own fine skirts made her dizzy, as if the twinkly grey were a series of whirlpools any one of which she might fall into and drown.

The fog seemed to giggle. The hairy rat-snake things were back, and she thought maybe the giggling came from them. They didn't seem to have any eyes – or, for that matter, mouths – just furry, unpleasantly sinuous bodies, and rather a lot of small pattering feet. Yes, she could definitely hear someone laughing – she opened her heavy eyes, not having realized they were closed, and looked at the dancers. She had trouble focussing her eyes on all the bright moving figures, but a couple near her turned and she saw Peony in Rowland's arms; and then the laughter in her ears grew louder. Who was laughing? She shook her head, which only made it throb.

"What is it?" said Katriona; but Rosie's lips refused to open, her jaws were clamped together. Slowly she stood up, and Katriona with her, still holding her hand. Now the fog seemed to be becoming visible in the Great Hall; there was a greyish sort of shadow cast by nothing in particular, hovering near the far end of the Hall, across the long room from where she now stood, near to where the merrel sat hidden among the rafters. The laughter seemed to come from that direction. Rosie was curious; she would go nearer, and look. It was good to feel as if she wanted to do something – anything – in the middle of this horrible sick foggy inertia.

She tried to pull her hand out of Katriona's – she didn't need Katriona – but Katriona wouldn't let go. Very well, she would have to come, too. Rosie was now moving inexorably towards the strange greyish-black shadow that had no reason to hover where it did, still hearing – following – the laughter. It was odd that no-one else seemed to hear it. She noticed several people looking at her as she made her single-minded way through the dancers, dragging poor stubborn Katriona behind her. But why was no-one looking towards the end of the Hall, no-one saying, Who is that laughing? Perhaps because the laughter was for her, Rosie. Perhaps – since she had heard it first when she was thinking about going home – perhaps it was going to tell her how to go home, how she could give up this dreadful princess business, and go home, and be Rosie again.

She had to walk slowly because she still felt light-headed and not quite steady, and because Katriona was gripping her hand so tightly, and because Hroc was pressed against her other side, almost as if he wished to prevent her from walking the way she was going. She thought some of the other dogs were coming with them; at least one of them, probably Sunflower, kept getting between her legs, getting its paws caught in the fancy lace of her underskirt. They must look like one of those children's games, where you have to go somewhere while you all touch each other. But they wouldn't stop her. As soon as she knew what the laughter knew, everything would be all right.

As she neared the shadow, she saw that the dancing had stopped; they were all facing the bodiless shadow. Oh, so they *did* see it. The music had also stopped, or at least she could no longer hear it through the laughter. It was so loud now Rosie's ears were ringing with it; nonetheless she heard some commotion behind her, someone speaking: *No, no, let me go, you don't understand*. It sounded like Peony's voice.

The shadow was no longer bodiless. At first it was only as if a purple stain ran down it, as if some shaft of light had touched it from an unusual angle and produced this effect; but then the purple and the black and the grey began to wind themselves together and become a human shape. The human shape became a woman, tall and beautiful and terrible, as tall as Rosie, and her black-and-purple-and-cerise cloak fell round her in dangerous, shining folds.

"Well, my dear," said the tall woman to Rosie, who was still moving like a sleepwalker towards her. "We meet at last. We did not meet before, did we? I may have seen a hand or a curl – your hair is remarkably curly, is it not? – above the sides of your crib on your name-day, but I do not feel that was a proper meeting, crudely barred as I was from coming close enough to look you in the face. Well! So this is what the princess looks like – a tall rawboned gawk. I always did think your mother was common. The boys take after their father. It is just as well that one of them will be king – if there is any kingdom left for them." And she laughed.

It was taking Rosie an astonishing length of time merely to cross a few spans of floor. She thought it had something to do with Katriona, and she tried to turn her head and frown at her, but she could not; she could only go on staring at the tall woman in front of her. Very well; she did want to stare at her; she was fascinating. She was not polite – calling Rosie a gawk – but it was the truth. It was obvious this woman would have all the answers. Rosie wanted to talk to her. She wanted to ask her how she could go home again.

In the corners of her eyes she could see various soldiers and magicians and fairies moving in a strange, constrained way. They were trying to make the tall woman go away, thought Rosie wisely, she is spoiling the party, and they don't want her answers. Well, I do.

If she could have spoken aloud, she would have told Katriona to let go of her; the hand Kat was holding was numb, it was very unpleasant, it felt as if it no longer belonged to her. Even the dogs were trying to push her away from the tall woman. But Rosie wanted to talk to the tall woman and, it seemed, the tall woman wanted to talk to Rosie.

The tall woman moved a little to one side, never taking her eyes off Rosie. Beside her stood . . . a spinning wheel. Rosie blinked, startled and distracted. A spinning wheel of all things! And in that moment of distraction Rosie half felt someone tear themselves loose from the binding Rosie was half aware the tall woman had laid on every person in the room, and run forward; but whoever it was, they stumbled and stopped, ran and staggered, as if the way forward was very difficult. Rosie felt a sort of sympathy for them, trammelled as she was herself by Katriona and the dogs.

"Yes, a spinning wheel," the tall woman said. If she noticed someone trying to run towards her, she gave no sign. "A homely thing, is it not? Out of place in a grand room such as this one, in the middle of a grand ball. But I wanted a homely thing. You are a homely thing yourself, aren't you, my dear? And I wanted you to feel comfortable – as you are not comfortable in your present surroundings, are you? Such a pity, about your upbringing. The worst of your drawbacks might have been tempered with the right upbringing. Even your mother might have passed on to you – certain domestic virtues.

"Come, my dear. Come and spin. Forgive me if I don't demonstrate. It's such an unassuming skill, it has slipped my mind. Indeed, you can show me. I shall find it very interesting. And then I shall owe you a favour – and you have a question to ask me, do you not? Come and spin, my dear, and then I will answer any question you care to put."

Rosie was very close to the woman and the spinning wheel now. She couldn't at the moment remember if she knew how to spin – she couldn't remember having been taught, she couldn't seem to remember the feeling of the wool turning in her hands, the hypnotic, endless roll of the wheel going nowhere, the spindle filling up with thread – but she had a queer desire to lay her hands on this wheel, as if she knew exactly what to do with it – or perhaps she was eager to try because she wanted so badly to ask the tall woman her question about how she could go home again.

She wanted to reach out her hand, but that was the hand Katriona clung to, and she could not get it free, so she went to stretch out her other hand, and found that she was still holding the little gargoyle spindle's end. Her eyes went to the spindle on the tall woman's wheel, and she frowned in puzzlement; it was strangely elongated and sharp, sharp as a poniard at its tip, nothing like the thick, round-tipped spindles she had always been used to. What a very strange shape for a spindle!

She remembered now that she did not know how to spin. Katriona had said that she didn't need to know, that Rosie could do other things she and Aunt could not, but Rosie had guessed this meant she was sure to be as cack-handed at spinning as she was at sewing, and Katriona was trying to save her the humiliation. She felt humiliated now, remembering. And then she remembered offering to loan the gargoyle spindle end to Peony, to help her spinning, and Peony saying that if it was a charm, it belonged to their family, and it might have its feelings hurt or its usefulness spoilt if it were loaned away. Rosie needed a charm now so that she could spin something for the tall woman, and then the tall woman would answer her question.

Slowly she drew the gargoyle out, and held it before her. "If – if you don't mind," she said, and her voice sounded thick and hollow in her ears, "I would rather use my own spindle; I've never seen one like yours, and I'm sure I shan't be able to use it. . . "

The rage and hatred in the woman's face was so vivid and potent and suddenly *there* that Rosie took an involuntary step backwards, tripping over a dog as she did so; and the break in her concentration was much sharper and more complete this time. *Pernicia!* Rosie thought suddenly. Dear fate, this is *Pernicia!* And here I am wanting to ask her how to go home again!

But Rosie had been spelled very powerfully, and she could not run away nor shake herself free. She could feel the fog squeezing her, and the rat-snakes wriggled and chittered. But her hands, for a moment, were her own, and she squeezed Katriona's hand as the hand holding the gargoyle pressed it to her breast like a shield; and then the running, reeling footsteps she had heard off and on during Pernicia's speech were directly behind her, and as Pernicia's eyes turned briefly to this unwanted distraction, Peony half-ran past her, precarious as a drunk woman, her hand outstretched to grasp the daggerlike spindle –

– and Pernicia opened her mouth, and swept up her arms, to perform a curse that would blast Peony into dust, and hurl Rosie forward despite Katriona and the entire complement of Lord Pren's kennels, to impale herself on the spike as if it were the spear it looked like –

– when from over Pernicia's head a great white bulk moved, spreading its huge wings and giving the wild berserker shriek of the hunting merrel, which chills the blood of the oldest huntsmen, who know that it is too wise and too wary to stoop on a human being –

– and Pernicia, not having noticed the merrel, or perhaps not knowing that the creature who made that noise will not attack a human being, or that this one was chained on a short chain strong enough to hold it, faltered for just an instant –

– and Peony touched the point of the spindle, uttering a tiny cry as it pierced her forefinger, and the first bright drop of blood spilled out, and Peony lurched first to her knees, grasping at the frame of the wheel, and leaving a smear of blood as she fell to the floor –

– and then there was a great roaring, and the floor seemed to heave under Rosie's feet, and she could feel neither the gargoyle in one hand nor Katriona's hand in the other, nor all the dogs wound round her legs –

And then she knew no more.

PART FIVE

Chapter 20

S he was still breathing with Peony.
Well, that was a good sign; it meant both of them were still alive. But it certainly wasn't her own lungs that were pumping her breath in and out, and this made her, distantly, vaguely, a little apprehensive. She'd never felt quite so *inert* before, breathing with Peony. Perhaps she was just very tired. She was very tired. She lay enjoying the luxury of not even having to do her own breathing for a minute or two.

She couldn't just now remember why she was so tired. She tried to cast her mind back, but it seemed as inert as the rest of her. This last season had been busier in the Gig than usual, it was true, because some kind of odd magical trouble had been making mischief for everyone . . . everyone . . . especially at Foggy Bottom . . . Her memory made an incomplete lurch and recoil that juddered through her physical body. Almost she began breathing for herself again – almost she thought she heard a ragged, desperate voice mutter, "Come *on*, Rosie" – but then she flopped back into the queer passivity that held her. But she half remembered that it was early spring, not midwinter, that she had lost three months somehow. . .

Breathing *with* Peony?

She gasped, and it was her own gasp, and with it she realized that there were fingers pinching her nose, and a mouth over her mouth, forcing air down her throat and then backing off to let her exhale; again; and again; and again; and that this had been going on for some time. When she gasped, the fingers slackened, and she heard a hoarse voice say, "Rosie?"

It was dark, or perhaps her eyes were too listless to see as her lungs had been too listless to breathe. She nonetheless sensed the solid bulk of the speaker's body bending over her, and lips just brushed her cheek when they spoke her name. She would have liked to answer – she would have liked to say, "Who are you?" – but she could not. She went on breathing, jerkily, as if learning a new skill; and the arm that slid itself under her shoulders and raised her to a sitting position seemed a familiar arm, as the hair that tickled her cheek seemed familiar hair, and the smell of the breath and the skin of her rescuer was a familiar smell. Not Katriona. Not Aunt. Not Barder. Not Peony.

Narl.

"Narl?" she said in amazement; or she thought she said it, but her voice was little more responsive than her eyes or her heavy limbs.

She could feel him looking around – perhaps the darkness was not so dark to him – feel his alertness, his watchfulness, as he knelt beside her with his arm round her shoulders. She could not remember. Those missing three months; wearing dresses; breathing with Peony. . .

Ikor. Woodwold. The princess' birthday party.

Pernicia.

A little mew of fear escaped her, and she shivered, despite the unmerited bliss of Narl's arms round her. He put his lips to her ear and said, "We are all right for a little while. We'll need to move soon, but right now you go on remembering how to breathe for yourself. I can carry you a while if it comes to that. Although neither of us would enjoy it much" – there was a ghost of a laugh – "and before that, we have to have decided where we're going."

It took her several more breaths to knit together enough strength to ask a question: "Where are we?"

"We're still in the Great Hall. You're where you fell after you asked to use your own spindle" – the ghost of the laugh again – "and Peony and the merrel interfered just in time."

"What are *you* doing here?"

There was a pause so brief Rosie wasn't sure there had been a pause at all. "Watching out for my horse-leech, of course. My business has been a lot duller, these last three months."

Rosie remembered Barder saying, "The joke is that Narl won't take a stranger's horse, because he'd have to tell 'em what the fee is."

"I didn't see you," she said.

"No."

A typical Narl answer. Rosie knew herself to be smiling, and felt a little better. She could almost stand up. Not quite.

"Why is it so dark?"

"The lights all blew out – and the fires – after Peony touched the spindle and the floor leaped up. It'll be dawn soon."

"The *floor* leaped?"

"Yes. It seemed to want to be rid of Pernicia."

At least it seemed quiet and floorlike now. Rosie concentrated on breathing again, waiting for dawn, and trying to force some vigour back into her limbs. She could feel her hands and forearms lying over her lap, limp as sleeping puppies; and her feet flopped at the ends of her legs, as if they had no idea what they were for. She could hear no sound but her own breathing, and Narl's, and a faint purring, echoing noise itself rather like breathing, which seemed to come from all round them. She almost thought she imagined it. Then she thought she didn't. She considered the rustly silence.

"Where – where is everyone else?" she said at last, fearfully.

"Oh, they're here too," he said matter-of-factly. "They're just all asleep."

"Asleep?" said Rosie. "Like I was asleep?"

"They're breathing," he said.

Sleep is the sister to death. "Is Peony breathing?"

This time there was definitely a silence before he answered. "Rosie, I – I don't know. Pernicia grabbed her as the floor curled up round her – round Pernicia, and then threw her as a hand might throw a ball. She took Peony with her. Then the doors slammed shut and everything went dark."

Rosie put her hands over her face, and leaned against Narl's shoulder, and one arm curved round her and the other hand stroked a gentle path from the crown of her head to her shoulder blades, again and then again. She thought wretchedly of the many nights she'd lain awake thinking of just such tenderness and such an embrace, and now, when it came – "Rosie, love," said Narl. "We're going after her. Just wait for it to get a little light, so we can see what we're doing."

Rosie blearily opened her eyes, and peered over Narl's shoulder. Were not solid black shapes beginning to differentiate themselves from the grey of what was merely air?

As if in answer to her thought, Narl said, "There should be more light; I can feel that the sun's over the horizon."

Rosie's eyes were idly focussed on a bit of darkness that had gone a strangely ragged grey. She supposed she must be looking at a tapestry on a wall with a curiously contrasty and dramatic pattern; funny that she couldn't remember any such; but it might have been something new, from the arrival of the royal party. Or could some splash of Pernicia's magic have washed up a wall and changed the colours of a tapestry?

Rosie blinked, and frowned. Narl was facing the wrong direction. "Narl – look over here."

Narl cautiously let her go, and turned round. She propped herself on her hands and resisted the impulse to collapse full-length on the floor again. They both looked further along the wall she was facing, and found more large ragged grey rectangles at regular intervals. Narl slowly climbed to his feet, and leaned down and pulled Rosie to hers; and she found that she could stand.

Still slowly, Narl steadying her, they moved among the huddled dark shapes that Rosie could half recognize as human bodies, a glint or sheen giving away that they were all dressed in their finest party clothes. It was an eerie landscape, something out of a fairy tale; magic was never as comprehensive as this, not in real life.

The grey rectangles were windows, and the reason the

morning light could not get through was because of the thick tangle of thorny branches growing just outside them. Narl had designed all, and made many, of the window catches for the glass panes at Woodwold, and he pulled open the nearest casement without hesitation, and warily put his hand through it. "They're wild roses," he said, sounding as bewildered as Rosie had ever heard him. "Briar roses – a great hedge of them, as if they'd grown here for two hundred years."

"Woodwold," said Rosie, thinking of the conscious, listening presence of the house during the last three months, suspicious of what it did not understand – and it understood very little about most of the creatures that went loose upon the earth – but loyal to its family, short-lived and precariously footed though its members were, and steadfast in their defence. She remembered it murmuring, *Rosie.* "Woodwold is protecting us."

Narl stood a moment longer, staring out at the wild impassable weave of rose stems, many of them as thick as his wrists, the thorns bigger than a fleethound's fangs. "Woodwold is protecting the sleep of its people," he said at last. "But also keeping us imprisoned. We must go after Pernicia, not only for Peony's sake, but, I guess, if any of these people is to wake up again."

"Us?" said Rosie. He had said that once before. Her heart rose and sank simultaneously, leaving her feeling rather dizzy; but that might have been only the remains of the fog that had held her last night – if it was last night – and the magical, poisoned sleep. "Katriona. Is Kat asleep, too?" Kat was supposed to come with me. Kat was supposed to keep me alive long enough to. . .

She turned away from the supporting wall, took a tentative step away from it and Narl, and found that her body was mostly back in her control again. She was also beginning to remember more about the end of the ball. If she had woken up where she had fallen, then Katriona should be there, too. . .

She was. Rosie saw the sparkle of her overskirt first, the deep emerald that set off her dark hair so well; an inquisitive ray of sunlight had made its way through the rose stems and had found the green and decided to play with it, sliding down the hollows and twinkling off the gentle rise and fall of Katriona's side. Rosie knelt beside her. Her face looked peaceful, and her breathing was the slow light snore Rosie remembered from the cottage, when the three of them shared a bedroom. One of Lord Pren's hounds had his head comfortably pillowed on the skirt round her feet: the animals were asleep, too. Rosie took Katriona's shoulder and shook it gently. "Kat," she said. "Katriona." Katriona didn't stir.

"Rosie." Narl, standing behind her. "I don't —"

"No," said Rosie, and one tear slid down her face. You were supposed to come with me, she thought. You *promised*. "Narl— why aren't you asleep?"

She heard him shift, as if uneasily, but his voice, when it came, was cool and neutral. "I've a bit of – cold iron, that was given me, long ago. I welded it into my smith's chain when I made the chain. It's some protection against some things. The sleep's hers, but Woodwold interrupted before she finished the job, I reckon. You could say she didn't have time to notice me."

He wasn't lying, but he wasn't telling her the truth either. She turned round to look at him. He wouldn't meet her gaze, but looked instead across the twilit landscape of the room, the series of hummocks of all those sleeping bodies, the sharp angular peaks of furniture, the sparks of glancing sunlight.

She followed his gaze, and then couldn't; it was too eerie, too – spectral. The rustle of breathing could have been the whispering of restless ghosts. She looked back at Katriona, lying sleeping with a half smile on her face. She touched her cheek, knowing she would not awaken, still half hoping she would. She thought of Aunt, somewhere in the Great Hall, and of Ikor, and of all the royal magicians and fairies – even Sigil – lying asleep, the most powerful magic wielders in the kingdom; all asleep, except for Narl. And herself, having breathed Narl's breath.

"Narl," she said. "Tell me the truth. The rest of it, I mean."

Narl sank down beside her, and, to her amazement, reached for one of her hands and began to play with the fingers. This was an utterly un-Narl-like gesture. "I'm a fairy," he said at last. "Didn't you know?"

Didn't she *know*? "I – of *course* I didn't know. You *can't* be a fairy," Rosie said. "You're a *smith*."

Another silence. "It happens occasionally. You know the stories."

"They're all from centuries ago!"

"It doesn't happen very often."

Rosie, overwhelmed, fell silent. She took her hand away from him and wrapped both arms round her knees and put her head on them. She tried to find something to think about that was still itself, after the last three months, after last night, after Narl's revelation. Oh, Gorse, she thought. You were wrong. I'm not who I am – nor is anyone else – and besides, they're all asleep. She wanted to laugh, but she thought if once she started, she wouldn't be able to stop.

"There are a lot of fairies asleep in this hall," she said. "Why not you?"

"I don't know."

When it became obvious that he was not going to say any more, Rosie said with asperity: "This is going to be a *long* conversation. Why did you think I should know you are a fairy?"

"The animals know."

Rosie digested this. It was true that the animals would know, but it was also true that it was not the sort of thing they would pass on without an animal sort of reason. They might have told her if she had asked, but it wasn't anything it would ever have occurred to her to ask. Which meant that Narl couldn't talk to animals himself, or he'd know all that. She flushed, and scowled – it would have been too humiliating if he hadn't needed her to translate when he'd asked her to.

He was watching her closely, and saw the scowl. "Rosie, I'm sorry. I've never told anyone – not since I left home, and that was a long time ago. I barely remember it myself, most of the time."

Rosie shook her head, still scowling. "Why not? You're obviously – well, you must be pretty good," and she gestured at their surroundings.

Narl grimaced. "I'm a seer."

Oh. Seers were notoriously unreliable. Although they usually told wonderful stories – many of them earned their livings as bards. It figured that Narl hardly spoke at all. And was a blacksmith.

"But – won't working with iron all the time give you rheumatism?"

Narl sighed. "No. It's in my family."

"*What's* in your family?," said Rosie, holding on to her temper.

"Fairy smiths. Those old stories are mostly about my family."

Rosie stared. The stories about fairy smiths tended to be about eight-foot giants laying out taralians with back-handed blows from the hafts of their axes, or hammering all night to shoe the horses of the king's cavalry so they could trot across the flooded river on top of the water and meet with a very surprised invading army on the other side. . . And then there was that story of the Prendergast seer who had decided where Woodwold would be built.

"That – bit of cold iron," said Rosie. "Where does it come from?"

Narl pulled at the short chain round his neck, finding the link he wanted by feel. It was nothing to look at. The rest of the chain was a proper forged chain; what he held now between thumb and forefinger was a little irregular knob of iron, some broken-off, discarded bit, too small to bother salvaging for another purpose. "It came from round here," said Narl. "Somewhere. About forty great-grandfathers ago, Lord Pren and I are cousins."

"Is that why you came here?"

Narl shook his head. "No." He hesitated, and added, "But then Rowland didn't come here looking for the princess either."

What if—? No. Narl had been in Foggy Bottom long before Katriona came home from the princess's name-day with a baby. But . . . how much *can* a seer see? She thought of some of the stories the seer-bards told: by that standard, a lot. How much does a seer see in a true vision, supposing he knows he's having one? Enough to know that to save a princess – to save a kingdom – someone's fortieth-great-grandson needed to be in the Great Hall someone was founding, eleven hundred years later?

"Does Lord Pren know?"

"No. But I think . . . Woodwold does. I think it recognizes this," and he touched the small iron nub on his chain with a finger.

He took a deep breath, like a man nerving himself for a single-handed rush at a massed enemy, and plunged into speech. "Rosie – I'm not a very good fairy. I'm a much better smith. You'd have been better off – much, much better off – with Kat. Or Aunt. Or even Ikor. The problem with Ikor is that he saw you, Rosie, as the reflection. The princess is the solid one, for him. So he never understood Rosie."

Rosie stared at him. So far as she knew he had never met Ikor, let alone heard him talk about the princess, let alone seen them together, let alone. . . "Narl . . . how did you know that Peony . . . that I . . . that I am the princess?"

He spoke as if he were now in the midst of battle, and his every word was an arrow that flew at him. "I've always known. I knew there was something about you that first day you walked into the forge – knee-high to the horse I was shoeing and more chatter than a squirrel. Seers *see*, you know, and even bad ones learn when they're seeing right even though they mostly see wrong. And – things are true, in a smith's yard. It's like there were two of you – the solid one that talked all the time and loved horses and all the other beasts, and a sort of . . . radiance, that followed you, human shaped, like a shadow, only rainbow coloured, which did everything you did. I don't know when I understood what it meant. By the time I knew I already *had* known" – he made Rosie's gesture of frustration at that point, running his hand through his hair. "It was like finally having a name for a bird or a flower you see every day or every season. Rosie. Princess." He paused for a moment and added, "The – the princessness of you only shone out like that at the forge. I looked. That's why I never said anything to Aunt or Kat about it. All I did was – er – I arranged it that my forge is unusually prone to disturbing the vision of other fairies with rainbows and foxfire. Even Nurgle sees them when she brings the laundry. Anyone who saw you trailing your radiance would think it was that. That's something a seer can do: give other people visions as false as his own." He paused again and then said heavily: "I will help you the best I can, you see, but it won't be a very good best."

Rosie shook her head. "That's not how the stories go. Fairy smiths are always terribly powerful."

"Those are fairy tales," said Narl. "I'm real."

"Just like me," said Rosie sadly. "I'm real, too. I just don't know, real what."

Narl made a gesture towards her, hastily cut off, that Rosie couldn't identify. She unclasped her hands, straightened her legs out, and looked at her crumpled, dusty, once-fine skirts. "If we're going to go – wherever we're going to go, I need some other clothes," she said. She looked across the long stretch of floor to the stairs, and shivered.

"I'll come with you," said Narl.

The journey to the princess's tower was made without incident, though it was not pleasant. The corridors were all too long and too dark and too silent, and Rosie was still suffering the after-effects of her poisoned sleep, and felt cold and strengthless. The last long flight of stairs was very long indeed, and without Narl's hand under her arm, half lifting her up each riser, she thought she might have sat down at its foot and never moved again.

Even the princess' tower room was dark with the stark coils of late-winter rose stems wrapped round its windows, and the fire asleep in the hearth. Rosie staggered feebly to her window seat and pulled herself up the step to look out. "Narl," she said.

Narl had remained by the door, looking up, perhaps at Eskwa, still hanging over the lintel. He joined her and together they peered through the thorny barricade to a great opaque weave of grey rose stems stretching away from them, swelling and falling over the invisible walls and roofs of Woodwold. It was a bleak landscape, as alien and frightening as the Great Hall and its sleepers, and far more unfamiliar, for every landmark, every familiar roof line, had disappeared, and a cold hard grey light lay over everything like a sheen of water. "I've looked out of this window several times a day every day for three months," she said, shoving gingerly at a hindering rose stem, a mere thumb's breadth in diameter, in the hopes of improving her view, "and I can't even tell you what we're looking at." Could it be a heavy dew that made the light glare so? "I can't see anything but the rose stems, can you? I can't even see where the park begins. It's almost as if we're floating in a cloud, or an island in a bog."

"I hope not," said Narl.

The spiderweb hung empty in the corner of the window frame.

Rosie looked at it intently, willing herself to find one tiny bobble at some gossamer crossroad which was a tightly-curled, sleeping spider, but she could not find one. "What is it?" said Narl.

"Nothing," muttered Rosie. "I can't find the spider. She's been here right along – since we came here three months ago."

"Maybe she decided to go downstairs and see the ball," said Narl.

"I hope she started in time to find a good window frame first," said Rosie.

She climbed down from the window seat and rummaged among the boxes under her side of the bed. She had forbidden the maids to touch her old clothing, but after the first week she hadn't checked; looking at her beloved boots and trousers and the leather waistcoat darkened by the damp affections of hundreds of horses and scratched by the enthusiasm of many small and medium-sized clawed feet, only made her more miserable. She held her breath as she tipped the lid back. . . Yes, there they were, folded far more neatly than she had left them. She had so longed for the opportunity – the excuse – to put them back on. . . She pulled the things out and began to dress. She noticed that everything (except the waistcoat, which was beyond recovery) had been beautifully cleaned before it had been stowed away, and this only made her more wretched. Last she rescued her spindle end from the pocket of her ball gown, and slipped it into her trousers. She muttered, "Let's go," in a muffled voice, and kept her eyes resolutely on Narl's feet as he turned away from the window to join her again.

She felt a slight resistance as she stepped across the threshold into the hall, as if the air had gathered itself together and pushed back at her. She paused and looked up, as Narl had looked up.

It was dark in the hall, and darker still above the door; but Eskwa glittered in the darkness. *Eskwa both binds and cuts. If you have need of either, he will answer to your hand.* She could barely reach the lower edge of the blade, even standing on tiptoe; she would need a stool or something to stand on, to unhook it from whatever held it. But as she thought to go in search of the stool, the sabre came softly away from the wall and slid into her hands. She stood staring at it; swords and sabres were outside her practical experience. "It will do as a lamp," she said, turning the blade a little as one might turn a faceted gem in candlelight, "even if I don't know anything else to do with it. Do you?"

Narl shook his head. "I have no warrior training. And it is your hand it came to."

No-one awake, their footsteps seemed to say to her as they descended again. She had loosened her belt and cautiously tucked Eskwa through it, and the blade laid a little track of light in front of their feet. *No-one awake. No-one awake.* No-one awake but Narl and me. No-one awake. Down they went, down and down, as they had gone up, with no other sound but their footsteps, until they heard the soft tidal sound of hundreds of people breathing in their sleep as they turned on to the final flight of stairs.

They paused at the foot of those last stairs. To their right ran a corridor and a series of smaller parlours Lady Pren had set up as places where weary and overwhelmed party-goers might retreat; by the faint moan of breathing, some people had. To the left were the series of corridors that led at last to the kitchens and cellars. Rosie dreaded re-entering the Hall, but that was where the main doors were. "I suppose we should try the front doors first? It doesn't seem very likely, but it . . . who knows what the rules are in a fairy tale?"

Narl nodded, and they made their way as quickly as possible across the floor, Rosie half trying not to look at any of the figures she scuttled round, half hoping to see Aunt, or Barder, or even Ikor or Rowland. Or Sigil. She did see Lord Prendergast, inelegantly sprawled, one leg somehow thrown over the body of someone who could only be one of the royal magicians, and an important one, too, by the jewels at his breast, and the beribboned gold chain in his hair. One of the ribbons had fallen into his open mouth, and he made a slight gagging noise as he breathed. Rosie stopped and brushed it clear.

Their path did not take them near the dais where the king and queen had still been standing when Pernicia appeared; Rosie would have avoided it even if that had been the shortest way.

Despite icy-dank early-spring draughts (and a collision of incompatible smoke-suppressing spells that caused great ashy belches from one of the enormous fireplaces) the huge central doors of the Hall had been left open since the official beginning of the ball, so that people could come and go as they pleased, including members of the royal family walking out to the tents in the park. (Ikor had hated this, but agreed that it was the sort of thing the princess they had created would do.) The big doors, which opened outwards, were now closed; slammed shut, Rosie wondered, by the force of an explosion of rose stems? The doors might now as well have been walls; they barely creaked when Narl and Rosie pushed unhopefully against them. There was a small door cut out of one of the big ones, which opened inwards, and it still opened, but outside the rose stems were so thick not even sunlight could break through. Rosie looked at Eskwa, as if the sabre might tell her what to do, but it said nothing; and she did not wish to try Ikor's blade against Woodwold's defence. It wasn't till then that one more implication of the breathing silence came to her: Woodwold itself was asleep. There were no whispers of *Rosie*. The doors were sealed against them as well as against Pernicia. No-one awake.

As Rosie turned away from the doors, she saw something in the corner of her eye, and saw Narl's head begin to turn just as she snapped her own round. Movement.

Someone was staggering to his feet. Not two feet, but four. Hroc. And then Sunflower, the spaniel bitch. Then a lower, lurching, drunken shadow: Flinx.

"*Flinx!*" said Rosie. "What are you doing here? Did you come with Kat? Oh, I'm so glad to see you!"

But Flinx sat down at some distance from Rosie, with his back to her, and tried to wash a front paw; and promptly fell over. He hissed, furiously, and his hair bushed out; but that didn't work right either, and some of his hair stood on end and some didn't, giving him a look both rakish and clownish. He hated it, and hissed again, ears flat back and eyes like midsummer bonfires.

"Flinx, I'm sorry," said Rosie. "I'd stroke you, but you'd only bite me, wouldn't you? In the temper you're in. And if you missed, you'd only be angrier." She spoke aloud, for she knew her words were more for her comfort than for Flinx's; but she knew, by the angle of his back-turning, that he was listening to her, and that her placatory tone would be registered.

Several more sighthounds had woken up: Milo, and Tash, and Froo. Tash had lain by Rosie's chair every evening since she had come to Woodwold and, when the draughts were bad, across her feet. Froo was a romantic, and loved Rosie because she was the princess; she reminded her a little of Ikor.

And Spear: she hadn't known Spear had come to the ball, nor how he might have done so; he did not stray far from his pub any more. He appeared out of the darkness in the back of the Hall, his wiry half-long coat, dark during Rosie's childhood, now almost as white as the merrel. He placed each foot with utter deliberation. He of them all walked the most steadily, as if he were habituated to overseeing mere physical unreliabilities, and the after-effects of poisoned sleep were no worse than the standard infirmities of old age. He came straight up to Rosie and with no apparent hesitation, reared himself (a little stiffly) on his hind legs and put his front paws on her shoulders, which had been his standard greeting since she was ten years old and strong enough to bear his weight. He did this with no other human; but then no other human had taken her first steps clinging to his tail.

When he dropped back to the floor again, Rosie saw one more approaching shadow over his shoulder. This one was very small and low to the floor – less than half the size of Flinx. Throstle.

Throstle was moving slowly, but he did not stagger. He walked up to Rosie and put his head on her foot. He weighed so little she wouldn't have known he was there if he hadn't caught her eye first; but he hadn't been a sleeve dog most of his life without learning a good deal about how to make his presence felt, even among people who couldn't talk to him as Rosie could.

She and Narl and their ragged, wombly, teetery crew stood still in the middle of the scene of desolation and tried to think about what came next. The dogs, without seeming to organize themselves, had meandered round till they were all facing more or less in the same direction. There was a tiny bump against Rosie's ankle, a meek plucking at the floppy top edge of her boot, and she leaned down (carefully, on account of Eskwa) to scoop up Throstle: and discovered two mice looking at her beseechingly. *Us too*, they said. *Uss tooo.*

Their silent voices were familiar. *You're from Foggy Bottom*, said Rosie. *How did you get here? Where are your brothers and sisters and cousins?*

They are still in Foggy Bottom, they replied. *We came in your — your box.* (There was at this point a vivid mouse-eye view of the inside of a box full of not-very-well-packed bits and pieces moving at speed on the back of a coach.) *When you came here.*

Why?

To be near you, Princess, they said, surprised that so obvious an answer needed to be supplied. *We all wanted to come. But we thought it would not . . . do you a service with the humans here if there were . . . suddenly many more of us in this other place. So we . . . chose.*

Throstle wagged his tail. "Oh well," said Rosie, "if they're friends of yours. I wonder if Lady Pren knows?" And she dropped Throstle into her biggest pocket, offered the palm of her hand to the mice, and, when they had ticklingly climbed on to it, dropped them on top of Throstle.

Flinx had already set out, towards the stairs at the back of the Great Hall, making a determined, if still slightly unsteady, way through the sleepers. "That way?" said Rosie.

"I don't know any reason why not," Narl said.

Flinx led the procession through the corridors away from the formal parlours, and down wide, worn stairs into the kitchens, where the fire slept with the cooks and the men and the maid and the spit boy. And the cat. Flinx looked at the sleeping kitchen cat with disdain. Rosie paused long enough to shift the spit boy, who, if the fire woke up before he did, was going to be himself roasted, as Narl saved the cook from drowning slowly in her bowl of batter. "I don't suppose we dare touch any of the food?" said Rosie; Narl shook his head. Then they went on.

Flinx led them steadily, walking more strongly, and Spear walked beside him through the kitchens. But as they went down another flight of stairs, they descended into darkness, darkness so heavy that Eskwa faded to a ghostly crescent shape, and cast no light. There would have been torches on the walls, but they had no fire to kindle them with. "Oh, but—" began Rosie.

Narl, a step below her, reached up and took her hand. "I can lead you through the dark," he said. "This dark, anyway." She curled her fingers round his wide palm and followed. The animals all moved together, close enough to touch their neighbours, so as not to lose each other. Just before the darkness became absolute, Hroc dropped back from Spear's heels to insinuate his head under her other hand. They reached the bottom of the stairs and went on. The flooring was rough stone, and Rosie picked up her feet like a carriage pony. Her nose and ears and skin could sense the openings of other passages; she wondered if Flinx and Spear were still at the head of the procession, and if Narl was following them.

She felt, strangely, perfectly safe, her feet taking slow, careful, blind steps into the dark of an unknown tunnel underground. She felt wistful about all the other underground ways she would have liked to learn more about. Here were the roots of Woodwold, here were the first founding places; she might have been able to hear . . . to hear some buried, secret language telling her what she needed to know, some old but mortal trick she might use against Pernicia, some trick so ancient Pernicia would have forgotten it: some trick Narl's forebear might have left for their aid, eleven hundred years ago.

By now the pitchy blackness was thick and tangible enough to prove a fifth element, unjustly omitted from the usual list: not air or water, not earth or fire, but dark. She stopped, and listened, and her companions stopped, too, and, with the sharpening of the other senses blindness provokes, she could feel them turning their heads, searching for what had disturbed her.

But all was silence. Woodwold was asleep, too; down here Rosie was sure she could have heard what she had had only echoes of in the walls upstairs. Pernicia had sent even Woodwold to sleep. But Narl was awake, and had woken her. And Hroc was awake, and Milo and Tash and Froo, and Flinx and Spear, and Sunflower and Throstle and two mice from Foggy Bottom. And what about the rose hedge?

She stood a minute longer, listening, waiting; the others stood patiently, for she was their princess.

The dogs picked it up first, of course; she felt the ears pricking, the heads – and the hackles – rising; and she could feel the buzz of an inaudible growl through the top of Hroc's head. Then she and Narl, too, could hear the soft pat-pat of small feet in the silence of the corridor.

Fox. Even human noses can recognize that smell. It stopped at some little distance from them, and said, *I have come to be near the princess. Will you let me pass?*

The dogs made no move as it approached, neither making way for it nor barring it. Rosie felt soft padded forefeet touch her knee, and a cold nose her wrist. *Z e l*, she said. *You jumped into Peony's arms, that night. Ikor looked at you and. . . But where have you come from?*

I don't know, he said. *I have just woken up. It was dark. And then I heard your company. May I come with you?*

Yes, said Rosie, *but do you know where we are going?*

Pernicia, sighed all the silent dog-voices around them. *Pernicia*.

Zel was silent for a moment, and then he said, *I am here. I will come.*

They went on, and then the dark began to grow a little less, and Rosie could see dog-heads and dog-backs, and then a smaller puff of darkness became Flinx, still in the lead; and then there were stairs again, and they went up. The smell told them where they were before they reached ground level: the smell of very well kept horses, and of the bins of corn in the storage room the stairs led to.

The long stable was in twilight, rose stems growing over the windows. The door to the courtyard at the end of the central corridor stood open, but there was little more light through it; although the immediate way was unblocked, there were thorny branches hanging down from the lintel and curling round the side posts, and a tangly greeny-grey of hedge not far beyond.

The horses, too, were asleep, and grooms lay in the aisles, some of them fallen down on the harness or horse rugs they were carrying. Rosie looked anxiously at the row of pitchforks hanging on the wall, but the only one missing was found slid harmlessly from the lax hand that had held it.

All the horses were asleep. She had no reason to expect otherwise. Nor had she led the little party here; Flinx had, or Spear, or Narl. Perhaps this was merely the shortest way back to the surface from the kitchen cellars. Perhaps they would have to go back down into the darkness and try the other tunnels. Try them for what? A way out? She doubted that Woodwold's underground maze ran any further than Woodwold's hedge of briar roses.

There was a quick scrambling noise not far from them, and then a long elegant blood-bay head with straw in its forelock was thrust out over a half door: Fast. Rosie broke into a run – thus finding out she could again do so – to open his door, and put her arms round his neck; and then they went to find Gorse. He had just finished opening his own door when they came to him: *A useful skill, he said, but one I have been careful not to overuse for fear of someone finding out I can do it. That is how I came to you that night, a season ago.*

And Fast?

A prance from Fast: not a very good one, for the sleep still lay on him, but neither of the horses seemed as sick from it as those who had fallen in the Hall had been.

Fast merely jumped his fence. He is young, and impetuous, and he loves you, Princess.

Fast bit her shoulder, lovingly, and not very hard, but Rosie looked at her friends in the striped twilight and thought: one reluctant princess who is really a horse-leech, two horses, a few hounds, a spaniel, a very small terrier, a fox, two mice, and a cat. And a fairy smith who says he's better at smithing. And we are seeking to confront a wicked fairy who is planning to destroy our entire country, and the only people who might help us are asleep. I suppose it is a confrontation we want. I don't *know*. This was what Katriona was supposed to do. Oh dear. I don't suppose there's any point in finding our way to the dairies or the poultry houses, and picking up a cow and a few chickens. I wonder what happened to Pernicia's spindle when – when Woodwold threw her out of the Hall? Without her conscious volition, Rosie's hand felt for the friendly wooden spindle end in her pocket.

She looked at Narl and saw he knew the shape of her thoughts. "Do you have any idea what we do now?"

Narl shook his head. After a moment's silence he said: "I'm afraid it's your call. In spite of the iron I'm carrying, the pressure of the magic here is making me stupid. Of the magics. That's part of the problem. They strain against each other like the parts of a badly made tool you're being forced to use – you don't know which bit is going to fly to pieces first but you know something will. I should be able to give you a little warning if the balances shift dangerously, but that's about all. I told you you would have been better off with Kat. But . . . there must be some way out even if I can't think of it. Magic can't do everything."

Right, thought Rosie. It can only kill you or ruin your life or destroy everything that means anything to you. Fine.

It took them the rest of what might have been the morning, although the light did not change as on an ordinary day, to test the immediate boundaries of the briar hedge. Neither Narl nor Rosie believed there would be a way through, but, like trying the front doors in the Great Hall first, the venture had to be made. They asked the horses to stay where they were, just outside the stable doors, where there was a little rose-roofed clearing about the size of the Foggy Bottom wrights' yard; the other, smaller, animals, and the two humans, pursued the inner circumference of the hedge.

There was indeed no way through. There were places a thin determined body could slide carefully along for some little distance – when it was between some wall of Woodwold and the hedge, the ancient and pitted stone facing of Woodwold was only slightly less cruel to human skin and clothing than the thorns of wild roses – but these never led anywhere. Even the mice said they could find no path that lasted more than a few dozen mouse-lengths. *There's a* stretchy *feeling about this hedge*, said Hroc. *Like a leash made of green leather. There's a give to it that makes you think it's not serious, but it won't let you go very far. It's there to hold you in.*

Several times Rosie tried to speak to Woodwold, but there was never any answer. She might, in the tension and anxiety of present circumstances, have begun to believe that she had never heard Woodwold saying *Rosie, Princess*, never felt the eerie awareness of the house watching her; but the quality of Woodwold's silence now was not that of something that does not speak but of something that has been shut away, trapped, barricaded. Rosie stared at the impassible hedge and thought of herself during the last three months.

Then she thought: I wonder what a bird might find, flying above this – prison? Perhaps there is some answer in the fact that we have seen no birds. She sighed. It was beginning to be difficult to ignore how hungry she was, and thirsty; they would not be able to go very much longer without risking a drink of water. Her eyes went longingly to the water butt outside the stable door.

She tried to remember some of Aunt and Katriona's conversations about spell breaking. This didn't come up very often in a place like the Gig, but it did occasionally. "Never attack a spell head-on," Aunt had said. "That's where it's strongest. You need to sniff out where the weak places are. All spells have them;

it's just a matter of finding them . . . and, of course, being able to use them. If a spell has been very powerfully made, the likes of you or I won't be able to."

Magic can't do everything. Think! We cannot get out through the doors – the house doors, nor the stable doors. We cannot get through the hedge. The tunnels again? I don't think so – none of those other passages felt more – more – Pernicia *must want to find me; she must know she's been cheated. She must know – because* Peony *must be still alive.* Rosie's thought faltered here. *Peony is still alive, and we must find her. Pernicia – never mind Pernicia now.*

But she flung the sleep over us as Woodwold threw up the hedge. We're deadlocked.

Magic can't do everything.

I wonder what a bird might find.

We haven't tried up yet.

She looked at the low snaggy ceiling, at the cracks of glarey grey light; and then she looked down at Eskwa. *Eskwa both binds and cuts.* She did not want to cut Woodwold's guard of roses; but could a gardener not bind back stems that were growing where she did not want them? She looked at the massive, formidable weave above and round her and shook her head; but she laid her hand on Eskwa nonetheless and felt it once again slide into her hand.

Bind, she said to it. *Can you bind back a space for us to look through?*

She held the blade over her head, so the tip of it slipped through the twining branches, and she felt it quiver, like a hunting dog on point. And there was a creaking noise, and a scraping, grinding noise, and the rose branches shook; and then there was a tiny hole, just over Rosie's head, and it grew, the branches now writhing back like snakes, curling up on themselves like rope. Eskwa drew her on, tugging at her hand, its blade pressing against the hedge like a hand drawing back a fold of cloth. Rosie began to walk round in an ever-increasing circle as the space she had asked for grew larger and larger; till the courtyard in front of the stables was almost completely clear. . .

And then Eskwa faltered, wavering in her hand, its tip falling from the circle of the hedge; and she saw that its blade was almost entirely eaten away, the crescent of it now barely wider than a tapestry needle. In astonishment she looked again at the pulled-back rose stems and saw that they were, indeed, bound, by a fine gleaming network of silver like a spiderweb. *Oh*, said Rosie. *Oh. Thank you. I'm sorry. I – I think I needed to ask. I didn't know what else to do. I – I hope Ikor can make you fat again.* She stroked a gentle finger down the back of the long curved tapestry needle that had been a sabre, and then she went into the stables and hung it in the scabbard loop of Gorse's parade saddle, which was the most honourable place she could think of for it.

And then she came back out to the courtyard again and stared at the sky, as everyone else was doing already; as everyone else had been doing since the gap first opened. There was a high thin cloud cover that seemed only to intensify the glare as it hid the position of the sun; and the sky itself was a funny colour, almost violet. Up is still up, she thought. And I don't know what we might do for a ladder.

She felt small padded feet at her knee again, and Zel's nose in her hand. She looked down at him, and he raised his nose, telling her where to look; and then Narl's hand was over her shoulder, pointing at a particular bit of sky, a particular odd swirl of cloud, an angular swirl, rather like a tall narrow castle with too few windows standing in a wide barren landscape. The funny colour was very noticeable just there, as if this were the place where the violet – lavender – purple – was leaking through to taint the sky.

"Even if you're right," said Rosie, *Even if you're all right, and frankly, I don't believe that even – er – the person we have to find can have conquered the sky, how would we get there?*

Jump, said Fast.

Rosie stared at the castle, which looked more and more like a castle the more she stared at it. She was beginning to get a crick in her neck. The hole works both ways, she thought. We might be able to get out. Or Pernicia might be able to get in. "But—" said Rosie.

"I don't think that is the sky, you know," said Narl.

"Yes," said Rosie. "It – it feels like that to me, too. I'm not even a fairy, and it makes me feel stupid, and as if everything is about to come to bits."

She thought for a moment, but there wasn't much to think about. Where would she rather meet Pernicia? Here? Or somewhere else? Not here. Not with Katriona and Aunt and Barder and the queen and the king and the princes and the Prendergasts and Ikor and I suppose Sigil asleep and unrousable, protected only by a few thorns. "Fast says we can jump," Rosie said.

"That's as likely as anything," replied Narl.

The best jumpers will jump, said Fast. *That's Gorse and me and the hounds. The others must ride. The cat has to go in a sack. Cats always use their claws, even when they promise not to.*

I will jump, said Flinx with scorn. *I jump better than any huge ugly beast with bones that are too long and whiskers that are too short and hard flat feet.*

Narl was absentmindedly rubbing at a rose scratch on his cheek. "Wait a minute. We are all tired, hungry and thirsty. Tired and hungry we can go on with a little longer, but I think we have to try the water in the water butt before we – er – try anything else."

"We don't dare," said Rosie. "If we fall asleep there's no-one left to—"

Spear said, *I will drink the water. I am too old to jump and too big to ride. If it sends me to sleep – well, at least I will no longer be thirsty.*

Spear, began Rosie, distressed.

He was already walking towards the water butt. *And*, he added with the dispassionate tranquillity animals assumed so easily and human egotism found almost impossible to bear, *if I am asleep, I will not have to see you leaving me behind.*

Everyone watched as Spear reared up and put his forefeet on

the rim of the water butt, bent his long neck and drank. The sound of his lapping in that silent courtyard was as loud as thunder. He had a long satisfying drink, and the watchers all jealously swallowed dryness and tried not to stare too fiercely for signs of drowsiness as he dropped to all fours again. He sat down, had a scratch, yawned –

Everyone held their breath.

– finished yawning. Stared back.

One minute, two minutes. Three minutes. How long do we have to wait? thought Rosie. Four minutes. Five.

I believe, said Spear, *that this water is just water*.

There was a general rush for the water butt. Rosie found the grooms' cup for herself and Narl – No drooling, said Rosie, shoving Fast's nose aside just in time. Flinx paused in his dainty sipping to give Fast a glare worthy of the Prendergast majordomo facing a footman who has just dropped a tureen.

Then they organized themselves to leap into the sky.

Gorse took Narl and Zel; the hounds – all but Spear – ranged on either side of Gorse, waiting for Rosie. Rosie knelt down in front of Spear, and put her hands on his narrow shoulders. He licked her nose. *It is all right*, he said. *I will wait for you*.

We will be back soon, said Rosie, knowing that this was the sort of useless, pretending thing that humans said; but Spear had pity on her and said only, *Yes*.

Rosie stood up, turning away from her old friend; gently patted the pocket that again contained Throstle and two mice; she could feel them trembling. She patted the pocket with the spindle end to give herself courage, and then looked at Fast. *I don't know how to ride*, she said.

I know, said Fast. *Hold on to my mane, and let Sunflower sit within your arms. You may fall off on landing but you mustn't fall on take-off*.

Narl looked perfectly at ease on Gorse's back; Rosie, trying to figure out how to scramble up on Fast's, wondered how he got there. The bigger, more muscular horse perfectly suited the bigger, burlier rider; Zel's nose over Narl's arm and brush under it slightly spoiled the effect, but they looked as if they might be off one of the tapestries in Woodwold's Great Hall, illustrating the noble deeds of Prendergasts through the ages. It only then occurred to Rosie that Narl – like everyone present last night – was dressed in fine clothes (if by now a little the worse for wear and thorn rents). She didn't know he had any fine clothes. She hadn't noticed before, she thought, because he looked so comfortable in them – rather as he looked on Gorse's back – unlike herself, who in three months of wearing ladies' clothes hadn't once felt at ease in them. Oh *well*, she thought. Who cares? But she did care. Narl's clothing, black and brown and grey and mostly of leather, fitted him too well to be borrowed; on the proud golden Gorse, he could have been anyone. Only the smith's chain gave him away.

She thought of Peony, who always looked graceful and serene and unwrinkled, and considered, for about the space of an inhale but before the exhale, if she could possibly learn to hate her friend; and decided she could not. I wonder if Narl is hoping that if he rescues Peony. . . She spent a moment trying to imagine Narl as the romantic lover, kneeling at his beloved's side, taking her hand reverently in his and covering it with kisses. . . To her own dismay, she started to laugh.

Narl turned his head at once, amusement bright in his eyes. "It's harder on a slab-sided beanpole like the one you drew," he said, thinking that she was laughing at her attempts to climb astride; "but there's a barrel just there, which is what I used. You don't think I'm one of these crack jockeys that vault from the ground, do you?"

Fast followed her and stood quietly as she eased herself on. *Fine. Now let your legs hang down as straight as they'll go, and get your* seat bones *out of my* spine. Rosie hastily shifted her weight forward, and beckoned to Sunflower, who bounced from barrel to Rosie's lap with too much enthusiasm and nearly hurtled off the other side as a consequence.

She overheard a quick consultation between the two horses, flick-flick-flick, of bunched muscles and aiming; they weren't bothering to lay it out for any human that might be listening in. Flinx was ignoring them all, but Hroc added something that had to do with the shorter legs and lighter weight of the hounds – since there wasn't actually much vocabulary, in the human sense of the term, in beast-speech, cross-species communication, so long as the topic was mutual, was feasible if a bit rough – and then they lined up, facing in the same direction, looking at the castle above the briar hedge. Fast gave a sort of wriggling sway, like a cat readying himself to pounce, and Rosie felt his hind end sink as he gathered himself together. She grabbed as much of his mane as she could round Sunflower, and tried to squeeze her legs in the little hollows behind the swell of his shoulders: and then he sprang into the air.

Chapter 21

They were flying like birds. The great thrust of the horses' hindquarters was long since spent, but something drew them on, faster and faster, as if they were sliding down a slope, except they were far from the ground, and going up – and up – higher and higher, and the air was thin and icy cold. But – were they going up? There was something wrong with Rosie's sense of direction, and the world, or the sky, or both, were spinning round her.

She closed her eyes, but that was worse, so she opened them again, opened them to see the purple-stained castle clearly in front of them. They seemed to be hurtling towards *it*. . . "No," she said, or gasped; "this isn't right; too soon, not now." And she threw herself off Fast's back, Sunflower leaping clear, and hit the ground – some ground – with a bone-jarring smack, not daring to roll on account of the little creatures in one pocket and the hard knob of the spindle end in another. The wind was knocked out of her and she lay dazed for a moment, unable to get up.

Everyone else struck the earth just beyond her. Fast lost his own balance and fell; Gorse staggered and lurched and remained upright, while Narl half slithered and was half thrown off his back, Zel also leaping clear; most of the hounds did somersaults. Rosie didn't see Flinx land, and only saw him a minute or so later, nonchalantly walking towards the rest of them, but he was wearing several small heathery-looking twigs behind one ear and a long dust-smudge down one flank. Zel was the only one who seemed never to have lost his poise; Sunflower had none to lose.

She sat down next to the half-stunned Rosie and licked her face. Throstle and the two mice crept out of Rosie's pocket and lay panting as she was still trying to pummel air back into her own abused lungs. Flinx sat down and began to wash.

Rosie shook her head, and levered herself upright. Fast was walking towards her, a little stiffly. *Anyone hurt?* she said. Fast tossed his head. *No*, said Gorse. *Only a little rubbed backward.*

They were standing at a kind of boundary between a scraggy sort of wood behind them and an almost-barren landscape with a little low scrub before them. There were standing stones scattered about, strange unwelcoming shapes at strange menacing angles.

The castle itself rose from the scrubland like the biggest standing stone of all.

It was twilight, but of dawn or sunset or something else they could not tell; the low lavender-grey clouds hid the motion of the sun here, too. It was a heavy, drab sort of light that did not feel like any sort of daylight any of them were accustomed to – worse than the glarey grey light of the briar-shrouded Woodwold – and instinctively they drew closer together.

Rosie looked first at the wood behind them, wondering if it had any relation to the briar hedge round Woodwold. These were trees, not rose stems, even if they were no sort of tree she knew, and she thought they were not friendly; they seemed a kind of vegetable version of the heavy, unnatural light. She could sense nothing beyond them, neither building nor hill. She looked at the darkness among the trees and was sure it was not unoccupied, and that they were being watched, although she could see nothing, and the only rustles she could hear could be explained by the roaming breeze round them.

Narl said softly, "This place is – sticky with magic. I can almost feel it on my skin, like blown sand, and it coats your tongue when you open your mouth. I think no Foggy Bottom housekeeper's charm could shift it. It's why neither the light nor the ground – nor those trees – look or feel right. You know we are being watched from the wood?"

Rosie nodded.

They stood, huddled together, a little longer. Rosie turned away from her contemplation of the low ominous wood and stared at the tall malevolent castle. When she looked over her shoulder, she saw the first eyes, blinking at her from the shadows; they, too, were violet-grey. She did not attempt to speak to their owner.

"Come on, then," she said in a voice she was pleased to find steady. "We have an appointment elsewhere."

She stepped forward, Narl beside her, and the animals followed. She had taken three or four steps when she knew she had crossed some boundary; as her leading foot took her weight, the foot tingled, and briefly the sky, or the castle, or whatever bit of mid-air Rosie had been looking at, gave a great writhe, and became Pernicia's face; she was smiling. And then the smile was only a gaunt wisp of cloud, and Rosie's other foot moved itself forward and planted itself on the ground, and it tingled, too, although Pernicia did not reappear. Rosie felt Throstle and the mice rearranging themselves as if the pocket had grown suddenly smaller.

Narl said nothing, but as the animals crossed the boundary, the horses snorted and bobbed their heads, Flinx hissed, and there was a faint grunt from Narl a step or two later as Zel landed on his shoulders, scrabbled briefly, and then bestowed himself round his neck like a collar. Sunflower made a little yip; the hounds were silent, but suddenly there was a dog head under Rosie's hand again, and she was glad enough to bury her cold fingers in the longer fur on the back of Hroc's neck.

She thought the journey across the barren land could not have taken very long, for she seemed no hungrier at the end of it than she had been at the beginning, and, now that she was no longer thirsty, she was beginning to count everything in terms of her hunger; or perhaps she was now so hungry she would not feel any hungrier. The light had not changed either, growing neither brighter nor darker, but she felt that the light in this place was an even worse indication of the passage of time than her stomach. It had nonetheless felt like a long journey, and dread of the ending will often make a journey short.

But here they were.

There was a moat round the castle, but there was no water in it. Standing beside it, looking down, Rosie thought it was hard to see just what was in it; it seemed to be a long way down, and weren't those . . . rocks? . . . of some kind? Something greyish-brownish-purplish and lumpy, something that cast some kind of shadow; but they were weirdly blurred somehow, and weren't they . . . moving?

"I would not look into the moat any more," said Narl in the same gentle voice he had used earlier, but Rosie jerked her eyes up as if he had shouted at her.

They turned away to walk round the moat and the castle; but the strange, pushed-pulled, unbalanced, something-just-behind-you-that's-always-moved-when-you-turn-to-look feeling was suddenly very much worse, and they were all tripping and stumbling, although the ground was not that rough, and jerking their heads round to look at things that weren't there. The horses blew repeatedly through their nostrils, raspy, rolling, I-don't-like-this snorts, and the dogs made little grunting noises that were neither barks nor growls. Sunflower and Tash, the youngest of the hounds, forgot themselves so much as to whine, but everyone else pretended not to notice.

Flinx rematerialized from the outskirts of the company and began winding himself round Rosie's ankles. His fur was full of sparks, and they bit painfully through Rosie's trousers, which then clung to her legs and chafed. *What do you want*, Rosie said, too tired and hungry and worried and impatient to bother remembering that this is a bad question to ask anyone, and worse yet to ask a cat.

Flinx stopped dead, so that Rosie nearly tripped over him, and Hroc gave a little *woof* of annoyance. Flinx ignored the dog, but gave Rosie a resentful look. Rosie pressed the heel of her hand to the bridge of her nose, as if trying to push undesirable thoughts further in. I'm sorry, she said to Flinx. *I have never been any good at—*At random, she said, *The sky is very violet today, isn't it?*

Her impression was that Flinx was more amused than mollified, but he stopped rubbing against her legs, and trotted beside her for a time. Rosie could feel him thinking, but he was silent for long enough that she had the opportunity to notice that he was the only one of all of them who was not blundering over his own feet. She felt him notice her noticing – there was a certain sense of "at last" about it – and then he said: *The things that aren't there are not there in different ways. Some of them are almost there and some of them are nearly not-there.*

She could feel that Flinx was making a supreme effort to communicate plainly, but she could think of nothing to say in return but *thank you*.

"I think," said Narl, "that something is changing."

Rosie could *feel* something pushing against her left side, something lumpy, as if a bag full of rocks were being driven into her; but there was nothing there, though she had to lean forcibly against it to avoid being shoved into Gorse. Gorse himself was walking diagonally, as if something were pushing at his left hip; and Froo was bent in a half circle, as if a very narrow something were bearing against the midpoint of her right side. None of them, except Flinx, was walking normally. At Narl's words they came to a ragged halt. Flinx sat down and began unconcernedly to fluff up his tail.

"Flinx says that the – the things that aren't here aren't here in different ways," she said.

Narl said slowly, "Yes. This seems to be a – neither here nor there sort of place. And the things here are neither here nor there either."

"Only they don't seem to – upset Flinx's sense of balance," said Rosie.

"Perhaps cats are neither here nor there all the time," said Narl, and Flinx, picking up the gist of this through Rosie, gave Narl a thoughtful look before returning to his tail.

But he paused again mid-fluff to stare searchingly at a particular portion of blank air. Rosie, nervously, looked where he was looking, and, more or less reluctantly, so, too, did everyone else.

Rosie couldn't decide if it was more as if an invisible door opened and let them out, or whether they merely formed themselves out of nothing. Whatever they were, they made you sick to look at them; not sick because of their horribleness, but sick like a person who doesn't like heights looking down a very long way. Looking at them made you dizzy and gave you a headache, and you suddenly felt you no longer knew which way was up and which down, and you wanted something to hold on to, except that there wasn't anything to hold on to, except each other, and that wasn't any good because all the rest of you felt exactly the same.

Except Flinx. Rosie dragged her blurred, aching eyes away from them – whatever they were – and looked at Flinx. Flinx was still sitting, but sitting to attention, watching the things come (if come was quite the right word) closer, for closer they undoubtedly were; and when they came right up to them . . . Flinx said suddenly: *Tell that foot-hammerer to mind his other makings. He says he bends air as he bends iron; let him do it now.*

And then he leaped to his feet and all his hair stood on end, so he was a super-Flinx, large as a wildcat, and he screamed, the several-octave range of a cat about to plunge into a cat fight, and then he shot off . . . *towards* the upside-down-making things that approached them.

He says he bends air – ? What? There were often cats at the forge, Rosie remembered, perched here and there, staring at nothing; but cats stare at nothing wherever they are. *That's something a seer can do: give other people visions as false as his own.* "Narl," Rosie said with difficulty. "Can you – can you make – can you make *lots* of Flinxes?"

Narl stared at her. She could see by the tension in him that he was feeling the same strains she was; but she was not as strong as he, and while he clasped his hands together till his arms strained at his sleeves, her right arm was being dragged upwards into the vacant air while her left hand was trying to crawl up her spine. "Back in the Hall," she said, "you said about seers. . ."

Understanding leaped into Narl's eyes, and he glanced towards the approaching things, and at Flinx, still yelling and streaking back and forth under the bits of them that seemed to touch the ground, which should have been feet but weren't – the bits above what should have been feet extended a great way up and sideways – and Rosie, following his look, had a brief, wild impression that they were tripping over him, or maybe that they were turning to give chase, as if in the place they came from they were a sort of dog, and recognized, even in this place, which must have seemed very queer to them, a thing like a cat, meant to be chased. But there was only one of him, and no sane cat would attack a pack of dogs; these things were closing round him. . .

And then there were a dozen Flinxes, twenty, twice twenty, all of them spitting and squalling, all of them with their hair standing on end, all of them shooting back and forth among the dizzying things, and the things were now making noises of their own, rather like wind keening under eaves, and the fact that the things now seemed to have a great many more sticking-down bits, as if they'd grown a great many more legs, gave an impression rather like a dog's hackles rising in reverse. The by-now-several-times-twenty Flinxes stopped hurtling back and forth through the crowd of the things (Rosie wondered how all the false Flinxes managed not to run into each other, and thought perhaps they simply ran *through* one another), and took off in several-times-twenty directions, and the things all scattered and went after them.

The landscape was empty again, and the little company all stood up straight and sighed, and relaxed. The strange grapplings that had seized them were gone. And here was Flinx, looking pleased with himself, having returned from nowhere anyone saw him returning from, giving a last lick to a nicely smoothed-down tail.

They had come a little further from the castle during the confrontation with the unbalancing things, and now they looked round to reorient themselves. The castle had, somehow, got behind them. As Rosie turned to find it again, she heard Sunflower whine: not a miserable whine this time, but a small intrigued considering whine.

These things looked rather more human: upright, swinging what might be arms, walking with two legs; although what they walked on and from where was a little obscure, since they seemed to be walking out through the doorless wall of the castle, and across the moat on a level with the ground, although there was nothing there for them to walk on. They stalked across the invisible bridge, and as they came to the rough tussocky ground beyond it they spread out, so that the rank of them coming towards Rosie and her friends was twenty or thirty bodies wide. Faceless bodies; they had head shapes at the top of their body shapes, but there was no glint of eyes, no irregular shadows from the hollows and protrusions of other features.

Sunflower began to bark and leap, rushing back and forth in front of her companions, wagging her tail feverishly, sometimes curling herself up into a circle and spinning round and round in place, uttering little cries, half whimper, half yelp, which was all what she did any time there were visitors at Woodwold and she was neither out hunting (when she was the model of a sober, dedicated retrieving dog, and never made a gesture or a sound without direction from her huntsman) nor locked up somewhere. She obeyed about half the Prendergasts; if any visitor were so unlucky as to meet her with only one of the other Prendergasts in attendance, they were on their own to face the barrage.

These are mine, she said to Rosie. *Tell the fairy*. And she galloped off towards them.

Rosie didn't have to tell Narl; there were a hundred Sunflowers before she'd gone more than a few bounds; two hundred before she arrived at the marching first row of things. The Sunflowers leaped on the things, striking them in what might have been their groins and their stomachs. The ones she knocked down immediately she began to lick furiously, especially around the face regions; and convincing-looking arms rose up to try to fend her off. But she was an old hand at this game, and she knew how not to be fended. Those things that had not immediately been knocked down, she circled round behind and flung herself at backs of knees, smalls of backs; more of them fell down, and she began to lick them, too. They didn't like being licked; they thrashed and wriggled, and made snatches at the Sunflowers which were never where they had been when the snatches began; and tripped up those few of their fellows that some Sunflower or other hadn't already managed to hurl down.

There were, by now, more Sunflowers than there were things, and the Sunflowers not occupied in licking amused themselves instead by running across the supine (or occasionally prone, in which case the attending Sunflowers rootled relentlessly about the head to get at where the face should be) bodies of the things, landing heavily and taking off again with a great deal of thwacking and scrabbling.

The things seemed to be growing thinner, as if the false Sunflowers were licking the magic away, and that magic was all there was of them.

Quite suddenly the Sunflowers standing on the bodies of their victims started thumping abruptly to the ground as the things disappeared. The false Sunflowers began to disappear, too. There were six left when the last thing flicked out of existence; and then there was only one Sunflower. She looked round to check that her duty was done (for a moment Rosie could see the faithful, thorough hunting dog in her expression), and she came trotting back towards Rosie, grinning hugely, with her tongue lolling out of her mouth.

She permitted herself to be patted and praised, leaning against Rosie's and then Narl's knees. The big hounds all looked deeply embarrassed; they had spent their lives looking the other way from Sunflower's excesses, unable to understand how she could be the same dog they knew out in the field, attending to business. She looked round at them with a glint in her eye, knowing full well what they were thinking. Then she sighed, stood up, and shook herself: and looked over at Flinx, who was looking at her.

Flinx stood up and wandered, as if carelessly, and thinking of something else, in the general direction of Sunflower, who stood still, watching, her tail a little raised. He paused and looked round, as if suddenly aware that he was, by some strange chance, very near to Sunflower; and then he walked the last few steps towards her and raised his face. She lowered hers, and they touched noses.

Not bad, said Flinx. *Not bad at all*. Sunflower's tail gave a slow, majestic wag.

"Well," said Rosie, and patted Narl's shoulder as she had just been patting Sunflower's. "Are you all right? Er – thank you."

Narl shook his head, and his other hand reached for Rosie's patting hand, and held it. "Rosie—" he began, and stopped. "Rosie, whatever happens—" and stopped again. He smiled at her, a funny, half-sad smile (*Ironface! Smiling!* Rosie heard the animals murmuring round her; *the Block, cracking*, from Flinx), and said, "I'm too tired and stupid to put it into words, and if I weren't so tired and stupid I wouldn't be trying. Don't thank me. It's – it's an honour to serve you, Princess."

"*Don't* call me *Princess!*" shouted Rosie, snatching her hand away, feeling as if he'd struck her across the face.

"I'm sorry," he said wearily; "but we'd better get used to it, hadn't we?" He turned away, and began to walk slowly back towards the castle.

After a moment she followed him, and the animals closed up round them, and soon they were walking side by side, but neither of them spoke.

When they arrived at the edge of the moat again, they found their own footprints in a patch of rough sand, setting out in the other direction; they had come all the way round, and, except for the not-door and not-bridge that Sunflower's things had used, they had seen nothing resembling a way in.

Somewhere, Rosie thought, Pernicia is waiting. Is she watching us? Has she known of us since the moment Eskwa opened the rose hedge?

Is she scornful? Is she – worried? Are we not what she expected?

Is Peony still alive?

Rosie's mind bucked away from that last thought, and instead she said to herself crossly, But Pernicia should *want* to see us. And Rosie wrapped that thought round with an irrational irritation similar to what she would have felt if she had turned up at someone's farm to look at a horse and found no horse and no-one at home. She should *want* to see us.

She should want to finish what she started.

Rosie's irritation drained away, and she was standing in the middle of nowhere with a few friends round her, and the little wind that blew past her smelled of dust and emptiness.

How do you build a bridge out of nothing and unlock a door you can't find?

All that was around them was dirt and sand and stones. And the things at the bottom of the moat that weren't stones. She took the gargoyle spindle end out of her pocket and looked at it. She was thinking about the twentieth fairy gift at her name-day, the one just before Pernicia had come, the one that had given Pernicia the shape of her curse. Katriona had told her about that, too, the last day in Foggy Bottom.

You could spin thread till you had enough to make rope; you could make a bridge out of rope. "If I only had something to spin with," she said, and ran her other hand through her hair in her characteristic gesture of discontent or dismay.

"Much too short," said Narl. "Try mine." He plucked a hair from his head and held it out to her.

Rosie hesitated. She remembered what had happened with Peony's bit of cloth and embroidery silk. But to spin something they might all walk on, even from a fairy gift . . . especially since she didn't know how to spin; she only knew what it looked like, from watching Kat and Aunt. She held the spindle in one hand, as if telling herself, or Narl's single black hair, or the magic-sticky air, what she wanted, and then she gave the hair a twist, as if it were fluff from a sheep she wished to mould into thread; and she closed her eyes.

Immediately she felt something – something – coiling and looping and winding through her fingers, and she felt the spindle end spinning and spinning and spinning till her fingers were hot with friction, and heavy curls of something were falling down her arm, and piling up at her feet, and at last she felt the spindle being snatched out of her hand, and Narl's voice, almost laughing, in her ear: "Enough! Enough! Imagine if I'd given you two hairs!"

Cautiously she opened her eyes. Around them in great silky waves lay . . . the something. Black it was, as black and glossy as Narl's hair, and it shimmered in the sullen light as if it were breathing. She picked up the end of it that still lay at her feet, and discovered a kind of supple rope, as big around as her two hands could grasp, but as light and flexible as Narl's single hair had been. "Can we make this into a – a bridge?" she said.

"I have a better idea," said Narl. "I don't see a door, do you? And I bet the roof's no better. Let's squeeze her out. She'll know where the doors are in her own house." He handed her the emptied spindle end, and she automatically gave its nose a rub before she put it back in her pocket.

"Squeeze. . . ?" said Rosie.

But Narl was already paying out arm's lengths of the black rope, letting it coil up at his feet, then kneeling, and measuring it a second time, squinting up at the castle as he did so, muttering under his breath, "Not as if the best eye in the world is going to give us much help here."

She felt tired – no, she felt exhausted – and dull, and could not imagine what he had in mind; and then he stood up, holding the rope in both hands, with the lengths he had measured between, and *flung* it –

It seemed to blow up and away from them, like a single hair on a current of air so gentle you cannot feel it against your face. It spiralled for a while, and then it floated, and drifted – and then it seemed to stop, seesawing, like a hair in a weakening draught; and Narl put his hands round his mouth and *blew*.

The high centre of it shot up, as if awakened from sleep, dragging its languorous loops behind it, and at the peak of the castle it drooped a little, hung, and then fell, over the roof of the castle, one end caught by the crenellations, the other sagging towards the moat –

But Narl was already running round the edge of the moat, shaking out the black rope behind him, and just before he disappeared round the far side of the castle, he took another handful of rope and gave it a yank and a flick, and Rosie saw the caught bit fly up in the air again, and then come softly down on the far side of the castle.

Narl hastily tied the loose end round his waist, and was pulling the other in as quickly as he could, backing towards Rosie as he did so. "I don't think we want this to touch the bottom of the moat," he said, and handed her the long end, while he untied the other. "Pull," he said. Rosie, bemused, pulled. What could a rope made of nothing and one human hair do against the walls of a castle?

She pulled. The rope seemed to clasp at her hands, as if it were a sentient member of the party, consciously trying to apply its own strength; she almost heard it trying to speak to her. If a house can speak, she thought wildly, why not a rope made of nothing? She took a better grip, scraped her boots in the ground a little, dug her heels in, and *pulled*.

There was now an odd sort of smoke, or fog, rising off the castle, or dripping down its sides, and a strange vertiginous gleam where the rope touched its walls, a quaking, precarious gleam that made no sense if you looked at it, made no sense in the same way the castle hanging in the sky over the briar hedge round Woodwold had made no sense, made no sense and made your head spin and your balance waver the way the upside-down things that had chased the Flinxes made no sense. The way the things in the bottom of the moat . . . Don't look in the bottom of the moat, Rosie told herself. Don't look at the contact point between a rope that doesn't exist and a castle with no doors. Just pull. *Pull.*

She glanced over at Narl; his face was drawn into deep lines with the intensity of what he was doing, and she felt a tiny foolish stirring in her breast, a stirring of hope. If he thinks. . .

She realized she was nearly tipping over backwards; the rope was lengthening – or the castle wall was yielding to pressure. Sure it was: easy as squeezing whey from a stone, like the brave tailor in the story. In the story it was cheese, and he only said it was a stone. Don't look. Don't think. Just pull. She resolutely looked away from the castle and the moat, backed up a step, two steps, to keep the rope taut. The smoke, or whatever it was, was growing thicker; and it was enough like ordinary smoke that it made her eyes water, it caught in her throat and made her cough. *Pull*. She looked to her left: she could still see Narl through the increasing murk, but the animals, beyond him, were little more than huddled shapes.

You loathsome child, spat into her mind; she flinched, and might have slackened the rope, but the rope itself reached out and wrapped itself round her hands. She stood, wondering if she were trapped, seeing out of the corner of her eye Narl taking another step backwards as he kept the tension on his end of the rope, feeling the pull on her own wrists, staring at her helpless hands, feeling the weight of the spindle end hanging in its pocket, tapping against her thigh. *Rope?* she said tentatively. The rope did not reply; but she no longer felt trapped, but embraced.

Look at me.

Rosie jerked, startled, grasping at the rope with her fingertips, looked up. Pernicia stood there, carrying something in her arms.

Someone. Peony.

You cannot have her, Rosie said without thinking, without thinking to whom or how she was speaking. *You cannot have her*.

Peony lay lightly in Pernicia's arms, as if she weighed no more than a hollow doll. Perhaps Pernicia was very strong; perhaps the uncanny air of this place bore Peony up; perhaps the magic of the poisoned sleep also robbed her flesh of its living weight. That it was Peony herself and no false semblance Rosie was sure; she did not believe that even Pernicia could make so fine a replica of her friend that Rosie would not see through it at once. There was the faintest of frowns on Peony's face, as if she knew, somewhere in the back of her sleeping mind, that something was not quite right.

You cannot have her. It's me you want.

I want neither *of you. But I will have* both.

No. Not Peony. It is not her fault.

Her fault? Her fault? It is not her fault that she agreed to this shoddy despicable charade? It is not her fault that she seized my spindle's end? But I do not care whether it is her fault or not, any more than I care that a stupid hulking girl was first-born to the king and queen twenty-one years ago rather than two hundred and one. I have been waiting my time, and it has come.

Her words rang or bellowed or crackled or reverberated strangely in Rosie's head, or her ears. Rosie had never been quite sure how she spoke to animals, nor how they spoke to her, other than that something happened besides the ordinary sounds and gestures most people heard and saw animals make. And each animal had an idiom, a vernacular, a little different from every other animal; for some animals, like dogs, elaborate their speech with sneezes and barks and growls and tail waggings and ear flattenings and yawnings and pawings and bowings and many other sounds and gestures, while some animals, like most insects, had speech that was little more than a series of clicks and ticks in a kind of code Rosie happened to have the key to (mostly).

Pernicia's speech seemed to be all of this, as if dogs and cats and cows and horses and hawks and beetles were all speaking the same things simultaneously – except that they would not use the same signals, the same expressions – and although Pernicia stood silent and motionless with Peony in her arms. With the rough discordance that should not have been comprehensible but was, there was something else, and the something else was in the grey and purple fog that slid and swirled round the castle. Rosie swayed a little, and the rope, drawn close round her wrists and forearms, held her up.

Yes, I am speaking to you in that brute speech you favour. It suits you, said Pernicia. *It suits you so much better than any human tongue. It suits who you have become, country maid, simpleton, beast-girl. Who you are. Because is not what you have become what you are best suited for? Have you not spent many hours wondering why you are as you are, why it fits you so well, these last three months, and why the last three months did not? For that alone it was worth waiting till your final birthday, thinking of you wondering. It took me but a moment, when I realized the truth, why you had remained hidden from me for so long, when I looked for you so eagerly. I had been looking for a princess.*

Rosie shook her head numbly. It was true what Pernicia said, that Rosie was not a princess, but she knew that already. She knew that Pernicia said it to hurt her, but it did not hurt her; and she wondered if the only reason Pernicia chose to speak to her in this way – in this clumsy, cacaphonic beast-speech – was to humiliate her. Pernicia would not have thought to ask the animals where to find the princess, and they would not have told her had she asked; and as she had not thought to ask them, she had neither thought to punish them for their refusal. Pernicia's words did not hurt Rosie, but fear of what she might do – was planning to do – to Peony hurt her very much.

She could no longer see Narl, nor the animals, nor the castle; she was alone in the purple-grey murk with Pernicia, and Peony's life lay between them.

Come to me, said Pernicia, and her words yelped and roared and hissed and sang and clicked and tapped. *Come to me. You want to save your friend; then come and try. You will not succeed; but I have had more bother over you than you are worth and perhaps watching you fail will be some recompense for my trouble.* She bent swiftly, with little eddies of fog scuttling out of her way as she moved, and the long folds of the black-and-purple-and-cerise robe she wore rearranged themselves, and Rosie noticed there were long rents in them, as if, perhaps, they had been caught and torn by thorns. She laid Peony at her feet.

Peony sprawled, limp as a child's toy or a sleeping baby. Her hair was coming free of the crown of inheritance the king had placed on her head, and tumbling round her, and the superabundance of her princess's ball-gown skirts made her look tiny among them. They seemed to froth over the edge of something into nothing, although Rosie could see neither the something nor the nothing, wrapped as both were in the muddy haze.

She remembered that she had been only a few steps from the lip of the moat when Pernicia had appeared, standing, apparently, on the naked air over the moat, emerging from the unbroken wall of the castle. Was the moat still there? Was the castle still there? But then none of this landscape existed as landscape should; they had come here from leaping into the sky. But if Pernicia had dissolved all of it into this thick, grimy fog, what was she, Rosie, standing on? And if the castle was no longer there, what was the rope that still held her pulling against?

Rosie shook her head; the fog in her mouth tasted foul. She tried to free herself from the rope, but it would not let her go. You don't exist, she thought. Go away. I have to try to reach Peony.

But it would not let her go. She stepped forward, and it writhed beneath her stepping foot. A loop felt its way round her like an arm round her shoulders. She could feel it round her ankles, leaving her just enough space to take small steps. It was strangely squashy to walk on, like a bog before you begin to sink; and she remembered the old bog-charm Aunt had wound round her long ago, and how much she had resented it. That had been before she was a princess, when she had understood her world, and been happy in it.

The rope still grasped her hands, but now it seemed to lead her on, as Rosie might have led a skittish horse. It held her steadily, gravely, confidently. She took another step forward, and another – if the moat was still there, she was now over it – but walking was more difficult now, and her feet seemed to grope from one swaying, spongey, irregularly placed loop of rope to the next, sliding anxiously along, fearing that the in-between would not hold her securely enough, that her foot would slip over the edge into nowhere. She was panting for breath, and now she gripped the rope as strongly as it gripped her, leaning against it, feeling for its narrow yielding roundness against her feet, pressing its coils against her sides.

But she was still sinking, or perhaps she had not climbed high enough; when she neared Pernicia and Peony, her face was nearly level with Peony's as she lay at Pernicia's feet. Rosie reached out with her rope-tangled hands to touch Peony's face, and heard Pernicia shout an *AHH!* that made whatever Rosie was standing on vibrate like a young tree in a strong wind; and then she stooped.

Pernicia's stooping seemed to take a very long time, as if she were a merrel plummeting down upon its prey from half a league overhead, and Rosie watched those long-fingered hands reaching to seize her as she scrabbled Peony towards her – Peony slid as if she were still lying on the polished wooden floor of Woodwold's Great Hall – and together Rosie and Peony fell backward into the pliant rope with Peony half on Rosie's lap and half in her still-pinioned arms. With some part of her mind Rosie registered that Pernicia's hands were covered with scratches, as if she had recently had to fight her way out of a briar. But she felt one of those hands brush her shoulder, and she cried out, for that fleeting touch felt like the slash of a knife, and she glanced towards it, expecting to see blood soaking through her sleeve; and then there was a rustle and a rush and a whispery, tickly blur, and Pernicia screamed, a hoarse, horrible scream, in rage and surprise, and threw herself backwards; and there was a small terrier clamped to the hand that had just touched Rosie, and two mice dangling from her cheek and chin.

And then Rosie was falling, falling, clutching Peony as best she could, falling against the soft rope, as soft against her face as if she lay against Narl's hair, and then she staggered, for the coils had given way to two human arms, and her feet had struck the ground. She twisted one ankle painfully, but the arms held her safe, her and Peony. Together they laid Peony gently on the ground, Rosie straightening up just in time not to be knocked on to her friend's body by a horse's foreleg banging into her side. The fog had thinned, now racing by her in streaks and tatters on the capricious gusts of wind that also clawed through her hair, and made the little huddle of animals and people all lurch against each other; but she could see very little, only more racing fog. And now here was Narl, offering to throw her up on to the back of the horse: Fast.

"The castle's gone," Narl said, raising his voice to be heard over the low evil howl of the wind. "Your rope pulled the top off, and this wind is taking the rest. I'm not sure what happens now, but it won't be friendly. She'll pull this wind to her soon and. . . You must get away from here. If anyone can save you, Fast can," he said, but his words were almost blown away before she could hear them. He said something else: about the animals holding the way. "Go on."

"She wants both of us," shouted Rosie, leaning against Fast and grasping his mane against the increasing buffeting. . . The wind was full of voices now, yammering and bellowing and clattering: Were they all Pernicia's voice?

Narl knelt and grasped her ankle and heaved, flinging her up Fast's side and down across his back with a jerk that hurt her hip joint. "Can't you hear them on the wind? It's you they're after – she's after. She only took Peony as a hostage – because she missed you. They'll follow you, and leave us, and I can just about make them think we aren't here anyway. We all have to leave this place – it's breaking up round us. Stay on the human road! Remember! Now go. Go!"

She had just enough time to wind both hands in Fast's mane; as she laid herself as best she could along his back she felt the wild strength of him bound into his full speed within a few strides, the wind trying to peel her off his back like a knife pares an apple. All round them she heard the evil magic in Pernicia's thwarted fury rising and rising to a pitch that might yet shatter the world.

Fast can save me? From what? For what?

For a little while she was wholly absorbed in the experience of Fast's running: the power, the terrifying power of it, the surge of the hindquarters, the stretch of the stride, the bunching together in preparation for the next surge, all compacted into a single motion and translated into the torrent of his speed. She had seen him run many times, for after her successful interference on the subject of his manners, she had been invited to watch him train; and, upon its being very obvious to the Master of the Horse how pleased he was to see her, she was also invited, as a kind of good-luck charm, to the occasional match-race that some other owners of some other horses misguidedly begged Lord Prendergast for. There was a flat clear stretch along the riverbank of about a league and a half that was used as a racecourse, for Lord Pren would not send Fast away to race elsewhere; he said *he* had no doubts about Fast's speed. And Fast was so clearly faster than any other horse he had ever run against that no other owner dared cry foul.

Rosie remembered standing beside Fast just before one of these contests – she wasn't bothering to try to talk to him; his mind was full of spinning glittery fragments of running, wanting to run, waiting to run, being nothing but running with a bay coat stretched over it – and looking up into his rider's face, and seeing a curious expression of determination settle upon it as he picked up the reins: the look of a man who is about to jump over a precipice.

She hadn't understood it at the time. She understood it now.

But someone – many someones – were running with them, even as Fast outstripped them. Dimly she could see sleek bodies beside them: other horses, dogs, wolves, foxes, wildcats, deer; Fast ran past all of these. She caught glimpses of slower animals: cows and sheep, bears and badgers, and of smaller animals, otters and martens and rabbits and hedgehogs and cats; and there were tiny streaks of motion she thought were mice and voles and squirrels. Overhead she could just make out the shapes of birds flying among the rags of cloud, and darting shapes that might be bats.

She thought they were all running and flying in the same direction, Fast driving among them like a ship through the sea, although she could be sure of very little, for the wind of Fast's speed whipped tears from her eyes. But as they ran she realized that those that ran with them were in fact opening and holding a way for them, and that beyond the animals that were her friends were other creatures that were not her friends, who would stop her if they could.

Rosie could see, now that she had guessed what to look for, the occasional wicked face, rough and square or delicate and oval, tall or short, human or half human or goblin or imp, peering at her through the ranks of her friends, reaching out hands or claws or thick twisting or biting magics, to grasp her as she ran by; but none of them could reach her.

Stay on the human road, Narl had said. They were running through desert places, like the land round the castle; and then they ran through trees, sometimes widely scattered, sometimes in groves; but always there was a clear way for Fast to go, clear and nearly straight, and his hoofs seemed barely to graze the ground before he hurtled forward in his next tremendous stride. Stay on the human road. She could not tell if they were on a road or not, only that the animals had chosen the way.

The fog cleared slowly and the light grew brighter, and the landscape grew slowly less flat. There was a piece of hill line she could see through Fast's streaming mane that looked familiar, and then they shot past a curious little basin of valley that teased at her memory till she remembered, and, remembering, understood: they had passed the northern boundary of the Gig from the wasteland where no-one went. They were now running over the ground where King Harald had fought the fire-wyrms; the valley they had just passed was called the Dragon's Bowl, caused by the fire-wyrms melting the landscape in rage when they could not defeat the king. She had not been here since she was small; Aunt used to collect bdeth near here, although in recent years she had stopped using it. "The Dragon's Bowl is too far to walk on these old bones," she said, when Rosie had once asked her; it had been a sennight's journey for the three of them, during the autumn expedition to collect all the wild things Aunt and Katriona would spend the winter making up into charms or storing away for the next year.

Fast was still running as swiftly as the footing would allow him, but she could feel his lungs beginning to labour, and his neck and shoulders were wet with sweat. She did not know how long they had been running, but she was tired from hanging on, smooth as a good horse's flat-out gallop was to sit over, and neither of them had had anything to eat in much too long. The way they were going was narrowing, too, and she could see more and more of those malign faces looking at her. Her friends were no longer running with them, but holding their line, struggling to hold their line, to hold Pernicia's creatures back.

The first deviling that broke through Fast dodged round, scarcely breaking stride; but the second one was bigger, and the third was not alone, but stood against her with six friends. Fast gathered himself together and leaped over them; Rosie shot up his neck when they landed, but she stayed on. Where are we? she thought. Fast – even Fast – cannot run the whole length of the Gig. But then where are we going? Has Pernicia's host overrun the Gig? What is happening in Foggy Bottom, at Woodwold?

But Fast was running the length of the Gig. They were on a road she knew, the road from Mistweir to Waybreak.

The blood vessels stood out now on Fast's wet hide, and she

could see the huge red hollows of his nostrils, and hear the saw of his breathing. She tried to call to him, *Fast, Fast, slow down, slow down, do not kill yourself*; but he did not answer her, not even with a flick of his laid-back ears. She thought, he is right, if they catch me it is all up for all of us; but what does he think I can do even if I get back to Woodwold – if Woodwold is where we are going? She took Peony because she knew if I lived I had to follow; but now. . .

What is it I'm supposed to do?

Ahead of them the line broke, and a scatter of deer, red and roe and fallow, scrambled dazedly across their path and a mob spread out before them. Fast was now running past Moonshadow; Rosie could see fields and rooftops, but she saw no human beings, and no animals but the ones that lined her way.

Fast faltered and then deliberately slowed, pulling himself together as if showing off for a mare, prancing, tail and crest high, towards the glowering creatures that blocked their way. Rosie half thought, half made herself believe that these creatures trod uneasily on the human road, that the roughness of their quick steps was not only due to their eagerness to seize her and pull Fast down.

One of the enemy made a feint towards her and Fast, and a little group of deer and sheep blocked it; Rosie saw a bear rise up behind them, and another of the invaders was snatched and thrown over the heads of his companions. Fast swerved to one side, and back, leaped over some heaving tangle on the ground, and Rosie, struggling to maintain her seat, did not notice in time – someone, or something, had her leg, and was about to drag her to the ground.

Fast sat back on his haunches and swung round, but the goblin swung, too; Rosie beat ineffectually at its face, but it only sank its fingers more firmly into her flesh. If only she had some weapon – where the cloth of her trouser leg was strained by the goblin's grasp, the gargoyle spindle end drove painfully into her thigh. She worked her hand into her pocket and pulled it out, cracked it sharply across her attacker's face, and felt the goblin's hold loosen. Fast gave it an awkward punch with a hind foot, bending round and aiming as if he were planning to scratch his own shoulder, and it fell to the ground. Fast straightened out with a jerk that almost finished unseating Rosie and shot off again, through the remains of the throng, and pressed on. Rosie didn't quite have the chance to stuff the spindle end back into her pocket, and tucked it into her waistcoat instead; old friend that it was, she spared a thought for the sound of that *crack*, and hoped it had been only the goblin's skull.

Fast's hoofs no longer grazed the earth with every stride, but struck it hard and jarringly; but he was still running, and they appeared to have outrun Pernicia's army – as well as their own friends. The little respite they had had outside Moonshadow had seemed to give him a second wind, and while he no longer ran lightly, he ran resolutely. Between her own and Fast's breathing and the wind in her ears Rosie could hear nothing else; it was a very silent and empty landscape they were running through, thundering through the square at Treelight and later across Smoke River's big common. Still she saw no people nor any animals; they saw no-one, not even a butterfly.

And there was the briar hedge, climbing up over Woodwold's outer wall and spilling down the outside. They were thundering down upon it, on the main road from Smoke River, a wide and clear way: clear enough that Rosie could see the hedge from far away, see it grow ever closer and closer. . .

They had not outrun all of Pernicia's army. Some of it was waiting for them.

Those that stood against them stood quietly, watchfully: expectantly. They had known that what they waited for had to come to them at last. They had had no need to cry warning – not of one horse near foundering, and one weaponless rider – they had no need to do anything. What they waited for raced towards them, and would fall at their feet without their having to lift knife or stick or bare claw or fang. They stood with their backs against the briar hedge, many of them so knotted and twisted themselves that they were not immediately evident, especially not to eyes as weary as Rosie's and Fast's. But as Rosie's eyes adjusted she saw how many of them there were: several ranks of them standing out from the wall. Silently. Patiently. Waiting.

She could feel Fast's uncertainty and alarm but she had no suggestions for him. He slowed nearly to a canter, looking right and left, as she was looking; but while those that waited for them were most thickly grouped just in front of Woodwold's gates, half invisible among the rose stems but marked by the road, where the road turned towards Foggy Bottom the way was blocked by tall armoured creatures, clanking as they moved, as they turned their heads to look at her. Rosie could not see if they wore their armour like humans, or if it grew from their flesh.

And then something hurtled past them, growling, and jumped at the faces of those standing in front of Woodwold's gates. Hroc. And behind him Milo and Tash and Froo, all of them red-eyed and streaked with foam from the speed and distance they had run, following Fast. Pernicia's creatures gave way, a little, in surprise, and their stolid, irresistible, waiting strength was against them because the hounds were quick and agile; gaps appeared in the enemy line in front of the briar hedge. And Fast, who had come to a halt when the hounds shot by, leaped forward again, and Rosie found herself shouting at the top of her lungs, shouting, too, with her inner voice, half aware of the armoured creatures blocking the road to Foggy Bottom rolling forward to close in behind her, "Woodwold!" *Woodwold! Let us in!* And, as a token, she pulled the gargoyle spindle end from her waistcoat, and threw it into the heart of the hedge.

And the hedge pulled itself back, like two ladies drawing back their skirts, the stems wrinkling themselves away and then hoicking themselves upward, their tips rising higher yet above the walls and then diving down again to wind their way among the thick bony mat of branches already there. But the gates remained shut: all fifteen by twenty foot of them.

Fast was running again, the last few strides he had left in him to run, surging into his speed again with his neck-cracking starting bounds: Rosie saw, out of the corner of her eye, a chain with some horrible spiked sphere on the end of it whistle harmlessly past his hindquarters as the end of the armoured line drew close to them.

But if Narl's gates did not open she and Fast would merely shatter themselves against the bars. The gates were too high to jump, and the bars were much too close together to squeeze between, even for a child. But Fast ran forward, ears pricked, committed to his decision, and much too near the end of his strength to have any left for a final tendon-snapping swerve to one side: and Rosie closed her eyes. *Narl*, she said, despairingly; but beast-speech could not carry as far as Narl was, wherever he was, nor was there anything he could do to cold wrought iron, even if he, who had no beast-speech, had heard her plea.

With her eyes closed, she saw the animals that made up the bars of the gate turn their heads to look at her, at her and Fast. She saw them leap to their feet – the lion shaking his flower mane, and the bear his flower ruff, the hare bounding upright and the snake writhing aside like another rose stem; and the ones first on their feet turned and pressed against the slower ones, the hedgehogs and the tortoises, the toads and the badgers, and cats picked up confused kittens and dogs sleepy fox cubs, and a centaur and a unicorn herded foals and fawns; and birds seized wiry vines and tender shoots in their beaks, and moles scrabbled and beavers paddled, as if cold iron were mere earth or water; and the central bars bowed aside.

Even so, Rosie felt iron bars scrape by her on either side, bruising her shoulders, painfully wiping her legs off Fast's sides and tossing her feet over his rump; and then Fast staggered forward as if released by a rope breaking, falling to his knees and then lurching to his feet again, and Rosie, looking down, saw chafe marks on his shoulders, and, looking behind, on the points of his hips. But they were through; and here the hounds were as well, Tash only a bit rumpled, Froo limping, Milo with a bleeding slash in his side – and Hroc with the gargoyle spindle end in his mouth, carrying it as gently as he might have carried a straying puppy.

There was a brief, terrible noise, like the noise someone might make if iron bars closed on them suddenly; and Rosie had to nerve herself to look round. Behind them the briar hedge rose, unbroken, the iron gates invisible among the rose stems.

Rosie, shaking in every limb, slid off Fast and stood beside him. He stood unsteadily himself, taking deep, deep breaths, heaving in far more air than one horse could possibly hold, the steam rising off him in clouds like a cauldron boiling. *Fast*, said Rosie. *Fast! Listen to me. You must walk. You've run too far, and all your muscles are going to seize up on you. Fast, can you hear me?*

He said nothing, and he was by now shivering so hard she could not see if he made any gesture of agreement. But he raised one forefoot and dropped it like a stone, and then one hind foot; and then the other two, one after the other. Rosie grabbed a handful of mane and pulled; but Fast had stopped again, and his nose dropped till it nearly touched the ground, and there was a whine in his breathing she dreaded to hear.

Walk, damn you!

A tiny voice, so faint she almost didn't hear it: *Can't.*

Yes you bloody can! She thumped his shoulder with her fist, which was like thumping a block of meat on a slab, and then pinched the tender skin behind the elbow, and Fast twitched a little, and she saw his head begin to swing round and then back as he countermanded his instinct to bite the little stinging thing that was hurting him. He staggered forward again, stiff as an old cart horse, but he was walking.

She turned away from him to see to the hounds; all but Hroc were lying full-length on the ground, panting so heavily she thought they must be bruising themselves against the hard earth. Hroc was sprawled mostly upright, with the spindle end between his front paws; he flattened his ears when he saw Rosie turn towards him. Short way, said Hroc. *We did not go by the human road. No-one was after us.*

Are you all right?

Yes, said Hroc. *Milo's is just a scratch. You see to Fast. I thought we would get here first.*

Rosie would have laughed if she hadn't been so worried. She took up the spindle end again, rubbing the dirt from its grin before she put it back in her pocket; and then she went after Fast, who was still walking, feeling for the ground with each foot as if he had gone blind.

It was only then that she registered that the drive was clear of rose stems. The courtyard outside the stables had had no way out when she and Narl had stood there after the princess's disastrous ball – except the way Eskwa made. She looked at the sky: it was no longer grey-purple, but cloud-grey, drizzly, Gig grey, ordinary grey. She couldn't feel very hopeful with poor Fast gasping and stumbling beside her, but when she put her hand on his shoulder for comfort she felt at least she had a little to give him. The dogs heaved themselves to their feet and followed.

It was a long walk, and an eerie one, for the tall curtain of rose stems still hung on either side of the drive, as if they were walking down a roofless tunnel; nor was there any sound but what they made themselves. Rosie tormented herself by pretending she could see through the woven roses enough to discern a tree or two that stood just by the drive, or one of the pavilions erected for the ball; but she did not really believe she saw anything but more rose stems.

By the time they could see the courtyard opening out at the end of the way (much to Rosie's relief), while Fast was still taking small clumsy steps, he no longer stumbled, his nose had come a few inches up off the ground, and his breathing was no more than hoarse. When they came within sight of the stables, Rosie ran forward as quickly as she could, which wasn't very, looking despairingly at the liveried groom who still lay sprawled in sleep in the corridor just outside Fast's door, and pulled down the beautifully folded horse blanket that hung on it. Fast was nearly at the door when she met him with her armful. *No*, she said. *You have to keep moving.* Where was Spear? She discovered she could take on yet one more worry: Had something happened to Spear? She threw the blanket over Fast and buckled it. The dogs all collapsed again. *Spear?*

And there he was, trotting stiffly towards her. *Spear – can you keep Fast moving? I'm sorry. He must walk – so must the others*, she added, looking round at heaps of panting dogs. *But Fast especially. Tepid water, little and often – but he mustn't stop moving –* she was chivvying him down the aisle and into the courtyard as she spoke – *Spear, can you do it?*

The four-legged scourge of obstreperous human drunks gave the seventeen-hand horse and the way-worn fleethounds a measuring glance and answered mildly, *Of course I can do it.*

I'll be back as soon as I can.

Rosie started off hurrying and then thought, Back soon? From what? What do I have to hurry towards?

She stopped on the far side of the courtyard, a few steps before she had to. Because while the drive was open, Woodwold was still swaddled in rose stems, just as she had left it. She looked up at the sky again, but drizzly Gig grey no longer comforted her. She listened to the silence, knowing what it meant; knowing what she would find when she went back into the Great Hall. I should be hurrying, she thought, for the danger is no less than it was; I have merely eluded it again, for the moment. But I do not know my course. I haven't even rescued Peony – I don't know where she is, nor Narl and the others. It's all very well, what Hroc said – *no-one was after us* – but I'm now inside the briar hedge again, and they're still out there, with Pernicia's army, who will be a lot quicker to grab the next lot because the first ones got away.

What have I done, after all? she thought. What have I done? I suppose Pernicia will just come for me again; and I may have killed Fast. Maybe Narl can get Peony right away . . . maybe if they go far enough, Peony will wake up . . . then, at least, out of all of us, Narl and Peony. . .

She sat slowly down at the edge of the courtyard, and wrapped her arms round her pulled-up knees, and rocked back and forth, her mind empty. She hardly noticed when two hounds came up to her and pressed themselves round her, rather as they had done at the princess's ball, as if they were holding her together, as if they were aware that she needed holding together. Vaguely she felt Hroc licking one ear, and someone else – Froo, she thought – licking the other.

She was half asleep when the words – if, after all, they were words – entered her understanding. She could not say she heard them, for the taking in of meaning was as much deeper in and other-than-human than animal speech as animal speech was deeper in and other-than than human. It was as though meaning grew somewhere in the centre of her body, as if the marrow of her bones were talking to her.

She felt in her body that Pernicia's castle was gone. She felt that there had been a hard place that hurt her – she could almost feel where it had been, low under her left ribs – that had disintegrated, fallen back to the earth it was made from; that the sun and the rain upon it would make good earth of it in time to come, not merely the crumbled remains of the castle as it was now, lying like a shattered vase upon a floor, still glinting with the paint the maker of it had laid upon it, a tint of dark magic. For now the important thing was that it was no longer a castle, could no longer be a castle; its maker would not put it together again. And Rosie had done this, Narl had done this, Flinx and Sunflower and Zel and Hroc and Throstle and all of them had done this. Weaker, Rosie thought, very dimly, for it was difficult, in this deep-in place, to put anything in human words. We have weakened her.

It was not everything, but it was something. They had, all of them together, done something.

She felt the effort round her, under her and over her, the effort to speak so that she could hear, and know that she was not alone with five hounds and a horse, willing and loyal though they were, little, flimsy, squashy creatures, almost as fragile and insubstantial as she was herself.

Woodwold. Woodwold was talking to her. *Rosie. Princess. I am here, too*. Woodwold was awake.

Slowly she uncurled herself, finding it strange that she could do so, that she appeared to be this light, airy, bendable creature; she weighed so little it seemed to her surprising that she did not float away like a leaf. How precarious, to stand on feet, to carry what substance one had in this scanty and attenuated manner. . .

She shook herself and took a deep breath. Hroc and Froo came to their feet and looked at her expectantly. She turned to look towards where the Great Hall lay behind its embrace of rose stems, and then found her own feet and ordered them to take her there. She went unerringly to a certain snarly mess of rose stems, visibly no different from any other along the great hummocky hills of rose stems beneath which lay Woodwold, and prised them apart with her hands; and they permitted themselves to be prised.

She ducked, and stepped underneath, and began, carefully, to part those that now wound across her way; and they, too, permitted themselves to be moved aside. She caught herself on a thorn, once, and a drop of blood fell from the tip of her forefinger; and she held her breath, and thought of Peony, and then she put her hands out again to pull at the next layer of rose stems, and saw another drop of blood fall twinklingly from her finger and on to a hunched brown elbow of stem; and then she was through the next low, twisted arch, and reaching for the next beyond it.

She came after some little time to the old doors of the Great Hall, and here she stood on tiptoes and brushed at the stems that hung round it as if they were no more than cobwebs; and they broke and fell aside at her touch as if they were cobwebs indeed. The sunlight seemed to fall on her more strongly than it had before, and she turned round and saw behind her two hounds, and a great tall arch stretching through the rose hedge; and yet, as she had made her way through it, the partings she had made had only been enough to let her through if she crouched and held her arms close to her sides; and once Froo had yelped as, following her, she misjudged. She took a deep breath, and turned back to the doors, and flung them open – the old doors that had been opened for the first time in over a century for the princess's one-and-twentieth birthday, and which had required four men on each to persuade them – and the light rushed in to brighten as much of the floor as it could reach.

But most of the Great Hall was still dark from the gnarled rose stems over its windows. That's the first thing, she thought. She went to the tall window nearest her, scrambled up to stand on its sill, fumbled with the latch, and put her hands through against the rose stems, pushing at them as if they were no more than an odd sort of curtain, but pushing gingerly, on account of the thorns; her finger still throbbed where she had caught it before. The thick branches creaked, and gave, and she pushed a little more vigorously, and they rustled as they parted, and the sunlight came in, and she noticed that it looked like sunlight, that it was no longer grey and gloomy, and when she peered up, the sky was blue, and the shreds of cloud that drifted across it were white. And when she looked again at the rose stems, she noticed that they were now covered with leaves, which was why they had rustled; but they had been bare and brown but minutes before.

She clambered down from the windowsill and went on to the next, and pushed back the suddenly green rose stems from that window, and then the next, and the next; and when she came to the last, she saw flower buds among the leaves, although the princess's birthday was in early spring.

Only when there were no more windows to free from their blindfolds did she turn to look into the Hall.

It was almost worse, being able to see, because it emphasized how wrong what she saw was. She found Katriona at once, and knelt beside her again, stroked her hair. She was still breathing. She was still asleep.

The deep, bone-marrow knowledge stirred in her, and she knew that from this sleep, magical and malicious as it was, the sleepers would take no harm, unlike the sleepers found in the broken fastnesses, years ago, where the princess might have been. Woodwold could do this much for the little creatures that walked under its roofs; it had watched over other little creatures for hundreds of years, and it understood hurt and harm and the will to do evil. But it did not comprehend sleeping and waking any more than it comprehended walking and breathing; this was why (Rosie thought) Pernicia's sleep had first confused it, but had failed to hold it.

Woodwold had done what it could. Now she must lead the way.

Rosie stood up, looking round her wildly. She was taking deep, involuntary breaths, and at first she thought she had made more of an effort climbing window frames than she had realized, and then she thought she must be fighting off some lingering odour of the sleep-spell, and then she thought she was probably frightened; but as she sucked in the air and expelled it violently she knew that none of these things were the real reason she stood and panted: what she was was *angry*.

She couldn't ever remember being so angry – not even when she had knocked down the man who had been beating his horse instead of trying to free the trapped wheel of the cart – not even when she had found the whip scars, invisible under the sleek hair unless you were looking, on the colt who had been afraid of Narl because he had no beard – not even when she had first begun to realize what Ikor's message meant to her, to Katriona and Aunt and Barder – and Peony and Rowland and Narl – and Jem and Gilly and Gable, and Crantab and Hroslinga – and all of the Gig – the whole country – not even then. She was bursting with anger; her skull throbbed with it; her hands, hanging at her sides, felt hot and swollen with it.

Pernicia, she shouted. *We have business, you and I.*

There was a low laugh, and Rosie spun round, and saw Pernicia walking in through the open door of the Hall. "How very sweet of you to be angry with me," she said. "Such an invitation, anger. I might have been delayed a little longer, else." She was carrying a cane in her left hand, which Rosie had not seen before, and there were several red marks on her cheek, and she had her right hand tucked into her long dark-streaked robe with the thorn tears in it; and Rosie's deep knowledge reminded her of the ruined castle, of what the destruction of that castle meant. *We have weakened her.*

"I could almost – er – adopt you for that; the last one-and-twenty years have been difficult for me too, and I could use a good lieutenant. I have never had a good one."

Rosie made a spitting, inarticulate noise.

"But it has gone too far for that now, has it not? That is almost a pity. One of us must die, you know; the magic will pull your whole dreary Gig apart else; I couldn't stop that now even if I wished to. Although I don't wish to, you know; I want it – and the country – nice and whole. To do as I like with.

"But I hadn't expected there to be two of you; my mistake. I almost wonder if it might be worth saving one of you – do I mean saving? Perhaps not quite as you would mean it. But – no. I'm sure it has gone too far for that. . ." She raised the cane, waving it gently in the air like a fan, and then paused, and dropped its tip a hand's breadth or so –

Fairies didn't carry wands. Except in direst need.

– as if to aim it like a weapon.

Magic can't do everything. Rosie hurled herself upon her, seizing her throat between her hands.

Chapter 22

As the two of them struck the floor, Pernicia underneath, Woodwold cried out, a shriek of wood and iron and stone, a convulsion like an earthquake; and sleeping bodies slid across the heaving floor, rebounding off each other and off pieces of equally unsettled furniture, and there were muffled, confused cries, as of sleepers caught in a nightmare.

Rosie was dimly aware that something was going on round the two of them, but she had no consciousness to spare for thinking about it; her entire focus was in keeping her hands round Pernicia's throat. She knew she had succeeded so far only because Pernicia had not imagined anyone attacking her directly, and had had no immediate ward against it; but Rosie could feel hundreds of tiny threads of magic, tickly and horrid like centipede legs, pulling at her fingers; and the cane, the wand, whatever it was, was beating at her back, and every time it hit her there was a nasty, miserable sensation like hitting your elbow on a door, and every time it was raised it left behind it a feeling like burning. She tried to hold in her mind that image of the castle she and Narl and the animals had pulled down; she tried to remember that they had weakened her; she told herself Pernicia hadn't turned her into a paving stone or an octopus yet; and as long as she had her hands locked where they were, she wasn't going to be able to prick her finger on a spindle. . .

But Rosie would not last long in the strangling cloud of Pernicia's magic. She could already no longer see what she held;

sometimes it seemed to be a fire-wyrm, or a goblin, or a taralian; sometimes it was only a wild-faced woman with hatred in her black eyes as they stared into Rosie's; and Rosie had only just enough strength left not to be drawn to return her gaze. Rosie's back was on fire from the blows, and the numb, banged-elbow feeling was creeping slowly down her arms, and she would soon no longer be able to keep her fingers closed; and her hands furthermore seemed to be increasingly weighed down and muffled with something like slug slime and spider silk. She thought she heard voices, but she could not tell if they were animal or human, nor if they were speaking to her or to Pernicia. She thought she saw human figures moving, but her eyes seemed obscured, as if sticky webs were being woven across her face as well as round her hands, and these humans, if that was what they were, moved oddly, gropingly, uncertainly, as if they were not sure if they were awake or asleep and dreaming.

She thought she heard the clatter of iron-shod hoofs.

Gorse flung himself through the open door to the Great Hall as he had flung himself through the hole in the hedge and the just-horse-width bow in the iron bars in the gate that had greeted Narl's great fiend-scattering shout as they had borne down upon that confused and unhappy army. The bars bounced off Narl's knees with a sound like wet dough being slapped on a kneading board as Gorse leaped through, but Narl, Peony still in his arms, stayed on his back; perhaps the gate was growing accustomed to the work, or perhaps it recognized its maker, and stretched wider. Narl had followed the hounds, the short way, but he had known – or at least guessed – that Rosie and Fast had won their way through because as they neared Woodwold they met more and more unfriendly creatures, but which were less and less inclined to interfere with them, as if their commander had forgotten about them while greater matters pressed elsewhere.

Gorse's iron shoes slipped on the dancing-floor, and he scrambled to keep his footing, and to prevent himself from stepping on any of the half-awake people who lay there, bewildered, and slow from a too-heavy sleep, unable to get out of his way. He gave a short, raspy neigh that in a human would have been "oh *no*" and he put his head right down, to see where he was sliding to, and his hindquarters down for balance. Both he and the humans were further dismayed and disoriented by the fact that the floor itself was moving, in abrupt little heaves and eddies like water striking rocks or discomfited by wind. One or two people had managed to climb to their feet, seeming to have difficulty deciding whether they needed worse to cling to some support or to clutch at their heads, as if the heads seemed riskily loose on the shoulders.

Rowland hauled himself upright by grasping a table edge, and then grappled his way from chair to chair to fall against Gorse's shoulder; even half awake he had recognized the burden that Narl bore before him. Peony was still wholly asleep; she did not stir, while many round her were stirring. Narl slid off the sweating Gorse, and carried her to the nearest table – the floor was now only making tiny tremors, like a horse shaking its skin free of a fly – and laid her down gently. Rowland snatched two pillows off two chairs and placed them, clumsily, for his hands were still not quite his own, under her head.

Narl turned to the two struggling figures he knew to be Rosie and Pernicia, though he could see neither. Pernicia's magic and Rosie's fury wrapped them round, and he could not tell the one from the other, nor much more than make them out as two vaguely human shapes in the fiery turbulence of their battle. Fate and all the gods! he said silently to himself, too frantic to say anything aloud, incapable of coherent words, and sure as well that there was nothing he could say that would be of the slightest use, and so he need not try: Rosie! Could you not have waited till there was someone to help you? He knew that whatever was happening, Rosie had little time left; his only wonder was that her rage and despair had protected her this long.

Where was Katriona? Or Ikor? Or Aunt? He looked wildly round, and that was when he noticed that not everyone in the Hall was waking; no fairy nor magician was doing so, not only those of the Gig, but those of the royal party as well. Katriona herself lay nearly at his feet; he knelt down beside her. Woodwold's pain and distress had rolled her on to her back; her mouth was a little open and her face was drawn and unhappy, as if she were half remembering something important left undone. He touched her cheek, sending his thought towards her, wherever she might be, and knew at once he could not rouse her. He tried a moment or two longer, thinking to find at least a clue to what held her; but she was too far away, and he could feel that what stood watch over her would clutch at him, too, if he stayed, for he, too, was a fairy.

As it was, he was already half lost; he could feel the Great Hall round him, and the twitching floor under his knees; but he could not take his hand away from Katriona's face, and he could not stand up and turn round; there was a great cold weight on him, bearing him down. With a great effort he brought his other hand to the iron chain he wore round his neck, and seized the little ancient knob of it that he had welded there; and with the touch of it he could jerk his other hand back with a gasp.

It would need some great magic to rescue these sleepers. And all those who could wield it slept. Pernicia had planned well. If she won, there would be that many fewer real and potential rivals or enemies for her to dispose of; if she lost . . . she still won, because this country would be uninhabitable without its fairies and magicians to negotiate the long tricky series of truces with its native magics. And three-quarters of the best fairies and magicians had been in Lord Prendergast's Great Hall for the princess' one-and-twentieth birthday party.

He could not think of it now. He would think of it later. Now there was Rosie, gone into battle alone, a battle she must have known she would lose. Did she think he would not follow her, to the ends of the earth if necessary?

But then, what could he do against Pernicia?

He stood up again, hoping for inspiration, and did not see Zel trotting up behind him. Zel went round Narl's ankles, and stood by Katriona, looking into her face. Narl took one step, two, three, towards the small, terrible whirlwind that contained Pernicia and

Rosie; and as he walked away, Zel put his two front feet on Katriona's breast and said, *Katriona, you must wake up and help us*.

Narl knew nothing of that; his eye had been caught by a faint pale stir high over his head. He looked up, and the merrel was standing on its rafter, half spreading its wings; it looked down at him, and he felt it was trying to catch his eye.

The merrel. The merrel was awake.

Merrels have the best far-vision of any creature; a merrel can see a harvest mouse running up a stem and into its grass globe while the merrel hangs a half a league above the earth. Narl, who had no beast-speech, could nonetheless hear it telling him, in the nearly human language it had learned over its long years of imprisonment above Lord Prendergast's Great Hall: I can see her. *I can see your friend, your companion, your dear one, bound in a death embrace with the fairy who has sought her life for twenty-one years.* I can see her.

The merrel sat high above the floor of the Hall, bound short by links of cold iron, which no magic can loose. Narl took a deep breath, and swept together all the magic that was in him, and held it, and looked at it, and then he brought the experience of all his years at the forge, working cold iron in fire and earth and air and water; and he seized the magic as if it were the raw material he was accustomed to, and bent it and shaped it, drawing it long and thin, setting a point and an edge to it; and the magic struggled like an angry colt, for he was not accustomed to shaping magic, and it is at best a much less obedient servant than is iron. No magic is willing to be handled as if it were some common, dull thing, inert but for the hands of its worker, and still less may it be easily forced to the will of, of all people, a smith; and, furthermore, into this magic he had to hammer some of his own being, some sympathetic tie to the qualities of iron, and this was worse yet, for it was like weaving fire and water together. The magic nearly escaped him many times, for it would have none of what he would have of it, and in the back of his mind he knew that what he strove for could not be done, by the laws of the world.

But he felt the thing in his hands become the weapon he needed, created perhaps more out of his own dire extremity than of anything else, and briefly he quailed, because he was not sure what it was he had made. But it was all he had, and he had no time to try anything else. And so he grasped it, aimed it, and flung it at the chain round the merrel's ankle. He bit back a cry as it left his hands, for his magic-spear burned like the fire of his forge; and he was caught in a back-draught.

Katriona woke to the sound of the roof on Woodwold's Great Hall being ripped apart, and the scream of a hunting merrel. She looked up and saw the merrel that had lived in the rafters of Lord Prendergast's Hall for as many years as Rosie had been alive, beating its great wings, and flying up, up, out through the ragged, smoking hole in the roof, two or three broken links of the chain round its ankle glittering in the sunlight, the whiteness of its beating wings as dazzling as the sun itself. It flew up into the sky till it was lost in it.

Katriona looked round, trying to remember what was happening, wondering why everyone seemed to be lying or crawling about on the floor, wondering why she felt so sick and lost, feeling as if she had just been dragged a very long way through some thick, cold, horrid, slobbery material, that had blocked up her eyes so she could not see the way, and her nose and mouth so she could not breathe, and clung to her limbs so she could not move; she would be there still if it were not for whatever had so determinedly dragged her . . . absent-mindedly patting the young fox which was standing beside her, looking at her thoughtfully. It had called her by name and asked for her help, she suddenly recalled – and as suddenly recalled a day almost twenty-one years before when another fox had asked if she would come to the rescue of a fox who called her by name. She had not heard a fox speak since Rosie was a baby.

She staggered to her feet. It occurred to her as quickly as it had occurred to Narl, though she could not yet put sense to it, that only the ordinary people were waking as she was waking, the fairies were all asleep – asleep – why were they asleep? – and then she began to remember, as if it were all something she had dreamed, the night of the princess' birthday party. Pernicia. Pernicia would be sure to lay her baleful sleep the heaviest on other fairies – Katriona could still taste the foul gumminess of it on her tongue – on the magicians, on the royal family themselves, those who had hoped, had striven, to defy her.

But worse yet, Pernicia had torn Rosie away from her, Katriona; she had felt her hold loosen and break before the sleep, the awful sleep, struck her down. She remembered Peony struggling through the crowd towards the two tall women facing each other incongruously over a spinning wheel – she did not remember any more after that, only her knowledge that she had lost Rosie. How long had she been asleep? Where was Rosie?

She turned too quickly, still dizzy from sleep and waking, and almost fell. *We have been to the castle, Rosie and I and the others*, said the fox at her feet. *We pulled the castle down*.

Pulled the castle down—? Unbidden, Katriona's memory produced a picture of the barren plain and the standing stones and the unfriendly eyes and the castle, where she and Aunt and Barder had once briefly stood. Pulled it down? Hope surged through her and made her hands and feet tingle with warmth, and she felt healthy and strong – and amazed, for she remembered the tales of the people who had woken out of Pernicia's sleep at the broken fortresses. And perhaps it was because she was thinking of castles and fortresses, and that her feet were planted so firmly on Woodwold's bare floor that briefly the bone-marrow knowledge stirred in her, too, and she heard a voice that was no voice speaking at a pitch no human ear could imagine, and it said *I am here. For Rosie. Princess*. At that moment Katriona raised her eyes and saw the briar roses twining round the windows and hanging over the open doors and knew who it was who spoke to her. *Thank you*, she said, not knowing if it could hear her or not; not knowing if it could understand gratitude. *Thank you*.

But where was Rosie? She looked again at the hole in the roof, and when she dropped her gaze this time she saw a seething roil of magic near the feet of a haggard man.

Narl – she had not recognized him. His face was grey with pain, and he was missing some of his hair, as if it had been burnt off. He held his hands in front of him, curled loosely to his breast; she glanced at them and saw that the palms were swollen and cracked and bleeding, and the sleeves of his fine coat had been tattered to the elbows, and his forearms were marked as if with tongues of fire. "Narl – " she said, horrified.

He shook his head, and her eyes turned to follow his. She could see through the roil of magic only slightly more clearly than Narl, but she knew that what she saw was the final confrontation between Pernicia and Rosie, and that Rosie was, inevitably, losing.

The merrel stooped so swiftly that neither of them saw it, neither of them nor Pernicia either; lightning is slower. The merrel's talons seized Pernicia and wrenched her out of Rosie's slackening grasp as Woodwold opened a gulf in the earth just beneath them. Katriona thought she heard Pernicia scream; but if she spoke any magic, it did not save her, nor did the merrel's hold falter. Katriona ran forward and grabbed Rosie's shoulders, pulling her back just in time, muttering a few hasty words to loose Rosie from the snare of magic that still clutched her, and a few more words begging that Woodwold might leave some floor under the both of them while she did it; as it was they were pitched backwards, and Narl put out his wounded arms and caught them both, and Katriona and Narl staggered out of reach, hauling Rosie with them. Katriona noticed that two long snowy pinions had caught in Rosie's hair.

Pernicia and the merrel plunged deep into the earth, and the gulf round them spasmed, spewing raw, dry, mouldy earth and fragments of ancient root and stone; and then it snapped shut with a sound like hundreds of anvils banging together, and the noise fell upon everyone as hard as a giant's blows, and their breath was knocked out of them. But the floor where those two had disappeared rose like a mountain, and avalanches tumbled down its sides, and there was a roaring, echoing noise like many angry taralians in a narrow valley, and there was so much fine grit in the air that as the people in the hall opened their mouths to drag their breath in again after losing it to the recoil of the closing of the pit, their mouths and throats were instantly full of it, and they coughed helplessly, and their lungs ached. Frightened, baffled people pressed themselves back, nearer the heart of the house, away from the front of the Hall and the mountain that had risen up there, dragging their still-sleeping comrades to what safety they could.

One of the walls of the Hall cracked and buckled and fell down, and the sounds the splintering wood made were like human screams. The walls on either side of it tottered and bent towards it, like grief-stricken friends towards a fallen companion, like Katriona and Narl over Rosie; the wreckage shot across the broken floor, dangerous chunks of lath and plaster thrown skidding up miniature peaks and launching themselves into the air on the far sides, though the central mountain was beginning to subside again in showers of chips and clods of earth. Tapestries belled out as if blown by the breath of giants; several were torn from the wall, and one skimmed round the stricken room like a bird before it fell upon what had been the high table; half of the table still stood, while the other half was a ragged heap of broken posts and planks and food and serving ware.

Rosie was only half aware of the destruction round her. Katriona had peeled the worst of Pernicia's binding magic away from her face and hands, but as shattered furniture and bodies slid this way and that across the writhing floor, Rosie was separated from both her and Narl and, dizzy and nearly helpless, fetched up against something solid. She groped at it, and discovered one of the legs of the high table at the end that was still standing, and slowly worked her way upright. The bowed body next to her was familiar, its arms braced against the tabletop, but it took her a moment to recognize it: Rowland, bent protectively over something, and once she knew him she guessed what, or rather who, that something was. Rowland looked up then and recognized her; and in a lull in the diminishing sounds of destruction he said hopelessly, "Is there anything you can do?"

Rosie stopped herself from shaking her head. She found an

overturned chair with a missing back but four sound legs, righted it, and knelt on it, looking into Peony's face. Her face was thinner and paler than it had been – last night? Was it still only last night? – and her breathing, as Rosie bent low over her, sounded strained, as if a weight pressed on her breast.

Rowland moved back a little, as if to give Rosie room, or as if he couldn't bear to look any longer, to watch Peony's life ebbing away from a wound neither of them could see.

Rosie, tired and bruised and miserable and shaken and sick as she was, felt her own life beating strongly in her, and reached out and took Peony's hands. She stared at her friend's face for a moment, at the face so like and unlike her own, and then she let go with one hand long enough to reach in Peony's pocket, and find there the spindle end she had made for her, and drew it out, and put it between Peony's hands, and clasped her own round them. One of the merrel's feathers came loose from Rosie's matted hair, and drifted down to lie on Peony's breast.

Something – something – some non-magic moved between them. Princess, not-princess, two young women who had traded places, who had pretended to be one young woman, who had become two other young women. Rosie with her strength and her careless energy, her generosity to everything that lived; Peony with her gentler kindness, her subtler understanding, and an elasticity that had never been a part of Rosie's nature.

Narl came up beside her. There were stained scraps of cloth wrapped round the palms of his hands, but when he put his gently round hers, Rosie felt him adding his strength of hope and love to her own, and she cared about nothing but that he should help her bring her friend back to life.

Katriona was moving through the Hall, waking those who still slept, against whom Pernicia's savage, ensnaring spell had struck hardest, the fairies, the magicians, the royal family. She had a long way to go to reach these, and even with Zel providing a safety line the way was ugly and dangerous. The king and the queen and the three princes she awakened first, drawing them back tenderly and carefully from the sticky, heavy emptiness where their spirits had been suspended; and several of the queen's ladies, who had pulled their queen and her family bodily away from the wreck of the Great Hall, burst into tears. Osmer woke up first; he looked round, half hearing the nearest lady's attempt to reassure him that the wicked fairy was gone and he was safe, and an admiring amazement came into his face. "I've been *asleep*? I wish I'd seen *that*!" Katriona discovered that she could still smile, and moved on.

She found Barder, who was easily awakened, and Aunt, who was not, and Ikor, who was harder yet, and even after his eyes were open, Katriona could see the ends of nightmares in them, gleaming like toads' backs. She turned then to the other Gig fairies, and when she had recalled them, Aunt and Ikor had recovered enough to help her awaken the other royal fairies and magicians; it took all three of them to awaken Sigil, whom they might not have found at all but that they were sure she had, after all, attended the ball. She had lain under a fallen-down tapestry, and she was so small and drab, even in her ball clothes, that she looked like a crumpled fold of vague foresty background to the bright woven scene of ladies gathering flowers. She opened her eyes with her head on Ikor's arm, facing a window, and the first thing she saw was briar roses: "Dear Woodwold," she said.

Lastly, and as gently as they could, they woke Lord and Lady Prendergast and their sons and daughters, who woke to find the Great Hall, the oldest part of their ancient and beloved house, destroyed, and for a little while the thought of a wicked fairy defeated and their country and future monarch saved seemed too small a victory to them.

Katriona wearily moved back towards the table where Peony lay, where Rowland stood and Narl and Rosie crouched over their joined hands. The stallion, Gorse, stood behind Narl, and several dogs were scattered round the table's end. One of them – her name, Sunflower, swam into Katriona's mind – had her feet up on the edge of the table, where she could just raise her chin high enough to stare into Rosie's face. Gorse was as bedraggled as a wild moor-horse, and had strange marks on his flanks, as if he had squeezed through a space too narrow for him; the dogs' chests were all matted with foam. Katriona guessed that this was part of the story of how they had pulled down Pernicia's castle; and wondered what else she had missed while she was asleep. But those stories could wait.

Katriona was exhausted. *Never attack a spell head-on*, Aunt had said years ago. *You need to sniff out where the weak places are. All spells have them; it's just a matter of finding them . . . and, of course, being able to use them.* Katriona could not have found nor used the weak spot of Pernicia's spell. Not alone. She looked down at a small pointed red-furred face looking up at her. *I am still here*, Zel said. *I am still here.*

They were all still here, and they were all still alive.

She stood at the end of the table, looking down at the top of Peony's head, at Rosie's face, fierce with concentration; and Narl looked up at her and said, half shouted, "Kat! Wake up! Don't you want to *keep her?*"

Katriona did not at first know what he meant, but she responded to the desperation in his voice, and saw that Peony, now alone in all the Hall, remained asleep; and obediently she put her hands out, and laid them as gently as she could on the burned backs of Narl's hands. But with that contact she realized the intricate interlacing of energies at play beneath her palms – discovered, too, the secret Narl had been hiding in his forge for many years – and suddenly understood what Narl had meant. Her fingers bit down against Narl's skin, and she put every mote of magic she had left in her into the work, for Pernicia was gone, and she could use her last strength as she chose.

Aunt looked up from where she was rubbing the temples of a young fairy with a headache, catching a whiff or a whisper of what was happening among the remains of the high table; Ikor, in one of the anterooms strapping the sprained ankle of one of the grandest of the royal magicians, leaped to his feet and ran back into the Hall, shouting, "No, no! You cannot! No—"

Rosie leaned forward, round the globe of hands, and kissed Peony on the lips.

Everyone's hands collapsed inwards as the spindle end shattered; Rosie felt an eerie, sucking sensation against her palms for a moment as she involuntarily fell forward on to Peony's breast, and a queer, fluttery, disorienting sensation in her own breast and throat, as if something were being pulled out of her and drawn into her friend. Narl and Katriona both took a sudden, hasty step backwards. Rosie sat up, spitting Peony's hair out of her mouth as Peony said, "*Oof*. Rosie, you weigh a *ton*."

It was at this moment that the cook came howling up from the kitchens saying that Lady Prendergast's terrier and two mice were lying asleep in the centre of the kitchen table with a single long black hair twisted round them in a circle, that nothing could pass that boundary hair, and would some fairy please come and get these animals *off her table*?

Chapter 23

Woodwold was not the only house that had suffered in the final confrontation between Pernicia and the princess and the princess's allies; all over the Gig there was wreckage as if by tiny, violent, very local storms, or duels among goblins or a fire-wyrm or two. There was a great deal of work to be done to set all to rights. But no-one's village had been flattened, and friends and family gave housing and help to those who had been unlucky; and the crops and the animals were largely unhurt, although the latter in some cases had strayed so far some humans suspected they had been ill-sent or driven, especially when, after their initial journeys, hitherto stolid beasts showed a tiresome new urge to wander. And, of course, as soon as the news of Pernicia's final defeat went out (and everyone shook themselves and stared at each other and said, "How could we ever have imagined that Pernicia had just *gone away*? That was a very powerful spell!" And everyone was a little annoyed, especially because no-one could remember the end of the ball and the appearance of Pernicia, which must have been one of the best stories if anyone could tell it, but then, it was king's business and magic, and all's well that ends well), everyone in the Gig was a hero. This pleasant knowledge helped the work go a little quicker, as did the amount of volunteer labour that poured in from all over the rest of the country, to hear the tales of heroism firsthand in return for some digging and dragging and sawing and hammering and heaving and putting together. The volunteer labour and free goods came even more thickly when the announcement of the wedding went out.

Prince Rowland Jocelyn Hereward and Princess Casta Albinia Allegra Dove Minerva Fidelia Aletta Blythe Domina Delicia Aurelia Grace Isabel Griselda Gwyneth Pearl Ruby Coral Lily Iris Briar-Rose's marriage was celebrated only six weeks after the death of Pernicia and the merrel beneath the ruins of Woodwold's Great Hall. The princess insisted that she wished to be wed in the Gig, from Woodwold, and the Prendergasts – whatever damage had been done to their family's ancient home – were incapable of saying no to her about anything whatsoever, aside from the fact that it was a tremendous honour. (And, of course, as a result of the prospect of the princess' wedding, every royal fairy and magician put their minds to the work of restoring the Prendergasts' Great Hall, which was the only possible location in the entire Gig for such an occasion as a royal wedding, so that it nearly put itself back together and was, furthermore, now glistening with powerful new spells and good wishes, fully sound and solid and complete by the day. The new Great Hall, indeed, was so lofty and beautiful that the king's bishop was almost reconciled to having to hold the most important wedding of this generation in the barbarian, backwater Gig instead of at his own noble cathedral in the royal city.)

Rosie and Narl were the bride and groom's First Friends (although the queues of attendants behind both of them were several dozen strong, and there was a certain amount of sniffing and eyebrow raising that a horse-leech and a smith, however dear the friendship, should come at the heads of the columns). Both of them felt extremely silly in the royal get-ups they were expected to wear, but both felt so complacent about their part in what had occurred, with this wedding as its culminating feat, that they almost forgot to mind. (Since Rosie had begun to let her hair grow so that she could braid the merrel's feathers into it, at least the ladies assigned to her hairdressing for the wedding, unlike those who had tried to dress it for the princess's ball, had had a little to work with. Rosie's godmothers' gifts appeared to have stayed with her even when being the princess had left her, and her hair grew at a cracking pace, as if it had been impatiently waiting its opportunity for the last seventeen years. But the curls, while initially just as bumptious as ever, began to hang out of their own weight as they spilled past her shoulders. The royal hairdressers had taken full advantage, thinking, rightly, that there was fairy work in it somewhere, but grateful that this tall young woman would not spoil the show.)

Rosie privately thought that Narl was taking Peony's marriage remarkably well, but when, a week later, they had seen the wedding party set off for the royal city, and Rosie was beginning to realize just how much she was going to miss Peony (who, with twenty-one new names to choose from, had chosen to remain Peony), she couldn't stop herself from saying something about it to Narl. At least they might be able to share their sense of loss.

But Narl was off-hand. "We'll all miss her. Lovely young woman, and clever with it. She'll make a splendid queen; she has all the right instincts, and the grace to make what needs doing get done."

Rosie said, only speaking the truth, "I can hardly imagine Foggy Bottom without her. "

"You'll miss her worse than I, of course," said Narl. Whistling in a curiously lighthearted way, he returned to his hammer and his fire. Rosie blinked. He had been whistling like this for the last seven weeks. Narl never used to whistle. Of course everyone was tremendously relieved at having the curse off the country for good, and the future queen officially heir-selected by the future king, and married to the man who both she and her country liked best as her consort, but . . . Rosie still did not clearly remember everything that happened during the destruction of the old Hall. She remembered that she and Pernicia had been grappling with each other (she seemed to remember attacking Pernicia with her bare hands, but rejected this as crazy); more particularly she remembered the white streak out of the sky, and the merrel's last words, *Goodbye, friend*. She knew that it was the merrel who had saved her.

And she knew that Narl and Katriona – and possibly her own spindle end – had done something besides just wake Peony up.

Her final meeting with Peony had been extremely painful.

Even if they did manage to keep a courier busy round the year with their letters to each other (and any sort of writing was not Rosie's favourite activity; it came approximately second to embroidery), even if Rosie did go up to the royal city at least once a year herself, their friendship was going to be nothing like it had been for the last six years. Peony herself would become – was already becoming – someone else than she had been; she had to. Rosie supposed that even she herself would change. What had happened to them wasn't like losing your best friend so much as it was like losing your shadow or your soul; you barely knew it was there sometimes, but you knew it was crucial to you. There had been tears of joy and despair on both sides; that Rosie would stay where she was, in a world and a life that suited her, and that Peony had found a life that suited her – that suited her as if she had been born to it – and people who loved her. Most particularly one person who loved her: Rowland.

"But I can't –" she said, as she began to understand what had happened. "But I'm *not* –"

"Neither am I," said Rosie, through her own tears. "I'm *really* not. I wasn't, even when I was supposed to be. I just *wasn't*. Even when Ikor. . ." She stopped. Ikor had not spoken to her since the ball; had not come near her. If, as had happened once or twice during her visits to Woodwold, she entered a room that he was in, he left at once. At least she had seen him that once or twice, and so had seen Eskwa, regrown and shining, hanging from his belt.

Peony looked at Hroc's head on her friend's knee, and Sunflower's head on her foot, and at Fwab singing the chaffinch spring song on the windowsill, and the cook's cat just happening by the doorway where they were sitting in one of the little anterooms off the Great Hall (the latter alive with the hum and bang of feverishly working, magic-augmented carpentry), just happening to sit down there for a wash, her back to the embarrassing tedium of human tears. "The animals know. The animals will always know the truth of it."

The animals knew. They still called Rosie *Princess* and she had heard the tale that had gone round after the wreck of the Hall and what came of it: *Pernicia is dead. Rosie and Oroshral* – which was how Rosie learnt for the first time that the merrel had a name – *killed her. Rosie is staying here. Peony is going back to the city to be the princess instead.* " Yes," said Rosie. "But they're not telling. Except each other. And they'll stop that too, soon enough. They'll close it down. Zel –" who was so puffed with importance for having become Katriona's familiar there was almost no bearing him –"is already trying to, because he knows Kat's worried. He hasn't learned yet that Kat is *always* worried." She added, less easily, "And, Peony, it – that I talk to animals—should never have happened. That it did happen may have been – what made the rest happen. Or made it possible to happen – that Pernicia's curse didn't work. That we found a way out. That I'm – you're – we're still here."

Peony took Rosie's hands in hers and squeezed them painfully. "You're sure? You're *sure*?"

"It doesn't matter if I'm sure or not, it's done," said Rosie, but seeing the look on her friend's face she added, "I was *there*, remember? If I hadn't been sure, it couldn't have happened. Whatever did happen," she amended, remembering Narl's and Katriona's hands on hers, and the queer feeling that she had somehow gone invisible, or insubstantial, and that the spindle end, just before it imploded into emptiness, had been the only real thing about either herself or Peony. But she had felt something pass between her and Peony when she kissed her, something that had come trudging up from the depths of her own being, something she herself had called out, and Narl and Katriona had given the capacity to come in response to that call. Something she hardly recognized as hers, except that she knew by the small surprised blank it had left behind when it moved that it had been there all her life till then, and had planned to stay there for the rest of her life as well, something that hopped quietly over to Peony when their mouths met. "Think of Rowland. Just keep thinking about Rowland." And Peony smiled through her tears.

Rosie had been called into the queen's private room once, too, the day before the wedding. Rosie had been uncomfortable at going to meet the woman she knew to be her mother, remembering, too, that the queen had known, when the deception was still a deception. The queen had stared at her as if trying to remember something. "I am sorry," the queen said to the Foggy Bottom horse-leech, "I cannot think who you remind me of. It is very rude to stare – even for queens. Especially for queens." She smiled, and Rosie thought of the story Katriona told, of her standing in her father's kitchen making supper when the king's messengers had come to offer her a throne. Rosie smiled back, and then curtseyed (not too clumsily; three months of being the princess' first lady-in-waiting had had some effect), having no idea what to say.

"You are my daughter's best friend," the queen said slowly. "I want to remember you clearly till I can come to know you. For you will come up to the city sometimes to see your friend, will you not?"

Rosie nodded, a lump suddenly in her throat, and then croaked politely, "Yes, ma'am."

"I hope we can be friends, too. Something about your face – whatever it is – I think my daughter's heart chose its friend well. I would like to be your friend, too," said the queen.

The queen held out her hands, and Rosie knelt as she took them, and bowed her head over them; but the queen freed one of her hands, and stroked Rosie's head, and touched the merrel feathers. At that moment the door of the queen's chamber opened, and a little round person walked in; Rosie looked up.

A little, round, elderly, white-haired person; a fairy. Sigil. Rosie knew her at once. Knew her as she had not known her own mother and father because they were the king and queen and she had thought about them too much in the three months between Ikor's arrival at the Gig and her first meeting with them in over twenty years; knew her because in the unexpected shock of this meeting she had no guard against knowing. She remembered that face bending over her – her hair had been grey then, not white – bending over her when she had been too small to do anything but lie in a cradle or in someone's arms, and smile, so that they would smile back. Sigil.

Rosie drew her breath in on a sob. It had all been half imaginary to her till then – the three months as a lady-in-waiting seemed the most imaginary of all – and she now wanted it to be imaginary, now that her own mother no longer remembered. It had all been – just possibly – some great mistake from the beginning. But she looked into Sigil's face and knew it was not. She, Rosie, had been born a princess; and she had chosen to forsake her heritage for ever. To her horror, the tears poured down her face, and she could not stand, nor move away from the queen, the queen who did not know whose hand she held.

Sigil was there at once, kneeling beside her, smoothing her wet cheeks with her small dry hands, and whispering to her in a voice Rosie remembered singing old lullabies. "There, there, my dear, it is always hard to lose a friend; and you are losing yours ever so dramatically, are you not?"

Rosie gulped and nodded, staring into Sigil's eyes, knowing that Sigil knew what Rosie was remembering, and why Rosie wept. As Rosie's tears slowly stopped, Sigil cupped the tip of Rosie's chin in her hands, hands that had once cupped her entire face when she had been only three months old, and said, "Live long and happily, my dear. Live long and happily. You have earned it, and I think – I believe – you may have it." She shook Rosie's chin, gently and fondly and familiarly, and whispered, "All will be well. *All will be well*." Rosie, through her tears, looked up at her, suddenly remembering the spider that had stowed away in Ikor's sleeve during the long journey in search of the twenty-year-old princess, and had, perhaps, been the same spider that had hung in the corner of the window in the princess' bedroom at Woodwold.

All will be well. Some day the queen would remember the young fairy who had sat on her bed and held her hand, and told her about her four-year-old daughter. Some day the queen would remember that she had looked over Peony's shoulder at their first meeting in Woodwold's park, had looked into Rosie's eyes. Magic can't do everything. All will be well.

Sigil kissed Rosie's forehead and stood up, and Rosie bent her head once more to the queen, and stood up also, and took her leave.

Rosie had not seen Sigil again, except briefly, at the wedding, at a distance, a distance one or both of them were careful to maintain; and now they were gone, her family, her past, what might have been her future. . . She shook herself, and took a deep breath, and thought, Peony *will* make a better queen. She even gets along with Osmer. And she'll have Rowland to help her.

Her mind reverted with relief to the sound of Narl's lighthearted whistling. Of course he was happiest when he had more work to be done than any six ordinary smiths could do, and at the moment, not only was the rebuilding of the Gig still going on; his was the only fully operational forge within it.

The centre of Foggy Bottom seemed to have been the eye of the magic-storm, and the centre of Foggy Bottom was the village square. Everyone assumed that this had to do with the wainwright's yard, which opened on to the square; but the wheelwright's yard was there, too, and Narl's forge. Whatever the reason, for half a league round it, as cleanly as if someone had measured it, no damage had been done to any field or tree or fence or building; and perhaps this was the reason why so many of the wandering animals had found themselves there, and why so many of them seemed to want to return there even after they had been fetched home. The condition of the other smithies was causing some frustration on the part of the other, less fortunate, smiths; usually a smith only has to hang a few pointy bits of iron round the area he wants to make into a smith's yard and he can get on with his making more or less untroubled; but in the Gig for nearly a year after Pernicia's death the iron bits round every smithy but Narl's kept falling down, or being rearranged overnight by persons or presences unknown, and perfectly sound bellows developed holes the moment they blew on smiths' fires, and the fires themselves flared and collapsed maddeningly, and iron broke instead of consenting to being worked, and the level of magic-midges was so dire that the smiths themselves were batting away at them.

No-one, however, had been quite so ill-spirited as to accuse Narl of being responsible for any of this, nor of himself being a fairy (there hadn't been a smith who was also a fairy in so many years it never occurred to anyone to think of such a thing unless he or she had restless children to keep amused with fairy tales), especially after it was discovered that if he forged the pointy bits of iron to mark out other smithies, they stayed where they were put. No-one but Aunt, Katriona and Barder ever heard the full story about the journey to the castle in the wasteland beyond the edge of the Gig.

But even too much work didn't make Narl lighthearted. Narl didn't know how to be lighthearted.

"But, Narl," said Rosie. "Aren't you going to . . . I mean . . . *really* miss her? Peony, I mean," she added in amazement, as he looked across at her blankly. She was sitting on a bale of hay and plaiting (badly) a few of the longest stems together.

Narl stopped whistling, and straightened up from the shoe he was measuring against Fast's foot, and looked at her thoughtfully. "Not as much as I'd've missed you," he said.

Rosie felt herself turn flame red, and then the blood all drained away from her head and she felt dizzy. She looked at her plaiting and let it drop on the ground (where Flinx, who, since the advent of Zel, was spending more time at the forge, examined it briefly for news of the mice he was sure lived in the hay bale). "I thought you were in love with her," she said in a very small voice.

"In love with –?" said Narl.

There was a pause. "Well," he said, as if commenting on the weather or the number of horses waiting to be shod and house- and shop-fittings to be cut and ploughshares to be mended, "it happens I'm in love with you. Have been since that day Rowland and Peony met. No, before that. That's just the day I knew it. Not having been in love before – and old enough to have long since decided it wasn't going to happen – I didn't recognize the signs."

Rosie couldn't say anything. She stared at the ground. After a moment she heard Narl moving towards her, and the toes of his boots appeared in her line of vision, and then one drew back, and Narl knelt and tipped her face up with one scarred hand till he could look into it. "I wasn't going to say anything about it," he said quietly, "because you seemed so determined to have nothing to do with me except as your old friend the farrier. "

Rosie stared at him as if he had turned green or grown wings. "Narl, I've been in love with you *forever*."

"That's all right then," he said, smiling a little, and Rosie remembered the animals saying, *Ironface! Smiling!* And Flinx, *the Block, cracking*. That had been a terrible day, the grey grim waking after the princess' ball, Peony missing and Pernicia waiting, and a terrible moment: Narl had just called her *Princess*, like slamming a door shut between them.

Narl's smile grew fixed, as if he wasn't sure how to say what he wanted to say next, and when he spoke at last he sounded so wistful and forlorn Rosie heard an echo in her mind, a great white bird chained to high rafters saying, *Will you come and talk to me again some time?* "Then will you marry me?"

"Oh yes. Yes. Yes. Oh. But you'll have to come and live with us, you know."

Narl, who lived behind his forge in two small rooms full of old tools and things he hadn't figured out how to mend yet, flinched.

"Oh – please," said Rosie, and grabbed his dangling hand, suddenly feeling that whatever happened next she would burst with it.

"What will they say?"

Rosie shook her head, still hanging on to his hand. "I don't care." She thought about it a moment, and then, surprised, and realizing it was the truth, said, "They'll like it."

"They will, will they?"

But she realized he was laughing at her, and she flung her arms round his neck and kissed him, and his arms closed round her, and drew her down next to him. They were out of sight of the town common and Fast's groom was safely at the pub and this bit of the courtyard ground had been recently swept; and it was a quiet afternoon, and no-one came bursting through the courtyard gate with the latest ironmongery crisis. The kiss went on quite some time, till Fast, standing tied to a ring and wearing only three shoes, turned his head round to see what was going on. It sounded rather enjoyable.

Well, finally, said Flinx. *Did you ever know two humans so thick?*

But Fast was a romantic. He could hardly wait to go home and spread the news at Woodwold, but he had to have four shoes first. He switched his tail, and nodded his head up and down hard enough to jerk at the ring, and began to paw the ground. And the hay-bale mice, taking advantage of Flinx's preoccupation, shot out of the back of the bale, dodged their way out of the yard, dashed across the common, and arrived, panting, to tell their relatives at the pub about the princess and the fairy smith.